PRINCESS
OF
BLOOD

TITLES BY SARAH HAWLEY

GLIMMER FALLS

A Witch's Guide to Fake Dating a Demon
A Demon's Guide to Wooing a Witch
A Werewolf's Guide to Seducing a Vampire

SHARDS OF MAGIC

Servant of Earth
Princess of Blood

PRINCESS
OF
BLOOD

SARAH HAWLEY

ACE
NEW YORK

ACE
Published by Berkley
An imprint of Penguin Random House LLC
1745 Broadway, New York, NY 10019
penguinrandomhouse.com

Copyright © 2025 by Sarah Hawley

Penguin Random House values and supports copyright. Copyright fuels creativity, encourages diverse voices, promotes free speech, and creates a vibrant culture. Thank you for buying an authorized edition of this book and for complying with copyright laws by not reproducing, scanning, or distributing any part of it in any form without permission. You are supporting writers and allowing Penguin Random House to continue to publish books for every reader. Please note that no part of this book may be used or reproduced in any manner for the purpose of training artificial intelligence technologies or systems.

ACE is a registered trademark and the A colophon is a trademark of
Penguin Random House LLC.

Book design by Daniel Brount

Library of Congress Cataloging-in-Publication Data

Names: Hawley, Sarah, author. | Hawley, Sarah. Servant of earth.
Title: Princess of blood / Sarah Hawley.
Description: New York: Ace, 2025. | Series: The shards of magic; [2]
Identifiers: LCCN 2025010365 (print) | LCCN 2025010366 (ebook) |
ISBN 9780593818381 (hardcover) | ISBN 9780593818398 (ebook)
Subjects: LCGFT: Fantasy fiction. | Novels.
Classification: LCC PS3608.A8937 P75 2025 (print) |
LCC PS3608.A8937 (ebook) | DDC 813/.6—dc23/eng/20250318
LC record available at https://lccn.loc.gov/2025010365
LC ebook record available at https://lccn.loc.gov/2025010366

International edition ISBN: 9798217188741

Printed in the United States of America
1st Printing

The authorized representative in the EU for product safety and compliance is
Penguin Random House Ireland, Morrison Chambers, 32 Nassau Street,
Dublin D02 YH68, Ireland, https://eu-contact.penguin.ie.

For the fighters and the dreamers.

AUTHOR'S NOTE

Princess of Blood deals with emotionally difficult topics, including violence, murder, torture, gore, self-harm, alcohol abuse, explicit sexual content, and explicit language.

PRINCESS OF BLOOD

1

THE BLOOD TREE ROSE BEFORE ME, TALL AND IMPOSSIBLY ancient. Its branches had been bare the last time I'd been in the vast stone chamber leading to Blood House—during the immortality trials, when the tree had shown me a lifetime of my sins—but now they were covered with crimson leaves. The stone tiles beneath my feet felt alive. Power thrummed through the chamber, an invisible current that brushed against a strange new inner sense.

I shivered at the sensation, just one sign of the tremendous and frightening change I'd undergone.

I wasn't human any longer.

I was a faerie—and the new leader of Blood House.

Welcome, Princess Kenna, a voice whispered inside my head. Liquid, female, throbbing like a pulse.

"How do we get inside?" These words were spoken out loud, and I turned my head to look at the speaker. Lara, my former mistress and the excommunicated heir to Earth House, looked as exhausted as she sounded. Like me, she had one arm around a drooping, distant-eyed woman with a shaved head and skin newly lined with scars: Anya

Hayes, my best friend from the human world, who I'd thought dead until a few hours ago. She'd been unresponsive but capable of walking when we'd left the corpse-filled throne room, but she'd sagged more with every step. Now she seemed barely conscious.

My chest hurt unbearably as I looked at them. The three of us had survived months of danger and a night of carnage, but at what cost? Lara had been stripped of her magic, her family, and her home; Anya had been tortured in unimaginable ways.

"I'm not sure yet," I told Lara. "I need to figure out what the trap is."

All six Fae houses in the underground city of Mistei had dangerous traps at their entrances. They were tests only house faeries could pass, while intruders were killed gruesomely. Fire House burned unwelcome visitors with a curtain of flame, Earth House drowned them in a tunnel of water... What would the faeries of Blood House, who could magically manipulate bodies, have done to keep their borders safe?

They were *my* borders now, I supposed. The entirety of Blood House had been massacred five hundred years ago by King Osric, but now Osric was dead and the house had been resurrected in the form of... me. Just me. The six Sacred Shards that had brought magic to this world had gifted me with immortality and magic, and in exchange, I was supposed to "restore the balance." Whatever that meant. However one person could possibly do that.

My gaze ran over the entrance hall. The checkered black-and-white stone tiles were etched with the faces of monsters, and the gray walls were carved with beings of all types, too: Noble Fae, Underfae, and the dark, twisted Nasties that inhabited the lowest levels of Mistei. The Blood Tree dominated the chamber, reaching its gnarled limbs towards the distant ceiling, and beyond it was an enormous silver door covered in spikes.

I wondered if the Blood Shard was listening to my thoughts, since it had spoken in my head in that dark, welcoming voice. *Any help?* I thought towards the room in general. *A hint on what the trap is?*

The Shard didn't respond, but a coil of metal around my bicep did. Caedo—my bloodthirsty, shape-shifting dagger—was currently in the form of a spiraling armband, but it writhed like a serpent beneath my sleeve and sank sharp teeth into me.

I yelped in surprise, looking down at my arm. "Was that necessary?"

"What?" Lara asked, sounding confused.

Caedo nipped me again. *You wanted a hint*, the dagger said, its voice metallic and genderless in my head.

I eyed the projections on the door. If Caedo could drain a body in seconds, it made sense the house entrance could as well. Now I needed to figure out how to get it to not kill my friends.

"Can you hold Anya?" I asked Lara. My arm should have been aching from supporting her for this long, but I didn't feel the physical exhaustion I would have expected after the throne room fight and the long walk here. The Noble Fae were stronger and more resilient than humans, and I was one of them now.

I was *immortal*. It was unfathomable.

Lara nodded and looped her arm more firmly around Anya's waist. I let go, heart pinching with grief when Anya wouldn't meet my eyes. Did she still believe I wasn't real? She sagged into Lara's grip, shivering in her flimsy taupe garments.

She needed to get somewhere safe and warm. I would empty any number of veins to make that happen.

I walked around the tree, trailing a hand over its rough trunk. The leaves whispered and sighed. There was a pulse beneath the bark, one that sped until it mirrored mine. It was simultaneously welcoming and unsettling.

Ten more steps took me to the silver door, which was easily twice my height. The spikes covering it were as long as my forearm. Surely I wasn't supposed to impale myself every time I wanted inside.

Then I spotted a sculpted silver wolf's head on the right side of the door, nestled between several spikes at chest height. Its mouth was gaping, and when I bent to peer inside, I saw sharp teeth guarding a cylindrical silver rod.

I'm supposed to stick my hand in there? I asked Caedo silently.
Yes.

The nature of the trap came clear. If a house member grabbed the handle, the door would allow them inside. If an enemy tried, the wolf's teeth would slam together, and the door would consume them.

I hesitated before sliding my hand into the wolf's maw. Even knowing I was the new Princess of Blood, it was a relief when the door didn't immediately bite my hand off.

The metal rod warmed under my palm, and the door started vibrating. A rumbling sound filled the air, like the purring of some enormous cat. Without any effort on my part, the door began to open. I extricated my hand as it slid to the side on smooth tracks, revealing a blackened opening. The air emanating from within smelled dusty and stale, with a faint, aromatic spice beneath.

There were more spikes at the edge of the door, thick ones that had been slotted into the wall. If someone tried to run through the door while it was open, I imagined it would either slam shut, or the points would shape-shift to skewer the intruder.

Welcome home, the Shard whispered in my head.

My skin tingled, and something in my chest—not my heart, but something dark and burning that wrapped around it—pulsed with awareness. The magic that filled me recognized its echo everywhere. A new sense had come to life inside me, like hearing without ears or feeling without touch.

I turned to look at my friends. Lara's face was taut with apprehension, her brown eyes wide as they darted between me and the entrance. Anya still stared at nothing, lost inside her head.

"Blood Shard?" I whispered, not sure where it was or how I was supposed to address it. "Can I bring them with me?"

Claiming a new house member is no small matter, the Shard said in a dark purr. The tree trunk glowed red in one spot, and light began spreading across the bark in branching rivulets. *You must be certain.*

I faced the heart of that crimson shine. "I'm certain."

"Is the Shard . . . talking to you?" Lara asked softly. At my nod, she looked even more anxious.

"I want them to be members of Blood House," I told the Shard more firmly.

Lara made a pained expression, though she didn't protest. This couldn't be easy for her. Earlier this night she'd been the first daughter of Earth, heir to a house of water and greenery. Now she was a magicless outcast, forced to take shelter in a house of bloodshed and death.

The bark parted, revealing a chunk of garnet-colored crystal. It was hand-sized, curved on one side and jagged on the other. Awe filled me. The Shard had been formed during the destruction of another world beyond the stars, if King Osric was to be believed. It was the echo of a dead god, a vessel containing a fragment of magic that had been launched through the heavens to find a new home.

And it had chosen me to wield that magic.

Crimson light pulsed from the stone with each word. *Then claim them.*

"You approve?"

Nothing you do is for me to approve.

I wasn't sure I liked that. The Shard had been a god once—it was supposed to tell me what to do, how to be a princess.

I am not the one who came before, the Shard corrected. *I am magic and memory. The Shards are woven into the fabric of this world—we do not rule.*

I wrapped my arms around myself, rubbing up and down. The blue gauze of my half sleeves was wrinkled and dotted with flakes of dried blood. If it didn't rule... apparently I did. "How do I add them to the house?"

Set the intention in your mind. If you will it, I obey.

The Shard *was* the house, I realized. Or maybe we were all part of something larger, connected by the magic we shared. The tree, the house, the Shard, Caedo... and me.

I closed my eyes, breathing in and out slowly. *I claim these two as members of Blood House*, I thought.

It is done, the Shard whispered back.

It was that easy? I opened my eyes again, then beckoned Lara and Anya forward. "You're part of the house now."

Lara looked mistrustfully at the spiked door. "Are you sure? What if it stabs me?"

"It won't," I said, though my underarms were growing damp from nervous sweat. Putting my faith in the honesty of a sentient rock was difficult, but that sentient rock had also saved my life and given me magic tonight, so I tried to project confidence.

Lara's eyes were reddened from grief and exhaustion. Her green ball gown was torn and spattered with blood, and her wavy black hair was tangled. She swayed, then visibly pulled herself together, spine straightening as she looked at the entrance with determination. "So long as there's a bed in there, I don't care." She shifted Anya into my hold, then walked forward, took a deep breath, and stuck her hand out as if testing whether the door would slam shut on it. When it didn't, she let out an audible sigh of relief.

Anya looked nearly asleep on her feet. "Let's get you inside," I whispered.

The entrance loomed, silent and dark. Whatever lurked inside couldn't be worse than what filled the rest of Mistei, and there would at least be a bed to fall into. The thought of that made me want to cry.

So I urged Anya forward, Lara fell into step beside us, and we made our way into Blood House together.

The door slid shut behind us with an echoing clang. It was pitch black. Everything was still and silent except for a distant trickling sound.

"It's dark," Lara said unnecessarily.

"Maybe I can find a torch."

A vibration went through the floor. A faint red glow sparked in the distance, followed by another. A line of torches came alight one by one, outlining the borders of a vast room.

The house was waking up.

Once the torches on the ground floor were burning, more swelled to life a level above, their fire unusually red. The light sparked up and up, revealing six stories in all. Each level was lined with silver-railed walkways that overlooked the central space, with spiraling staircases anchoring the corners of the room. It had the same layout as Earth House's main hall, but the decor was startlingly different. Earth House was bright and verdant, with a floor of packed soil dotted with flowers and trees. Blood House was paved with gray marble that sparkled in the torchlight, and the garnet-hued walls were coated with silver filigree. The courtyard was anchored by a tiered fountain.

The liquid in the fountain was running red.

"Oh," Lara said, sounding dismayed.

"Oh," I echoed, feeling something more akin to awe.

A deep sense of comfort and safety filled the room—the same

comfort I'd once felt as a servant in Earth House. The house's magic was wrapping us in a soothing blanket of welcome, letting us know we were home. The couches against the walls looked plush and inviting, as if they wanted us to rest. But the fountain was spilling blood, and the filigree wasn't the only shining ornamentation in the room—axes, swords, pikes, and spears rested in wooden racks and hung from brackets over the couches, as if the faeries of Blood House had never relaxed without a weapon close to hand.

A mix of softness and violence, beauty and death.

I brought Anya to a settee tucked beneath the curve of a staircase. It was upholstered in burgundy velvet, and a sword hung from the wall beside it. Dust puffed up as the couch took her weight, and she curled up on her side, closing her eyes.

Lara was exploring the room, trailing her fingers over the walls and furniture. She wrapped her hand around the haft of an axe, stared at it contemplatively for a few moments, then let go.

The weapons deserved investigation, but the liquid music of the fountain drew my attention. I crossed to it and sat on the dust-rimed edge, watching the fall of blood. The air was spiced with the coppery rich scent, and I didn't find it nearly as disgusting as I ought to. *Whose blood is this?* I asked Caedo silently.

The first princess began it with the blood of her enemies. You can add some from your next kill.

A cold shiver raced down my spine. I was a murderer now, and the dagger expected me to kill again. Worse, *I* expected myself to kill again. Illusion and Light House would be regrouping after the battle in the throne room. There would be violence as Mistei grappled with the question of who would rule next.

Ash-gray eyes filled my mind. Copper hair, a smile that flickered like flame, hands that had burned. A voice that had whispered promises in the dark and cruelties in the light.

I didn't want to think about Prince Drustan of Fire House, so I shoved the vision away.

The first princess had morbid taste, I told Caedo.

The dagger seemed amused as it pulsed against my skin. *You will learn to appreciate blood.* It slid down my arm like liquid, circling my wrist. I watched, fascinated, as it stretched narrow tendrils over my hand, mapping the spread of tendons before sending shoots over my fingers. It looked like a separate skeleton laid atop mine. Those metal bones were anchored in place with rings between each knuckle, and the tips sharpened into claws.

I dipped one claw into the eddying blood. Tiny ripples spread from that point of contact, and I felt Caedo sipping lightly, absorbing the liquid. The bond between us had strengthened with my new magic, and the dagger's thoughts and thirst lay alongside mine.

You make a fine monster, Caedo said.

I pulled my hand away from the fountain abruptly. When I looked up, Lara stood a few feet away, watching me nervously. "Kenna, what is that?"

The reddish torchlight winked off the metal bones and sank into the dark crimson jewel that had settled over the back of my hand. "My dagger," I said, willing it to take that shape, and the metal instantly reformed. The unfaceted gem capped the hilt, and the blade was silvery bright. "It belonged to Princess Cordelia." The last Blood princess.

As a human, I shouldn't have been able to wield Caedo, but it had been starving and without a mistress when I'd found it in the bog before my terrified flight to Mistei. The first taste of my blood had bonded us, and now I didn't know if—or how—we would ever be parted. It was alive but not animal, a piece of magic so old it had taken physical form. It existed to drink and to serve—and now it served me.

"That's what you used to kill Garrick during the Earth trial," Lara said, staring at it.

I nodded, feeling slightly nauseated at the memory of plunging the dagger into his gut. Not just at what I had done, but at how much I had enjoyed it.

"And Osric?"

"Yes." That had been even more gratifying than killing Garrick, but I wouldn't feel guilty about that pleasure, not after what Osric had done to Anya and everyone else in Mistei who had suffered under eight hundred years of tyrannical rule. "It drinks blood."

Lara looked ill at the thought. "Where did you even find it?"

During the immortality trials, I'd told Lara I'd found it in Mistei, but she'd been so absorbed by the trials she hadn't pushed for more details. "In the bog," I admitted. "Back when I still lived in Tumbledown."

Her jaw sagged. "You had a magic dagger all along and didn't tell me?"

Her hurt expression made my stomach twist. "I'm sorry. I didn't tell anyone. I was too afraid of losing it."

She looked away. "I think I'm just tired," she said, rubbing her forehead.

It was long past midnight. "Me, too." At the words, Caedo liquefied and crawled back up my sleeve to curl around my bicep. "Will you stay with Anya while I find the bedrooms? I don't want to leave her alone."

After a pause where it looked like she wanted to argue with me, Lara nodded.

I moved quickly, ducking into corridors on each floor of the house to get a sense of the layout, though I didn't explore past the first few doors. The torches struggled to life in front of me, but even with that illumination, there was an eeriness to the empty halls that gave me goose bumps. Definitely a place to explore during the day, when the ceiling crystals would reflect the light of the sky far above.

The house appeared to be laid out in a similar manner to Earth House, which meant the ground floor would hold kitchens, dining rooms, bathing chambers, libraries, salons, laundry facilities, and other public spaces. The next floors would hold more gathering spaces before sprawling away towards the far reaches of the house where Underfae and less prominent Noble Fae lived. The upper three floors of this central area would contain bedrooms and gathering spaces for the most prominent members of the house, with a corridor on the top floor reserved for members of the ruling family.

I jogged up the spiraling stairs towards the top level, running my hand along the silver railing before realizing how dirty my palm was getting. The staircase was beautiful under the dust, with a banister that looked like swirling liquid and balusters shaped like swords.

The flooring on the upper level was black marble veined with red, topped with a garnet-hued carpet runner. Candles burned in alcoves behind stained glass, scattering light across the hallway in crimson shards. While the wooden doors of Earth House had been carved to depict natural scenes, the silver doors of Blood House were engraved with scenes of battle, healing, and revelry. I peered at one depicting a ballroom full of Fae, Underfae, and Nasties. Their positions were ecstatic and wild, and when I looked closer, I saw figures twined together carnally at the edges.

A jolt went through me. Blood House wasn't just the house of warriors and healers, was it? It was the Fae's house of the flesh. And though Fire House might claim hedonism as their preferred virtue, pleasure was sacred to all the Fae.

I didn't want to think about pleasure or Fire House, so I turned to a door that showed a vast battle and opened that one instead. The torches were sluggish to spark, but soon they were blazing brightly, casting a more natural golden light than the flames in the entrance hall.

The red carpet was soft beneath my feet, and the walls were white marble veined with silver and gold. Like Lara's room back at Earth House, there was a main living space with a desk, vanity, wardrobe, fireplace, and sitting area, then a folding screen that sectioned off a sleeping area. The black lacquer screen was patterned with crimson swords, and the large four-poster bed behind it had a plush red comforter beneath a gauzy drapery. Even covered in a layer of grime, the room was beautiful.

The bed was large enough for the three of us, and tomorrow we could clean out more rooms. I stripped the blanket and shook it out, sneezing as dust puffed up. It was amazing the fabric hadn't rotted, but the house's magic probably had something to do with the generally decent state of things. The torches still burned, the fountain still flowed, and overall the place looked as if it had only been locked up for a few years, rather than five centuries.

Once the bed was remade, I returned downstairs. Lara leaned against a wall, looking close to passing out, but she nodded when I told her I'd prepared a room. The sound of my voice startled Anya awake, and she sat bolt upright.

"It's all right," I soothed. "We're going somewhere more comfortable."

She actually met my eyes, and relief fluttered in my chest, mingling with the worry. She looked so tired.

"You'll be safe," I promised. "It's just the three of us. No one else can get in."

Her chin dipped the tiniest amount.

Once we'd gotten Anya settled on a couch upstairs, I opened the wardrobe and was relieved to see an array of dresses and nightgowns. Like Earth's enchanted wardrobes, it knew what was needed. Lara took a voluminous white nightgown, I took a red one, and we slid a gray one over Anya's head.

Then the three of us settled into bed together, side by side like sisters. The torches extinguished, responding to our needs. The darkness left behind was heavy but not frightening. With spice and dust in my nostrils and the soft breathing of my friends in my ears, I fell into a deep sleep.

2

A SOFT EXCLAMATION WOKE ME, AND I SAT UPRIGHT. BLINKing sleep away, I looked for the source of the sound. To my left, Lara still lay unconscious, clutching her pillow tightly. To my right, the bed was empty.

Anya stood by the folding screen, arms wrapped around herself as she stared at me. The ceiling crystals had turned the room the gray hue of predawn, but I wasn't sure if they were reflecting the sky outside or if they'd responded to Anya's desire to see her surroundings.

"Anya?" I whispered, climbing out of bed.

"It was real," she said. "You're actually here."

Pain and relief mixed inside me. "Yes, it's me."

She'd once been solidly built—not as curvaceous as Lara, but with flaring hips, strong legs, and a bosom I'd been envious of for approximately a decade. Now she looked waifish, the gray robe swallowing her up. She'd lost weight during her imprisonment, and she seemed even smaller without her long golden-brown hair. A narrow scar spiraled over her right cheek, and her hazel eyes seemed dim.

"How is this . . ." She shook her head, clutching the robe tighter.

"Were you there, too?" Her voice broke, and my heart broke with it. In the brothel, she meant. King Osric had stolen her, the way the Fae had stolen countless humans. He'd seen her beauty and wanted it for himself, so he'd taken her.

Or maybe he'd seen her beauty and wanted to destroy it. Like throwing a fragile vase to hear the sound it made as it shattered.

"I wasn't... there," I said, feeling a sick surge of guilt. I'd been in Mistei for six months, and that entire time, Osric had been raping Anya and torturing her with illusions. I'd mourned her while she was suffering. "They made me a servant in Earth House."

"A servant," she echoed hollowly.

I began to walk towards her, then froze when she flinched and squeezed herself tighter.

"Your skin," she said.

I looked down at my hands. They looked normal to me. "My skin?"

"Last night, in the torchlight. It shone."

Realization snatched my breath away. The Noble Fae all shimmered with a hint of magical radiance. Not enough to cast light in the dark, just enough that when sunlight or torchlight struck them, they seemed dusted with glitter.

"Something happened to me," I said, feeling a surge of anxiety. The change was too large, too profound, for me to comprehend all at once. Instead, I sampled it in pieces. In the throne room it had been the revelation that my new magic allowed me to control bodies. At the entrance to Blood House, I'd realized my endurance was heightened. Now... I apparently sparkled. Even my skin was no longer my own. "I'm Fae now."

She let out a soft cry, then fled.

I followed, slipping around the partition that separated the main room from the sleeping chamber. The crystals crusted over the ceiling sparked to life, casting a golden glow that was somewhere between the rosy shine of early morning and the bright radiance of midday. The house had apparently been letting us sleep in.

Anya stood behind a couch in the sitting area. Her fingers clenched the velvet back so tightly her knuckles were white. "Stay away," she hissed.

"It's still me," I told her, chest hurting like she'd stabbed me. "Nothing else has changed. I'm still the Kenna you've always known."

That wasn't true, though, was it? The Kenna she'd known had been wild and fun, prone to romping through the woods and exploring the bog outside Tumbledown. A girl who wore trousers and was usually spattered with mud, whose biggest dream had been to become a merchant. That girl had had simple needs, simple angers, and simple wants.

Nothing was simple anymore.

Anya swayed. "Nothing feels real," she said so quietly the words almost didn't make it to my ears. "You don't feel real." There was a pause before she spoke again. "I don't feel real, either."

"It's real," I said, heart aching. "But you don't have to understand it all at once. I don't even understand it myself." Her face was closed off, so I cast about for anything that might help. "Are you hungry? I can find food."

She looked at me mistrustfully, then slowly nodded.

"I'm hungry, too," Lara said. She stood beside the folding screen, clutching her robe to her throat. Her black hair was mussed from sleep, and she looked nearly as tired as she had the night before.

Would Blood House even have food? There were orchards, vegetable patches, and stables full of animals below Earth House, thriving on faerie magic despite the lack of natural sunshine, but the magic also created items out of nothing. In the Earth House kitchens, I'd only needed to long for a certain treat before it appeared.

"I'll go see if I can find something," I said.

An expression I couldn't identify passed over Lara's face. "You're not a servant anymore. I should be bringing a tray up for you."

"You're not a servant, either. I'll go look." Then, realizing Anya had never gotten a proper introduction, I gestured between them. "Anya, this is Lara. She's Fae, but you don't need to be afraid of her. She's from Earth House."

"I am not from Earth House," Lara said sharply. Then she turned and disappeared back into the sleeping area, and I heard the rustle of blankets.

My head was starting to hurt, and with it came a rising tide of anger. Not at Anya for her mistrust or at Lara for the bitterness that came from losing so much, but at the people who had caused so much pain. King Osric, Princess Oriana, and all the rest of the Noble Fae who manipulated and hurt and used others.

Anger at myself, too. Because here I was, immortal and newly magical, and I couldn't do anything to fix this pain for my two closest friends. I could find breakfast, though. So I forced a smile for Anya, promised to return soon, and went exploring.

THE HOUSE SEEMED CLEANER THIS MORNING. THE LAYER OF DUST was thinner, as if invisible hands had tended to it overnight. Magic pulsed and thrummed everywhere, little currents that raced through the walls and danced inside the torches, and contentment radiated from the stones.

Blood House had a reason to live again.

Did all Noble Fae feel such a strong connection to the magic inside Mistei, or was this a power reserved for the house heads? I felt like a spider perched in a vast web, reading messages in the vibrations.

I passed a suit of armor that looked as if it had been knocked askew, and when I thought about straightening it, the house instantly obeyed, making me jump.

This must be related to being the new princess, I decided, slightly unnerved by the ability to affect my surroundings with a thought. I hadn't felt this web of magic outside of house walls, and the flavor of it—if that was the right word to use for a new sense that wasn't sight, taste, touch, hearing, or smell, but somehow none of them and all of them simultaneously—was the same as the magic burning inside my chest. As if the house and I were cut from the same piece of cloth, resonating with each other on a mystical level.

There would be multiple kitchens throughout the house, but the one on the ground floor near the entrance hall was the largest and served the royal family and other elite house members. I headed towards it, passing woven tapestries, silver sconces containing red-burning torches, and more racks of weapons. Another small fountain sat in an alcove, shaped like a silver goblet tipping to pour blood into a bowl. It should have been an upsetting sight, but instead the bright tinkle of drops sounded like a giggle to my ears.

The house didn't speak words in my head the way the Shard or Caedo did, but emotion permeated the air. It had been lonely, it told me on a sigh of feeling that made the torches flicker. Now it wouldn't be anymore.

As I passed the fountain, I wondered if that was entirely the blood of enemies or if some had come from the massacre all those years ago. Had the house cleaned the gore up the way it had apparently begun to dust itself, or had it drunk it instead? There must have been so much carnage—a sixth of the population of Mistei slaughtered in a single night.

I stopped, heart slamming hard. King Osric had gotten into Blood

House through a secret back entrance. Did it still exist? Because if Osric knew about it, others would, too.

I needed to talk to the Shard, but I wasn't sure how to. Asking out loud had worked the night before, but it had been nearby at the time, ensconced in the tree. Did I always need to petition before the tree, or could I communicate with it some other way?

We had to be connected through our shared power. I closed my eyes, focusing on the heat of magic inside me. I imagined it as a deep liquid pool in my breast and tossed the question in like a stone. *Blood Shard. Can you hear me?*

After a pause, a voice filled my head. *You learn quickly.*

It was the only way to survive in Mistei. *Is there still a back entrance?*

A vision filled my head of a rocky hill with a jagged gap between boulders. Underfae in Illusion colors piled stones in front of the entrance, and then dirt was shoveled over that. An asrai poured blood over the soil, dampening it. Finally, I saw Princess Oriana, hands outstretched and face pensive, growing grass and tangled shrubs over the dirt as Osric watched. Soon the entire hill was smooth again, as if the entrance had never been.

The blood was Princess Cordelia's, the Shard murmured. *It made the barrier whole, and a new opening cannot be carved by anyone but you.*

The tension left me. *Why did Osric do that?*

He wished for Blood House to be forgotten—even by the ground itself.

How terribly sad. I was here now, though, and Mistei would be forced to remember.

The kitchen was vast, with three long stone worktables, multiple bread ovens, and two fireplaces large enough to roast whole stags in.

Counters and sinks lined the brick walls, and cabinets stretched to the ceiling. I started opening them, but the shelves were empty.

Lara appeared in the doorway, still in her white robe. Apparently she'd decided not to go back to sleep, after all. "Anything?" she asked.

I rubbed my forehead. "No."

She scowled at the cabinets. "Where is food usually kept?"

She'd never been in the kitchens of Earth House before, I realized. Her brother Selwyn had mingled with the servants, but Lara had always kept herself apart, the way Oriana had wanted her to.

Pain speared my chest at the thought of Selwyn's easy smile and shy confidences. It was easy to see him in Lara—they had the same brown eyes fringed with short, dark lashes, the same rounded face shape. He'd been *good*, the way no one down here was good, and now he was gone because Drustan had sacrificed him for his coup.

"There would normally be staples in the cabinets," I said, trying not to think about my part in that tragedy. "Bread, cheese, pickled vegetables, salted jerky, things like that. Meat, fresh vegetables, and fruit would be kept in cold cellars a level down." Like the root cellars of the human world, except chillier thanks to magically unmelting blocks of ice. "But I doubt there's anything left. Nothing good, anyway."

"We have to leave to get food?" Lara sounded dismayed by the idea.

"Let me think." I closed my eyes, reached for the pool of magic, and passed the question along.

The house can provide food using its magic reserves, the Blood Shard replied. *Not forever, though.*

That explained the midnight snacks and extra treats Earth House's kitchen had snuck me. The houses could spark their own torches, change the quality of the overhead light, and provide a changing array of outfits—apparently they could manufacture food from nothing but magic, too.

How do the house's reserves get filled? I asked.

It will regenerate on its own, but the process will be slow without a supply. If you add to the house, that will help—every member is part of the magic, and the whole is stronger together. Or there are other ways.

Other ways?

The Shard slipped another image into my head of a faerie wearing scarlet silk and a spiked black crown pouring a pitcher of blood into the fountain. It was followed by a more gruesome one: a corridor piled high with corpses wearing red and silver, their blood pooling on the floor and sinking into the gaps between tiles.

"Kenna?" Lara's hand brushed my sleeve, pulling me out of the vision.

"The Shard," I said by way of explanation. Tears pressed at the backs of my eyes. The house was still functioning today because it had fed on its own sorrow.

Lara withdrew her hand. "Oriana told me she communicates with the Earth Shard. I never knew how." She shook her head, looking at her feet. "I won't ever know how."

She would never take her place as princess. She would never rule over Earth House and protect the faeries who lived there. Lara had rarely seemed to want that future, but it had been expected of her, something to cling to as a certainty in the midst of so much chaos. What did she have now?

Just me. And I hadn't even been able to feed her yet.

I turned to face the cabinets, determined to figure this out. "Bread," I said out loud, shaping the wish in my head.

One of the wooden doors rattled. When I opened it, a loaf of bread sat on one of the shelves. It had scored lines on the top and a dusting of white over the crust, and it took seeing it to realize how hungry I was. My stomach growled, and I grabbed the bread and ripped a hunk off to hand to Lara before shoving one in my own mouth.

"Cheese?" Lara said hesitantly.

She might not have powers, but she was a lady of Blood House now, and the magic obeyed. A hunk of white cheese appeared on one of the long stone tables. We tore into that, too, shoving the sharp cheddar into our mouths.

Anya had always loved cheddar. A silent wish made an apple appear, and I found a collection of silverware, dishes, and goblets in an enormous pantry and began putting together a meal for her on a freshly washed porcelain plate.

A vibration came from the floor and shivered up my legs, and I paused in my work. "What was that?"

"What was what?" Lara asked between mouthfuls. She'd gotten adventurous and requested hot chocolate, and a mug steamed at her elbow.

"I felt something."

We fell silent, listening, but the air was silent. The vibration came again, and the back of my skull prickled as the house wordlessly urged me to hurry to the entrance, because someone was outside.

Trepidation crept through me. Who was it? No one I wanted to see, probably. "Can you bring this to Anya?" I asked, handing the plate to Lara. "We have a visitor."

"Who?"

I shook my head. "I don't know." The threads of magic woven through the house shivered again, and I got an impression of dark velvet and cold midnights. "A Void faerie, I think."

She grimaced. "Do you have to go?"

The house nudged more insistently. I rubbed my temples, wishing I was in a better state for this. "Yes, I do."

She nodded, mouth tense. "Be safe."

I left the kitchen and passed through the inner hall. The house door slid aside at my approach to reveal the Blood Tree—and a familiar black-clad figure standing beneath it.

Lord Kallen of Void House had come to see me.

3

"PRINCESS KENNA," KALLEN SAID, INCLINING HIS HEAD. HIS voice was a smooth baritone, as perfectly composed as the rest of him. "I hope you are well this morning."

His pale face was solemn, and his midnight-blue eyes seemed black in the reddish light of the hall. His straight raven-dark hair hung loose to his shoulders, and he wore full Void black with no adornments, as usual. His sword was strapped to his hip, but the opal brooch that had once marked his allegiance to King Osric was gone.

The King's Vengeance had been part of the king's undoing. He'd been a traitor—a rebel—all along.

"Lord Kallen." I nodded in return, reminding myself I was no longer a servant obligated to curtsy to Fae nobility. "If you're looking for information, your blackmail material has expired."

That was usually why Kallen sought me out—to threaten me into sharing whatever I could about Drustan, Earth House, or any random information I'd happened to overhear. His leverage had been the fact I'd been cheating in the trials, but everyone knew that now, and I'd slit the throat of the king who had tried to execute me for it.

"So it has." His expression was unreadable. "And, no, I've come to escort you to the meeting."

I felt a prickle of alarm. "What meeting?"

"Drustan and Hector would like you to join them in an hour to discuss who will be king."

My stomach dropped. "Already?"

"War does not wait." Kallen's eyes drifted over me. "You may want to change."

I should have already changed. This was not how I wanted him to first see me as the Princess of Blood, with bare feet, tangled hair, and a rumpled nightgown. I tucked my toes under the hem of the robe, feeling the flush of embarrassment.

A meeting with Drustan. Shards, I wasn't ready for that yet. I pressed a hand to my belly, willing my nerves to settle.

"We don't need to leave for another thirty minutes," Kallen said, watching me closely. "If you need a few moments of privacy."

I scoffed, not very convincingly. "Why would I need that?"

His expressions were always subtle, but I read the skepticism in this one. He knew why. Kallen always knew everything. He was a spider, spinning his webs in darkened corners and waiting for hapless insects like me to stumble into his trap.

My face felt hot. He'd known I would sleep with Drustan before I had. *Are you fucking the Fire prince?* he'd asked before Drustan and I had even kissed. *You will be soon, I'll wager.*

And like a predictable little fool, I had.

This hurt, and I didn't know what to do about any of it: Drustan, Lara, Anya, my new magic, my new position, the decisions I was expected to make. Blood House needed to throw its support behind a ruler to break the stalemate between Fire and Void, but how could I choose a king when I didn't know what made a good one? When I didn't know what either of them would do with power?

One moment at a time, I told myself. The future was too vast to deal with all at once, but I could survive in smaller chunks. A second, a minute, an hour. One foot in front of another, each breath in sequence, and soon I would be partway through a journey that would have seemed impossible to start otherwise.

I straightened my shoulders and notched my chin up. "I'll be fine."

Kallen's mouth turned up slightly. "I know you will." He approached with slow, deliberate steps, as if testing whether I might flee. "The tree is thriving again," he said, gesturing at the new crimson leaves.

"It is." There was even a crow in the branches, preening its glossy black feathers. Birds were rare in Mistei—I'd seldom seen any outside of Earth House—and I wondered if the resurrection of the magic had drawn it here to roost.

"And the rest of the house?" he asked.

I eyed him warily. Something had changed between us over the past months. He'd blackmailed and threatened me, but we'd also danced, and last night he'd saved my life. But he was a collector of information, and his brother wanted to be king. "Forgive me if I don't share any details."

He stopped a few feet away. "Probably wise. You are well, though?"

"I suppose."

"It must be quite the change."

To become a powerful immortal after a lifetime as a poor, vulnerable human? "An understatement." There was something in his watchful air that made me want to confide in him—or at least tell *someone* how overwhelming this all was—but Kallen couldn't be trusted. Even if his ultimate loyalties had come clear last night, there was still so much I didn't understand about his motivations.

He nodded. "You will have to learn quickly."

Annoyance sparked. "I'm aware."

"But you will," he said, seemingly unaffected by my irritation. "It's something you excel at."

My breath hitched at the unexpected praise, delivered so matter-of-factly. "We have to adapt to our circumstances in order to change them."

His sword hand flexed at his side. "A fact I know well."

We were dancing around too many topics, and I wasn't sure why he had come to retrieve me personally. Except . . . No, I did have an idea. "Are you going to ask me to support Hector?"

Kallen looked surprised at the abrupt question. It was rare to break through that cool composure, but sometimes I managed it. "Obviously. Though you are capable of making your own decisions."

His equally blunt response startled me in return. The Fae talked around everything, preferring metaphor and insinuation to outright stating their intentions. "I don't know anything about him. How do you expect me to throw my support behind someone who's given no indication he'd be a good ruler?"

"Has Drustan given you a better indication that he'll be a good ruler?" he asked, brows rising.

The question hit me like a slap. Kallen certainly knew I'd been sleeping with the Fire prince, but did he know I'd practically worshipped him? That I'd thought him a true idealist and a champion for the greater good? That I'd believed in him so fervently I'd risked not just my life but the lives of others in the name of Drustan's supposed principles?

I'm not afraid to die for this, Drustan had told me, gray eyes burning with intent. *No one who works with me closely is.*

When the supposed idealist was the only one left standing, that said something. When that same idealist quickly moved to cement his grip on power, that said even more.

"No," I said. "Which is why I'm not supporting him, either." Then, because I didn't feel like discussing Drustan anymore, I turned away. "I'm going to change."

Kallen's voice followed me. "I'll be waiting."

NEITHER ANYA NOR LARA WERE IN THE BEDROOM. I CALLED their names, and a door across the hall opened to reveal Lara. "What?" she asked. Her eyes were red and puffy like she'd been crying, but there was a guardedness to her expression that told me she didn't want to talk about it.

"Where's Anya?"

Lara pointed towards the end of the hall. "She picked out a bedroom."

They both had, apparently. Behind Lara, I saw at least a dozen dresses piled on the floor in a mass of shimmering red and silver fabric. One had been laid out with more care over a chairback: a navy blue gown trimmed with red ribbons.

Her wardrobe back at Earth House had been full of blue dresses.

Lara followed my gaze, then frowned and stepped into the hall, closing the door behind her.

"Is Anya all right?" I asked, pretending I hadn't been staring at the mess Lara had made of her new room. "Did she eat?"

Lara shrugged, picking at the folds of her robe. "She took the food, but she won't talk to me."

I hesitated over whether or not to say anything about Lara's own emotional state, then took the wary look in her eyes into account. "Thank you. I'll check on her."

"Who was out there?" Lara asked.

"Lord Kallen."

Revulsion washed over her face. "Why?"

"He invited me to a meeting with Hector and Drustan."

"Princess Kenna," she said slowly, as if the title were too heavy on her tongue. "I still can't believe it."

"I can't, either." Guilt gnawed at me, because what had I done to deserve this when the Shards had judged her so harshly? We'd committed the same crime, after all.

"Where is the meeting?" Lara asked.

"I don't know. Kallen is bringing me there."

"The King's Vengeance? You're going to end up gutted."

"He's not the King's Vengeance anymore. And Drustan's more likely to murder me at this point, since I refused to support him last night even after—"

My jaw snapped shut. Lara didn't know about my history with Drustan, I realized with a surge of anxiety. I'd been keeping so many secrets from her.

She made a soft, pain-filled noise. "I want to rip his heart out for what he did to Selwyn." Then she stormed back into her room, slamming the door behind her.

The guilt intensified. If Lara ever found out the role I'd played in recruiting Selwyn to Drustan's cause, she'd probably want to rip out my heart, too.

A sense of déjà vu came over me as I approached the door Lara had pointed out. Anya had chosen the last bedroom before the servant stairs. If this had been Earth House, it would have been my old room as Lara's handmaiden.

I knocked lightly. "Anya?"

There was no reply.

I turned the knob slowly and opened the door, peeking inside. This wasn't the fine bedroom of a noblewoman; it was one of the adjoining servant's chambers. There was a dusty wooden desk, a single chair, a wardrobe, and a narrow bed in the corner—just like my old room.

Anya was curled up on the floor at the foot of the bed, facing the wall.

I hurried towards her, worry rising. "Anya?"

She startled and turned to face me, tucking her knees tighter against her chest as if protecting her vulnerable belly. The skin beneath her eyes was smudged with exhaustion.

"Are you all right?" I asked, crouching beside her.

She made a soft noise and blinked heavy eyelids. "Sleeping."

"On the floor?"

She nodded. "Safer."

I hesitated, wondering what to do. The floor wasn't comfortable, but there had to be a reason she wasn't in the bed. A glance at the quilt showed that it was free of dust, either cleaned by Anya or the house's magic.

Safer, she'd said.

Her last bed hadn't been safe at all.

"Maybe this time I won't dream," she whispered, closing her eyes.

I clenched my fists tightly, struggling against the urge to scream at what had been done to her. Anya's cheeks were hollow, and the shadows under her eyes spoke of deep fatigue. If she was able to rest, even if it was on the floor, that was good.

"Sleep well," I said softly. "If you get hungry again, you can ask the kitchen to give you food. The magic works like that."

She didn't reply.

I pulled the blanket off the bed, draped it over her, and left.

Back in the bedroom that was apparently now mine alone, I let out the scream that had been trapped in my chest, muffling it in my palm so Lara wouldn't hear. My best friend was lying on a stone floor. And instead of watching over her, I had to attend this damned meeting.

I yanked open the wardrobe, wishing for armor rather than silk. It didn't offer that, but it did present an array of dresses with metal embellishments. I chose one as red as the blood I wanted to spill on Anya's behalf. It was simple enough to put on without assistance, with a silver clasp that pulled the fabric in at the waist. The sleeves were long and tight, terminating in points that covered the backs of my hands and secured with rings around my middle fingers. Small metal spikes marched in a line from collar to wrists. A dress that threatened pain—though the back was shockingly low. When I looked over my shoulder in the mirror, I could see the line of my spine down to my waist.

Caedo had wriggled up to curve around my neck. The dagger looked good with the rounded jewel settled into the hollow of my throat, but my back prickled to be so exposed. It wasn't enough to be a beautiful creature; I wanted everyone at that meeting to know my teeth were sharp.

An idea came to me, and the dagger re-formed itself. A wedge-shaped head settled below my collarbone, fangs bared, while the rest of the dagger stretched out to loop around my neck and trail down my spine in sinuous curves. When it settled into place, it looked like a snake slithering over my shoulder, with the jewel from the hilt placed in the middle of its head.

"I like you like this," I told Caedo. The spikes on my sleeves might prick if someone were to grab me, but if anyone touched my back, they would bleed far worse.

There wasn't time to properly fix my hair, but there was oil in the attached bathing chamber that I dripped onto my curls before using my fingers to gently detangle them, starting at the ends. I bound my hair back in a bun, then quickly applied cosmetics—a smoky gray shadow and black liner for my eyes, a crimson paint for my lips. My cheeks were pale, the freckles standing out, but I didn't bother with rouge. The woman I wanted to be today wasn't the type to blush.

Surveying myself in the mirror, I felt a jolt of unreality. This was my face, but it was also a stranger's face. The dark shadow made my amber eyes look more vivid, while the crimson on my lips was reminiscent of blood. My skin glittered faintly.

I brushed my fingers over the jeweled snake head resting on my sternum. "I don't know what to expect," I admitted to Caedo and the mirror. "What to do." Even with my new powers, I was at a disadvantage. The other house heads had centuries of experience and strong opinions about who should rule. They would expect me to capitulate to what they wanted.

Caedo thrummed against my skin. *You'll do whatever you have to.*

KALLEN'S EYES WIDENED SLIGHTLY WHEN HE TOOK IN MY CHANGED appearance, but he said nothing other than "Blood House attire suits you."

We left the house behind, heading up a sloping corridor towards other parts of Mistei. He hadn't spoken since complimenting my dress, and the growing awkwardness felt like a tangible weight against my skin. "You said the meeting would be with Hector and Drustan," I said to break the silence, "but it clearly includes you as well." It had been like that under Osric's rule, too—Kallen had always been seated at the high table.

"Yes. It will be Hector, you, me, Drustan, and one of his allies—and possibly Oriana, if she deigns to accept the invitation."

A shiver raced down my spine at Drustan's name. The last time I'd seen the Fire prince, he'd been demanding my support after a night of betrayal and violence. The time before that, we'd been naked in each other's arms.

"I'm not sure what Drustan expects to have changed overnight," I said, trying to feign nonchalance.

Kallen's sidelong glance said I hadn't fooled him. "Perhaps nothing has changed in the group members' fundamental positions, but Drustan is correct that we need to resolve this soon. Illusion will be scrambling to determine which of Osric's relatives has the best claim to the throne. Light might be split right now, but I suspect they'll ultimately back Illusion. The only way to stand against those two houses is to form an alliance ourselves, which means we need to come to an understanding."

Just like the old rebellion—Fire, Void, and Blood against Light and Illusion. Maybe this time Earth could be shaken out of its longstanding neutrality. Oriana had refused to take a side last night, but in the light of morning, she might realize the mistake she'd made.

"Did Osric have children?" I asked, wondering who his successor might be.

"A few over the centuries. Mostly accidental, and he murdered all of them as soon as they expressed a hint of ambition." At my appalled look, Kallen shrugged. "If you'd met them, you wouldn't consider it a loss."

"Even so. He killed his own *children*." That shouldn't shock me when he'd done so many other awful things, but it did.

"Osric was as paranoid as he was powerful. He murdered his siblings for the same reason, and he never took a consort. Not that there's much precedent for consorts seizing power after a house head's death, but it's happened a few times."

I was woefully ignorant of the majority of Fae history—yet another way I was unqualified for this position. "Then who's left to step into his place?"

"It's rumored a few children may have been passed off as the offspring of other court members, but at this point the likeliest candidates are only distantly related to him. Cousins of cousins, things like that. They'll choose based on a mix of bloodline claim and magical power."

When the Fae lived forever, family trees became unreasonably complicated. Most faeries were less than a thousand years old—they were too fond of murdering one another—but that was still a long span of time for families to establish their bloodlines.

The path curved into familiar territory. A ramp on the left spiraled up to Fire House and the sitting room outside it where most of my affair with Drustan had been conducted. My pulse accelerated as we approached. The last place I wanted to see Drustan again was one where we'd been naked together.

Thankfully, we passed the ramp, and some of the tension in my chest loosened. "Where are we meeting?" I asked.

Again Kallen slid me a look. Did he know where I'd met the Fire prince for our assignations? How often I'd met him?

Of course he did, I thought bitterly. Kallen had eyes everywhere, and that was before one considered his ability to disappear into shadows.

"Drustan has chosen a room in neutral territory," he said. "One he swears is known by few."

"You said he's bringing an ally. Who?"

"A faerie from Light House."

"Gweneira?" Roland's brother Lothar was dead, and she was the only other member of Light House I knew Drustan had been plotting with.

Kallen paused mid-step. "Did you meet with her? I was unaware."

"No."

He resumed his even pace. "Then you must have seen her with Drustan at some point. Perhaps while spying for me?"

I felt the bite of satisfaction at the annoyance in his voice. Kallen didn't like not knowing things. "Perhaps."

"And neglected to tell me." He clicked his tongue. "I shouldn't be surprised. I knew you were withholding information."

That startled me. "You knew?"

His look said that was obvious. "Kenna, you did everything you could to avoid me, and when you couldn't avoid me, you lied to me."

Fear prickled over my skin, even though Kallen didn't hold any leverage over me anymore. "If you knew that, why let me get away with it?"

He was silent for too long. "You provided a few grains of truth. It was still worth it."

That wasn't a real answer. He'd had all the power in that situation. In addition to blackmail material, he'd had strength, connections, wealth, magic, and a deadly reputation. He could have made our arrangement far more worthwhile by applying even a fraction of that power—which meant he'd chosen not to.

We turned into a narrow hallway leading to a library. A tapestry hung halfway down the corridor, and Kallen stopped before it. He looked over his shoulder, then held his free hand up, fingers slightly curved. The shadows thickened where the walls met the floor, then crept over the ground in a thin layer, painting the stone a darker gray. A ward of some kind?

He brushed the fabric aside, revealing a plain wooden door. "Ready?" he asked.

I wasn't, but I nodded anyway.

Kallen knocked on the door in a syncopated pattern, then opened it. My heart pounded like the wings of a bird startled into flight. I took a deep breath, pushed my shoulders back, and walked inside to face Drustan, Hector, and the impossible choice I was expected to make.

4

My eyes instantly found Drustan. He stood beside a granite table, posture straight and hands folded at the small of his back. His long hair was a shining copper that rivaled the gleam of the torches, and his scarlet-and-gold tunic stood out starkly against the backdrop of gray stone.

"Princess Kenna," he said. "Thank you for joining us."

It felt like a fist was squeezing my heart. His voice was distant and polite, as if we were mere acquaintances. As if he wasn't the first person I'd ever lain with, as if I hadn't given myself wholly to him and his cause . . . as if he hadn't watched without protest as I was sent to my death.

I despised myself for that ache. Drustan had always made his priorities clear: the revolution first, everything else after. It was my fault for being naïve. I'd imagined myself the heroine of a grand love story, while to Drustan I was nothing but a side character in the legend of his own rise to power.

Drustan was waiting for my response, but it was hard to make my tongue work. I felt small and foolish and oddly lonely now that Kallen had slipped away to stand at the wall. I cleared my throat and forced myself to speak. "Drustan."

His lips thinned. He'd clearly been expecting more of an acknowledgment than that.

A low chuckle came from the table. Prince Hector lounged in a brocade-upholstered chair, looking like a slash of night against the gold fabric. His eyes were the same blue as Kallen's but narrower, making him look perpetually skeptical, and his lips had a sideways tilt, halfway to a sneer. His posture was relaxed, but something in his bearing and the sharpness of his stare made me uneasy. He had always struck me as restless, full of barely contained energy, like an animal pacing the boundaries of its cage.

"Hector," I said, dipping my chin slightly. He would have to earn my respect, too.

Hector's brows rose fractionally.

A third faerie sat opposite Hector. Lady Gweneira of Light House was delicate-boned and lovely, with oak-brown hair cut as short as a young boy's. Her brown eyes had a catlike quality. "Princess Kenna," she said. "How interesting to meet you."

"Gweneira is Roland and Lothar's cousin," Drustan told me. "She aided me in planning the revolution."

"Yes, I know." I nodded at Gweneira. "It's interesting to meet you, too." If she wouldn't say it was a pleasure, I wouldn't, either.

Drustan was smiling now, but that didn't mean anything. He put that smile on the way other people picked up weapons. "Oh, you know? Is that something you overheard while spying on me?"

Did he expect me to be sorry for eavesdropping? "Yes." I covered my discomfort by studying the room. The bare walls glittered with fragments of mica, and an empty fireplace was recessed into the back wall. There were no furnishings other than the table and chairs.

Drustan approached me, and my body tensed. He stopped within arm's reach and leaned in, lowering his voice. "I regret we can't speak privately first. Are you . . . Is your house well?"

My skin felt hot under the pressure of his gaze. Something burned in his eyes that didn't match that polite tone. "Well enough," I said, taking a step back. "Will Oriana be here?"

"Is it to be like that, then?" he asked so quietly the words were barely a breath.

"Kallen told me you invited her," I said, ignoring the question. "I'm curious if you expect her to actually show up." Despite my outward show of confidence, my stomach felt knotted.

"Unlikely," Hector said at the same time Drustan said, "She'll be here."

"Do you speak for Earth House now?" Hector asked sharply.

Drustan's lips lifted into another of his easy, charming smiles, and he left to take up his position beside the table again. It was as if the interlude between us had never happened. "No," Drustan said, "but unlike you, I understand what motivates others." His eyes touched on me lightly, as if illustrating his point.

What did he mean by that? Paranoia twisted up my spine, and I was regretting wearing red. Drustan's tunic was a brighter shade than my dress, but it still looked uncomfortably like I'd dressed to match him. Had he chosen the color to imply an alliance between us?

Damn the Fae and their double meanings and hidden agendas. The meeting had barely begun, and my head was already hurting trying to unravel the undertones.

Hector was smiling, too, but it was a hard slash of a grin, more akin to showing teeth. "Not everyone plays by your rules, Drustan."

"You and your feral dog were late to this alliance. You don't know a thing about my rules."

For a moment I didn't understand what dog Drustan was talking about, but when Kallen let out a soft chuckle, realization hit. He looked mildly amused at the insult, but anger moved swiftly through me. Kallen and Drustan had fought back-to-back the previous night. Whatever the complicated politics here, he deserved more respect than that. "Feral dog," I repeated. "Is this how a potential king treats his allies? If so, we are off to a very telling start."

Drustan looked startled at being told off. Kallen's attention flicked to me, but I couldn't tell what he was thinking. Except he raised a brow, and then I could. I had called him the king's dog not that long ago, hadn't I?

My face felt hot at the memory. Maybe I was inconsistent, but so was Drustan, and if he expected loyalty from this group, he needed to do better than that.

"Hector did not consult me before inviting Kallen to the meeting," Drustan told me. "I do not appreciate being caught unawares."

"You invited Gweneira without consulting me," Hector pointed out.

"Because she was essential to this victory," Drustan shot back.

"She is not a house head."

"Neither is your brother. And what has he accomplished, other than murdering everyone who looked at Osric the wrong way?"

Hector worked his jaw. "Kallen was cultivating external allies to aid in overthrowing the king. With Elsmere's aid, we would have struck at Samhain—"

"But you didn't," Drustan interrupted. A crackle of flame danced in his irises, and when he clenched his hands on the back of a chair, the air above his knuckles wavered with heat. "Gweneira was instrumental in recruiting members of Light House to our cause. I will not apologize for inviting her because of your wounded pride." His mouth twisted. "I'm surprised Kenna hasn't commented yet again on how a potential king treats his allies, but perhaps she reserves her judgments for me."

I found myself wishing for wine despite the relatively early hour.

It would make this meeting far more tolerable, and it would give me something to do with my hands, which were currently clutching my skirts.

"She's Roland's cousin," Hector told Drustan. "Surely even she understands my concern."

"Are you going to address me directly?" Gweneira asked. Her voice was low and melodic, making me think of the sound of a wooden flute. "Because if you were to ask my opinion of Roland, I'm sure it would match yours."

Suspicion tightened Hector's expression, but he didn't reply.

Tension filled the room. Shadows coiled around the legs of Hector's chair, and the air surrounding Drustan remained blurred with heat. Kallen was stroking the hilt of his sheathed sword as if imagining using it. Every person here was dangerous, and I wanted nothing more than to fade back while they snarled at one another, but my position was precarious. Any respect I had been afforded because of my new title would be lost if I didn't assert myself.

"What is your opinion of Roland, Lady Gweneira?" I asked her.

"Thank you for asking," she said, inclining her head. "My opinion of Roland is that he was a brute and an insult to the traditional ethics of Light House. He craved power but lacked the imagination to seize more of it, and it's a shame he wasn't cut into a thousand pieces centuries ago. His death was not slow enough for my taste, and I would dance over his grave every morning if it wouldn't take up too much of my valuable time."

I blinked at the vicious words, which were spoken with perfect serenity.

Hector scoffed. "So why didn't you cut him into a thousand pieces?"

"There is a benefit to predictable evil, particularly when Osric was such a force of chaos. And Roland was so certain of his grip on power that he never considered betrayal might come from within his own house."

I looked at Gweneira more closely, trying to take the measure of this new ally. The Noble Fae tended to be composed, but she was nearly preternaturally still, the way Kallen often was. Her simple white dress draped in perfect folds to the floor, as if it had been carved from marble. She wore no jewelry, only a belt adorned with a golden ornament shaped like a sparrow. Light faeries were fond of bird imagery, since the animals traveled closest to the sun. The pouch hanging from her belt presumably contained light-focusing crystals—as placid as she looked, she could burn a hole through anyone in this room.

Kallen abruptly turned towards the door. "Someone's approaching."

How did he know? But then I remembered the darkness he'd cast outside and how he'd once told me he would know if anyone "disturbed his shadows."

Drustan gave Hector a smug look. "Oriana."

We waited for the coded knock, and my shoulders barely relaxed when it came. I wasn't looking forward to seeing the Earth princess after she'd abandoned Lara. But when the door opened, it revealed a tall, thin asrai with a pale blue face and long, gray-blue hair. Surprise straightened my spine as I recognized Alodie, the head servant of Earth House.

She curtsied and held out a folded piece of paper. "Princess Oriana sends this in her stead."

Hector laughed. "Drustan, you certainly understand the motivations of others."

Drustan made an irritated sound and strode forward to snatch up the missive. While he read, Alodie smiled at me, though her eyes were sad. We had been friends once—perhaps still were—but she had always been bound by duty, and we served different causes now.

Drustan's jaw clenched. "Oriana will not be coming."

"That's it?" Hector asked.

Drustan tossed the missive on the table before seating himself. "Read it yourself."

Hector didn't move, but I picked up the paper and ran my eyes over the elegantly penned lines.

> *Despite the poor judgment of members of this house who participated in last night's violence, Earth House remains neutral. We await news of what Fire, Void, Light, Illusion, and Blood decide.*

A soft breath left me as rage dug sharp claws into my heart. That was Selwyn she was speaking of so dismissively. Her *son*, who at only sixteen had possessed the courage to rally Earth soldiers to attack the throne room. Her son, who had died at Osric's hand, proud and defiant despite his fear.

"What a coward," I whispered as the paper crinkled under my tight grip.

Alodie looked down at her feet.

"Eight centuries of suffering under Osric wasn't enough for her, apparently," Drustan said, anger evident in every line of his body. "So long as her hands remain clean, she will allow anything."

Furious as I was with him, I couldn't find fault in the sentiment. Neutrality sounded ideal in principle—to be a watcher of history, to document the truth without bias and stand apart from the violence so easily inflicted by others—but in the face of monstrous evil, it became complicity.

"May I bring a response to the princess?" Alodie asked.

"She doesn't deserve a response," Hector said, tapping his fingers on the table. "Let her wallow in her righteousness. We waste precious time trying to shift her opinion when there are lives at stake in all of our houses."

"I agree," Gweneira said.

I looked at Alodie, whose head was still bowed, and sorrow joined my anger. Earth House was full of people I'd come to care about. Oriana's choices became theirs by default.

"Very well," Drustan said. "We send no response."

Alodie curtsied again. "My gratitude for the audience." Then she was gone, slipping out the door with the quickness of a darting fish.

Drustan raised his hand and cast a ward over the door, shimmering and orange as a summer sunset. That magical boundary would stop noise from leaving the room—I knew because he'd used it during our meetings, and not just because we were whispering secrets.

Not a memory to think about right now. Unsure what else to do, I took the seat opposite Drustan. I looked a question at Kallen, but he shook his head and remained standing with his hands clasped behind his back.

"Gweneira," Drustan said, "will you tell us about the current state of Light House?"

"Chaos," Gweneira replied, leaning in. "There are more of Osric's loyalists than there are supporters of the revolution, but as I'm sure you know from your own houses, there are many who have kept their opinions private and chosen the path of least risk. Osric's death will sway more to our side if we can capitalize on that momentum—which I am doing my best to accomplish."

"Who else is positioning themselves as Roland's successor?" Kallen asked.

"Torin and Rowena."

Hector made a face. "I'd tried to forget about them."

Feeling embarrassingly ignorant, I cleared my throat. "Who are Torin and Rowena?"

Gweneira turned her cool brown eyes to me. "Torin is my cousin. Rowena is his consort, but they plan to oversee the house as equals."

"Oh. Is that . . . common?"

"Not at all. But the two of them have been acting as one for six hundred years, so this isn't a surprise." She paused. "It would be best for everyone if they did not prevail."

"They're insane," Hector told me bluntly.

"Don't discount them," Gweneira said. "They are sadists in Osric's vein, yes, but they're also cunning."

A shiver went down my spine. "But you might take over the house instead?"

She nodded. "My claim is weaker than Torin's by blood, but I'm indisputably the leader of the faction that supported Drustan, and the house will always preserve itself above all else. If I can gather enough to my cause, the rest will fall in line."

Drustan rapped his knuckles on the table. "I would like to discuss the military resources we each bring to this alliance, since skirmishes will undoubtedly begin soon. But first, we have a pressing matter to decide. An alliance cannot function without a leader."

Hector straightened in his chair. Every eye in the room landed on me.

Anxiety surged in my chest, and my magic swelled with it. Ribbons of crimson power began twining around my fingers, startling me, and I fisted my hands in my lap to hide the evidence of my emotional response.

"Kenna," Drustan said, "I understand last night was a difficult one, but you've now had some time to think about it, and we must close ranks. Do I have your support?"

Anxiety escalated to panic. This wasn't just my life at stake—it was the fate of all six houses. Tens of thousands of lives. I shot to my feet and started pacing. "Gweneira supports you, doesn't she? Why does it matter what I think?" There were four houses represented in this room, and Drustan already had half of the vote. The best I could do was tie it by declaring for Hector—which I was equally unwilling to do. I knew nothing about him except for a few very frightening rumors.

"I am not a princess yet," Gweneira said. "I cannot speak on behalf of Light House, and by the time I can, we will already be in the midst of war."

"Then Oriana needs to have a say," I said, seizing on any reason not to have this decision come down to me. "Why not try one more time to win her over?"

"Why not make the choice yourself?" Drustan snapped, clearly losing patience. "You have been gifted an enormous amount of power, but with that comes the responsibility to use it. It is an *honor* to be in this meeting, particularly considering where you came from."

I flinched. *Where I came from.* The pathetic little human, elevated from her pathetic little life. He probably thought showing me his cock had been an honor, too. Bitterness lay heavy on my tongue. "I told you, I want proof that you're fit to rule."

Flames flickered in his eyes. He shoved his chair back and stalked towards me, and the heat of his approach smacked against my skin. "You are the most—"

Kallen was suddenly there, positioning himself between Drustan and me. "You know her terms."

Drustan looked even more incensed at Kallen's interference. "I am to perform tricks to earn a crown I've already won?"

"If you'd already won it, it would be on your head," Kallen said with cutting precision.

"We do not have time for this."

"Perhaps you do not. I am sure Hector would be happy to provide Kenna with whatever she needs. Some written policies, perhaps?"

Hector made a face. He would not, in fact, be happy to do that. "Certainly," the Void prince said.

"You want written policies?" Drustan asked me over Kallen's shoulder, looking incredulous. "Shall I detail foreign relations with faerie courts you've never heard of? Break down our system of tithes? I'm eager to get your keen political insight on matters you have no experience with."

I sucked in a breath, stung by the words—and by how true they were.

"Drustan," Kallen said warningly. "If you want her support, you have to actually motivate her to support you."

Drustan sneered at Kallen. "Oh, I motivated her plenty, trust me."

Kallen's jaw clenched, and his hand brushed the hilt of his sword. But his reaction was nothing compared to the rage that swept through me at Drustan's insinuation. Caedo had been coiled at my neck, but at a thought, the dagger slithered into my hand and took form. I stepped around Kallen, pointing the blade at Drustan's throat.

"I used to fuck you," I said bluntly. "There, I've said it."

Drustan's eyes widened. "I didn't mean—"

"Whether or not we used to sleep together has no bearing on my decision now," I continued, talking over him, "or on the way you will treat me. Which is with respect." The dagger trembled in my hand. "This is new to me, and I'm doing my best."

There was a heavy pause while we stared at each other. The contempt was gone from his expression, replaced by something weary and . . . sad?

No, I thought. He wasn't allowed to grieve something he'd destroyed.

He bowed his head. "You're right," he said, surprising me. "Forgive me, Kenna."

A lump grew in my throat. Was that apology even genuine? Did it matter if it was? Regardless of sincerity, he'd apologized in front of others, and a strategic faerie might say the appearance of contrition was more important than the actual substance of it.

I wasn't like the rest of the Fae, though. I had to believe in something. "Thank you," I said, lowering the dagger. I stepped back until I no longer felt the radiating heat of his body.

Drustan took a deep breath. "I am sympathetic to your uncertainty," he said, clearly grappling for politeness. "What would put your mind at ease?"

Hector's eyes flicked between Drustan, me, and a spot over my shoulder. Kallen was still lingering behind me, and I didn't understand why he had come to my defense or why he wanted Drustan to treat me better. It would only be to Hector's benefit if Drustan enraged me.

"You know what I care about." My voice wobbled despite my desire to remain composed. "Or you should know. We talked about it often enough."

He nodded. "The people."

So he did understand. "Yes. All the people whose lives will supposedly be so much better under your rule. That's what I care about, not your tithing policy."

Was that regret in his eyes? "I do care about them, Kenna. This isn't just a power grab."

I didn't know if I believed him anymore. My lips felt too dry. I licked them, and the movement caught Drustan's attention.

"I'll draft some policies for you," he said. "But you need to make a choice soon, or—"

Kallen abruptly unsheathed his sword, making me jump. "Someone is coming," he said, striding towards the door. "Is anyone else expected?"

"No." Flames gathered in Drustan's palms, and when he closed his fists, he held two daggers of fire. He cast a vicious glance at Hector. "No one else knew about this meeting."

Hector stood, drawing his own sword, and Gweneira pulled a crystal lens from the pouch at her belt. I squeezed Caedo's hilt, wondering what new disaster was on its way.

The ward only worked one way when it came to sound passing through. Footsteps sounded in the corridor, and I heard the tapestry being brushed aside. Then the knob turned, and the door opened.

A faerie wearing purple stepped into the room. He was slender, with cheekbones sharp enough to cut, and his hair was the same startling crimson shade as Karissa's, the failed Illusion candidate from the trials. A relative? He wasn't carrying visible weapons, but considering the type of magic he wielded, that meant nothing.

"Lord Ulric," Gweneira said. "What an unexpected pleasure." She didn't put her crystal away, though.

Ulric smiled. "Sheathe your swords. I mean you no harm."

No one moved. My skin crawled. Of all the magic the Fae exhibited, Illusion House's powers unsettled me most. How did I know what I was seeing was real? The Fae operated on some sort of unspoken code to keep the peace, but we had moved far beyond keeping peace last night.

"Why are you here?" Drustan demanded.

"To deliver a message from Queen Imogen, rightful ruler of Mistei."

Kallen had been right, I thought with a sharp bite of nausea. War did not wait. We hadn't even begun discussing who Osric's successor might be, and the new queen's emissary was already here.

"Imogen?" Gweneira asked. "An interesting choice."

"She must not have been paying attention last night if she thinks we'll call her queen," Hector sneered.

"The succession is set," Ulric said. "This is how power moves in Mistei."

"Right now, power moves however we wish it to." Hector glanced around the room as if to ensure we were all with him. I nodded slightly when his eyes touched mine. Our supposed alliance was a mess, but I wasn't going to accept someone I'd never heard of as queen, particularly if she was related to Osric.

"I am not here to argue the matter." Ulric reached for a leather pouch at his belt, then stilled when Kallen, Hector, and Drustan all took a step forward. "It's just a letter." He pulled a scroll out, then set it on the table and backed away, hands up.

Gweneira put her crystal away to retrieve the scroll, which was marked in shimmering purple ink. She read it silently, and her jaw dropped. "Imogen calls an Accord."

"What?" Drustan snatched the paper out of her hands and read aloud. "'Mistei deserves a peaceful transition of power. I am sympathetic to the chaos unfolding in your houses and across this kingdom, so in the tradition of Queen Brigitta, I hereby declare a month of Accord, to end on Lughnasa. Let us celebrate the ending of one dark era before the beginning of a brighter one.'" He lowered the paper. "This is . . . unexpected."

Lughnasa was the next major holiday, positioned halfway between the summer solstice and autumn equinox. I moved closer to Kallen. "What is an Accord?" I whispered.

"A formal peace period declared during times of unexpected unrest," he murmured, lips barely moving. Even he looked startled by this development, though the expression was subtler on him. "Queen Brigitta last declared one twelve hundred years ago, when her sister tried to usurp the throne at her coronation."

It had been hard enough keeping track of the limited history I'd learned in the Tumbledown schoolroom; now I would need to be familiar with events from over a millennium ago. "And what is the point?"

"It offers time for negotiation to resolve the conflict peacefully. More realistically, it's time to prepare for battle."

"The Accord will last thirty days," Ulric was saying, "starting with a silvered state dinner tomorrow night. Invitations are circulating throughout Mistei as we speak."

"How generous of her," Drustan said bitingly.

"Imogen is not Osric," Ulric replied. "She is not eager to plunge the realm into war."

"She still expects our surrender at the end of the month, I presume." This came from Hector.

"She trusts that you will see reason by the end of the month." Ulric looked at Gweneira, and the light shimmered in his blue eyes in a way so beautiful it had to be an illusion. "Torin and Rowena have already accepted the Accord—and pledged the support of Light House when it is done."

Gweneira's lashes flickered. "They cannot pledge what they do not control."

Ulric shrugged. "And yet there they are, at Imogen's right hand. For the rest of Mistei, that is authority enough."

"And Oriana?" Drustan asked.

"She has accepted the Accord as well."

Oriana had responded to Imogen's invitation while ignoring ours. A fresh sense of betrayal poured over me.

"I will leave you to your secret meeting," Ulric said, emphasizing the word *secret*. "But I look forward to seeing you at dinner tomorrow night."

"Thank you for your courtesy in delivering the message," Gweneira replied.

Ulric bowed, then backed out of the room, closing the door behind him.

As soon as Ulric was gone, Hector turned on Gweneira. " 'Thank you for your courtesy'?"

She looked at him coolly. "Ulric values etiquette, and not all of us negotiate at swordpoint."

"Do you think there's negotiating to be done?" Kallen asked, sheathing his blade.

"This is a much gentler approach than Imogen could have taken."

"She needs this time." He strode to the table to study the letter. "She'll want to gain public support, considering the legacy she's inheriting. And Osric's guards were well trained and equipped, but the larger Illusion House army is poorly maintained. Osric grew lazy in his perceived omnipotence."

Drustan, Hector, and Gweneira resumed their seats, so I did as well, placing Caedo back at my neck. My heart was still racing from the unexpected visitor. "How did he know where to find us?" I asked.

Gweneira frowned as she stroked the metal bird on her belt. "They're probably watching our houses. We'll need to be more cautious, and we should set patrols."

"What we should do," Hector said, smacking his fist on the table, "is ignore this invitation and strike while they're unprepared."

"We aren't any better prepared," Kallen replied. "As individual houses, perhaps. But a civil war won't be won on the strength of one army—or the outcome of one battle."

Hector grimaced. "I hate when you're reasonable."

"You must hate me all the time."

Hector made a noise that was half grunt and half laugh.

Drustan glowered at the curling paper with its shimmering ink. "She's already sent the invitations," he said. "If we attack, we'll lose popular support. No one's ever broken an Accord."

"Who is Imogen?" I asked. "What is she like?"

"She's a distant cousin of Osric's, and if you'd asked yesterday, I would have described her as a shallow hedonist dedicated solely to her own pleasure."

"Osric thought the same," Kallen said. There was a thoughtful crease between his brows. "It's why he allowed her to live, even though she's rumored to have a great deal of magic. She seemed to have little interest in anything but wine and merrymaking."

It was a reminder of how close Kallen had been to the king. He hadn't just been Osric's sword—he'd been a confidant of sorts.

"She found a strategy for survival," Gweneira said. "And she's popular in the house, which can't have been easy with Osric ever vigilant against challenges to his influence. I suspect she's been laying the groundwork for this for a while."

A single flame was dancing across Drustan's knuckles, back and forth. "Thirty days," he said. "While she tries to force Mistei to fall at her feet."

"The Accord doesn't begin until tomorrow night," Hector said. "We wouldn't technically be breaking it if we attacked Illusion House before then."

Drustan shook his head. "That argument will not play well with the masses, and I don't want to start my reign by spitting on an ancient tradition."

"*Your* reign," Hector repeated scornfully.

The two started arguing again, but I ignored them. Instead, I moved to the fireplace, staring into the cold ashes. "A month," I whispered. That meant extra time for Imogen, Torin, and Rowena to gather support and ready their armies. They would only grow more dangerous over the next few weeks. It would offer us time to do the same, though.

And it would give *me* time.

"Kenna," Drustan said, raising his voice over whatever objection Hector had just made. "To get back to what we were discussing—"

"No," I said firmly, spinning to face him. "If you want to win my support, you know what to do. I look forward to reading your policies." I gave Hector a stern look, too. "Both of your policies."

Hector's eyes narrowed. "I look forward to convincing you, Princess Kenna."

The muscles at the sides of Drustan's jaw flexed. Then he nodded stiffly. "As do I."

5

I STORMED TOWARDS EARTH HOUSE, MY SKIRT RIPPLING BEhind me like a flag snapping in the wind.

The rest of the meeting had gone as poorly as the start of it. We'd agreed to send rotating patrols through the territories surrounding Fire, Void, and Blood House, but no one could agree on the particulars. Drustan wanted Fire's soldiers to be solely responsible, since he knew they were committed to the cause—the implication being that Void's soldiers weren't. Hector had then accused him of wanting to send spies into Void territory, to which Drustan had commented that Void House would know all about spies. They'd eventually settled on sending sentries in mixed groups, but it hadn't been pleasant getting there.

Gweneira was unable to spare many soldiers for those watches, since the situation within Light House was so volatile. I was even less helpful. It had been embarrassing to listen to everyone else plot and bicker, painfully aware that there was only one purpose I served.

Everything would have been different if Oriana had come.

Ahead, an asrai carrying a bolt of fabric emerged from the water tunnel leading into Earth House. Her brown skin shimmered blue at her cheekbones and the edges of her forehead, and her hair was the color of sapphire where it floated around her shoulders. Hatheryn—not an Underfae I'd worked closely with, but someone I'd seen around the house and been friendly with. She was responsible for the mending and cleaning for Lady Rhiannon, the matriarch of one of the stronger bloodlines. When she spotted me, she gasped and curtsied.

"You don't have to—" I started, but she was already hurrying past, giving me a wide berth like I was a disease she might catch.

I slowed as I approached the tunnel. Sunlight speared through the lake water, turning it turquoise, and colorful fish swam past the mystically enforced barrier. Despite the beauty, a gnawing unease filled my stomach. At my neck, Caedo quivered with the same tension. We didn't belong here anymore.

Stopping outside the entrance, I shouted, "Princess Oriana!"

The passageways of Mistei often echoed—whether with footsteps, music, or screams—but the water absorbed the sound. I waited for a few minutes, then yelled again. "Oriana! I need to speak with you."

A cluster of orange fish that had been hovering near the entrance darted away. More minutes passed, but Oriana didn't emerge.

Did she know I was here? Blood House had informed me when Kallen had shown up. She was probably ignoring me on purpose, as she'd ignored the summons to the council meeting.

Fresh anger filled me. All that power, and Oriana stayed in her luxurious rooms and did nothing. Didn't fight, didn't speak up, didn't protect her own family. "I'm not leaving until you speak with me!"

A dark green fish with trailing fins drifted up to the curve of the tunnel wall. It paddled lazily, the edges of its scales glimmering gold in the water-thickened sunlight. The black eyes fixed on me were more intelligent than they had any right to be.

Oriana definitely knew I was here.

"You coward," I told the fish bitterly. "Don't you care about anything besides yourself?"

The fish flicked a fin and swam away.

No entreaty, no insult, could shake Oriana loose from her sanctuary. A few times servants appeared at the far end of the tunnel, but each time they hurried back inside the moment they spotted me. Eventually no one else emerged.

My throat hurt, and not just from prolonged shouting. Lara was waiting for me back at Blood House, and the thought of why that was infuriated me all over again. Oriana hadn't just abandoned Mistei—she'd disowned her own child.

The green fish had returned a few times to inspect me. It lingered now between wavering fronds of lake-bed grass, the golden scales above its eyes gleaming like a crown. "Don't you want to know how Lara is?" I asked the fish, lowering my voice. Surely Oriana cared deep down, beneath the layers of politics and polish. After Selwyn had died, after Lara had been stripped of her magic, I could have sworn she'd looked as if her heart were fracturing.

The fish watched me, fins combing lazily through the water.

I sighed, shoulders slumping. This had been a fool's errand. If Drustan hadn't convinced her to attend the meeting, if Osric's death hadn't convinced her to do something, *anything*, to make Mistei a better place, what hope did I have?

It would have been nice to shout at her, though.

I stepped back—and the corridor tilted. The floor tipped so precariously I staggered, and vertigo spun my head. When I regained my senses, the entrance to Earth House stood to my right—less than a foot away from my grasping hand.

I yelped and leapt away from it. A laugh floated to my ears. "Oriana?" I gasped, clutching my head as a fresh wave of dizziness washed over me.

The water tunnel was to my left now. Fish swarmed around the glassy arch as if in a feeding frenzy. My vision flipped upside down, and I lost my balance, tripping forward... just as the entrance shifted and reappeared directly in front of me.

My knees hit cold stone. The lake curved blue around me. A droplet fell from the magically restrained ceiling.

Then a wall of water crashed down and swept me away.

The impact knocked the breath from me, and there was no air left to replace it. Water poured into my lungs, icy cold and then burning. Shock and horror hammered me as the current spun me up. Colors flashed past my eyes—sunstruck turquoise, the flash of fish, the brown and green of the lake bed. Then a darker blue as I was flung into a deeper part, away from the sun.

Panic filled me as the water wrapped cold fingers around my ankles and dragged me down, down, down. Sharp pain ripped through my ears, and a horrible pressure filled my chest as my lungs struggled against something they were never meant to hold.

Air, I needed air, where was the air? *Help me, please, help...*

I was screaming without making a sound, thrashing against nothing as the water filled me up. As it killed me.

My vision wavered, and the terror was joined by bleak despair. This was how it ended. Kenna Heron, the herbwoman's wild daughter, who had loved well and hated better, was going to die alone. I'd finally had power in my hands—the power to change things, to save people, to make this miserable world a tiny bit happier—and in less than a day, everything was lost.

In the end, I'd amounted to nothing at all.

Blackness grew over my vision like mold. My limbs moved sluggishly. I was heavy now, filled with my own death. Magic raced through me, but it couldn't create air where none existed. The gleam of garnet around my grasping fingers flickered faintly through the black. It was the last thing I would see—the power I'd had so briefly and let slip away.

Something grabbed my waist like a giant's fist. There was no breath left for it to squeeze from my lungs as it yanked me through the water, and I was too weak to struggle. My eyes closed against the dark and the pain as a ferocious current ripped past my skin.

Air suddenly burst around me. Bright, windy, sun-warmed. The enormous hand released me, and my knees hit rock so hard my teeth clacked together. I collapsed forward, slamming my face into the ground, and pain burst at the bridge of my nose.

The water inside my lungs surged out all at once, leaving my chest deflated and sore. When I sucked in a breath of summer air, I immediately started coughing.

"What—" My voice was too raw to come out properly, and the sound was strangely muffled. Water streaked down my face, dripping from my sodden curls and weeping eyes. I rose to my knees, trembling from the effort.

Princess Oriana stood before me, lips pursed and arms crossed. She wore a dark green gown, and her golden hair hung loose, as though she'd been in the middle of having it combed when she'd come to my aid.

The pain in my ears disappeared as my ruptured eardrums healed. Sound returned—birdsong and the lap of water. The sunlight was so bright it was nearly painful.

No one survived the death promised by the house entrances. "You saved me," I said, voice hoarse. More tears leaked from my eyes to drip onto my soaked bodice.

"I did not do this for you," she said coldly.

My head was so muddled I couldn't make sense of the words. Where were we? I looked around and realized she'd brought me to a small island in the middle of the lake covering Earth House—the same island where Lara and I had once sat sharing secrets and looking at the stars. The water rippled, disturbed from my near drowning. Wind-smeared clouds dotted the sky, and a copse of trees rustled in a breeze that drew goose bumps from my chilled skin.

The saturated blue of the sky, the green of the leaves, and the golden sheen of sunlight made my eyes sting. I'd spent the last six months almost entirely underground, and while Mistei glowed in its own way, the world above had a heartbreaking sort of brilliance.

I wouldn't have seen the sky again if it weren't for Oriana.

"Why did you do it?" I asked, wiping my wet cheeks.

"I will not allow Earth House's defenses to be used on behalf of anyone else." There was fury in her hazel eyes, and her fingers dug into her arm like claws.

"On behalf . . ." I shook my head, then regretted it when the movement elicited a rush of nausea. I was still dizzy from the battering I'd taken in the waves. "I wasn't trying to use it for anything."

She gave me a withering look that reminded me painfully of one of Lara's classic expressions. "Not you. Though you also behaved abominably. My servants were afraid to leave the house."

An unpleasant feeling twisted my stomach. The Underfae, afraid of me? The only people who should be afraid of me—the only ones I *wanted* to be afraid of me—were the Noble Fae.

Not that Oriana could fear me in this state. Pride gave me the strength to struggle to my feet, though my legs were shaking, and I seized my anger like a blade. "You should have come talk to me if it bothered you that much. And what do you mean, not me?"

Disdain crossed her face. "Foolish girl. The Shards' gift is wasted on you." My jaw dropped at the stinging words, but she continued speaking before I could defend myself. "It was obvious as soon as you started staggering around. Seeing visions, were you?"

"Seeing—" I broke off, realization spearing through me. "Someone from Illusion House was there?"

It hadn't been vertigo. It had been magic. Someone had tried to kill me.

"You couldn't tell," Oriana said, sounding disbelieving. "The magic of the body, and you still couldn't tell someone was there."

My face grew hot with humiliation. "Did you see them?"

"No, but I will not aid Blood House any further. The only reason you live is because Earth House will not be used as anyone's sword. We remain neutral."

There was that word again, sharp as a slap. "Neutral," I spat, clenching my fists tightly.

"Yes, neutral."

I took her in—all blond beauty, all poise. The lauded Princess Oriana, known for her composure and unflinching commitment to the traditions of Earth House. I'd seen this woman kill, though, her vines tunneling into a criminal at King Osric's behest. I'd seen firsthand her ruthlessness and willingness to cheat to achieve her ends. She had no right to speak of neutrality.

"You didn't fight against Osric," I said, voice trembling from how deeply I despised her. "You won't fight any new tyrant who takes his place. Do you fight for anything but your own skin, I wonder?"

She sucked in a breath. The blow had struck true. "I cannot expect you to understand the deep history of the Fae, nor Earth's role in it. You may call me a coward—"

"Oh, so you were listening earlier."

"—but you are a mere *child*, full of a child's passions." Her lip curled in a sneer, revealing the even white of her teeth. "You imagine yourself righteous. You imagine yourself just. So you will seat another king on the throne and hand him your trust and the well-being of your people, as if a new king can ever be the answer to everything."

To everything? No, but it was an answer to something. Drustan and Hector hadn't earned my loyalty yet, but at least I was in the room, having those conversations. At least I was weighing options, trying to make the best choice—not just for me, but for all the faeries and humans who suffered down here. "What else would you have me do? Let another Osric seize power?" I shook my head. "I suppose you would accept that gladly so long as you remain safe."

Spots of pink burned on Oriana's cheeks. It was gratifying to see her flushed with anger, her eyes full of something besides cold disdain. "Someone must look upon history impartially—"

A nasty laugh came out of me. "Save the speech. I've heard it before." She'd been full of speeches like this, which Lara and Alodie had dutifully repeated as if passing on sacred truths. Princess Oriana, great and noble leader of the great and noble Earth House, always standing apart. Better than the rest.

Caedo quivered against my throat, the metal vibrating in a reflection of my tumultuous emotions. I had a sudden vision of driving the blade into Oriana's flesh and watching her blood spill for a cause at last. *My* cause.

I shoved away the disturbing fantasy, unsure if it was Caedo's or mine.

Oriana clenched her skirts like she was imagining strangling me. "If only you could ask Princess Cordelia what comes of coveting thrones," she said. "Or any of the thousands of faeries she sacrificed for that cause."

"They chose to risk death for their principles."

She scoffed. "Do you think the servants truly had a choice?"

"I had a choice last night." I'd killed Osric because it was the right thing to do—not because Drustan or anyone else had told me to.

Her words were burrowing into me, though. I'd been a servant, yes, but I'd also had a magical dagger, new Blood powers, and immunity to Osric's wards. The Underfae of Blood House hadn't had anything like that when Princess Cordelia had decided she would never bow.

"The princess tried to help her people escape," I said, shoving aside the doubts. "It wasn't her fault Osric knew about the secret back entrance."

"She gambled," Oriana said flatly. "She gambled with her people's lives, and she lost. I will not."

"You gambled with Lara's."

Oriana flinched. "You have no right to speak about my daughter."

It was sometimes hard to believe this woman had birthed Lara. Lara took more after her father, with her hooded brown eyes, black hair, and olive-toned skin, but I saw echoes of her in Oriana. In the delicate arch of their eyebrows and their matching noses, in the roundness of their faces and their generous figures.

There was nothing of Lara in Oriana's heart, though.

"Is she your daughter?" I asked, throat thick. "Because last night she wasn't. You renounced her in front of the entire court for doing what you told her to do."

That was what infuriated me most. Oriana had raised Lara in an environment of perpetual disappointment, chastising her for the softness that made Lara a fundamentally decent person. She'd torn down her daughter's self-esteem in the name of strength, then insisted Lara needed help in the trials because of it. She had decided how that help would be delivered, too. And then when Lara had been punished for cheating, Oriana had abandoned her.

"You speak of traditions that are not yours." Oriana's jaw was so stiff her lips barely moved. "The Shards are an authority above all else. When they judged Lara unworthy, there could be no place for her in my house." There was a pause while she seemed to struggle against things unsaid. "No matter what I might wish."

There were shadows under her eyes. She'd lost both of her children last night.

Except she hadn't lost Lara—she'd thrown her away. "I made Lara a lady of Blood House, and the Shard didn't say a word. Did the Earth Shard actually order you to disown her?"

Oriana's expression was bitter as she stared at me. When she didn't respond, I knew the answer.

"You're a princess," I told her. "You can shape the world however you choose, love however you want to, save whoever you decide to. There are no rules for someone like you. Can't you see that?"

She sneered. "And now I know what sort of ruler you would be. Another small tyrant, wrapping her fist around the world."

My chest was filling with bleak disappointment. I'd provoked a response out of Oriana, but no matter how angry I made her, she wasn't going to change. She was never going to understand my point of view, and I was never going to understand hers. "The Shards should have taken your magic instead of Lara's."

"Maybe so," she acknowledged. "But they did not, and I will not change millennia of tradition because of the opinions of a young, naïve human."

"Not human anymore," I pointed out.

"Human in the ways that matter." She shook her head and stepped back, putting distance between us. "Your new king, whoever you choose to believe in with that naïve human heart—maybe he'll be good in the ways that matter to you, but he'll be horrible in different ways. All monarchs are. And you'll kill for him and say it is moral, and you'll let your people die for him and say it is right. Because you, Kenna the human, must always have someone to serve."

I felt cold, chilled by the wind and the water and the argument. "And you, Oriana the coward, will sit in your house and do nothing. That's how history will remember you, too."

Her eyes fixed on the horizon. "So be it." Then she raised her hand, and the water behind her swirled, churning faster and faster until it hollowed, the bottom dipping into a funnel. "I'm done with this conversation. You need to go back."

My throat hurt. How futile this had been. "If you change your mind," I said, already knowing the answer, "you know where to find me."

"I won't."

The whirlpool drifted closer to the shore. "I take it I'm supposed to jump into that?"

She nodded. "It will spit you out where you started."

I wasn't eager to risk drowning again, but there was no real fear of that anymore. Oriana wouldn't kill a rival house head. She wouldn't do anything.

"Before you go," she said, holding out her hand. "Give me the key."

"The key?"

Her lips pursed. "Don't pretend to misunderstand. I trusted you with something that belongs to Earth House. Give it back."

She was talking about the key to Earth's secret catacombs. "I don't have the key anymore," I lied. "I lost it in the battle last night."

"Liar." Her voice was a lash through the air. A bush behind her rustled and grew long thorns. "Yours is the only key not in my possession. I need it."

Lara had apparently handed her key over last night after being excommunicated. Why had she done that? Obligation? Shock? "I don't know who has it."

Hate shone from her narrowed eyes. "I will have it back, whatever it takes. And if you enter the catacombs again, you will not enjoy what you find there."

She delivered threats well, but would she actually follow through with them? "Even if I still had it, what would you do? Take a knife to the princess of another house and cut it out of my chest? Torture me into giving it to you?" Grim amusement joined my anger. In her smug self-righteousness, she had defanged herself. "Unless you're willing to break neutrality, I have nothing to fear."

She looked like she wanted to wring my neck. She wouldn't, though, and now we both knew it. "Do not come back to my house unless it is to return the key," she said viciously.

I had won that particular skirmish—but lost the rest of them. "Very well." The whirlpool called, but I hesitated. One more question hovered on my lips. One final offer, a chance to right a wrong. "Do you want me to tell Lara anything?"

A haunted look swept across her lovely face. "No. She's a lady of Blood House now."

Lara would get nothing from her mother, not even Oriana's regret. I couldn't speak another word to this horrible faerie, so I walked to the shore, preparing to jump into the whirlpool.

As my feet left the ground, I thought I heard Oriana whisper something behind me. Something that sounded like "Take care of her, Kenna."

6

WATER DRIPPED BEHIND ME AS I STALKED AWAY FROM Earth House. My hair had been ripped loose during my near drowning and hung wet against my bare back, and my sodden skirts stuck to my legs. Oriana probably could have made my return journey less damp if she'd felt like it, but any kindness towards me likely would have counted as breaking neutrality in her head. Or maybe she'd been feeling petty.

The outline of a hidden door gleamed gold in my peripheral vision, and my own petty heart took pleasure in that small victory. I would need to be careful about when and where I accessed them, but those catacombs were still mine.

The corridor looked empty, but paranoia bit at me, and I rubbed a hand over the prickling at the back of my neck. Who had my assailant been, and where were they now? How was I supposed to defend against someone invisible?

An invisible faerie still had a body, though. I reached for the well of my magic and imagined casting a net out, seeing if it would catch on bones, muscles, or the pump of a heart. I became aware of heartbeats pattering in the distance, but it was hard to pinpoint anything besides general direction, and they vanished as soon as my concentration wavered.

I'd relied on my eyes and ears my entire life. Now they might lie to me.

My breath shallowed, and I ducked into an alcove, pressing a hand to my chest. A servant was vulnerable in so many ways, but a princess was at risk in new ones. There were probably hundreds of faeries who wanted me dead, and unlike me, they had full command of their magic and the experience of centuries.

Everyone dies, Caedo said in my head. *A princess approaches death more frequently than most.*

I made a face. "That's not comforting."

Comfort won't keep you safe.

Wonderful. If I had to be saddled with a sentient, shape-shifting dagger that had a direct connection to my thoughts and demanded frequent blood sacrifices, the least it could do was offer emotional support. Not wanting to speak my fears out loud, I switched to thought communication. *This scares me, Caedo. I don't want to die.*

The dagger hummed at my neck. It was still shaped like a serpent—sharp teeth, scales, a ruby crown. An implied threat I'd imagined would keep me safe, but there was nothing a dagger, magical or not, could have done against what happened today. *You already died once*, Caedo said. *It created you.*

The words startled me. *What?*

In the maelstrom, the human part of you died. Now you are better.

Fear surged again, sending my pulse racing. The maelstrom of the Shards . . . No, I hadn't died in there. It was impossible.

The memory of that storm filled my head. Whirling and terrible, shot through with light as the Shards had discussed my fate. It had felt like I was being ripped apart piece by piece. My body had dissolved as my soul grew thin and ragged.

The Shards had saved me, though. Blackness had fallen, but I'd opened my eyes again a few moments later. Still Kenna, just with new powers.

There had been that period of darkness, though. The candidates who had succeeded had walked out of the maelstrom with their magic on full display. I'd slumped out of it, collapsing on a pile of corpses.

"Oh," I said, less a word than a whimper. Every part of me rejected the idea. Because if I had died, really died . . . what had been brought back?

Blood House always walks with death, Caedo said. *It is good to know the feel of it.*

I buried my face in my hands. "I don't want to talk about this anymore," I said out loud. The sound of my own voice felt essential. Confirmation that I was still here, still real, still *me*.

The thought sparked another. There were humans in Mistei who couldn't speak, but were they any less real because of that? Their tongues had been cut out, but they spoke with their hands and their laughter and their eyes. They still lived vibrantly, despite the Fae's efforts to crush them.

My breath hitched. Did they know the wards surrounding Mistei had evaporated with Osric's death? Did they realize the outer bars of their cage were gone?

A new purpose filled me. I hadn't been able to sway Oriana, but there was more to changing Mistei than that.

THE HUMAN LEVELS WERE DARK, DIRTY, AND CRAMPED. NO CRYStals shone from the ceiling to mark the passage of the distant sun.

Instead, torches guttered in wall brackets, leaving streaks of soot against the stone. There were no doors to offer privacy, and the air stank of sweat and excrement.

My wet hem picked up fragments of straw that had fallen from someone's basket. The first few rooms I passed were empty, and the main workroom—a large chamber with areas for mending, polishing silver, splitting grains, and other menial tasks—held half of its normal occupancy. Triana and Maude, my closest friends down here, should have been working at this hour, but they were nowhere to be seen.

I hesitated in the doorway, watching the workers. "Excuse me," I said.

Heads snapped up at the sound of my voice. A young man carrying a ceramic teapot stumbled into a table. The pot tumbled to shatter on the floor, and he followed it down with a sound of distress, kneeling to pick up the shards. Other humans bowed or curtsied, looking terrified.

Because I was Fae now, I realized sickly. My skin had a shimmer to it, and they'd likely heard the rumors. Yesterday I'd been one of them—luckier than most, and held at a slight distance because of it, but part of their number. Now I wasn't.

"Is Triana here?" I asked using sign language, hoping that would make them less afraid. "Or Maude?"

They stared at me mistrustfully.

"Did they run away?" I signed when no one volunteered any information. If so, I was glad. Anyone who could escape Mistei should, and quickly.

Still, no one replied.

My signing was slow and rudimentary in comparison to how the other humans spoke, since I was new to it and had had less opportunity to practice, but I kept going. "The king is dead. The wards are down. You can all run. You can go home."

A woman dropped her cloth and wrapped her arms around herself. She sobbed and shook her head.

"I can help you," I signed, confused by the refusal. We could cross the bog together, moving during daylight to avoid the will-o'-the-wisps. As a faerie, I might be able to see the path without help, or Caedo could show it to me again.

A princess should not leave her house, Caedo whispered. *You cannot abandon the ones who rely on you.*

Which ones? I wanted to ask. But there were only two other citizens of Blood House. *They can go, too,* I said stubbornly. *And then we'll come back together.*

Except no, we wouldn't, I realized with a tumbling in my gut. Anya should return to Tumbledown. She should run far away from this cruel kingdom, and as her friend, I should help her.

Would I ever see her again?

I couldn't think about that now. I focused on the people before me. "You can leave. I'll help you escape."

A bald man with a white beard glared at me. Bruno, one of Maude's friends, who was normally full of jokes and smiles. "You're lying," he signed.

The air rushed out of my lungs. "No," I mouthed, shaking my head.

"The Fae always lie."

There was a knocking sound behind me, and I turned to see Maude rapping the handle of a broom against the arched entranceway. She wore a brown dress and a stained apron, and her graying hair was scraped into a tight bun. She looked at me grimly, mouth pressed into a thin line. Then she pointed down the hall and jerked her head, instructing me to follow.

I did, feeling bruised internally. These had been my people a day ago, and now they looked at me like I was the enemy.

Maude led me to a scouring room. There were three women inside, scrubbing delicate silver cups that were washed separately from the more functional cookware. At the sight of me, they dropped the cups into the basins and fled.

Maude set the broom aside and leaned against the wall. She always looked tired, but today was worse. The wrinkles on her face seemed deeper, and her brown eyes were reddened. "What are you doing here?" she asked, hands moving quickly.

"The wards are down," I replied in sign language, much more slowly. "You can escape."

She scoffed and looked away—an insult on the human levels. She was telling me she didn't want to see my next words. "You lie. The Fae raised you from the dead, and now you're here to torment us."

Raised me from the dead. Cold prickles danced over my skin. "No, I'm not lying," I said out loud, feeling guilty even as I did so. It had always seemed unfair to open my mouth down here, to remind everyone I hadn't been mutilated the way they had. "I killed the king last night, and the border spell vanished with him."

That got Maude to look at me again. "*You* killed him?" Disbelief was evident on her face.

"Triana was there," I said, switching back to sign language.

Maude's eyes grew sorrowful. "She ran as soon as blood was spilled. After she saw you lying dead on the ground."

Triana had been one of the humans sent in as entertainment by King Osric—along with Anya. I felt sick remembering how both of them had trembled, utterly terrified. They'd been set free from the brothel they'd both suffered in, but Osric had thrived on torment, and he'd forced them to return to that misery just because he could.

At least the fighting had broken out before that particular entertainment could come to its twisted conclusion. Everyone had run, except for Anya. Which meant they hadn't borne witness to my resurrection or the cataclysmic events that followed. "What are people saying?" I asked. "You must know the king is dead."

"The king is dead," Maude confirmed. "And it does not matter."

"How can it not matter?"

"Our lives will be the same no matter who rules."

I pinched my forehead. She sounded like Oriana. *He'll be horrible in different ways. All monarchs are.* "Not if you leave," I signed, rather than arguing that a different ruler could, in fact, change Mistei for the better, so long as we chose the right one. "The wards are gone. You can go home."

She grunted. "Home," she echoed. The movement was almost violent. "I have no home."

"Your village—"

"Left fifty years ago. You think anyone in Alethorpe remembers me? You think they know what to do with a bent old woman with no tongue?" Maude was signing so quickly I was barely able to follow. "They'll call me Fae—" The end of the word was a complex movement my brain couldn't encompass in time. "They'll bar their doors and leave me begging on the street."

What had that sign been? *A dark thing* was my best guess, but the angle of the motion had implied heaviness. Some terrible burden to carry.

A curse, I realized, recalling the word from one of our later lessons. Triana had been melancholy that day, wondering what we had done to deserve this fate, and Maude had said a curse must have been laid over our cradles.

They'll call me Fae-cursed.

I started to deny it, but then I remembered a man who had stumbled into Tumbledown one afternoon dressed in rags and telling a tale of being stolen away by the Fae. He'd played the fiddle for them for a night of revelry, he'd said, and when they'd sent him away in the morning, the gold they'd paid him with had turned to leaves. He just needed some money from the good people of Tumbledown and he would be on his way...

A lie, certainly. I'd been ten years old, and even I hadn't believed him—and now that I knew what happened to humans in Mistei, it was even more obvious what a charlatan he'd been. He'd refused to play for us, his story had changed repeatedly, and his accent had been southern—a tourist's dialect, not one belonging to the towns that bordered faerie lands. Some in the village had thought him mad, but others considered him an opportunistic con man, there to fleece the superstitious northerners.

There were true believers in Tumbledown, though, quite a few of them, and tales of human abduction were common in the legends their ancestors had passed down. The faithful agreed he was faerie-touched—but he'd miscalculated his mark, because they'd also agreed anyone the Fae had discarded should be avoided at all costs. The faeries only took in the worthiest humans, and if he'd been set loose again, something was wrong with him.

Faerie-cursed, my mother had whispered that night as she'd barred the door against whatever evil that stranger might bring through it. *The hidden folk will punish us if we give shelter to a man like that.*

So he'd been sent on his way.

"They don't speak our language there," Maude signed when I didn't reply. "How do you expect us to explain ourselves?"

"I could go with you and interpret," I said, but Caedo's caution was still ringing in my head. *A princess should not leave her house.*

Mistei was on the brink of war. I'd been resurrected—I'd *died*—for the sake of the magic now burning within me, for the sake of Blood House. Would it be right to leave?

Alethorpe was a day's ride from Tumbledown, and Tumbledown

itself would take hours to get to over the hills and across the bog. There were humans who had been abducted from even farther away than Alethorpe. What would happen during those days or weeks away? What might happen to the precarious balance of power while I was shepherding the humans to safety?

Maude laughed, a ragged exhalation. "You will not," she said. "Even if we could leave here without dying. Even if that were true. You are one of them now."

One of them... "But also one of you."

Her pursed lips said she didn't agree.

I heard the sound of running feet, and then Triana skidded into the room. Shock, hope, and horror danced across her face. Then she launched herself at me, wrapping her arms around my neck. She held on tightly, swaying us both back and forth. Maude tried to tug her away, but Triana shook her head and clutched me tighter.

My heart ached, and I grinned into her short hair. She, at least, hadn't abandoned me.

Finally, she drew back. "It's true," she signed, looking me up and down. "You're Fae. An Underfae told me, but I didn't believe it."

I nodded.

Tears welled in her doe-like brown eyes. "How?"

I told her, speaking aloud considering the complexity of the story. How I'd been helping Lara succeed in the trials and how the king had found out and tried to kill me by throwing me into the swirling vortex. How the Shards had decided to keep me alive and gift me the powers of Blood House.

"They said I should restore the balance," I said, accompanying the words with the gesture for straightening something, though it was typically used in the context of a crooked picture frame or an uneven hem, not a broken political system. "Bring back Blood House somehow."

Triana looked enraptured. Her cheekbones were stark from poor nutrition, but her eyes were bright, and her reddish-brown hair was growing out after being shaved off. It was nearly three inches long now, every day of growth marking more time away from her servitude in the brothel. "It's like the old legends of the Fae-blessed," she said. "A real faerie story, the kind with a happy ending."

Was that the kind of story it was? There was a sudden knot in my stomach. My mother had adored those stories for the impossible dreams they promised, and I had learned to hate them for the same reason.

Maude cleared her throat. Her mistrustful expression had softened during my explanation, but she still kept a wary distance. "What if that isn't her anymore?" she asked Triana. "The Fae can make us see things."

Triana studied me so intently it felt like she was staring through me, right down to my bones. I held my breath, wondering what the judgment would be. Then she nodded. "It's Kenna. I see it in her eyes. Even the Fae cannot trick us that well."

Tears blurred my vision. How easily she gave me her trust. If our positions were reversed—if someone I knew had died and then returned as a type of creature who had hurt me terribly—would I be so generous? "Thank you," I told her, touching my fingers to my chin and moving them towards her.

Maude sighed, but I saw a change in her bearing, a gentling in her expression. "It is hard to believe in anything," she said. "They have taken so much."

The Fae had taken much. Our lives, our happiness, our freedom. But that didn't mean we couldn't take something back. "If you don't want to leave Mistei right now," I said, "do you want to come to Blood House? You can stay there. Any human who wants to can stay there."

Maude and Triana looked at each other. Then Maude dipped her chin slightly, and Triana turned to me with a wide smile and nodded, too.

7

No one else wanted to join Triana and Maude as the newest members of Blood House. *I'll think about it* was the most we got from Bruno after Maude spoke with him, but most of the others wouldn't even look at me.

I couldn't blame them. Faeries had never offered kindness or safety before, and Blood House had an ominous name and a taboo associated with it. When life had been full of raised fists, it was hard to believe in the promise of an open hand. I still hoped to convince as many as I could to leave Mistei and start over in the human world, far from this court's cruelty, but it would take time. Time I hoped we had.

We headed for the next level up. As we moved down that corridor, I spied the golden outline of a hidden door. I eyed it, wondering if we should use the Earth tunnels rather than walking in the open. It would take longer, since the paths in this portion of Mistei were particularly narrow and labyrinthine, but it would keep Maude and Triana away from other faeries until I could officially claim them as members of Blood House.

Unless Oriana was already in the catacombs, setting traps to stop me from roaming freely.

Four keys. Three in Earth House, one in Blood House. It would be an ongoing struggle for control of those spaces, especially now that the secret was out and the rest of Mistei knew there were hidden passages.

Maybe no one knew the extent of the catacombs, though. Selwyn had given his key to the rebels who had overwhelmed the throne room, but Drustan might not know there were passages beyond that one.

Maude and Triana looked around anxiously as we walked, jumping at every distant sound. I'd seen a teenage girl beheaded on the summer solstice for abandoning her post; they must worry the same could happen to them.

Seeing their fear, I decided on the catacombs. Oriana didn't want me there, but she also wouldn't kill me, and we were far from Earth House.

The corridor was empty. I opened my magical senses, listening for heartbeats. When I didn't detect anyone, I waved a hand over my chest. The necklace appeared, the slight weight of the key resting against my breastbone. "Want to take a back way?" I asked as I fished the key out from beneath my dress, letting the fine golden chain drape over my bodice.

Maude eyed the key suspiciously. "What is that?"

"There are secret passages in Mistei," I signed. Even if no one was here, I didn't want to say the words out loud. "Only a few people know about them."

Maude nodded. "If it's safer."

I turned towards the rectangular sliver of golden light. This door's outline was hidden in the stonework, and without the key, I doubted I would be able to see the whisper-thin seams. These doors were everywhere, yet somehow the sharp-eyed Fae never noticed them. They must be hidden by an ancient spell.

I held the key against the wall, and a crack appeared. When I pushed, the door swung open, revealing a blackened passageway smelling of mildew.

Triana looked at it doubtfully. "It's dark."

"This casts light." I raised the key to show her how it shone against the blackness. "And there are spy holes, too." Mostly pinpricks hidden within ornamental decorations, which the outside light passed through in thin shafts, but sometimes there were stained glass windows or narrow slits to peer through.

My skin suddenly prickled. I spun, looking around for whatever had triggered my instincts, but there was no one nearby.

"What is it?" Triana asked.

I shook my head, listening intently. The only sound was the soft gutter of flame as a torch wavered. I reached for my magic again and became aware of the surge of blood beneath my skin, like a network of rivers. Beside me, Triana's and Maude's hearts beat in a staggered rhythm, accelerating with what must be nervousness.

There was no one else around.

My uneasiness didn't dissipate. I looked more closely, trying to determine what had caught my attention. The walls were rough and uneven, the gray stone piled haphazardly. The next hallway over would have crystals in the ceiling, but we were still close enough to human territory that torchlight provided the only illumination. It gave the corridor a shadowed, uneven look.

Very shadowed, I realized as my eyes lingered on the far end. There was a corner past a spill of torchlight where the darkness looked thick as smoke.

Caedo was in my hand in an instant, edge sharp and gleaming.

"Show yourself," I commanded.

My magic-sense caught an echo of a heartbeat as the darkness shifted. Faint, like a whisper, but growing stronger as the black mist solidified into the shape of a familiar Void faerie.

"Kallen," I said, scalp crawling. When he was in mist form, my magic hadn't been able to identify the contours of his body or the beat of his heart.

And now he'd seen me using the key.

He dipped his chin in acknowledgment. "Kenna." His eyes moved to the open door, then back to me.

Maude and Triana had fallen back, clutching each other as they retreated half inside the secret passageway. They looked terrified, and I felt a swell of protective anger. "Why are you lurking in shadows?" I demanded, stalking towards Kallen.

He looked mildly surprised by my pique. "I always lurk in shadows."

A shiver raced over my skin. Did he know I couldn't sense him in that form? And *why* couldn't I sense him?

There must always be a balance, Caedo said in my head. *Different houses, different vulnerabilities.*

I had no idea what that meant and wasn't about to waste time discussing it. I stopped in front of Kallen, wrestling for composure. "What do you want? Trying to take me to another meeting? The last one went so well."

He looked pointedly at the dagger in my hand, but I didn't put Caedo away. If he felt menaced, it was his own fault.

Kallen's hands were relaxed at his sides, but it didn't make him look any less dangerous. His eyes were fathomless in the dim corridor, and his pale face might have been carved from stone. His posture was impeccable, as always, and the only spots of light on his attire were the silver buckles that closed his tunic and the hilt of the sword strapped to his hip.

Awareness prickled over my skin, a full-body shiver like I'd plunged a hand into a winter stream. Kallen always seemed so controlled, like he needed to keep a tight leash on whatever lurked behind those midnight eyes.

The only things that needed leashing were those too dangerous to let loose.

His gaze moved over me. "You're wet."

I was abruptly aware of how the damp dress stuck to my skin. The bodice and silver-studded sleeves had always been tight, but now the skirts clung to my hips and thighs. My hair hung down my back, the sodden strands cold against my bare skin, and goose bumps prickled over me.

"Your powers of observation are unmatched," I said, inserting sarcasm in the place of confidence.

His eyes flicked back up. "Oriana let you live."

Oh, for— "Must you always know everything?" I asked, exasperated.

"That is the traditional role of a spymaster, yes."

"You're not a spymaster any longer. Osric is dead."

His expression didn't change, but the air grew colder. "The official position may be vacant, but knowledge is always good currency."

I hated how hard it was to read him. Drustan was hard to read for different reasons—always smiling away his true intentions—but there was something about Kallen that got to me. No one could be that restrained all the time. One day he would snap, and then . . .

He stepped closer and lowered his voice. "What happened? Were you hurt?"

That couldn't be concern, could it? He probably just wanted to ensure Blood House remained intact so I could cast my support behind Hector. "No," I said. Then, when he kept watching me, the truth tumbled out. "A little."

More than a little. Physically it had hurt, yes. But in my head... Shards, it had been so much worse. Death's breath had been icy on my neck, and death was a greedy thing. How many times could a person dip a toe in that dark pool without being sucked fully in? How many times could I borrow breath before that debt came due?

Kallen's hand twitched at his side. "How did you end up in the water tunnel?"

"You don't already know?"

He shook his head. "My source only heard you shouting at the entrance."

The only people nearby had been servants of Earth House—which meant Kallen had leverage over at least one other person within Oriana's walls.

It wasn't surprising. He'd moved quickly to get me under his control, and while the speed of that blackmailing had been partially caused by my own recklessness, he'd had centuries to weave his web across the rest of Mistei.

"Someone from Illusion disoriented me, and I fell." It was embarrassing to admit, but we were supposedly allies now, and my allies ought to know about my enemies.

"Any identifying features?"

"They were invisible."

He made a soft, angry-sounding noise. "That's a rare skill to master, but there are still plenty of faeries who could have done it. Imogen may have ordered it, since the Accord hasn't officially started yet, but there will be many others who want to avenge the king."

"Yes, I'm aware." I looked over my shoulder to where Maude and Triana were huddled together. They were far enough away that they wouldn't be able to overhear, but I didn't want to leave them alone for too long.

Kallen's fingers brushed my chin, turning my face back towards him, and I sucked in a startled breath. "I'll find them," he said quietly. "And I'll have their head for hurting you."

My heart slammed behind my ribs. The tips of his fingers were cool and calloused. Those hands had killed countless people over the years—they could kill me, should he choose to. But he was touching me instead, more gently than someone like him ought to be capable of. "Why?" I whispered.

His jaw clenched, and his hand dropped. "Why did Oriana spare you?"

He always answered questions with other questions: an annoying habit. I could guess why he wanted to kill my attacker, anyway. A dead Blood princess was no use when it came to his agenda.

Bitterness slipped into my voice. "She thought it would be violating her precious neutrality to oversee my death."

"Perhaps." He stepped back, putting space between us. "Perhaps not."

Relief softened the tension of my muscles. It was hard to think when he was that close. "What do you mean?"

"She could have argued that interfering in any way would be breaking neutrality. The conflict was between Blood and Illusion; her house was merely the method of execution."

I shook my head. "That's the part she objected to. I'm sure she would have been delighted to see me dead otherwise."

He hummed. "Oriana can justify anything she wants to do. She would have found a compelling reason to watch you drown if that had been her aim."

I was quiet, considering it. Oriana clearly despised me, but she had rescued me. She'd engaged in the argument rather than immediately sending me away. She hadn't changed her political position, but she'd interpreted it in a way that let me live.

Why?

Maybe the key would have been hard to recover from a corpse. I didn't know how that magic worked or what it would take to call it out from beneath my skin without my permission. But maybe there had been another reason, one expressed in that whisper I wasn't sure I'd heard correctly. *Take care of her.*

Kallen was now watching Maude and Triana. "You've been busy since the council meeting. What are you doing with them?"

If he didn't have to answer questions directly, I didn't either. "Don't you already know?"

The torch guttered again, and light danced across his face. The shadows under his eyes deepened for a moment, giving him a ghostly aspect. Then the golden glow steadied, catching on the sharp line of his jaw and the blade of his nose. "I don't know everything, Kenna."

"You knew I was here."

"You were stalking through the halls, dripping wet. It drew notice."

All right, so this hadn't been a particularly stealthy mission. Once that whisper had reached Kallen's ears, it wouldn't have been hard to follow the rumors. I was used to going wherever I wanted, but a princess drew far more interest from observers than a human servant did—especially a princess who was soaked, scowling, and had been shouting in public. "Why did you come here?" I asked, fighting another burst of embarrassment. "You heard I survived. You didn't need to confirm it with your own eyes."

He opened his mouth, then closed it again. We stared at each other for a long moment while I waited to see if Kallen would answer a question for once.

The seconds ticked past. Apparently he would not.

I sighed, giving up. "Is there a purpose to this meeting besides your curiosity? I need to get them out of here."

"Are you rescuing them, like you did the woman in the throne room last night?"

So he also knew I'd brought Anya to Blood House. An awful thought struck me. "Did you recognize her?" I demanded. Osric had cast an illusion to allow his court to watch the solstice hunt. Had Kallen known all along that Anya was in the brothel being tortured? Had everyone known?

He cocked his head. "Should I have?"

"From the solstice."

A furrow etched between his brows. "I'm not following."

"She was taken," I said, voice sharp. "You must have seen it."

"She was one of the sacrifices?" Surprise shifted across his features. "Osric's illusion showed all of them dying. All but you."

So Osric had wanted to abduct Anya, but he hadn't wanted the other faeries to know. "Why would he do that? Why lie?"

"Her scars are . . . distinctive," he said after a pause. "Osric was covetous of what he saw as his. There were atrocities I only found out about decades later, and more I'm sure I'll never learn. He found pleasure in the secret as much as anything."

"She wasn't *his*," I snapped.

He was watching me closely. "A friend, I take it?"

It was none of his business who she was. "I need to return to Blood House," I said shortly. "Are we done?"

"Is that where the secret passageway goes? I'll walk with you."

"No, you will not." I glanced at Maude and Triana and saw them having a heated discussion. Triana made the sign for Void, and Maude made a sign I hadn't been taught but could intuit the general meaning of, considering the inclusion of the middle finger.

"Perhaps it's for the best," Kallen said dryly.

My head snapped to him. "Do you know sign language?"

"Some things don't require translation."

I eyed him suspiciously. If any faerie in Mistei knew how to speak the humans' secret language other than the servants, it would be Kallen.

He sighed, relenting. "I know the basics. It was difficult to convince anyone to teach me, but over the years I found a few humans who could be persuaded for the right incentives."

Persuaded. Did he mean blackmailed? Threatened? Maybe he'd offered rewards, though, because what could he do to these people that hadn't already been done?

"Why did you want to learn?" I asked.

"Why else? Information." He leaned in, lowering his voice even more. "And because most of the Fae don't realize how dangerous it is to trap a creature they don't understand."

"You call them creatures?" I asked, outraged. He was talking quietly enough that Triana and Maude wouldn't have heard, but I wasn't going to tolerate that sort of language.

"Only in the metaphorical sense. We're all beasts, Kenna. Good or bad, kind or vicious, whatever level of power we hold. When broken down to our basics, we become capable of anything."

"Then you must consider yourself a beast, too," I said, not really believing it. The Noble Fae thought themselves superior to everyone and everything.

"Yes," he said, surprising me. "A terrible one. And Osric never learned the lesson that a good hunter should know exactly what they've caught." He gestured at my friends. "The Fae chose to imprison and abuse a species they don't understand on a fundamental level. They decided to break them because they could, and then they decided there was no reason to pay attention to what the prisoners were saying to each other in their cages." He shook his head. "Cruelty aside, it's dangerously shortsighted."

He spoke like the humans might rise up and destroy the Noble Fae. And one had. I'd been able to do it because of Caedo and my new magic, but I'd *wanted* to do it long before that, and that had been entirely the fault of the Noble Fae.

What would Maude do with a weapon? What would Triana? Once the humans had freedom or power—once they knew how to believe in that freedom or power—what ruin might they be capable of visiting on their captors?

"What do you mean, the Fae don't understand humans?" I asked.

"Everything is condensed in a human lifetime. Hopes, hates, passions . . ." There was a pause after the word, and I wondered uncomfortably what Kallen imagined he knew about passion. "Humans have an intensity of purpose."

"The Fae have purpose. You've been plotting against Osric for, what, centuries?"

He inclined his head. "Perhaps *purpose* is not the right word. The point is that humans are capable of a great deal more than the Fae have ever acknowledged, and they are often unpredictable." His gaze was steady on mine. "Sometimes they will even sacrifice their own self-interest to help others—something many of the Fae will never understand."

"You clearly understand it, though."

He paused. "Perhaps because I know what the world looks like from a cage."

Because Osric had chained him in the role of the King's Vengeance in exchange for Void House's survival. "How old were you when Osric forced you to serve him?"

His expression grew grim. "Just old enough to be able to speak the vows."

My breath left me. "A child."

"I'm not sure I was ever that." Then he cleared his throat. "Does Drustan know Earth's secret passageways extend this far?"

The abrupt change of topic put me off-balance. "I don't know."

Then I scowled, realizing that had been the point of asking so suddenly. "I mean, this isn't one of Earth's tunnels, it's one of the, ah . . ."

"You're a good liar, but not that good." He eyed the door contemplatively. "This is how you cheated in the trials, isn't it? How you got into the labyrinth, how you learned so many things you shouldn't have known. These tunnels must go everywhere."

I rubbed my temple, feeling headachy and overwhelmed. Kallen was far too clever, and I was far too tired to keep up with his games. "Yes."

He hummed. "Oriana's been keeping a dangerous secret. She can't be pleased you still have that key."

"She isn't." And she would be even less pleased to find out another faerie—much less Kallen—knew about it. I grimaced. "Can you please not tell anyone else about this?"

"Why not?" His head was slightly cocked, as it often was when he'd spotted a vulnerability that might be ripe for exploitation.

I sighed, giving up all hope of holding my own in this conversation. "Because it's the one advantage I have in Mistei. Everyone else has soldiers, resources, alliances, *thousands* of faeries to support them. I have two house members—four now—and this key, and that's it." I shook my head. "What do you think Drustan will do when he realizes how far the tunnels go? What will Hector do?"

"They'll want the key." He looked at where it hung between my breasts. "I want it, too," he said, voice reverent. "The things you must have overheard . . ."

"Well, you can't have it," I snapped.

He met my eyes again. "I won't tell anyone. Not even Hector."

Dizzying relief swept over me. "You won't?" Then I remembered who I was talking to, and my relief shifted to suspicion. "There's a price, isn't there?"

"Consider it more of a request." His dark eyes gleamed. "I don't trust this Accord. Imogen, Torin, and Rowena will play politics in public, but they know what's coming as well as we do. They're going to be preparing for war. I want to know how."

"You want me to spy for you again." Frustration built in my chest. Would I never be free of his blackmail? My position in Mistei was too vulnerable to refuse, though.

He shook his head. "I want you to take me with you."

That made me pause, once again set off-balance. That was what Kallen did, though. He moved through conversations like they were sword fights—advance and retreat, feint and parry. He lured me in by sharing glimpses of the person hidden beneath that forbidding exterior, then struck to send the conversation spinning in the direction of his true objectives.

He was looking at me with such intense interest, though. Alive, maybe even excited, as if he couldn't wait for the two of us to go spying together. Kallen was rarely this animated, and a part of me I wasn't well acquainted with wanted to agree just to keep that look on his face.

Did he have any friends? Did anyone besides me let him share his philosophies about hunters and beasts? He'd come here because he'd heard I'd been hurt, not because he'd known I was going to use the key. Did anyone else care about his concern—or even believe him capable of it?

Maybe he hadn't been luring me in with conversation merely to manipulate me. Maybe I had gotten too close to the real person—the one who knew the view of the world from a cage and had sworn a vow to a tyrant as soon as he was old enough to speak—and he'd changed the topic in an attempt to regain the upper hand. Kallen didn't know how to be vulnerable, but he did know how to negotiate for information.

So here we were. Me in possession of a secret, Kallen manipulating the circumstances to gain access to that secret, too. An old pattern, yet the way he was looking at me, the way he'd said, *Take me with you*, with that pleading edge to his voice . . . that was new.

I cleared my throat. "Fine. But you can only enter the catacombs with me, and no one can ever know about it."

And then something truly shocking happened.

Kallen grinned.

8

W<small>HEN I WOKE FROM A NAP, THE CEILING CRYSTALS</small> gleamed with the last red of sunset.

I closed my eyes again, pressing my cheek into the pillow. After showing Triana and Maude around the house, I'd been overwhelmed by a wave of exhaustion. I'd slipped into a spiderweb-thin chemise, left my damp clothes in a pile on the floor, and crawled into bed.

It was tempting to search for dreams again, but a tapping came at the door and I realized what had pulled me out of sleep. "Come in," I called, struggling to a seated position.

The door opened, and Lara strode in. "Humans," she said without preamble.

I yawned. "What?"

"You brought humans."

"Yes, Maude and Triana. Are they all right?" I'd left them in their new bedrooms in a wing on the other side of the kitchen—they'd liked the idea of having a space entirely to themselves—and told them they were free to explore.

"They're currently making bread, so presumably." Lara cocked her head. "Are more servants coming, or can I have one of them?"

I blinked. "What? They're not servants. They're my friends."

"The younger one was dusting the staircase earlier."

I rubbed my eyes, wishing I was more alert. "I'll need to talk to them. That's not why they're here." They were here to be free, not to take up a different type of servitude. I grimaced, brain catching up to the conversation. "And what do you mean, can you have one?"

Lara gestured at the thick braid that hung over her shoulder. "My hair is atrocious. I'll take whichever one you aren't keeping as your handmaiden."

My mouth dropped open. Mistei was a month away from civil war, and Lara was concerned about her hair? "No. You can do your own hair."

"Not well." She toyed with the braid, running her fingers over the strands that had started coming loose. "And you're a princess now, so you're not going to do it. An Underfae trained in the cosmetic arts would be best, but I'll take what's available."

I bit down the angry words that wanted to fly out of my mouth. Lara could be difficult, but there was a reason for that behavior. Oriana had trained her not to show any vulnerability, so she lashed out and demanded things instead of admitting her hurts. "Things are going to be different from what you're used to for a while. We have to fend for ourselves." I shook my head, and some of my pique slipped out. "Who would you be doing your hair for, anyway?"

Her cheeks reddened, and she looked away. "I'm a lady of Blood House, aren't I? Ladies deserve respect."

The nature of the wound became clear. "I do respect you," I said, trying to soften my tone and only partially succeeding. "So does anyone who matters. But right now the house is just you, me, Anya, Maude, and

Triana, and I didn't bring the others here to be your servants. I brought them here to save them." I hesitated, wondering if saying this next part would wound her pride even more, but she was going to have to get used to this particular injury. "The same way I wanted to save you."

Her full lips compressed into a line. "Princess Kenna and her collection of broken toys."

My temper flared despite understanding why she was being confrontational. I threw the sheet aside and stalked over to her. "Do not talk about them that way," I said, planting my hands on my hips. "Don't talk about yourself that way, either."

She flinched and looked down. Her slippered feet shuffled over the carpet as she stepped back, then to the side, then returned to her initial place as if rejecting her own retreat. "How are we supposed to do this?" The demanding edge was gone from her voice—raw hurt lay there instead. "How do you expect us to succeed at . . . at anything?"

"You don't think we will?" I asked, though the same doubts festered inside me.

"It's three humans and me. What can we possibly be but a burden? What do we have to offer to you, to Blood House . . . to anyone?"

The anger fled, leaving me hollow. She'd been obnoxiously superior about her position here compared to the others, but there was the core of the issue, admitted plainly. *What do we have to offer?* Lara had no family, no magic, no standing in Mistei outside these walls, and she knew it.

"We have ourselves," I said past the lump growing in my throat. "You think I know how to do this? I have no idea what I'm doing. But I will *gut* anyone who tries to hurt us."

A house of five could become six and then ten and then more. We could become something Mistei had never seen before. The broken, the oppressed, the dispossessed—they could find a home here, and together we would show the Noble Fae a new type of strength.

Power could be gifted, but it meant more when it was seized.

Lara tugged on her ragged braid. "I'm useless," she said bitterly. "The humans at least have an excuse, but what am I? A failure."

"You're not useless," I said, heart aching for her even as the words sparked fresh irritation. "And the others aren't useless, either. Have you forgotten I was human yesterday?"

She yanked on her braid again, then shook her head. "You're different from the others."

I scoffed. "Nonsense. I'm just the only human you've ever gotten close to." She didn't even know sign language. How would she know what the others were like? "The three of them will treat you with respect, but you need to respect them in return. We're not going to win by being like the other houses. We're going to win by being different."

"Oh, Kenna. What is there to win?"

Disturbed by the question, I crossed to the wardrobe. When I opened it, the first garment that met my fingers was a black silk dressing gown banded with scarlet. I shrugged it on and tied it, watching the movements of my fingers. My skin might have a shimmer to it now, but it was also dotted with familiar small scars, earned through a mixture of childhood clumsiness, hard labor, and foolhardy fights.

The sight of those scars was comforting. Becoming Fae hadn't stolen those marks from me, even if my future wounds would heal seamlessly. It hadn't stolen who I was.

I finished tying the bow and faced Lara. "What do you want to win?"

She looked taken aback. "What?"

"What do you want? Because it doesn't have to be what other people want for you." Blood House might never have the same sort of power the other house heads aspired to, but if we lived—if we were happy, if we were safe, if we found meaning in our lives—that would be a victory.

"I—" She broke off, seeming even more consternated. "No one's ever asked me what I want."

"Because you were expected to be the perfect daughter and heir," I said, taking her hands in mine. "A duplicate of Oriana."

She flinched. "I failed at that, too."

"You didn't fail. You're just someone else." I swallowed the lump in my throat. "And you get to decide who that is. So what do you want?"

She needed to say it, but I needed to hear it, too. Because I wasn't perfect, either, and I never would be, and so much could go wrong if I didn't come to peace with that. I might give up my ambitions, telling myself nothing good was worth doing with a flawed hand. Or I might try to force myself to fit someone else's mold of the perfect princess, filing myself down until the person left was unrecognizable.

"I want to be respected," she finally said. "Not just by you. By everyone."

I nodded, encouraging her to continue.

"I want—" Her voice grew reedy, and she cleared her throat before starting again. "I want to be admired for something besides my parentage and my face."

I gripped her hands tighter. "Yes. What else?"

"I want . . ." She closed her eyes, and a shudder moved through her frame. "I want them all to be sorry," she whispered. "Everyone who's ever looked down on me. Everyone who's ever hurt me. I want to hurt them back."

Vengeance. She wanted vengeance.

"Yes," I said, feeling the same urgency in my bones. *"Yes."*

ANYA WAS IN THE KITCHEN WITH TRIANA AND MAUDE.

I paused in the doorway, heart leaping at the sight of her frowning as she smacked a ball of dough. I'd seen her like this many times before. She'd never been a good baker, but she'd liked kneading dough the best, rolling it out with the heels of her hands before picking it up to slap against the table.

"Vanquishing my enemy," she'd joked once when I'd commented on how she was pummeling the dough like it had personally insulted her. "Giving it a good beating before the burning."

There were three large bread ovens built into the wall at the back of the kitchen. The center oven was aglow, its brick floor carpeted with coal. A sweaty-faced Maude stood beside it, squinting at the embers. The oven must have reached temperature, because she briskly swept the coals and ash into a nearby trough, leaving the floor bare. She then grabbed a wooden paddle and hurried to the table where Anya was working. There were two other balls of dough there, which Maude quickly transferred to the oven floor. With those situated, Maude raised her eyebrows at Anya and pointed to the remaining dough.

Anya smiled.

A precious pain filled my chest, like I'd swallowed a beautiful glass bauble that had shattered inside me. Anya had the best grin in the world, dimpled and sudden, and I hadn't seen it in so long. She used her fingers to draw two furrows on top of the dough, then brushed her hands off and gestured for Maude to move it to the oven, too.

Then Anya saw me, and the smile slipped.

"Hello," I said, trying to pretend that change in expression hadn't hurt worse than seeing her smile to begin with. "What are you doing?"

Triana stood over a scarred preparation table, stirring a bowl with a wooden spoon. Unlike Anya, her expression grew warmer at the sight of me. "Use your eyes," she signed.

"Yes, I can see you're making bread," I said dryly. Cloth-covered proofing baskets sat on the counter, and one of the cabinets was open, revealing a sack of flour, a pot of honey, and other ingredients the house must have manifested. "But the house will provide cooked food if you ask it to. You don't have to make it."

Maude looked around mistrustfully, as if the house might start flinging food at her. "No," she indicated with a sharp jerk of her head and a slashing motion. "No magic."

"It's better this way," Triana agreed. "Something to do."

I refrained from pointing out they were already using magic, since the flour had come from somewhere. If this was what they wanted to do, I wouldn't argue.

Lara nudged me. "What are they saying?"

"That they don't want to rely on magic and that it's good to have something to do." I looked at Anya. "Do you know sign language?"

She shook her head. "I was kept . . . apart from the others."

Because Osric had been covetous of what he'd considered his.

Triana set the bowl aside, then moved to wrap her arm around Anya's waist. They had grown close in a shockingly short amount of time, and a small, shameful part of me was jealous. Then Triana rubbed her hand over Anya's shaved head before rubbing her own short hair, and I felt even worse for my pettiness. Of course they would have recognized each other as fellow survivors.

There was a message in that gentle rub of the head. *I was like you once*, Triana was telling Anya. Or maybe she was trying to tell Anya that her hair would grow again, with all the associated growth that came with it.

"Maude and I will teach you," Triana signed, pressing a finger to Anya's chest. She looked at me and made a gesture at her throat, asking me to provide the interpretation.

I cleared my throat, resisting the urge to cry at Triana's unhesitating kindness. "She says they'll teach you to sign."

"Can I learn, too?" Lara asked, surprising me. She had been staying close by my side, and while her earlier attitude towards the others had been petulant and entitled, now there was a hesitance to her bearing. "If we're all members of the house, we should understand each other."

No Noble Fae I'd ever spoken with—other than Kallen—had expressed a desire to learn the language. The humans were far beneath their notice, good only for the work they did or the entertainment they provided with their suffering. But Lara was making an effort.

I looked to Maude for the answer, because I already knew what Triana would say. Triana had welcomed me with open arms despite my new form and new magic; she would offer to teach Lara, too.

Maude's mouth was pressed in a tight line. Rather than answering, she turned to roll a stone in front of the oven to seal in the heat.

Triana walked over to Maude and tapped her on the arm. They held a discussion full of short, sharp movements, and then Maude shook her head and stormed out of the kitchen, skirting as widely around Lara and me as she could.

Triana looked at me apologetically. "She doesn't trust faeries."

"She hates me, doesn't she?" Lara asked, crossing her arms.

My head was starting to hurt. "It's not you," I told Lara. "Maude's been trapped here a long time. She doesn't trust any of the Fae."

"Except you."

A sad smile crossed my lips. "She doesn't trust me, either."

Triana rapped her knuckles against the table to get my attention. "I'll teach the faerie," she told me. "Who is she?"

I nearly smacked myself in the forehead. I'd talked about Lara many times when visiting Triana, but she'd never actually met her, had she?

"Can I tell them what happened?" I asked Lara quietly.

She scowled. "If you must." Then she stalked to a cabinet, opened it, and stared at the shelf balefully until a bottle of red wine and a goblet appeared. She proceeded to pour a very full glass before pulling a stool up to the table where Anya had been shaping the dough.

"This is Lady Lara," I told Triana. "Formerly of Earth House."

Triana made a soft noise, and I wondered if she realized why the heir to Earth House might be standing in this kitchen. When her brown eyes filled with pity, I knew it—I just hoped Lara didn't see that look, too.

Anya was frowning, fingers squeezing the edge of the table. She'd met Lara, but she didn't know the full story, so I picked through what to say that wouldn't injure Lara's pride too badly. "She was my mistress when I was a servant—I was helping her through the immortality trials." At Anya's quizzical look, I smiled ruefully. "I'll explain the trials later. A lot has happened." Far too much. I felt like I'd aged a decade in the span between winter and summer.

"So why is she here and not in Earth House?" Anya asked.

"This is humiliating," Lara muttered.

"There were three possible outcomes to the trials," I said, bracing myself. "Lara would either gain her full magic, lose all her magic, or be killed."

"I'm sure you can tell which one it was," Lara said bitterly, gesturing to herself. "Since I'm not dead, but I'm here."

"You . . . lost your magic?" Anya still looked wary, but she hadn't moved from her spot at the table.

"And was immediately disowned," Lara confirmed, drinking more. "Banished from Earth House, then taken in like a stray by Princess Kenna."

"Princess?" Anya whispered. She wrapped her arms around herself, swaying. "Kenna, *what*?"

Shards, I had gone about this all wrong. I'd left my friends alone in Blood House without any explanation of what was happening. Anya knew I had become Fae, but that was it.

The weight of this new life felt too heavy. So many secrets. So many lies. And there were so many people I'd sworn loyalty to—genuinely or not—that no one knew the entirety of who I was or what I had done.

A sigh slipped from my lips, and my shoulders drooped. "I'll explain everything, but I think we all need wine."

AN HOUR LATER, WE WERE EACH ON OUR SECOND GLASS, THE bread was cooling, and I'd explained as much as I could about what had happened since I'd reached Mistei, from my initial assignment to Earth House to the disastrous council meeting earlier that morning and the Accord we were all about to be subject to. My visit to Oriana I left unmentioned, since I hadn't decided what to tell Lara about that.

Maude had crept back into the kitchen partway through the story, perching on a stool near the ovens as she picked at some finger-knitting in her lap. Where she'd gotten the yarn was a mystery, but the house had a habit of providing helpful items. I took her presence as a positive sign. She still wasn't sure about me, and especially not about Lara, but she was listening.

The others had already heard pieces of the story, but Anya was the one with the most to learn. Her expression had grown stark when I'd first mentioned King Osric, and at the third instance of his name, she'd poured another glass of wine, hand shaking.

"Do you want me to stop?" I'd whispered.

"No," she'd said, frowning into her cup. When I'd reached for her hand, she'd pulled away.

Trying not to let on how much that hurt, I'd kept going.

There had been two other uncomfortable parts of the story—when I'd told them about spying for Kallen and when I'd confessed my affair with Drustan. Lara's gaze had nearly flayed me alive, but she hadn't said anything.

Not at first, anyway. The tale was done, Triana and Maude were discussing it while Anya stared into her drink, and I was approaching a cabinet, shaping a wish for cheese to accompany the fresh glass of wine in my hand, when Lara appeared at my elbow. She'd poured a third glass, too, but drinking didn't seem to have calmed her down.

"All this time," she said, gripping my elbow, her voice quiet but furious. "You were working with Kallen and Drustan *all this time*. You were sleeping with Drustan!"

I winced. Shame curled in my chest, and I covered it with a deep drink of wine. It tasted like black currants and smoke. I wished it was Earth House's crisp white wine instead, the vintage Oriana had served on the spring equinox. Whatever magic was woven into it had made me happy in a way that had grown rare.

That made me think of Drustan, though. I'd danced with him on the equinox, sun on my face and excitement in my heart.

"Are you angry?" I asked Lara, already knowing the answer.

"I'm annoyed you didn't tell me earlier." She swayed slightly, the alcohol clearly affecting her. "You were sworn to Earth House. Meeting with Drustan and Kallen was a betrayal."

"A betrayal?" My voice rose, and the others looked our way.

Lara wiped her eyes with the back of her hand. "To Oriana, anyway. I suppose it doesn't matter to me anymore."

The ache of regret was growing. "No, you're right. Not about Oriana, but . . . I should have told you. As my friend."

She sniffled. "Yes, you should have." Then she made a face. "Seriously, though. *Drustan?*"

"At the time, he wasn't... He hadn't..." I trailed off, not wanting to finish that sentence, because I knew why Lara was disgusted at the idea. Because of Selwyn.

I hadn't confessed to my role in that tragedy during the story, either. So much had been painful to admit, but that one had been too much to bear. It wasn't only grief tightening my throat until I thought I might choke; it was fear. Because if Lara knew I was the reason Selwyn had joined Drustan's rebellion, she might hate me for it.

"I didn't know what he would do," I said. "He promised everything in Mistei was going to change."

And it had.

She muttered a very un-Lara-like "Fuck," then ripped open the cabinet to reveal a plate heaped with cheese, grapes, and little jars of jam. It wasn't precisely what I'd envisioned, but it was close enough that I smiled despite the lingering pain.

"I can see the appeal, I suppose," Lara muttered darkly, ripping a grape off its stem. "Not personally, but he's always been lusted after on a grand scale."

And he'd wielded that charisma and sexual heat like a weapon. How many others had he recruited with sex?

We used to fuck, he'd said on the summer solstice before sending the Fire lady Edlyn to her death. *She was jealous.* And maybe Edlyn had been, and I could understand why Drustan had said what he did to save himself and the rest of the rebellion, but Edlyn had only been in that position because he'd asked her to start recruiting ladies from Illusion House.

He'd asked me if I wanted to help his cause, too. And I'd said yes, because overthrowing the king was right... but also because whenever Drustan's smile had been directed at me, I'd felt valuable in a way I never had before.

Maybe I should tell Lara that. A small piece of my hurt; a gift like the necklace she'd given me last night that I'd thankfully kept in my pocket, engraved with words that meant more than the object itself: *To my best friend.* "I thought he cared for me," I whispered, trying my best not to cry. "He made me feel important."

"You are important," she said past a mouthful of cheese. She still sounded angry, but this time it was in the way of a drunk making a passionate argument.

"Thank you," I said, torn between the urge to smile and weep. "But what hurts is I don't know how much of it was real. Because it felt real, but if it was a lie and all he was doing was trying to get information about Earth House..."

What did that make me? A fool at best. Desperate. Delusional. I'd given a part of myself—and I wasn't talking about my virginity—to someone who hadn't wanted it for the right reasons.

"If it was a lie, then he was too stupid to realize what he had." Lara gave me a boozy yet determined look. "I hope it wasn't a lie, though. Not because I want you to be with him, obviously, but because I want him to feel horrible about losing you. I want him to *suffer*."

"You're a good friend." My eyes were definitely misty now.

Lara handed me a piece of cheese. "Go on, bite it in half. Pretend it's his dick."

My laugh was loud and startled. I staggered, sloshing wine on her. "Damn," I said, reaching forward to wipe it off her navy blue skirt and accidentally spilling more.

She looked down at the spreading stain. "Maybe this is why Blood House always wore red."

That made me laugh more. Everything might hurt, but there were still good things in the world.

9

THE NEXT MORNING, I WAS EATING BREAKFAST IN THE kitchen and thanking my new Fae physiology for sparing me the negative aftereffects of wine when I felt the subtle vibrations in the house magic that indicated a visitor. I headed outside to find a Fire sprite in an orange tunic standing with his hands clasped behind his back, peering up at the crow perched in the Blood Tree.

Joy filled my chest. "Aidan!"

A grin split his ash-gray face. "Kenna. It's good to see you."

I ran over and hugged him. Though sprites were small compared to the Noble Fae, he stood only a few inches shorter than me. Aidan squeezed me back tightly before making an alarmed noise and jumping away. "Wait, you're a princess now." He bowed. "Sorry, my princess, I shouldn't—"

"Don't you dare start bowing and saying that *my princess* nonsense." We had spent too many events side by side, heads lowered as we waited for the Noble Fae to order us around.

"But you're—"

"Kenna. Just Kenna."

"I mean, you're not *just* anything anymore."

I shook my head, then gripped his hands. "How are you? We didn't get to talk after the throne room."

He'd been in the midst of everything as Lord Edric's manservant, but it had been such a whirlwind I didn't even know if he'd fought. He'd seemed uninjured afterwards, but he'd been obligated to leave with the rest of Fire House, and we hadn't gotten the chance to speak.

His face grew serious. "I'm well. But we lost some good faeries that night, and the house is still grieving. Everyone is tense, anticipating what comes next." He squeezed my fingers, then pulled his hands out of mine and clasped them together, looking nervous. "I suppose that's why I'm here."

So Aidan hadn't just come for a visit. My mood dimmed. "Drustan sent you."

He nodded. "Before I jump into it, are you all right? That night was . . . bad."

An understatement. "As well as I can be. I'm glad Osric is dead."

"Everyone is," he said emphatically. "You have no idea. Most people hid it well, but every time one of the dinners ended in an execution, I felt this intense collective wish for Osric to die. So many faeries were thinking it I couldn't identify them individually."

Sprites could sense secret desires. If Aidan had known how badly Mistei longed for Osric to die, and if he was here on some mission from Fire House . . . "Did you know Drustan was plotting a revolution?"

He nodded. "Edric has been involved for a while. During the trials, he was trying to convince Talfryn to join us. And my gift was occasionally helpful when it came to identifying possible allies."

There was no reason to feel betrayed, and yet I did. "You didn't tell me."

He shifted, looking uncomfortable. "To be fair, you didn't tell me, either."

He was right, and I was a hypocrite. "Edric was really trying to recruit Talfryn?" The other Earth candidate had been unflinchingly loyal to the ruling family of Earth House—I couldn't imagine him going against Oriana.

"It didn't work. He wasn't willing to fight unless house leadership did."

"Did Edric try to recruit Lara, too?" Or was I the only one Drustan had asked to do that?

"He tried to lead the conversation that way a few times, but she wouldn't even begin to have a discussion about what needed to change in Mistei."

Just like when I'd tried to talk to her. Oriana had taught Lara it wasn't safe to speculate about such things—and considering what had happened to Selwyn, she'd been right.

"Edric risked a lot," I said, throat thick with regret. Another young idealist, recruited to a war he might not survive.

Aidan's smile was soft. "He's always been brave."

And Aidan was in love with him.

This conversation was making me feel sick. Drustan had apparently been using more than just me to try to get his hooks into Earth House. How many other people would I find out had been his tools? How many others—like me, like Aidan—had been partially motivated by love?

"So, what does Drustan want?" I asked.

Aidan squeezed his hands together. "Well, first I'm supposed to ask if you know who has Selwyn's key to that passage."

My heart thumped. "What passage?"

"Between Earth House and the throne room." Aidan looked

apologetic. "It's not because he wants to attack Earth House or anything. I think he wants to see if it goes anywhere else."

So Selwyn hadn't told Drustan the true extent of the catacombs. And since Drustan wasn't asking about *my* key, Selwyn must have kept the true number of keys a secret, too.

"I assume Oriana has it," I said, keeping my expression blank. Whichever Earth rebel had been using the key, they'd either volunteered or been forced to return it to her—or she'd taken it from their corpse.

Aidan made a face. "Then Drustan's never getting it back."

It was never Drustan's to begin with, I wanted to retort. Then again, the key under my skin hadn't been mine to begin with, either. We all felt entitled to whatever we could seize.

He fished in his tunic, then pulled out a scroll. "I'm also supposed to give you this."

I took it reluctantly. "I wonder what promises he intends to make and then break this time."

Aidan winced. He was familiar with my history with Drustan. "You should give him a chance, Kenna. He has a vision. Good intentions. And . . . I know it ended badly, but I think he was trying to save you when he told the king what happened during the trials."

I wondered if Aidan judged me for helping Lara cheat. He wasn't acting like it, but it had to sting knowing Edric had passed the trials all on his own while Lara had had help the entire time. Knowing I'd lied about it, too.

But we'd both lied to each other. We'd both omitted. When our secrets were deadly, what other choice had we had?

"Maybe," I said. Almost certainly. Drustan had only said that when it had seemed like Lara and I might be branded revolutionaries. Better for the king to think us cheating, incompetent fools. "That doesn't mean I forgive him."

I slid my nail under the glimmering orange wax seal, then unrolled the letter.

Kenna,

I'm sorry to hear about the attempt against your life. I should have known you would try to change Oriana's mind. You were lucky this time, but for your own sake, I ask that you not be so reckless again.

The chiding tone to his concern rankled. Had going to Earth House been reckless? Maybe. But that recklessness was the reason I was in this position to begin with, and I wasn't going to become docile for his convenience.

You asked me to prove my right to the throne by speaking of its people. To that end, I enclose below a list of every human whose duties bring them to Fire House. I plan to invite them within house walls for safety, where they will become paid servants for as long as they wish to stay. If they do not wish to stay, I will make arrangements for their release after we know the direction of this initial conflict.

Some of my anger faded. It was a good start. The humans had always been property of the crown, not belonging to any house, and the crown had never paid them for their labors. I liked that he was immediately addressing that portion of the injustice, even if I didn't like the idea that they would need to wait for release. The humans would have to accept that offer, of course. If they didn't trust me, they were unlikely to trust him, either.

I also plan to abolish any restrictions against cross-house romances, and the changeling practice will end immediately. You know how important this is to me.

I did. Interbreeding between houses was forbidden, and the children of those unions had been shunned before Osric's time and exiled after it. For the past eight hundred years, those babies had been traded for human infants. The changelings grew old and eventually died in the human world, separated from the magic that could give them eternal life, while the humans grew up enslaved.

Drustan had lost someone because of that monstrous policy. Mildritha, a lady he'd loved as both a friend and something more. She'd had a child with Lara's older brother, Leo, and now both of them were dead and the baby lost.

I will also endeavor to reintegrate the communities of outcast Fae.

"Who are the outcast Fae?" I asked Aidan.

"Faeries who were excommunicated from their houses. Usually for crimes like thievery or spying—if the faerie they committed the crime against was important enough—but also for failing the immortality trials."

That would have happened to Lara if I hadn't taken her in. "Where do they go?"

"There are a few enclaves lower down, nearly at the level of the Nasties. They're forbidden from going anywhere near court."

An idea began to simmer at the back of my mind. Blood House needed to grow. We needed our own soldiers, our own patrols. If these outcasts didn't have a house . . . might some of them want to join mine?

It was worth investigating. I looked back at the letter, reading the few sentences that were left.

There is far more to ruling than these small decisions, and I will share more detailed policies with you soon, but they are a start. I have been preparing for this role for a long time. You believed in me once, Kenna—try to believe in me again.

Drustan

I traced my finger over my name and then his, written in his elegant script. "Do you believe in him?" I asked Aidan. "Do you think he would be a worthy king?"

Aidan nodded without hesitation. "I do."

"I suppose you have to as a member of Fire House."

"That is part of it, but not all of it. He's been good to the people he governs." His face grew serious. "I will not go against my prince or my house, Kenna. In the end, I will always choose that loyalty over any other. No matter what happens."

My stomach sank. He was telling me something important—that as much as our friendship mattered to him, Fire House mattered more. As it probably should, since it was his home and part of his identity. When we'd both been servants, subject to the whims of our masters and with little influence over Mistei's politics, house loyalty hadn't mattered so much. Now that I was a princess refusing to support his prince . . . it did.

"I understand," I told him. "I will not judge you for that loyalty."

He smiled, though I saw regret in his eyes. "You're a good friend, Kenna. I hope our causes never come into conflict."

They would, though. They already were. And my friendship with

Aidan—like so many things I cared about—was more fragile than I'd realized.

I HESITATED OUTSIDE ANYA'S DOOR. I'D COME HERE AFTER TALKing to Aidan, wanting to check on her, but now I found myself standing with my fist raised yet unable to knock.

Most relationships had boundaries. Whether it was a small connection or a deeper one, a friend or an acquaintance, there were lines that couldn't be crossed, topics that couldn't be broached, limits past which someone would say, *No, I don't want to know you better.* Or *No, I don't want to spend more time on you.* Or *No, I just don't care that much.*

Growing up, there had only been two people whose love didn't have boundaries: my mother and Anya. I'd just discovered the edges of my friendship with Aidan, and my first impulse had been to go to the person who had always accepted me exactly as I was, who had never said no to seeing even the worst parts of me.

Now I kept remembering how her smile had vanished when I'd walked into the kitchen last night.

I took a deep breath and knocked.

There was no response at first. Then an animal-sounding moan came from within. "Please," came Anya's broken voice. "No, please."

Fear swamped me. I shoved the door open, running inside. "Anya?"

She was lying on the floor, arms wrapped around herself. Her eyes darted rapidly behind her closed lids, and her mouth opened on a wheezed exhalation. Her face was so wet, it looked like she'd been crying for hours.

"Anya!" I knelt beside her, gripping her arm and gently shaking. "Wake up."

She lurched awake with a scream, nearly knocking her forehead into mine. She shoved me so hard I fell backwards. "No," she spat. "No!"

"It's all right," I said as I struggled back to my knees. "It's me. It's Kenna."

She looked frantically around the room. "No," she whimpered. "I was drowning. I know it."

She smelled like alcohol. There was a purple stain on her sleeping tunic and an empty bottle lying beside her. She'd brought the leftover wine upstairs.

Worry knotted in my stomach. She'd enjoyed a few glasses of wine on occasion in Tumbledown, but I'd never seen her like this. Never bleary-eyed and stinking, looking at me like she wasn't even seeing me. "You weren't drowning," I said. "I promise."

She pressed a hand against her cheek, then pulled it back to look at the moisture on her fingers. "Not real," she whispered. Then her face crumpled. "How do I make them stop?"

"The nightmares?"

Her voice grew louder. "How do I make it all stop?"

My nails bit into my palms. "Anya—"

She shook her head. "Go away, Kenna."

"But I—"

"Go away!" She flung the bottle at the wall. It shattered, sending fragments skittering across the white marble floor, and the last drops of wine splattered around them like blood.

I pressed a hand over my pounding heart. "I can't leave you like this."

Her face went cold. "You already did."

Then she grabbed her pillow and curled up again, facing away from me.

Grief howled through me. I struggled to breathe past the feeling crushing my ribs. My fingers and toes were numb as I staggered to my feet, and I could hardly see past the tears that threatened to fall. "I'm so sorry," I whispered.

She didn't reply.

I cried all the way down to the kitchen, where I found Triana sorting spice jars that hadn't existed the night before. She looked haggard after the late night, but her eyes widened at the sight of me. "What is it?" she signed.

I sobbed, pressing a hand to my mouth. "Anya. She had a nightmare, and . . . and she didn't want me there."

A look of mingled pain and understanding came across Triana's face. She placed a hand on my shoulder, giving me a little shake before signing, "It isn't your fault."

Wasn't it, though? I hadn't taken care of Anya in the bog. I'd run ahead, trusting that she would follow, and she'd been stolen by Osric's minions because of it. "She hates me now," I whispered.

Triana shook her head. "Not you. She hates everything."

Wasn't I part of everything? I ran my shaking hands down my face, feeling the wetness of tears. It was nowhere near what I'd seen glistening on Anya's cheeks and soaking her shirt. "What do I do?"

"Listen. Wait. Be there."

"And if she doesn't want me there?"

"Send someone else instead." Triana narrowed her eyes at the cabinet, then opened the door and retrieved a steaming mug of lemon-and-honey-scented tea. Maude didn't want to use the house magic, but Triana was apparently learning. She set it down to sign the next words to me. "I have nightmares like that, too. Send me."

I nodded, feeling a curl of gratitude in the midst of the crushing despair. "Thank you."

Triana picked up the mug again, smiled sadly at me, then hurried away.

I went to the sink and splashed my face with cold water. It reminded me of the lake swirling around me, and I hurriedly shut the tap off. Then I pressed my hands to my face and let out a muffled scream.

How was I supposed to manage any of this? How was I supposed to fix Mistei when I couldn't even help my best friend?

I heard the *tap tap tap* of heeled slippers and turned to see Lara blow into the kitchen, a scowl on her face. She was wearing silver today, with hints of red velvet visible through slashes in the sleeves. She planted her hands on her hips. "What is this I hear about you going to Earth House?"

I groaned. "Lara—"

"Because I went for a walk and overheard two servants talking, and they said you went into the water tunnel." She looked incensed. "Why would you do that?"

I felt empty and aching and broken. "Because Oriana didn't go to the council meeting, and I was angry with her." Because I was too much of a coward to make the decision of who should be king.

"So you decided to try to kill yourself?" Her voice hit a dangerous pitch.

"I didn't," I protested. "An Illusion faerie made me trip. And Oriana saved me."

Her nostrils flared. "You spoke with her."

"I did." My shoulders tensed, bracing for the force of her displeasure.

Her eyes seemed like dark pools. "You didn't tell me."

Shame swept through me. "No, I didn't."

"Why not?"

I looked down, scuffing the toe of my black boot against the floor. "I thought you would be hurt."

"Hurt that you went there to begin with? Or that she still wants nothing to do with me?"

I looked up swiftly. "How did you—"

Lara let out a haunted-sounding laugh, then shook her head. "You're predictable, Kenna. Of course you tried to change her mind. You still don't understand how the Fae think."

"I had to try."

"I know." The creases beside Lara's mouth deepened with her frown. "I am hurt."

My stomach sank. "Because I tried to change her mind?"

Her voice grew bitter. "Being cast out is humiliating enough without everyone thinking I begged to be taken back."

Perception was everything to the Fae. More important than loyalty, more important than love. Lara had always hated being seen as weak. "The conversation was private," I reassured her, wishing I could sink into the floor.

She shook her head. "It doesn't matter. I'm more upset about something else."

My eyes prickled. Lara and Anya were all I had. The only spots of love left in my life, and I'd failed them both. "What?" I whispered.

"That you didn't tell me someone tried to hurt you."

The breath left me. That hadn't been what I was expecting to hear.

When I didn't reply, she strode forward to place a hand on my shoulder. Anger still simmered in her eyes, but her expression had softened. "Do you think this friendship only goes one way? You nearly died, and you didn't even tell me."

A tear broke loose, and I dashed it away. "I didn't want you to know I failed with Oriana."

"I don't care that you failed with her," she said fiercely. "I care that you nearly drowned. I care that someone tried to kill you. *That's* why I'm angry."

My throat felt thick. "I survived, though."

She rolled her eyes in a more typical Lara expression. "Obviously. I still want to hear about things like that."

I had knelt beside Anya a short while ago, wanting to save her from the demons that haunted her sleep. I'd asked Triana how to be there for someone who didn't want the help.

I hadn't realized Lara might feel the same about me.

"All right," I whispered. "I'll tell you."

She wasn't done lecturing me. "You have all the power now, but that doesn't mean you have to shoulder the burden or the consequences of it alone." She shook her head. "I've been useless for far too long, nothing but a decorative coward. Let me become something better."

I clutched her hands in mine. "You don't need to change a thing."

"You've at least learned to lie like a faerie." She sighed. "No, I know who I am, Kenna. I also know who I want to be. So let me be that. Let me help you."

Grief and gratitude mingled. Most relationships had limits, so I'd assumed this one did, too. And maybe it still did, but I'd also drawn this particular boundary where it didn't exist.

"All right," I said. "I promise."

10

STATE DINNERS WERE ALWAYS HELD IN THE SAME VAST cavern—the only place I'd ever seen that was large enough to hold the thousands of faeries attending. They were the few events all Noble Fae were invited to, regardless of their rank within a house.

I lingered at the top of the ramp leading into the space, taking in the sight. Pearly stalactites hung far above, and stalagmites strained towards them. In a few places, they'd met and merged into rippled, uneven columns. The hum of conversation echoed off stone as faeries greeted one another and moved to their tables.

"It's beautiful," Lara said beside me. "Imogen is making her mark."

She was. Shimmering rainbow fabric wound around the pillars, and what looked like enormous soap bubbles floated amidst the faerie lights overhead, each containing a dancing pixie the length of a finger. An invisible orchestra played while ribbon-twirling acrobats leapt through the aisles.

My eyes went to the dining table atop the dais. Drustan and Oriana sat at one end, while Hector sat at the other. In the middle were three faeries I'd never seen before.

Princess Imogen—I refused to consider her a queen—sat in the center. The bodice of her dress was pink, deepening to purple at the ends of her billowing sleeves. She had a large quantity of mink-brown hair piled on top of her head, and there was a fox-like quality to her features—high forehead, small nose, pointed chin. It was impossible to tell from here if her eyes were as purple as Osric's had been.

To her left, between Imogen and Hector, sat two faeries wearing white. Torin and Rowena of Light House, presumably, both glittering with diamonds. Torin had a sturdy build and hair like bronze, while Rowena was beautiful in the way of a sunrise, with pink cheeks and pale gold braids.

A single empty chair waited between Drustan and Oriana.

I pressed a hand to my stomach. "I'm nervous," I admitted. An understatement.

"She's not going to kill us at the dinner announcing the Accord." Lara tapped her finger against her chin. "At least not until after dessert."

I gave her an annoyed look. "Not helpful. And I'm nervous about more than that. I'm supposed to act like a princess, and I have no idea how."

"You'll do fine. Just sit there and look pretty."

Lara was the expert at that, not me. She was smiling prettily right now, fluttering a black lace fan and looking like she didn't have a care in the world. Her crimson ball gown was covered with silver netting and tied with black ribbons, and her dark hair was held back in a matching silver net. Blood House colors looked stunning on her, but it couldn't have been easy to put that dress on tonight, knowing it would remind everyone of the colors she used to wear.

My own dress was a deep oxblood red. The flaring sleeves were loose enough to allow Caedo to coil beneath, and the wide, straight neckline showed the line of my collarbones. It was simple as ball gowns went, adorned with small pieces of jet along the neckline and hem, but the fabric shimmered with the slightest movement, catching the eye with flashes of brighter red. My skin gleamed, too—that faint faerie luster that marked me as something no longer human.

Strange to look at. Stranger to be.

We'd helped each other get ready, trading off the role of handmaiden, and that help had been essential when applying the final accessory we both wore. A whisper-thin chain crossed my right palm, anchored around my wrist and fingers. It had appeared on the counter when I'd gone to retrieve cosmetics—the silver of the silvered event, an unspoken promise we were all making to keep the peace. Swords weren't allowed tonight as part of the tradition, and daggers were to be tied in place with ceremonial peace knots, but other than that, symbolism was our only protection.

I raised my hand, looking at the shine of the chain. "This is flimsy armor."

"No one's broken a silvered vow before," Lara said.

"There's a first time for everything."

"Imogen is trying to position herself as a more reasonable ruler than Osric. She isn't going to start her reign by declaring a formal peace and then immediately violating it in front of nearly the entirety of Mistei."

Lara was right. The Fae were liars, but they also cared deeply about appearances. They sent one another countless tiny messages in the form of jewelry, dress, posture, lingering looks, the brush of a hand over a throat or a weapon . . . What they couldn't say out loud, they often said in other ways. This chain was one of those messages, which meant that while it was on display, we should be safe.

Feeling a little better, I ran a finger over the chain, which was warming from my body heat. "I wish all events in Mistei were silvered." This would apparently be infrequent even during the Accord—just at the major gatherings.

"Then someone would definitely break the tradition." Lara moved her hand in artful twirls to make her chain shift and shine. "It has to be rare or no one would respect it."

I wasn't sure how she managed to look so confident and unruffled, considering the circumstances, but if she could do it, so could I. I breathed in, imagining a cord anchored to the top of my head that would pull my posture straight. Smiles didn't seem right for the Blood princess, so I thought of blank sheets of paper and icy winter ponds and shaped my face accordingly.

A few faeries were still entering, moving past us down the ramp, but we were verging on being late. We were going to attract notice no matter what—might as well get it over with. "Come on," I told Lara, picking up my skirts. "Let's give them something to talk about."

The low, thick heels of my boots clicked against the ramp as we made our way down. I had opted against the bejeweled slippers the wardrobe had tried to foist on me. Silvered tradition or not, I wanted to be able to run if I had to. As we walked down the central aisle, a shift in sound marked our passing. First came a breathless silence as faeries got a good look at us. I could tell what they were thinking—*Is that the human who became a princess? Is that the former Earth heir wearing Blood House attire?* Then came the swelling murmurs.

Prickles raced over my skin, and I felt hot and cold in waves. There were so many eyes on us, so many people whispering and judging. As a servant, I'd been unremarkable and overlooked. A curiosity at best, but mostly an accessory for Lara.

Now everyone was staring.

I focused on the dais, trying to pretend the rest of the room wasn't there. The replacement of King Osric and Prince Roland wasn't the only change the high table had undergone, and it was strange not to see Kallen up there. I wondered if he was watching me from whichever Void table he'd been seated at. Probably. No, definitely. Kallen watched everyone, but he'd always kept a particularly close eye on me.

Lara peeled away near the dais to take her seat at the last remaining empty table, and I mounted the steps alone.

Imogen smiled as she watched me approach. Her eyes were lavender, and my skin crawled. It wasn't the intense amethyst of Osric's eyes, but it was far too close.

Did she hate me for killing him? Or was she grateful, since it meant she could step into the vacated position?

"Princess Kenna," she said as I approached. "How good of you to join us." Her voice was a rich alto, as beautiful as the rest of her. A lace collar sprouted around her throat, held in place by metal boning, and her golden-brown skin was dusted with an iridescent powder that made her cheekbones stand out. The way she sat shining at the center of everything made me think of a carnivorous plant, petals spread in anticipation of whatever bumbling insect came too near.

"Princess Imogen," I replied. "I've been looking forward to this."

Her eyes narrowed. "*Queen* Imogen."

I made a noncommittal noise in reply to the correction, then circled around the table and took my seat between Drustan and Oriana.

The Earth princess looked at me neutrally from her spot on my left. "Princess Kenna."

Bitch, I wanted to say back. This was the first time she'd seen Lara since disowning her, and I hoped it hurt. "Oriana."

If she minded that I didn't greet her with her title, she didn't say anything.

The air was warm to my right, and I steeled myself before turning my head in that direction. "Drustan. I hope you are well tonight."

He certainly looked well, all leonine grace and relaxed posture. His tunic was golden as the sun and dotted with rubies, and two braids held the front of his long hair back from his face. "Kenna," he said, nearly a purr. "You look exquisite."

I did, but it was none of his business anymore. I reached for my wine. It was a light, translucent red that didn't taste nearly bitter enough for how I felt seated between these two.

The seating arrangement on the dais was purposeful, I was sure. Imogen had taken care to position Drustan and Hector as far away from her as possible, where they couldn't speak to each other. She'd placed Torin on her left and Oriana on her right—her closest ally and the neutral party on the dais. Rowena went beside Torin, of course, and Imogen had stuck me in the last spot.

Not that it mattered much where I ended up. Every other house head was tied to a section of this room—patches of Light white and Void black, the colorful shimmer of Illusion, spots of flame-bright fabric for Fire House and the green and blue of Earth. Looking out over the vast sea of the Fae, it became even clearer the issue of scale I was up against.

My skin prickled with the instinctual awareness of being watched, and I glanced down the line to find Torin and Rowena staring at me. Rowena was even lovelier close up, with sky-blue eyes, doll-like features, and a smile so bright I immediately distrusted it. Torin had Roland's heavy jaw, and his lips tilted with the same sneer the former Light prince had often worn. His wavy hair was cut short, just curling over his ears, and his pale blue eyes made me think of chips of ice.

I nodded at them in acknowledgment, since that seemed like something I ought to do, though my skin crawled as I remembered what the other alliance members had said about them. *Cunning. Sadists. Insane.*

Rowena's grin widened. She whispered something in Torin's ear.

I focused on the room again, hating how exposed I felt. Though most faeries were smiling, tension hung in the air. We might all be wearing silver, but that tradition hadn't been practiced in over a thousand years, and Imogen was Osric's blood.

Everyone was seated, which meant the dinner should begin shortly. Underfae would carry in the first course of salads, soups, bread, and other light fare, which would be followed by the meat and main courses, after which would come dessert. At that point Osric had usually clapped his hands to make some awful speech or publicly execute someone.

I wondered how long Imogen was going to make everyone wait in suspense before giving a speech. The revolt had only been two nights ago, yet here we were, sitting side by side as if nothing had changed in Mistei but the bodies on the dais.

Imogen clapped her hands.

The noise startled me, and I sloshed my wine and had to immediately set it down. Drustan gave me a sidelong look but didn't comment.

Silence had fallen over the chamber—the hush of dreadful anticipation.

"Citizens of Mistei," Imogen said, rising from her chair. Her voice echoed, and I wondered if she'd forced an auditory hallucination on everyone to sound louder than she was. "I know you must be anxious about what is to come now that King Osric is dead. It is tradition for Mistei's ruler to speak after the dinner, but I'm not going to prolong this unnecessarily."

My heart raced. I'd mentally prepared myself for a variety of awful outcomes after dinner, but I hadn't prepared myself for the possibility they might happen this early.

Imogen could still declare immediate war. She could use her Illusion magic to make me blind to danger. She could kill us all, and there would be no need for this farce of a peace month.

Imogen wore the same crown Osric once had—heavy and dark,

with brutal spikes that spoke of a certain type of power. It didn't fit with her delicate pink-and-purple dress, which had layers like overlapping flower petals, and I wondered what message she was trying to send with that contrast.

Her eyes swept over the crowd. "I am the new Queen of Mistei. As one of Osric's closest living relatives and a direct descendant of Princess Ceridwen, this is my right by birth and power. I claim it here, in front of you all."

Oh no. I glanced at Drustan, but his expression was unreadable. Because this was what he'd expected? Or because he had some other scheme boiling behind those calm gray eyes, ready to explode into violence?

"King Osric was a powerful leader," Imogen said, "but power needs to be tempered by prudence. I understand why Void, Fire, and Blood made the choice they did."

A whisper raced across the room. Her condemnation of Osric shook me, too. Speaking ill of the king had been illegal for an eternity in Mistei, and though Osric was dead and gone, part of me irrationally feared he might rise from his grave to punish anyone who defied him.

"To demonstrate that I am committed to being a more generous ruler," Imogen said with a smile, "I have declared an Accord. During these thirty days of peace, we will celebrate the ending of an old era and the beginning of another. You will learn how it feels to serve a merry queen instead of a cruel king."

"A merry queen?" I muttered under my breath, eyeing Drustan.

Despite his lingering smile, his eyes were narrowed in a way that told me he wasn't pleased. "It means she's going to try to win them over with hedonism."

One of the six Fae virtues. It was a strange strategy to my thinking, but that was because human rulers were expected to be either wise and temperate or strong and decisive. The Fae valued strength and cunning, but they also adored their pleasures. And wasn't Drustan proof of how effective that strategy could be?

I couldn't resist making that jab. "Upset she's stealing your approach?"

He shot me a swift, dark look before resuming the lazily amused expression of the Fire prince, as if Imogen's plans mattered little to him.

Imogen was still speaking. "I plan to enter into negotiations with the other house heads during this time so we can discuss the best outcome for Mistei under my rule—and how we can all be part of it." She spread her arms wide. "I'm glad we can all be here together at the dawn of a new era. Tonight is for eating, drinking, and dancing. This celebration—this *peace*—is my first gift to you as queen." Her smile turned sly. "And this is my second gift."

A metal sculpture appeared on the table in front of me, and I barely restrained myself from toppling backwards as if it were a venomous snake. It was several feet high with a wide base and tapered tip, like a furled rosebud with overlapping copper petals. Similar sculptures had appeared in front of the other house heads and in the center of all the tables below.

A delicate whirring sound came from within the copper bud, and the petals unfurled in a spiral. In the center was a single golden apple.

Drustan cursed under his breath.

"These apples were plucked from the Dreamer's Tree at the heart of Illusion House," Imogen said. "I hope you enjoy them."

Below, faeries were already reaching for the apples, jostling to get the first bite. A Fire faerie at a nearby table sank his teeth into the golden fruit, and a look of euphoria came over his face. Someone else snatched it from his hand and took a bite.

"Let the revelry begin," Imogen announced. She sat, spreading her skirts.

A cheer started at the Illusion tables, then spread across the room to Light's. Even some members of Fire, Void, and Earth House clapped along, grinning. Whatever Imogen had just done was apparently significant. "What is this?" I muttered to Drustan.

"The apples induce euphoria and some mild hallucinations," he said. "They never spoil, and if you eat more than one a year, it's rumored the craving for the next will become uncontrollable."

I hadn't been planning to eat the apple, but I certainly wasn't going to now. Imogen had taken a healthy bite, but none of the other faeries on the dais had touched their gifts. "Why is everyone so eager to eat, then?"

"Because they're rare and expensive. And because pleasure feels most potent when it's a step away from destruction."

A shiver moved down my spine at the dark words. Even humans were drawn to desires that cut, and that lure must be especially intense for the Fae, who were far more difficult to destroy.

"She's been preparing for this for a long time." The whisper came, surprisingly, from Oriana, who was looking contemplatively at the apple in front of her. "The tree only produces a few hundred each year. There's no way Osric would have allowed her to harvest them all."

If she was able to steal twenty a year, even if there were only a thousand apples in the room, she still would have been collecting them for fifty years. Which meant Imogen's ambitions were very old.

"It's an extravagant gift," Drustan replied.

"Very." Oriana picked up her wineglass, looking at the red liquid within. "A sign of things to come."

Even someone who'd grown up as poor as me recognized a bribe when I saw it. Watching the glee spreading through the room—the laughs and grins, the swift kisses, the dreamy-eyed gazes at the lights drifting above—I felt the sting of trepidation. It was easy to mobilize hate against a tyrant who hurt their subjects. What were we supposed to do against one who offered bliss instead?

The food was brought in then, some heaping plates carried by servants and others seemingly floating in midair. Acrobats skipped down the aisles, swirling their ribbons, while contortionists and jugglers followed. A troop of faeries dropped from the ceiling, dangling from swaths of fabric as they danced in midair.

The music grew louder and faster, careening exuberantly. Every empty wineglass abruptly grew full again. The Fae cheered and laughed.

The unease prickling through me intensified.

Drustan lightly nudged my hand, and a shock went through me at the touch. "Smile," he said through his own bared teeth. "It's just the opening move."

I swallowed, then nodded, forcing a smile to my own face. The opening move—and the game to come would be brutal.

11

NO ONE DIED AFTER DINNER.

It shouldn't have been as astonishing as it was, but Osric had set an eight-hundred-year precedent of butchery. I'd only witnessed a few months of his atrocities, and even I couldn't quite believe it when the tables vanished and a lively tune came lilting down from airborne musicians. The Fae began partnering off, dancing not just with members of their own houses, but faeries from opposing houses.

The first offered hand took me aback. The other house heads were already dancing; apparently I was expected to, as well. I took a turn with a minor noble from Earth House, then a faerie from Void, counting my steps and sweating my lack of grace. The third dance was claimed by Lord Edric of Fire House. Edric was an excellent dancer and an equally good conversationalist, but it felt strange—even wrong—to be in his arms. I was painfully aware of Aidan watching from the wall and that I was in the position he'd always longed to be in.

Edric was handsome, with a bright grin and dark eyes that crinkled agreeably. Glitter had been brushed across his brown skin, and tiny ruby cuffs were dotted through his cloud of black hair. His pupils were wide, and the drop of golden nectar at his lips told me he'd partaken of Imogen's offering. Fire faeries rarely denied themselves when there was pleasure to be had.

He'd been one of my favorite candidates in the trials, mostly because of Aidan, but also because he seemed decent, as faeries went. Always livening up a room with a laugh, a witticism, or an offered drink. He'd performed well, too—not the best, but far from the worst. The only trial I knew for certain he had failed was the Illusion trial, when he'd . . .

I frowned, trying to remember the specifics. We'd been in a ballroom, trying to . . . What had we been doing there?

I remembered standing in a spotlight at Lara's side. I remembered writing on a magically enchanted piece of bark while hurrying around looking for something. The specifics of what I'd been writing or what the test had been were hazy, though.

My skin crawled. It had happened, as promised. The Shards had modified our memories, obscuring the details of the tests so the immortality trials could be repeated in infinite variations.

I'd lost my rhythm, thrown off-kilter by the realization. Edric looked at me curiously, then slowed his movements. "Is anything wrong?" he asked as he started turning me in a gentle circle.

"I was thinking about the trials," I admitted. "I can't remember what the tests were."

"Ah." He nodded. "It's unsettling, isn't it? You don't lose all of it, but you lose enough."

"You don't remember, either?"

"No. This morning I did, but I realized during dinner that most of it was gone." His mouth tipped up on one side, but it wasn't a happy expression. "I can't say I like it."

Remembering my conversation with Aidan, I asked a new question. "Do you remember trying to recruit Talfryn?"

He looked surprised I'd mentioned it, or maybe that I knew about it. "Did Aidan tell you that?"

I belatedly realized I probably shouldn't have brought it up. "Ah—"

He chuckled. "Don't worry. I could never be upset with him, and it doesn't need to be a secret any longer. I know you've been on our side for a while. Drustan told me you were working closely with him leading up to the coup."

Working closely with him. I hoped my face didn't reveal my embarrassment about what that had entailed. "When did he tell you that?"

"After you killed Osric." His expression grew serious. "I just wanted to say—I'm sorry for what happened to Selwyn, and I understand why you might hesitate to declare Drustan king. But he's a good leader and a brave one, and every sacrifice weighs heavily on him. Especially that one."

My goodwill towards Edric abruptly faded. This dance had had a political purpose all along. First Drustan had sent me a letter through Aidan, and now he was sending diplomacy through a dance.

The music was slowing and sliding into a new tune—the music never truly stopped during Fae dancing, just morphed into the next thing—and it was a perfect excuse to step away. "Thank you for the dance, Lord Edric."

He looked like he wanted to say more, so I headed for the refreshment table to grab a chilled glass of white wine. I drank, then pressed the sweating glass to my brow to cool my heated skin.

Every sacrifice weighs heavily on him.

Did they? They certainly weighed heavily on me.

A dark figure appeared at my side. Kallen, looking so solemn I instantly knew he hadn't taken a single bite of those apples. He wouldn't, though. Kallen seemed the last person to want to lose control. "Here," he said, handing me a scroll sealed with black wax.

I took it, sliding it into the pocket of my dress. "What is it?"

"Hector's first policies."

So the Void prince was doing what I'd asked of him, too. "Drustan already sent me his."

Kallen gave me a sharp look. "Is the speed or the content more important to you?"

I shook my head, feeling another bite of guilt. "If speed mattered, I'd have already chosen, and maybe Imogen wouldn't have Mistei eating out of her hand."

"This was inevitable. Even with Drustan or Hector leading our faction, she declared the Accord too quickly." His eyes moved restlessly around the room. "At least now we know what we're dealing with."

"A villain bearing gifts?"

"She's setting high expectations. Maintaining them will be a challenge."

I made a face. "The Fae are practically drowning in gold. Surely it won't be that hard to keep bribing everyone."

"Everything has limits. And if she spends recklessly on one area, she neglects another. Something to keep an eye on." He faced me again. "On that note, when are you going to fulfill your promise to me?"

Apparently I wasn't going to get a reprieve from his demand to go spying with me. "So speed matters to you, after all."

"I never said it didn't." He leaned in. "Tomorrow night?"

I sighed. Kallen was relentless. "Fine."

"Send me a message telling me where to meet you." He stepped back, bowing slightly. "Enjoy the dancing."

"You, too," I echoed automatically.

He shook his head. "I never do."

"Never?" I asked, brows rising.

He paused. "Almost never." Then he was gone, moving away through the surging crowd.

The ballroom felt too warm, the music too loud, and there was a wild edge to the dancing. The faces spinning by were ecstatic, and many lips glistened with golden nectar. A day ago the Noble Fae had been ready to gut one another, and now they looked a few drinks away from an orgy.

"So this is the new Blood princess." The voice behind me was light and sweet, almost girlish. Dreading whatever uncomfortable interaction awaited, I turned to find Rowena and Torin standing before me.

Prickles went over my skin. The power-hungry Light duo were not who I wanted to be speaking with, much less by myself. "Lord Torin and Lady Rowena," I said, resisting the servant's urge to curtsy.

"It's Prince and Princess," Torin corrected, mouth turning down.

"I believe that issue is still in question." I squeezed the stem of my wineglass. It cracked under my fingers, and I yelped as the two halves fell to shatter on the floor, spraying wine everywhere.

Around us, faeries stopped their conversations to stare. Then drunken laughter broke out.

Heat swept over my face. Had I gripped it that hard? More likely this was a consequence of my new faerie body. It wasn't a noticeable change most of the time, but my strength, speed, and endurance were all slightly elevated.

I moved to pick up the pieces, but a servant was already there, bowing and apologizing as they swept away the shards. A second followed with a cloth to blot up the wine, and a moment later it was as if the accident had never happened.

Rowena laughed, a high-pitched ripple of sound. "What a charming way you have about you. Very . . . rustic."

I'd heard worse. Forcing myself to smile, I pretended this was a joke we were all in on. "Yes, it comes of the peasant upbringing. How are you enjoying the dinner?"

If my aplomb had startled them, they gave no sign. Rowena looped her hand through Torin's arm as she looked around. "It's lovely to see Mistei embracing such revelry. I've been in need of a new diversion lately."

Torin bent his head closer to hers. "You know I'll offer you any entertainment you wish," he murmured, stern face softening as he looked at her.

She grinned and patted his cheek. "I know, my love."

It was jarring to see them show such obvious affection for each other. Couples in Mistei tended to be restrained in public—Beltane orgies aside, as those fell into the category of hedonism—probably because caring for anyone was dangerous. But Gweneira had said they'd been acting as one for centuries, so perhaps they didn't care.

Rowena's gaze fell to me again. "*You* are certainly an interesting diversion. Tell me, whose claim do you support for the throne?"

I hadn't expected her to ask so abruptly. Fighting the panic that said I was a fool for not knowing the answer, I lifted my chin and narrowed my eyes in a way I hoped looked regal. "That's my business and no one else's."

"Oh," Rowena said, sounding enchanted. "What an intimidating facade you are trying to put on." She squeezed Torin's arm. "Isn't it adorable, darling?"

Torin looked me up and down like he might a pile of fly-ridden shit. "I would find it more charming if the new Blood princess were supporting Queen Imogen."

I felt clumsy and gauche. They saw right through me, as anyone with half a brain would. But I could hardly back down now. "Why should I?"

"Because to do otherwise is dangerous." Torin might gaze at Rowena with adoration, but when he looked at me his eyes seemed flat, as if there were no life behind them. "One human should not speak with the voice of an entire faerie house. One human is also vulnerable, should she not use that voice for the correct cause."

It was an overt threat. Pulse hammering in my throat and stomach buzzing with nerves, I raised my hand so the silver chain sparkled between us. "What good fortune that your queen has declared an Accord, then. And that I'm not human anymore."

Torin smiled, but it still didn't reach those cold eyes. "Strange things can happen in the dark."

A chill went over me.

Rowena looked at me sympathetically, leaning her head against Torin's arm. "They don't have to, though," she said in that girlish voice. "There's still time."

My breath was coming too fast. "You're threatening me at a dinner announcing peace?"

"It's not a threat," Rowena said, nuzzling her nose against Torin's sleeve. She didn't say what else it might be, though.

"Excuse me," a new voice interjected. "I believe this dance is mine."

A strong hand entered my line of sight, adorned with a familiar golden ring. Torn between opposing urges—the strongest of which was to run away from everyone and everything—I looked up at Drustan. The Fire prince looked unusually solemn as he waited for me to accept the offer.

Who did I want to be near least? Right now, it was an easy answer. I was too slow giving it, though, because Drustan leaned down to murmur in my ear. "People are watching, Kenna."

Of course they were. This was my life now—to be gawked at and speculated about. I nodded, then slipped my hand into his before turning to face Torin and Rowena. "Enjoy your evening."

"May your nights be peaceful, Princess of Blood," Torin replied.

Everything inside me felt tense as Drustan guided me to the floor. This was a different sort of trial than the one I'd just escaped, but I didn't want to endure it, either. Dancing with Drustan at a ball... I'd dreamed of this. I'd occasionally dreamed of him coming to my rescue, too, the way he just had.

As always, his touch felt too hot. Too *much*. The thick gold ring circling his index finger was warm, the metal having absorbed the radiating heat of all that barely contained magic.

I wondered how cold my skin felt to him, and if he'd ever minded. No one burned as hot as Drustan in Mistei; we must all seem chilled as corpses in comparison.

The dance was slow and simple, which was good in some ways and awful in others. I was too flustered for complicated patterns, but it also forced me to look up at his face rather than seizing the excuse to stare at my feet. I'd been near him at dinner, but this was different. More intimate.

His mouth wasn't tense, but he wasn't smiling, either. A neutral look. "That didn't seem pleasant. What did they say to you?"

"Veiled threats."

"Revolving around...?"

"Supporting Imogen or facing unknown terrors in the dark."

"I'll double the patrols around Blood House."

Don't, I wanted to say. Did I really need more Fire soldiers—which meant Fire informants—around the house? I shouldn't be refusing any defenses right now, though. "It's probably just bluster."

"It would make me happy to know you're safe."

My breath hitched. "Stop."

He looked like he wanted to ask what he should stop—but also like he knew the answer.

We separated and circled each other for a few wary turns, hands pressed together, gazes assessing.

"Did you get my letter?" he asked.

I nodded.

He clearly expected me to say more, but my tongue felt clumsy, and I didn't want to heap him with praise for making promises he might not keep. The silence stretched between us. He guided me a quarter turn to the right, one hand firm at my waist. I was excruciatingly aware of the eyes following our movements.

"Will you truly not speak with me?" he asked quietly. "You used to have so much to say."

My brows shot up. Was he going to bring this up now? "You don't understand why I wouldn't want to speak with you?"

"I do, but . . ." He bit his lip, then released it. "I miss what we had."

No, he didn't. He couldn't, or he would have fought harder to keep it. "You were using me to get to Earth House."

"Kenna. You know it wasn't just that."

"Do I?"

He frowned. "You have a very poor opinion of me."

"Yes," I said bluntly. "But you've earned my poor opinion."

"Because I told Osric about you? I was trying to save your life—and Lara's. He needed a reason to find you harmless."

Apparently we were going to discuss this. I could think of better places than a dance floor to do it, but perhaps he knew I would have done my best to avoid being alone with him. The music at least covered our words, and everyone else seemed too drunk to listen, anyway.

I looked at his handsome face, remembering how blank it had seemed as he'd watched me being dragged past him. He'd caused that, even if he hadn't meant to. Osric had craved death that night, and the king had needed the flimsiest of reasons to deliver it.

That wasn't the real issue, though. As bitter as I was that Drustan had revealed our cheating, I could also understand that it had perhaps been well intentioned. The lesser of two evils, as he'd probably seen it. Better for Lara and me to be labeled cheaters than traitors to the throne.

"Do you remember what came before that?" I asked. "Do you remember *why* Osric took a sudden interest in us?"

His jaw tensed, and he looked away. Oh, yes, he remembered.

"Because we were mourning Selwyn," I continued. "Because you killed him."

"I didn't kill him. Osric did."

A ragged noise tore out of me. "Yes, you did. He broke neutrality for you and gave you soldiers, and in exchange, you told Osric he was the true traitor. You might as well have shoved him into the magic yourself."

Drustan glared down at me, but he was still guiding me through the steps smoothly, his lead so confident it was impossible to falter. I hated him a little for how good he was at this, too. "You know why I did it, Kenna. Don't lie and pretend otherwise."

I bit my lip hard. "That doesn't mean it was right."

"Likely not," he acknowledged. "But it wasn't wrong, either. I made the choice that would preserve the largest number of lives."

"You made the choice that preserved *your* life."

"Two things can be true." The air around him wavered, and a small flame licked at one of the braids holding his hair back. "But you need to admit why you're really angry with me. It's not just because of what I did to Selwyn. It's because, according to your logic, you helped kill him, too."

The words hit me like a slap. I stopped moving, and his momentum carried him into my space, so close our bodies were nearly touching. He didn't back away.

"Damn you," I said softly, feeling the prickle of tears. Because he was right.

"I'm already damned, Kenna. However humans tally such things, I'm sure my sins have passed the point of forgiveness." He shook his head. "But this is Mistei, not the poor little village you came from, and it's not as simple as that. Nothing is."

Dancing couples swirled around us. We were an island in the midst of a sea, frozen in the push and pull of this shared torment. Choices taken and love discarded, his lust for power and my shattered illusions. We had both walked over bodies to get here.

I couldn't forgive him . . . because I couldn't forgive myself.

"You can't belong to two worlds at once," he said, lifting his hand to cup my cheek. "If you keep holding on to both, the strain will tear you apart."

I briefly closed my eyes. How sick that this should be how he finally touched me in public as equals. On the surface, it was like a story my mother would have told me—the human who became a faerie princess, who went to the ball and danced in the arms of her prince.

The stories hadn't been honest about how many people needed to die for that to happen.

"And if I never forgive you?" I asked past the ache in my throat.

He shrugged, looking tired. "Then don't forgive me. But make your decisions for better reasons than to spite me."

The words stuck a thorn into my heart.

"We need to find a way to work together," he continued. "Even if you hate me. Even if it's painful for both of us. A princess does not have the luxury of making choices based on personal sentiment."

The strings played an aching lament overhead. The Noble Fae turned in graceful circles in one another's arms. My lover looked down at me, the memory of a Beltane fire flickering in his eyes.

He was both right and wrong about me. Right in his wrongness, maybe, or wrong in his rightness. Maybe that was the point he was trying to make—that there were no easy answers. Humans had the luxury of black-and-white thinking, but the Fae existed in the gray.

His hand slid from my cheek to my shoulder, resting there like he didn't want to stop touching me yet.

I shrugged off his hand. "I will work with you in this alliance," I told him. "But I can't promise we're going to agree on everything, and I will not guarantee my support. I do, however, promise that I won't make any decisions based on our . . . personal history."

He nodded. "Fair enough."

The drums were coming in again, sending the dance into livelier territory. He stepped back, and the air cooled. For a moment I missed that magical heat.

Drustan bowed. "Always a pleasure." He turned away, and soon he was dancing with a new partner, laughing before he leaned to whisper in the lady's ear.

I went to get wine, careful not to hold the glass too tightly this time. Then I watched from a spot at the edge of the cavern, wondering what alliances were being woven tonight and what promises were being made under the cover of music. Drustan was dancing with a Light lady while Hector was dancing with one from Earth. Kallen was nowhere to be seen, probably doing something secret in the shadows. Imogen was surrounded by a cluster of faeries from Light, Illusion, and Earth House, while Torin and Rowena were sending frequent looks in both Gweneira's direction and mine. Gweneira was speaking with Lara, and the cynical part of me wondered at her agenda in getting closer to the only other Blood faerie.

The music, the laughter, the glitter—all of it floated on the surface, as insubstantial as foam on a pond. Beneath it, in the quiet dark and the subtle spaces between words, changes were being set into motion.

I felt the increasing anxiety of an opportunity passing me by. What was I doing drinking alone in a corner? What moves was I making for the game ahead? I had so much less power than the other house heads—which meant I needed to be so much bolder to make up for it.

Swallowing the last of the wine, I set the glass on the tray of a passing servant, then hurried towards the dais before I could talk myself out of it. As I mounted the steps, the faeries twirling nearby slowed their movements, turning their heads to watch.

I stood on the platform in front of all of Mistei, pulse racing and skin dampening with nervous sweat. "Blood House has been resurrected," I announced. My voice couldn't come close to filling the cavern, but Mistei's rumor mill would do the rest. "We're seeking new members."

Shocked murmurs went through the crowd. Most of the dancers stopped entirely, and even the fiddle music broke off.

Imogen watched me with narrowed eyes. I met that look and raised my chin, imagining a crown on my own brow. Not Osric's, heavy and cruel, but something that would make me hold my head higher to earn the honor of wearing it.

"Too many of you have been suffering under the rule of tyrants," I continued, staring Imogen down. "Blood House will be different. If you don't feel safe where you currently are, come join us. If you hate your masters, come join us. If you crave freedom, an escape, or a new start, come join us. Regardless of house affiliation, species, or magic—if you want a new home, you may have it."

That was as much of a speech as I felt capable of. I was no Drustan, with charm in abundance and all the right words to win people over. So before I could ruin the words I had managed to get out, I gripped my skirts, raising them out of the way as I descended the steps.

For a moment everything was silent and still. Then the music started up again, the Fae resumed their dancing, and the laughter and glitter swept back in, covering everything in layers of pretty deceit.

Nothing had changed on the surface. But faeries were watching me now out of the corners of their eyes—and the ones looking most closely were the servants. I smiled, feeling the heady rush of triumph. It was too early to know what changes would be wrought as a result of that speech, but at least they all knew the truth now.

Blood House had entered the game—and I was going to play by my rules.

12

THE NEXT MORNING, I WAS WOKEN BY A KNOCK. EXHAUSTED from the late night, I was slow to rise, but some of the fog cleared when I found Triana outside, smiling. "They came," she said, hands moving excitedly.

"Other humans?"

She nodded. "And faeries from the other houses, wanting to serve here instead."

My heart lifted. My speech last night had reached the right ears, and Blood House was about to swell in size. "I'll be down in a few minutes."

I threw on a red dress, securing it with an iron-gray sash, then hurriedly redid my braid, which had gotten ragged during the night. Then I woke Lara and convinced her to join me.

"It's too early for this," she said grumpily as we headed down the stairs.

"No, it's not." I couldn't stop smiling. "People actually came."

Her expression grew softer. "It was a good speech. Daring, too.

Imogen looked ready to stab you for seizing everyone's attention at her party."

"That's why it was important to do. If everyone keeps acting like this is Imogen's Accord, Imogen's party, Imogen's plan, then she's already won."

"No princess has ever tried to recruit members before. The Fae take house loyalty seriously—Gweneira said encouraging faeries to defect was about the most shocking thing you could have done."

"Do you know Gweneira?" I asked. "I've never heard you talk about her before, but you seemed close last night."

"I've decided to be more strategic and start cultivating allies for us." She looked almost embarrassed to admit she'd been playing politics. "Since she's on your council and fighting for control of Light House, I thought it would be a good place to start."

I grinned. "Lara, that's wonderful."

"We'll see if I'm any good at it. But Gweneira was interested to hear my opinions on Earth House, and when she found out I don't know much about other successful coups, she promised to send over some history books."

"So you're going to be my political advisor?"

Her smile was half grimace. "I have no idea what I'm doing."

"And you think I do?"

"I like Gweneira so far, though," Lara said as we reached the ground floor. "She's calm and reasonable. I hope she ends up in charge of Light House."

It was hard to imagine a Light faerie being reasonable, but their favored trait was discipline, and they supposedly cared deeply about justice. The danger came when the worst of them—like Prince Roland—defined what justice meant.

The door to the house was open, letting in the murmur of conversation. Maude and Triana hovered in the entrance, alternating between talking to each other and signing to the humans outside. Triana caught sight of me and grinned.

Maude was more hesitant to smile, but she seemed a bit happier than she had been the first day. She nodded at me, then signed the number 117 and pointed outside.

There were that many people here? I could barely believe it.

Sure enough, the entrance hall was filled. Approximately eighty were humans, ranging from children to the elderly; I spotted Maude's friend Bruno, who had apparently softened in his opinions, as well as other familiar faces from the workrooms. Most of the rest were Underfae, but there were five Noble Fae hovering at the back of the crowd, looking ill at ease. Their attire marked them as members of Earth House, and Lara made a soft noise of recognition before waving to them.

"You know them?" I asked.

She nodded. "The three teenagers are—I mean, they were Selwyn's friends. The two elder faeries often challenged Oriana about neutrality."

Earth House defectors here to defy the Fae's ancient traditions because of me.

I faced the crowd as Lara took her place beside me. "Welcome to Blood House," I called out. "I'm Princess Kenna, and I'm glad you're here."

The Underfae looked nearly as nervous as the humans, darting glances over their shoulders as if expecting someone to arrive at any moment to punish them. Betraying a house bore severe consequences, so I would need to claim them for Blood House quickly.

I tallied them up, finding a mostly even split between Earth, Light, and Illusion Underfae. I recognized most of the Earth faeries, though I didn't know them well. The servants were always on the move, and with so much of my time taken up with Lara, I hadn't formed the same bonds that the kitchen or cleaning faeries had with one another.

"This is my trusted advisor, Lady Lara," I continued, gesturing at her. "You are welcome to take shelter in Blood House for as long as you like, but you must swear fealty to not just me, but the other faeries and humans who live within these walls. We are a small house, and this needs to be a safe place for all of us."

A Light asrai stood near the front, watching me with sunlike eyes. Her long fingers were laced together at her heart, and it was hard to tell with those brilliant eyes, but she looked like she might be crying.

A shiver of unease went over me at the sight of her. Trusting the Light and Illusion Underfae was going to be difficult, I realized. They had come seeking shelter, but what guarantee did I have that they weren't spies? If I didn't take this risk, though, the house would never grow.

I could at least exercise a small amount of caution. "I'd like to talk to each of you to find out why you want to join the house and what you'd like to do in these walls. Can you please form a line?"

They moved into place, though many looked ready to bolt. *Let me know if anyone else comes near*, I silently requested of the Blood Shard. It hummed agreement in my head. I tasked Maude and Triana with managing the line, and Lara and I settled into a small study in the corridor outside Blood House and started the interviews.

The human interviews were fast and easy. I wasn't going to force them to explain why they wanted to join the house, so all I asked were their names, where they were from, and if they were interested in leaving Mistei once I could arrange transportation. Almost all said yes, though a few expressed the same concerns Maude had—that they doubted they would find welcome in their old villages. I informed them they would not be expected to act as servants and could simply rest until we figured out a path for everyone.

Once I'd spoken to each person and performed the mental task of adding them to the house, the Underfae began interviewing. The first two were a dryad and a brownie who had defected from Earth House, wanting to follow Lara. The dryad, Nadine, had apprenticed under Alodie and offered her services as our head servant.

Lara and I sent them out of the room while we debated to set a precedent for the others waiting outside, but there was no debate to be had. We knew them, and we would certainly need a head servant to manage the growing household. So I closed my eyes and communed with the Blood Shard, offering the two Underfae safety.

The next two faeries, both from Illusion House, wanted to interview together. One was a sylph wearing a purple shirt that was slit in the back to allow his long, filmy wings to poke through. The angle of his wings was odd—they stuck out crookedly rather than falling straight down his back. On his shoulder perched one of the more minuscule Underfae: a lavender-haired pixie the size of my finger, with the blueish-purple wings of a butterfly.

"Princess Kenna," the sylph said. He bowed as low as he might to a queen. The pixie flitted up from his shoulder at the movement, gave him an irritated look, then executed a bow of her own in midair. "I'm Jory," the sylph continued, "and this is Maela. We've come begging shelter."

"Will you tell me why?"

"Even with the king gone, I can't stand to stay in that house." Jory shuddered and wrapped his arms around himself. "Please let me stay, Princess."

I hesitated. It was easier to trust the faeries who had left Earth House because I knew what went on within those walls, but Illusion House was very different.

"You should show her," Maela told Jory. Her voice was light and tinkling, so soft I leaned in to hear better.

Jory sighed, then turned to present his back to me. His wings twitched, but instead of snapping up and out to lift him off the ground, they jerked into a half-extended position. The slit in his shirt allowed me to see where they merged with the pale skin of his back. The bases of his wings were covered in ropes of scar tissue.

"The king cut them half off," the sylph said sadly. "All because I dropped a plate when he was passing by. Now I'll never fly again."

I pressed a hand to my mouth. "I'm so sorry."

Jory turned to face me again. "It doesn't matter if Princess Imogen is better than him or not; she's still his blood. I can't stay there."

I looked at Maela. "And you?"

The pixie held out her arm, and I realized her tiny hand was missing—only a bandaged stump remained. "I stole milk for a babe who wasn't suckling. The weak are supposed to die naturally in Illusion House, so I was punished."

My jaw dropped. "They cut off your hand for feeding a baby?"

She nodded, her heart-shaped face set in lines of fury. "The day you killed the king. They haven't gotten around to throwing me out of the house yet, but they will."

She could have chosen to take shelter in one of the outcast colonies. Instead, she was here.

I sent them out of the room and discussed the issue with Lara. To my surprise, she was immediately in favor of taking them in. "They're from Illusion House," she said, "but servants are different. They barely have magic anyway, and you saw her hand. Illusion won't keep her no matter what. Why not let them serve here instead?"

I agreed, and so the decision was made.

Both Underfae looked shocked when I told them. "It's real,"

Maela whispered, looking at me in awe. "What everyone's been saying about you—it's actually real."

"What have they been saying?" I asked as I mentally added the Underfae to the list of people allowed into Blood House. I could still keep track of everyone, but the larger the house got, the more I understood why the other house heads had a few chosen people who could also add or remove house members. Once this was a community of thousands, there would be no way for me to keep track of who was coming and going.

"That you actually want to help people." The pixie's eyes grew bright with tears, though she was smiling. "We'd all forgotten how to hope."

Moved, I pressed my hand to my heart. "I do want to help. I *will* help."

The enormousness of the responsibility pressed on me, though. Hope was a flimsy reason for them to put their lives in my hands, and the concept wasn't an easy one for me in general. Life had taught me that believing in something without any tangible reason to—like the kindness of strangers, the shape of my father filling the doorway after years of absence, or a cure for my mother's illness—was asking for disappointment.

It was getting a little easier to hope, though, mainly because I'd stopped thinking of it as a wish and started thinking of it as an action. Hope wasn't just believing that the world could be good and beautiful and kind. It was knowing the world was awful and likely always would be . . . and trying to fix it anyway.

After they left, I silently communicated with the Blood Shard. *I want Lara to be able to add house members. Can she do that without magic?*

Yes, the Shard replied. *She is part of the whole, and just as the house will feed her or rouse her from sleep, I can also speak with her if you wish it.*

The Blood Shard's voice in her head was a small benefit compared to the powers Lara could have wielded, but at least there was a tiny piece of magic left in Mistei for her—and a large responsibility to go with it. *I want that.*

Then it is done.

I told Lara, and her eyes widened. "You can't do that," she said, pressing a hand to her throat.

"Why not?"

She looked overwhelmed. "Because . . . because you *can't*."

"Who was able to add members to Earth House?"

"A few of Oriana's closest advisors. Alodie, but only when it came to the servants. And Leo, when he was alive." Lara's brother, who had died on the king's wards trying to find a way out of Mistei for his lover and child. Lara's eyes grew sorrowful. "Oriana was going to give me the ability after I passed the trials. That's why you shouldn't do it."

"You're my closest advisor," I told her. "I'm not going to change my mind."

She pressed her fingers below her eyes as she did when she was trying not to cry. "Fine. How do I do it?"

I struggled to explain how I experienced the connection with the Shard. "You know how it feels to wish for something in the kitchens?" She nodded. "Well, it's like that—setting an intention and sending it outside of you to something that's listening. I think of my connection with the Blood Shard like a lake I'm throwing stones into. I toss out questions and see what answers float back up."

She was silent for a moment, brow furrowed, and then a look of wonder crossed her face. "It spoke to me," she breathed. "It was faint, but I heard it."

Bittersweet joy filled my heart. I wanted so much more for her, but at least she had this. "Then you can add the next few faeries to Blood House."

Our next interview was with a Light nymph, beautiful, glowing, and nude except for the wisping white mist that covered her breasts and hips. She told us she didn't want to stay in the fracturing Light House and was terrified of what Rowena and Torin might do once they prevailed over Gweneira—because there was no way they wouldn't, not when they were capable of anything. "I think Rowena poisons the servants who displease her," the nymph said, clasping her arms tightly around her body. "They always get sick. And . . ." She hesitated, shuddering. "Torin forced me to dance on broken glass for her once. As a present, he said, because the normal type of dancing had grown dull. She laughed the entire time."

The story was sickening. It sounded like something Osric would do.

The nymph wept when I told her she was welcome in Blood House, and then she threw herself on the ground and kissed my shoes, promising she would dance whenever I wanted her to. When I told her she should only dance if *she* wanted to, she looked at me with overflowing eyes and said, "I don't understand, my princess."

That broke my heart, too.

The stories from the rest of the Underfae followed a similar theme. Servants who had been mistreated, those who feared the war to come, those whose loved ones had been killed in the solstice punishments. People in search of a home. As I listened to them, my mistrust of the Light and Illusion faeries faded. Where they'd been born and who they'd been forced to serve wasn't their fault. I'd only ended up in Earth House because of a king's whim—I just as easily could have been one of them, mutilated and despairing, longing for an escape.

We saved the five Noble Fae from Earth House for last so as not to set a precedent that they were inherently more important than the others. Even within the strict hierarchy of the Fae, everyone deserved the same respect and dignity. Thankfully, those five faeries seemed to be in agreement, and after hearing their pleas to become part of a house that was willing to take a stand for a righteous cause, they were easy to welcome, too.

I watched the last faeries pass through the spiked door, guided by Maude and Triana. The house thrummed with happiness, its invisible threads of magic vibrating in welcome. That joy was infectious, but my own happiness was woven through with worry. These humans and faeries had risked so much to come here.

Now I needed to figure out how to keep them all safe.

13

I PACED UP AND DOWN A STATUE GALLERY IN NEUTRAL TERRItory, trying to settle my nerves. Tonight I was making good on my promise to take Kallen spying.

I stopped in front of the carved figure of Princess Clota, the first Earth lady, whose lush figure was wrapped in marble roses. This was where Kallen had first told me Drustan had set his sights on me. The Fire prince had followed me for a moment of innuendo—a moment to nudge me closer to becoming his ally in Earth House—and Kallen had been watching from the shadows.

I'd been so afraid of Kallen back then. Or afraid of the King's Vengeance, since that was the armor he'd been wearing at the time. A faerie with a bloody reputation who used threats and blackmail as currency. He was still that faerie, I supposed. He hadn't quite blackmailed me into this invitation, but it was close.

I felt a shift in the air, a cool current against my skin. Mistei was full of peculiar breezes—some from ventilation shafts, some with no explanation whatsoever—but this wasn't the first time I'd felt one when Kallen was nearby. I turned and saw a shadow curling through the corridor, moving quickly. It stopped a few feet away, and the darkness solidified before unraveling to reveal his tall frame.

"You move fast like that," I said, fighting a fresh spike of nervousness. Kallen might not frighten me the way he once had, but his presence wasn't exactly calming.

He nodded. "It's difficult to maintain over long distances, but helpful for bursts of speed."

"And for skulking around in poorly lit areas."

"That, too."

I took him in. He was wearing black, as always, but these clothes were more casual than his stiff formal tunics. His boots were scuffed, the leather well worn. An outfit for moving in, much like mine, though my trousers and loose shirt were dark red. In addition to the sword strapped to his left hip, a long knife was sheathed at his right.

"Can all Void faeries move like that?" I asked. "Turn into a shadow?"

"Only the most powerful. I'm better at it than anyone else, though." He said it matter-of-factly. Not a boast, just the truth.

"I wish Blood magic could do something like that. It doesn't seem fair that only Illusion and Void can disguise themselves."

His eyebrows lifted marginally. "You could make my heart explode if you wanted to, Kenna. You have plenty of skills of your own."

"I suppose that's true." I flexed my hand, looking at it. I hadn't dipped much into my new magic yet. What were its limits? Could I torture someone with a thought? Tear their arms and legs off without touching them? Destroy the part of their brain where reason resided?

All of those ideas were disquieting, but my gifts needn't only involve destruction. I could heal wounds. Maybe calm someone whose heart was racing or who couldn't draw a deep enough breath. And if I could give pain . . . I must be able to give pleasure, too.

I dropped my hand, feeling flustered at the thought. "So. Where should we spy?"

"I want to see who's coming and going from Light House. I caught a Light faerie setting a trap near Void House today."

"A trap?"

"A bushel of explosive powder hidden in an alcove."

Alarm spiked. "That's against the rules of the Accord."

He shrugged. "Without a criminal, can it still be called a crime?"

"But you caught them."

He reached up to rub his left shoulder, tipping his head to the side. "I don't know if he was following Torin and Rowena's orders or if he had a personal grudge."

"Did you ask him if he was following their orders?"

His face didn't change expression. "I did."

"And?"

"He stabbed me with a hidden knife. Una ripped him in two for it."

"You were *stabbed*?" I reached for him instinctively, wanting to check for wounds, then stopped. "Where?"

He lowered his hand. "It doesn't matter."

"Of course it matters."

He looked genuinely confused. "I healed. The main issue is that Una acted too rashly. She eliminated him before I could get deeper into the questioning."

I didn't care what Kallen's sister had done to the faerie who'd wounded him. I cared that he'd been hurt. "Where?" I repeated.

He hesitated, then tapped his chest a few inches above his heart, just below where he'd been digging his fingers into his shoulder.

I bit my lip. "Can I look with my magic?"

"If you need to practice. The injury is gone, though." Regardless, he faced me more fully, dropping his arms to his sides.

He was trusting me to use my Blood power on him, even after telling me how easy it would be to explode his heart. Nervous at that level of responsibility, I closed my eyes, reaching for the pool of magic inside me. It didn't feel like fire, but it still burned. Hot, liquid, deep. The magic surged to greet me, slithering through my veins and making my fingertips tingle.

Kallen formed in my mind's eye. The beat of his heart pulsed against my new senses, and as I deepened the focus, I discovered the countless tributaries of his veins, the sturdy structure of his bones, and the coiled strength of his muscles. Focusing on the left side of his chest, I hesitantly sent a tendril of magic towards him, shaping a wish to know if he was in pain.

My power found smooth skin, a thick slab of pectoral muscle, ribs, lung, heart, spine. All unblemished.

I wasn't touching him, but somehow I felt the shiver that went through him. I lingered in the sensation, marveling at being able to know someone else's body like this, from the inside out. I could feel the tension in his shoulders, the knot that had formed there that he'd been trying to work out.

Then I frowned as the edges of my magic brushed up against something else. Scar tissue, coiled around his ribs. Faeries didn't scar unless they'd been injured before becoming immortal, or unless certain herbs had been rubbed into fresh wounds to prevent them from healing correctly.

Who had hurt Kallen, and when had it happened? Could I heal that old scar? I had just started thinking about it, pushing my magic against the ridge of raised skin, when Kallen abruptly jerked away. My eyes flew open to see him looking at me with a tense expression.

The look was gone too soon for me to figure out what the feeling beneath it had been. "As you can see," he said crisply. "Uninjured. Let's not waste any more time."

"Very well," I said, though my pulse was tapping too quickly. Feeling the insides of him—the bone and sinew and that echo of an old injury—had been strangely intimate. I wanted to know more about how he was put together.

My lips hovered over the question of what had caused that scar. But he was blank again, deliberately cold, and I already knew he wouldn't answer.

"Lead the way," he said.

LIGHT HOUSE WAS THE CLOSEST TO THE SURFACE IN MISTEI, nearest the sun, and it was a long hike through the claustrophobic passageways and up narrow staircases.

We were in one of those staircases now, moving single file by necessity. The walls pressed in on either side, the stone damp beneath my fingers, and I was far too aware of Kallen following close behind.

"I can't believe these passages existed all along," he said, voice soft. We weren't near any spy holes or doors at the moment, but we were moving quietly anyway. "How far have you explored?"

Talking about this made me uneasy; it was a massive betrayal of Earth House. But I wasn't part of Earth House anymore, and Oriana had betrayed Lara, so what loyalty did I owe her? These tunnels were mine, too, which meant I could do whatever I wanted with them.

I wouldn't have chosen to involve Kallen, though. He wasn't the type to sit idle when he had access to a tool of this magnitude. He thankfully couldn't open or even see the doors without the key, but that just meant more opportunities for him to badger me into taking him spying.

"Far," I settled on. "But nowhere near all of it."

"Down to the Nasties?"

I shook my head. "I couldn't find a route that deep, but I'm sure it exists."

"To the places where the trials were held?"

I hesitated. "Yes."

"You killed Garrick."

I stopped and felt the whisper of air at my back as he nearly walked into me. I spun to face him. He was a step below me, and it brought our faces to the same level. Far too close, but I wasn't going to be the one to retreat. "How did you know?"

His eyes flicked to my neck, where Caedo was coiled. "He was drained of blood. Once I saw you kill Osric, I knew it had to have been you. I just couldn't figure out how you had gotten into the forest without being detected."

"Do you remember the trial?" I asked. "I don't anymore. Only brief flashes."

Wilfrid, the Void candidate, lying dead in a pool of blood. Lara swinging a branch into Markas's head and Garrick trying to kill Lara. And driving my dagger into Garrick's gut before twisting the blade, taking joy in his suffering . . . yes, I remembered that, too. I just couldn't remember why we had been in the forest to begin with or what test had been set for us.

"Not the specifics. I was there when they brought Garrick's body back, though." Kallen regarded me with a neutral expression. "It looked like you made it hurt."

I felt a deep spike of discomfort at someone else knowing the crime I'd committed. "He tried to kill Lara."

"You don't have to excuse it."

"Do I not?" At his steady look, I sighed. "I suppose I don't. Not in Mistei."

"Not to me, at any rate."

He was too close to be having this conversation. Those serious blue eyes saw far too much. "You don't care that I was cheating?"

"Lara was cheating. You were forced into it."

"I don't think that absolves me."

He shrugged. "I don't think there's anything to absolve. We all manipulate the system however we can. We just have to be prepared for the consequences."

I felt suddenly chilled, and I brought my hands to my arms to rub up and down. The fabric was fine, sliding smoothly over my skin. I wished it was something rough enough to catch at my fingers and rub me raw. "I didn't suffer those consequences, though. Oriana didn't, either, and she's the reason it happened." No, Lara had taken the consequences for all of us.

He was quiet, watching me rub my arms. His fingers flexed at his sides before he clenched them into fists. "It would be nice to believe in justice, the way Light House does."

Kallen never seemed particularly well rested, but there were moments he looked downright weary. "You don't believe in justice?" I asked.

"Not in the sense that good people will be rewarded and bad people will be punished." His mouth turned down slightly. "Sometimes it's hard to believe in goodness, too."

I laughed softly, the sound scraping up my throat. "Sometimes I don't believe in it, either."

"And yet you're the main argument for its existence."

The words took me aback. I let out another laugh, startled this time. "For goodness? I've killed people, Kallen. I enjoyed killing Garrick and Osric."

He looked deadly serious. "They deserved it."

"And that makes me good?" I shook my head, squeezed my arms

tighter. "I think a good person wouldn't want to kill to begin with. I think they'd always strive to be kind." Like Anya had always been. A smile on her face, a helping hand when she could afford it. Infinite forgiveness, infinite generosity.

And look what had happened to her. Maybe Kallen was right, and justice was an illusion.

"It's not black and white," he said. "What is the point of having ideals if you never dirty your hands to make them happen? If a kind person isn't willing to stop a tyrant, what use are they?"

We were debating philosophy when we should be spying on Light House. But Kallen's opinions were intriguing, and I didn't want to stop the debate, and he was looking at me like he didn't want to stop, either.

"Justifying evil in the name of good?" I asked. "That seems like a slippery slope."

"Do you think killing Garrick was an act of evil?" He sounded genuinely curious.

No, I didn't, and that should probably concern me. "I think I shouldn't be the one to decide that."

"I'd argue you are the only one who gets to decide that. Good or evil, right or wrong. The answer is almost always somewhere in the middle, and the important thing is that we don't lie to ourselves about that."

My skin felt electric. The argument was waking me up, invigorating me and making me think. I'd been reacting out of fear to so much these last six months, but right now it was just the two of us in a darkened stairwell, away from any listening ears or prying eyes. That privacy made me feel safe enough to ask the next question. "Do you ever feel guilty about what you've done?"

"Always." His eyes held the dark of a winter's night.

"Always," I echoed, feeling a surge of relief. It wasn't just me grappling with the weight of all this violence. It wasn't just me who felt conflicted and broken sometimes. Kallen, untouchable and feared as he was, felt it, too. "You say that, but you still don't believe in goodness? You clearly want to do the right thing."

"I am not good, Kenna," he said, voice sharpening. "That word has nothing to do with me." His eyes moved to my lips, then to my neck and the weapon that was now practically a part of me. "But I do understand wanting."

Shivers chased over my skin. I wanted to say that the desire to do the right thing and the ability to feel guilt were both fundamental parts of goodness. I wanted to tell him he was wrong to think the word had nothing to do with him. But the argument got lost somewhere between my brain and my tongue.

Why was he looking at me like that?

I blinked a few times, feeling like I was surfacing from a dream. Why were we having this debate to begin with? This was supposed to be a mission. Something like blackmail but not quite, like we were allies but not quite.

Kallen wasn't my friend. I didn't know what he was, but it wasn't that.

I let go of the desire to keep engaging in this strange argument and turned to start climbing again. "What I want right now is to get this done with so we can both go home and rest."

For a moment there was no noise from behind me. Then I heard the brush of his foot against the stairs, and we resumed the climb in silence.

14

I PEERED THROUGH A PEEPHOLE AT THE BRIGHTLY LIT STAIRS leading to Light House's entrance hall. This was as close as we'd been able to get. The Earth Shard had supposedly carved these passages long ago—or rather, a house head must have worked with the Shard to do so, since the magic of the old gods seemed to work in symbiosis with the princes and princesses—but house territory was sacrosanct. There would be no tunneling in or out of Light House itself.

The stairs bustled with activity as Noble Fae and Underfae came and went. The atmosphere was palpably tense, full of lowered voices and furtive looks. Light House was in conflict right now—Torin and Rowena positioning themselves with Imogen, Gweneira aligning herself with the rebel faction, and each with a portion of the whole loyal to them.

"Anything?" Kallen whispered.

I shook my head and stepped aside to let him take a turn.

He moved into place, hunching slightly to put his eye to the wall. After a while, his shoulders tensed. I leaned in, wishing there was room for both of us. "What is it?" I asked quietly.

"Soldiers," he said, stepping aside to let me look.

Six Noble Fae were walking two by two down the stairs. One wore white leather, but the remaining five were more heavily armored than most soldiers I'd seen, with golden breastplates, greaves, and gauntlets beneath snowy white capes. Their round-topped helmets covered the top half of their heads, with a thin strip of metal extending from the browband over the nose, and their sword belts also held knives and what looked like small metal nets dangling from hooks. Several were carrying bulging fabric sacks, and as they passed, I heard a faint clinking sound.

Kallen tugged my arm, pulling me gently away from the wall. We headed back down the tunnel, stopping periodically to look through other openings to make sure we were keeping pace with the soldiers.

"Do you think they're patrolling?" I asked at one point as we waited for them to catch up. Our route didn't match theirs perfectly, since the tunnels twisted and changed elevation unexpectedly, and we'd gained time by climbing down a ladder to the intersection where Light House's stairs met the public areas. There were a few pinprick holes here, so it was possible for both of us to look at once.

"Could be. I don't like the look of those bags they're carrying, though. I would bet they're laying traps or scoping out ambush spots for when the Accord ends."

Thinking about ambushes made me think of strange things that could happen in the dark. "Torin and Rowena threatened me if I didn't support Imogen."

"Did they?" Kallen glanced quickly at me. "I saw you speaking with them at the dinner."

Of course he had. He'd probably been skulking around, listening in on conversations. He hadn't asked about my attempt to recruit new house members, but his network of spies had probably already told him about the people who had shown up on my doorstep.

"They can't murder another house head during the Accord, can they?" I asked. "The attack at Earth House was before it had technically started."

Kallen leaned back against the wall, arms crossed, while I alternated between looking at him and peeking out at the corridor. "There may still be violence, Kenna. You should be ready."

Dismay sank in my gut like a stone. "I thought it was a mandatory peace period."

"No, it is the appearance of a mandatory peace period."

I sighed, rubbing my forehead. "I hate faerie riddles."

"It's not a riddle. Fae politics have layers. The Accord accomplishes one major goal—preventing all-out war on a grand scale until everyone is ready for it. If that war can be negotiated around, so much the better. But we are very much still battling for supremacy, and if you, Hector, or Drustan can be eliminated or recruited to Imogen's side without causing her supporters to turn on her, that will place her in a stronger position."

"So we're going to be smiling at each other at parties, all while secretly trying to manipulate or kill each other?"

"Precisely." His lips twitched. "Much like any other faerie party."

I started to roll my eyes at that, then caught the flash of torchlight against a gold breastplate. "They're here," I whispered.

The soldiers reached the base of the stairs. Four of them split off, two heading in either direction to stand guard. The remaining two faeries—a golden-armored male faerie and the female soldier wearing leather, who I assumed was their leader—knelt and began fishing through their bags, pulling out smooth, circular pieces of what looked like glass or crystal.

"What are they doing?" I asked.

Kallen was watching through his own spy hole. "Shoring up defenses."

Confused, I watched the faeries turn to face the archway that separated this main hallway from the stairs leading to Light House. The stone around it was intricately carved. Two mouthless Underfae flanked the door, their robed stone bodies glittering with flecks of mica. Their feathered wings curved to meet over the entrance, and the design was crowned by a sun whose rays shot jaggedly in all directions. The art was beautiful but unsettling, because scattered through the figures' wings and all around them were dozens of carved eyes.

Light was the house of order and justice. Casting light on darkness—or so they liked to believe—and always watching for crimes in need of correcting.

Some of the irises and pupils had been carved with precision, but others were holes recessed into the rock. The soldier wearing white leather fitted a piece of crystal into one of those hollows. Her companion joined her, doing the same to another, then another, until twelve eyes had been filled with crystal or glass.

The leather-armored soldier pressed her hand to a gap in the wall. Her skin turned an illuminated, translucent red, the veins standing out starkly, and then beams of light shot out from the crystal-capped hollows, so painfully bright I closed my eyes. The afterimage showed twelve reddened lines at different angles.

A trap. If a Light faerie with strong magic focused their power into whatever empty space was behind that stone wall, bouncing it off mirrors or bending it mystically in some way I couldn't understand, those beams would hit the curved pieces of glass. And as I'd seen at the summer solstice, light concentrated through a lens could kill.

The house entrance would do the same thing to intruders if they were foolish enough to get that close, but Light House was preparing for conflict in the public areas, too. The lenses blended in well—if no one realized the carvings around Light House had changed, it would be a nasty surprise.

The soldiers moved on, and we followed. A few times we lost them due to deviations between the tunnels and the main corridors, but Kallen knew Mistei far better than I did, and he had a sense of where they might be heading. Between my knowledge of the catacombs and his knowledge of everything else, we were able to catch up to them on the ramp near Blood House.

Kallen and I watched through a narrow line of metal mesh at the edges of a painting bolted into the wall. I'd seen the art before—an image of a battlefield, bright with blood and framed in silver. The mesh was finely wrought, and from the other side it looked like an artistic embellishment at the edge of the frame. A hidden door glimmered beside us, and I quietly pointed it out to Kallen.

The soldiers had been placing lenses in small hollows throughout Mistei—Earth House wasn't the only one keeping secrets—and the leader's bag was empty. She tossed it aside, then gestured at one of the other soldiers.

The second faerie placed his sack on the floor. The fabric shifted. Something was alive in there.

He knelt to open the bag and pulled out a salamander, gleaming black with spots of green. It writhed under his gauntleted grip, four-toed feet flexing. Its eyes shone the same toxic green, and when it opened its mouth, a clear, viscous liquid dripped out.

The faerie dropped it. Then he pulled out his knife and skewered it.

I twitched at the sudden violence. The blade pinned the salamander to the ground, and as the faerie pressed down, his unarmored companion bent to whisper something to the creature, words I could only half make out in a language I'd never heard before.

Kallen cursed, low and rough.

"What are they doing?" I asked, fear starting to beat at my throat and wrists.

"It's poisonous. They're casting a spell to make it attack."

Rowena poisoned the servants, I remembered sickly. "Attack who?"

Then I heard the whisper of my name across the air.

Kallen unsheathed his sword, then reached for the door before I realized what was happening. "Open it," he ordered me.

"But—"

"Open it!"

"There are six of them," I argued. "There are only two of us."

"If they release that thing, it's going to find a place to hide, and then it will be singularly driven to find you. It's called the bonebreaker salamander, Kenna." He gripped my arm, fingers digging in. "A single drop of venom against your skin and your muscles will seize so hard your bones break. You'll heal and rebreak yourself over and over, and all that time, the poison will work its way through your skin and into your veins. When it reaches your heart . . ."

He didn't need to say more. I yanked the door open.

Kallen burst into the corridor. The soldier whispering to the salamander was dead before I even crossed the threshold. The faerie pinning the salamander down leapt back with a shout, dropping the knife, and the creature tried to scurry away, dripping toxic black blood, but Kallen swung his sword and severed the animal's head.

The five remaining soldiers swarmed him. He dodged a sword, then grunted as a dagger sliced across his cheek. He retaliated by stabbing the attacker through the eye, instantly killing him, but his next blow caught metal as a soldier raised an armored forearm to deflect it.

He was fast and deadly, but there were still four of them, and their breastplates and helmets limited where he could strike. I couldn't let him face them alone.

Caedo leapt into my hand. Heart racing, I lunged for the soldier who had been carrying the salamander, who had just unsheathed a new knife. He spun in time to catch my blade in his gauntleted hand, and there was a clanging sound as metal hit metal. The impact reverberated up my arm, and my fingers briefly went numb.

The faerie threw his body weight forward, knocking me into the wall. He grabbed my wrist, slamming my right hand into the stone again and again. Bones cracked under the onslaught, and I cried out as my fingers lost their hold on Caedo. The dagger swirled up over my wrist, clinging to me, but I couldn't grip it anymore.

I looked into the soldier's hateful eyes. Distantly, I was aware of Kallen shouting as he murdered a third faerie. His face was streaked with red. He was bleeding, he was hurt, and I—

The soldier sneered at me. "They would want you to suffer." Then he swung the butt of his knife into my cheekbone, shattering it.

I screamed at the burst of splintered pain. As he pulled his fist back again, I slammed my uninjured left hand against his armored chest, imagining shoving my magic towards his heart.

The moment my palm met his armor, my skull felt like it had been cleaved in two with an axe. There was a sucking sensation behind my ribs as something essential was torn from me, and a sudden silence fell in my head. The place where Caedo's thoughts had brushed up against mine was empty.

I cried out, sagging from pain and disorientation. My chest had been scraped clean, left hollow as a shell. The Blood magic that was going to save me . . .

It was gone.

Caedo? I cried out mentally, panic swamping me. The dagger didn't answer. The metal circling my wrist lay inert.

The soldier laughed. "Really?" He gripped my hair and dragged me back upright, then stabbed me in the gut.

Agony ripped through me, and a raw wail tore out of my throat.

"Kenna!"

Kallen's shout broke through the ringing in my ears. My vision fuzzed at the edges as I watched him chop off the fourth faerie's head. Blood flew off his blade, coating the painting in red spatters. Then he shook off his final assailant and leapt for the soldier who had stabbed me.

The faerie jerked the blade free and let me go. I collapsed, blood pouring from my stomach, then convulsed. It felt like I'd swallowed fire. My body was healing, but not fast enough, and there was no magic left to help it along.

My head seemed light and heavy all at once. "Caedo," I mumbled, eyes drifting shut.

A furious, bloodcurdling yell pulled them reluctantly open again. My lashes tangled, wet with tears, and my blurred vision was slow to clear. When it did, I saw Kallen fighting the last two soldiers at once, eyes blacker than night and face carved in lines of fury.

He was trying to save me, but it was too late. My dwindling life had formed a warm pool around me. I couldn't even move my lips to speak.

Kallen had lost his sword somewhere in the melee. He fought with a knife and his bare hand now, never pausing for a second even as a dagger sliced his bicep open.

Why wasn't he using magic? The thought was distant, confused. Had he lost it, too? What had happened to us?

Kallen leaned to the side, foot lashing out and slamming into a faerie's chest with shocking speed and force. The soldier stumbled backwards, reaching out to catch himself against the wall. Kallen turned into shadow for an instant, swirling around the other attacker's descending blade before reappearing in front of the one he'd kicked. He drove his dagger through the faerie's exposed armpit, teeth bared.

The soldier collapsed, blood gushing out of him and staining his white cloak.

The last faerie—the one who had hurt me—unhooked the metal

net from his belt and flung it at Kallen. It flared out, weighted at the edges. Kallen threw himself beneath it, rolling on the ground before lunging upright. The faerie dodged, but not quickly enough, and Kallen's blade opened a cut at the side of his neck. Kallen snarled, then threw his knife aside and grabbed the faerie by the throat. His fingers dug into the cut, widening it as they burrowed through skin, and then Kallen ripped the soldier's throat free in a gruesome spray of blood.

Then it was just him, standing with his chest heaving, surrounded by bodies.

I'd never seen anyone move like that. Never seen anyone *kill* like that.

My consciousness slipped, and time slipped with it. When I blinked, Kallen was kneeling beside me, pressing a hand to the wound in my stomach. "Easy," he said, voice ragged. His face was spattered with gore. "Come on, Kenna. Heal yourself."

My vision grew watery. I shook my head, then regretted it when the inside of my skull felt like I'd taken a hammer to it. "C-can't."

"You can. You *must*." He brushed the hair back from my forehead, leaving a wet streak across my skin. How much of the blood on his clothes and hands was his? Through the tear in his sleeve, I saw a cut deep enough to show muscle, though it was slowly knitting itself back together. "Breathe," he urged me. "Slowly. Calm your thoughts. Let your body do what it needs to do."

Noble Fae, I thought as I watched his injuries heal themselves. He was Noble Fae, and now I was, too. My body would heal like that—it just needed to heal itself faster than the blood could leave me.

Pain and horror were beasts that were nearly impossible to cage once they'd been released, so I focused on small things. The easing of air into my tight lungs. The feel of Kallen cradling the side of my head. The steady pressure of his other hand on my gut.

My chest had felt sickeningly empty since I'd tried to cast magic, but something unfurled around my heart at last. A hint of heat, a flicker of a magical pulse. Caedo's whisper drifted back into my mind, faint but furious. *Destroy them...*

The Blood power I'd somehow lost was still weak, but it crawled through my veins until it reached my injuries, starting with my gut before moving to my cheekbone and hand. My skin warmed as the magic added its efforts to the healing. I felt the gruesome grind of bone slotting back into place, followed by the soothing relief of something being put right.

I closed my eyes, overwhelmed and dizzy, drunk on the agony and the relief.

When I opened them again, Void faeries filled the hallway. One was bending to throw a corpse over his shoulder, and as he stood, others moved in to start cleaning up the blood.

How much time had passed? I'd only closed my eyes for a moment, but the world had shifted entirely.

Caedo was curled around my upper arm, quivering like a frightened animal. *Kill*, it said.

Relief filled me. I hadn't realized how accustomed I'd grown to the dagger's low buzz in my mind until it had been taken away. *They're already dead*, I thought back.

Too bad.

I called up a memory of the faerie's throat being ripped out, and the dagger gave a nastily satisfied hum.

I still didn't understand what had happened. One thing was clear, though: carrying Caedo had made me cocky. With a weapon like that, I'd thought all I needed to do was get close enough and victory would be mine.

Two familiar figures came running. Lara and Anya dropped to their knees on either side of me, Anya gripping my hand as Lara patted my shoulder.

"You're all right," Lara said. She was wearing a nightgown and looked like she'd just tumbled out of bed. "He said you were, but . . ." She sniffled and wiped a tear off her cheek. "I needed to see for myself."

"I—" My voice creaked. "How did you know?"

"He shouted at the door until the house got me. Kenna, what were you even *doing*?"

Anya looked down at me with wet, bloodshot eyes. She hadn't changed into nightclothes, but her tunic was rumpled like she'd slept in it. "Kenna the Fierce," she murmured.

My old nickname. We'd been Kenna the Fierce and Anya the Great and Terrible for a few imagination-filled years—children playing with sticks, dreaming up a world in which we could be heroes.

I'd been no hero today. The bodies had been carried away, but the scent of death was thick in the air. Blood and offal, the coppery tang of butchery—and none of it had been my doing.

I would have died tonight if Kallen hadn't been there to save me.

I turned my head, looking for him. He was standing in the midst of the Void faeries, head bent as he listened to something a soldier was saying. My lips shaped his name.

Kallen seemed to sense my attention, because he turned. A tremor went through me as our gazes locked. His face was still painted in blood, his posture weary, but his eyes . . .

Oh, they burned.

A moment later he was striding towards me. Faeries fell back, scrambling to get out of his way. Then he was crouching by my side, reaching out to gently touch my face. "Kenna," he said, voice rough.

"You killed them for me," I whispered.

Kallen's bloodstained fingers stroked my cheek. "I will always kill for you."

Anya looked at him askance, edging away. I felt nothing but swelling gratitude, though. My head still ached, and my well of magic felt nearly empty again after the task of healing myself, but the relief of having survived was sweet.

"Let's get you inside," Lara said. She was also eyeing Kallen warily, but it wasn't the suspicious hostility she'd exhibited even a day before. He'd come to get her, I realized. That was who had shouted at the Blood House door.

I started to sit up, but Kallen stopped me, moving his hand from my cheek to my upper chest to keep me in place. A gasp left my lips, and my heart thumped as his fingers lightly brushed my neck.

He studied his bloody hand against my skin before meeting my eyes again. "Do you trust me?"

My pulse fluttered. Did I? I didn't know if I was capable of much trust anymore. It was a precious, delicate thing, and delicate things broke in Mistei.

But he had fought for me. He'd been hurt trying to protect me, and for some reason, he was looking down at me like I was the secret to a puzzle he was desperate to solve.

"Maybe," I managed.

It was apparently good enough for him. "Let me carry you. You can ask the Shard to allow me into the house. Just for a short while."

"You're from Void," Lara said, distrust returning to her expression.

His fingers twitched. "That's not why I want to do this."

Why did he want to do it, then?

"I can carry her." Lara glanced at Anya. "We can carry her together."

The way we'd helped Anya that first night. Anya nodded, and my mouth quivered as a tender ache bloomed in my chest.

"No," Kallen said. "I need—" He made a frustrated sound. "I have to, Lara. She can disinvite me immediately after, but I need to carry her. *Please.*"

Lara looked as shocked as I felt. Had Kallen ever said *please* before?

He looked messy and tortured—not the icy, controlled spymaster anymore. Tonight had rattled him badly for some reason. A fine tremor moved through his fingers where they rested against my skin.

Lara raised her brows, asking me the question.

Invite a faerie from another house in. I'd never heard of anyone doing that before.

The Shard's voice slipped into my head. *It's been done. But you must be sure.*

A Void faerie in the heart of Blood territory when Mistei was on the precipice of war . . . it sounded like madness. But Kallen was more than Void House, the way all of us were more than who we swore allegiance to.

He waited patiently for my verdict, never looking away.

Yes, I thought to the Shard. *Let him in for a while.*

And then, out loud: "Yes."

Kallen's breath hitched. Then his hands were sliding under me, shifting me gently into the bed of his arms. I smelled death on him, but there was something beneath that, too. Something dark, complex, and compelling—like incense, wet earth, and cold winter nights.

Kallen stood, cradling me close to his chest. Then he turned and carried me into Blood House.

15

"Have you been in any of the other houses before?" I asked as Kallen carried me into the inner hall. I felt unaccountably nervous, like he might judge me for the fountain of blood.

"No." Some of the tension in his face and shoulders had relaxed after I'd allowed him to hold me. "This is the first."

"It must be a rare sort of invitation."

"More common before Osric's reign. As with all good things." He paused before the fountain and looked around. "It's laid out similarly to Void House."

"Earth, too."

This late at night, everyone else was abed—the house must have roused only Lara and Anya. They'd been following close behind, but now Lara swept in front of us. "You need a bath," she told me. "And some tea for the pain."

Anya seemed less certain. Her shoulders curved as she looked at Kallen, and she wrapped her arms around herself. It was as if, now that the immediate crisis was over, she was remembering her vulnerability. Now that we were away from the stench of death, I caught the sour echo of wine wafting off her. "I'll make tea," she said softly, then turned and nearly fled to the kitchen.

My temples throbbed, and I grimaced.

Kallen frowned. "Tell me where your chambers are."

"I can take her—" Lara started, but Kallen cut her a look, and she subsided.

Somehow I hadn't realized he planned to carry me to my room. I swallowed, looking up at him. "Back right staircase, top level."

His lashes lowered. "That's like Void House, too."

My fingers curled in the fabric of Kallen's shirt as he began climbing the steps. I felt an urge to apologize for burdening him. "I can probably walk—"

"No," he said firmly, and that was the end of that.

He carried me like it was no effort at all. The Noble Fae had greater endurance than humans, but he was stronger than most from what I'd seen. He'd killed six soldiers single-handedly tonight. He'd ripped someone's throat out.

It should have horrified me, but I found myself wishing I had managed to kill someone, too.

I directed Kallen to my room, and he shifted me in his hold until he could reach the doorknob with the hand hooked beneath my knees. Refusing to put me down even for that small motion. I wrapped my arms around his neck, fingers tangled in his blood-matted hair. He needed to bathe, too.

I envisioned him in my tub then—strong arms stretching along the rim as he watched me, steam rising around his bare torso. The imagining was so unexpected and visceral that an alarmed noise escaped my throat.

"Did I hurt you?" he asked, looking concerned as he carried me over the threshold.

I shook my head, cheeks starting to burn. My brain must be addled from nearly dying—that was the only reason to be imagining Kallen naked.

He moved through the sitting area quickly, heading for the bed. The thought of him placing me on those sheets filled me with a swift panic. "Wait," I said. "I'm covered in blood."

His steps slowed. "You need to rest."

"I need to wash first."

He put me down next to the bed, keeping one arm around me to support my weight. "Can you stand while I draw a bath?"

"Yes, but I can draw my own—" At his narrow-eyed look, I stopped arguing and nodded. "Thank you."

My body was healed, though the trauma and blood loss had left me shaky. I gripped the bedpost for support as he entered the adjoining chamber, and soon I heard the tub filling.

Why was he doing this?

I was coming to know Kallen better, but he was still an enigma. He'd played the hostage, the spy, the assassin, the traitor, and now the kingmaker, but I couldn't shake the feeling that whoever Kallen truly was didn't fit neatly into any of those categories.

The water cut off, and Kallen returned. "It's ready. Do you need me to carry you?"

Was he going to offer to strip me next? The idea was as disturbing as the vision I'd had of him in my tub, so I shook my head. "I'll be back." I slipped past him and closed the door, then removed my filthy clothes.

The hot water felt like a miracle. I lowered myself into the tub with a stifled moan, not sure how much Kallen could hear. Blood bloomed on the surface, and soon the water turned pink. I had to drain and refill the tub twice before it remained clear.

I soaped gently around Caedo, and the dagger nuzzled my fingers without nipping. Maybe Kallen could explain what had happened to us.

As I untangled my wet hair, I puzzled over the mystery of what he was doing in my chambers. He might have saved me for the sake of Hector's crown, but that didn't explain why he was fussing over me. Unless he was trying to earn my allegiance through demonstrations of kindness?

That didn't seem like something Kallen would do. That was more Drustan's method of winning allies.

Maybe he'd wanted to get a look at the interior of Blood House. But then why hadn't he found an excuse to explore? The only time I'd heard the door open was when Lara had come to check on me and drop off tea, and I didn't hear sounds that indicated the ransacking of drawers, either.

If he wasn't doing this for Hector's cause . . . he must be doing it for me.

I rinsed a final time, then grabbed a towel. As I looked down at the stained garments heaped on the floor, I realized I'd made a terrible miscalculation. Cursing myself, I wrapped the towel around my body and padded to the door. I opened it a crack. "Kallen?"

"Yes?" His voice came from closer than I was expecting.

My face was hot from more than the steam. "I don't have a dress."

There was a long pause. "Oh."

"Can you—"

"Yes." I heard him moving away, then the wardrobe opening. A moment later he was back.

I opened the door wider to grab the burgundy dress he held out, embarrassed that he was seeing me in nothing but a towel. "Thank you," I squeaked.

I shut the door, then tied my wet hair up messily before putting on the gown. It was soft and unstructured, without any laces or hidden fastenings to worry about, and I wondered if Kallen or the wardrobe was responsible for selecting the most comfortable item.

Kallen must feel disgusting with all that blood on him. I considered offering him the tub, but that disturbing vision nagged at my mind again, so I wetted a hand towel and left the bathroom to bring it to him. "Here."

He seemed surprised by the offer. "Thank you." He rubbed the towel over his face, hands, and hair, wiping away the dried gore.

I tossed the towel into the bathroom before returning. "Do you need anything?" I asked, twisting my fingers in my skirts. "Food, a drink?"

He shook his head. "Let's sit for a while."

I preceded him into the main room and sat on the velvet-upholstered settee. There was a steaming mug of tea waiting, and I recognized the scent of medicinal herbs wafting from it. I took a sip to cover my nervousness.

Kallen unbuckled his sword belt and set it on a nearby table. I'd rarely seen him without his sword, and the movement struck me as oddly intimate.

This was a huge amount of trust he was offering, I realized suddenly. To enter another house's territory alone, where he could be captured or killed, and then disarm in front of me. I'd been thinking of the risk in letting an outsider into the house, but the risk to him was substantial, too.

The cushion dipped as Kallen sat on the opposite end of the settee. He stretched his arm along the back. "Let's talk about what happened."

I grimaced. "I was useless tonight."

"Not useless." His fingers tapped a few inches away from my shoulder. There was still a restless edge to him, an unsettling intensity to the way he was watching me. "Let me teach you how to fight."

"What?"

"You need training."

He wasn't wrong. "I would have done better," I said, trying to preserve what was left of my pride, "but my magic stopped working."

Kallen's lips parted. "You tried to use magic?"

I nodded, wondering why he looked so alarmed.

"Fuck," he said softly. He withdrew his arm from the back of the couch and leaned forward, bracing his elbows on his knees. "I hadn't even thought . . . You don't know about Sun Soldiers? Or cold iron?"

"I . . . no?"

"Cold-forged iron is anathema to faerie magic. It drains us of our power if we touch it or try to cast against it. Those were Sun Soldiers, Light House's most elite fighters—and the inner layer of their armor is iron."

That must be why he hadn't used his Void powers to tear them apart. "I had no idea."

Some of the true believers in Tumbledown had hung horseshoes in their barns to prevent mischievous faeries from stealing livestock, but I'd never given the practice much thought. It had seemed like a silly superstition, but apparently it had been rooted in truth.

"Iron is also used to shackle prisoners," Kallen said. "To bind their magic and worsen their suffering. It blisters the skin, so the Sun Soldiers plate the armor with gold to diminish the effect. They can't cast light while wearing it, but it's an advantage for strong fighters because it forces combat to stay on the physical level. The net he threw at me was iron, too—they use it when they anticipate a Void faerie turning into shadow."

Now I understood why the soldier performing magic tonight had been wearing leather—and why prisoners' wrists always looked raw beneath their manacles. "I should have realized," I said, angry with myself at the oversight. I'd never questioned how Fae prisoners were kept under control when they had such terrifying powers.

"No, I should have told you." Kallen's tone was harsh with self-judgment. "I didn't even think about it, and you were hurt."

"You didn't know."

"But now I do." He gave me another frank look. "Let me train you, Kenna. Let me teach you how to survive down here."

Lessons in warfare from the former King's Vengeance. The thought was intimidating, and my pride stung, imagining all the ways he would find my skills lacking. But if anyone could teach me survival, it was Kallen, who had navigated centuries at Osric's side while plotting against him.

I nodded.

Kallen's expressions were usually subtle, but something had changed between us in the last few days—either I was reading him much better, or he wasn't bothering to guard his emotions as much around me. The relief that passed over his face was obvious. "Good. I want to meet you for nightly sparring sessions."

"Nightly?" My eyebrows shot up. "Don't you have better things to do with your time?"

"No."

I supposed preserving my life so I could choose Hector would be near the top of his priority list. I sighed, rubbing my forehead. The headache had diminished thanks to the bath and the tea, but I wasn't eager to get knocked down again. "Fine. Where?"

"There's a training room between our houses that will work. I'll come get you tomorrow night."

"You're not going to start swinging a sword at me tonight?"

He shook his head. "You need rest. But I am going to teach you more about iron—and find out what else you need to learn about being Fae."

He told me the dampening effect of iron required a direct touch of skin or magic, so anyone wearing it—either shackles or armor that surrounded that well of inner power—would be impacted no matter what. In terms of casting against someone wearing iron, as I'd attempted tonight, the effectiveness varied. If that Sun Soldier hadn't been wearing a helmet and I'd tried to liquefy his brain without touching him, my powers likely wouldn't have been lost. That was how Osric had been able to torture prisoners with hallucinations—Illusion magic impacted the mind, so it didn't spill over into the rest of the body to encounter the manacles.

In terms of the other executions I'd witnessed, Roland's ability to focus light so precisely had preserved his power, and when Oriana had torn a prisoner apart with vines, she'd kept the plants away from the iron at his wrists. Drustan and Hector, though, would have both briefly lost their magic the night of the first state dinner. Fire was nearly impossible to keep precisely contained, and Drustan had chosen the fastest death for the asrai he'd been tasked with executing—a mercy I now realized had come at his own expense. Likewise, when Hector had ripped a faerie apart with the dark holes he'd carved in the air, his power would have contacted iron when the victim was sucked inside.

"Blood and Illusion faeries seem like they have an advantage, so long as no one's wearing a helmet," I pointed out. "Since they can target the brain."

"They do, but only if the attacking faerie is well trained. Magic has a tendency to spill out and get messy during times of stress."

"Why would two houses have an advantage like that?"

"Why do Void faeries feel least powerful at midday and Light faeries feel least powerful at midnight?" He raised his hand, teetering it back and forth. "Everything in Mistei is a balance."

"Like how I can't sense your heartbeat when you're in shadow form."

"Can you not?" When I made a face, he smirked. "You should be cautious about revealing weaknesses like that."

"Except when it comes to you, I'm sure."

There was a wicked glint in his eye. "I strive to be the exception to everything."

The talk of battle led to an assessment of my own arsenal, and I had to admit I had no idea how to wield any of the weapons on the walls downstairs. I explained more about my bond with Caedo, and Kallen told me there were rumored to be other artifacts like that. When the Shards had exploded magic over the world, some of it got tangled in the trees and rocks rather than finding a home within Fae bodies, and over time those deposits gained form and sentience.

I wondered if the dagger's consciousness had grown in a vein of ore. Caedo didn't answer when I asked. I couldn't tell if it even remembered where it had come from.

At least now I had an answer to the mystery of why Caedo had gone silent and still when I cast against iron. It *was* magic. Pure magic, fallen from the stars. The dagger was part of me now, and the iron had stolen that power away like it had the rest.

Kallen seemed to enjoy playing the tutor. He was patient, approaching each topic in detail. "Magic isn't infinite," he told me, hands moving gracefully as he painted a picture in the air. "It can be depleted by overuse, though it always replenishes itself."

"I did know that one," I told him, tucking a lock of wet hair behind my ear self-consciously. As always with my hair, it didn't want to stay constrained, and tendrils were slipping loose. "I started to get dizzy in the throne room."

Kallen's gaze followed the movement of my hand. "That will get better with time. But it will always be more draining to kill with magic than to do anything else with it."

"Why?"

"If it wasn't difficult, what's to stop someone like Drustan from torching an entire battlefield? The magic keeps itself in check in ways we don't entirely understand." His gaze grew shadowed. "Some faeries have greater endurance when it comes to killing. Roland was notorious for his ability to execute prisoners without needing to rest. And Osric..."

I'd seen what Osric was capable of. That was what happened when limitless cruelty met raw power.

Kallen's eyes were distant, like he was looking at something beyond the room. "Osric cast more illusions during the first civil war than anyone realized was possible. He forced his enemies to run into swords or maddened them until they killed themselves. And he did it again and again in the years after. Centuries of executions, wherever and whenever he wanted to."

"His power was never depleted?"

"I'm sure it was, but no one would have been able to tell when, because he liked to force others to kill for him, too. It never ended."

Kallen's face had become blank. It was like watching a lake ice over, like watching something rare die.

I only knew the smallest portion of what he'd experienced, yet I couldn't imagine surviving centuries with Osric. "Kallen," I whispered, brushing my fingers over his hand.

He blinked slowly, dark lashes veiling exhaustion-shadowed eyes. I wondered when he'd last felt content or well rested.

Never, maybe.

"I would kill Osric again if I could," I said. "I'd kill him worse."

The words seemed to shake Kallen out of the trance he'd fallen into. He looked sideways at me, lips quirking the slightest amount. "You did plenty. It was a good death."

Was it? I thought of Osric's throat splitting under my dagger. His ragged screams, the lake of blood spreading beneath him, the fear in those purple eyes as I'd listed who I was taking vengeance for: Anya, Mistei... and me. "I don't know. It could have been more painful."

Kallen let out a soft sound, half laugh and half sigh. "I don't think anything would have been painful enough."

A lock of dark hair clung to his neck, still damp from the wet towel. He wore his hair shorter than many of the Fae, the ends brushing his collarbones. I wondered how often he'd had to wash blood out of the strands.

Maybe that was why he wore it short.

Silence lingered between us. It felt sad but not uncomfortable. The ghost of the past was in the room with us, and we were listening to its whispers.

"Will Light House know it was us today?" I asked quietly. "Will they seek vengeance?"

"My soldiers searched the area. No one was nearby, and the bodies are being disposed of, but depending on who else knew the soldiers' route, it may become obvious where they went missing."

I shivered. "The one who stabbed me . . . He said they would want me to suffer. He didn't say who *they* were, but it had to be Torin and Rowena, right?"

A muscle in Kallen's jaw flexed. "Yes. The bonebreaker salamander would have needed to be imported from Lindwic, and I'm sure it was expensive. But Rowena is a poison collector, and she can afford it."

Strange things can happen in the dark. "I suppose they'll keep trying to kill me."

"I'll kill them first," Kallen said darkly. He turned his hand over, lacing his fingers through mine.

I looked down at where we touched, my breath coming faster. It was an odd moment of intimacy, framed in the threat of violence. There were calluses on his palm and fingers that could only be explained by a lifetime of warfare.

He'd ripped out someone's throat with that hand.

My pulse was tapping too quickly. I felt the urge to squirm on the seat—away from him, towards him, some combination of the two. Gentle touches weren't something I was particularly used to. And gentle touches from him . . . I didn't know what to think of them.

"Do you think the council will be angry?" I asked, trying to act as if holding hands was a perfectly ordinary thing for us to do. "Drustan will probably say it was reckless to murder Light faeries in the public hallways. Bad politics."

Kallen's fingers tightened on mine. "Fuck Drustan," he said with sudden vehemence, eyes flooding black with Void power. The air chilled, and goose bumps rose on my skin. "They deserved worse than they got."

I felt a flush of heat despite the cold emanating from him. Part embarrassment, but also part . . . something else. Something strange and violent and complicated. "I'm sorry you had to do that for me."

"I'm not."

"Don't those deaths weigh on you?"

"Do they weigh on you?"

I hesitated, then gave him the truth. "I wish I felt worse about them."

The black leached from his eyes, leaving only midnight blue. "Would you take them back if you could?"

I shook my head.

"Even if killing the Sun Soldiers was bad politics?" he pressed. "Even if Torin and Rowena find out what happened tonight? You could tell them it was entirely my doing, try to preserve an advantage for later—"

"No." That much I knew. "You were trying to save me. You were in danger—"

"I wasn't really—"

"You were," I argued. "You were bleeding, Kallen. And the reason I nearly got myself killed is because I wasn't going to let you fight alone." I was squeezing his fingers too hard, but I couldn't seem to let go. "I'm not willing to watch someone who tried to help me get hurt. Even if it gives me an advantage later. Even if it's the right thing to do for Blood House, it's not *my* right thing to do."

And that might be my weakness. A wise ruler made sacrifices for the greater good; when the fate of thousands rested on one side of the scales, a true queen wouldn't weigh a single life against it.

But I wasn't a queen. Wasn't even a proper princess, really. I was a stubborn peasant girl who had inexplicably been given power, and my loyalty was fierce but finite. Kallen had earned it today.

I wondered if he was also thinking what a flawed leader this made me. But all he did was look at me with that unwavering focus. "Then the only thing that matters is what you can live with," he said. "And what you can't."

I wondered how many sacrifices he'd had to weigh over the years, how many times he'd selected the lesser of two evils—or if he'd ever selected the greater one. "What have you been unable to live with?"

He seemed surprised that I'd asked, but he always seemed surprised when my curiosity was directed at him. Everyone else in Mistei probably assumed they knew his answers already. "A few things. Not enough, probably."

"Will you tell me about them?"

He looked down at our connected hands. "Someday."

Disappointment settled on my shoulders, but at least it wasn't an outright refusal. He'd spent three long centuries making sure no one had any idea what he held sacred. That would be a hard habit to break.

"Someday," I said softly.

Kallen squeezed my fingers, then released my hand. I tried not to feel disappointed as he stood. "I need to get back to Void House to discuss this with Hector."

"Will he think it was a bad choice?" I asked, standing as well. I suspected Drustan would be disappointed we were risking public battles during a peace period when we were supposed to look like the reasonable ones, but I didn't know enough about Hector to understand what his moral code had room for and what it didn't.

"Hector doesn't waste time on questions like that," Kallen replied. "He'll say the soldiers opened themselves to retribution the moment they tried to plant that salamander. He cares less about what led to a particular outcome than what happens after—for him, once something is done, it's done, and there's no point wasting time wishing it was different."

That was an enviable way to live. An efficient way, too. It was probably how a king needed to think.

His first policy letter had been similarly blunt. He'd informed me that his first action as king would be to eliminate the changeling practice. *We can't bring back the children who died*, he'd written, *but we can make sure no more are lost because of narrow-minded bastards.* A similar sentiment to what Drustan had sent, but a very different tone.

I still had one major doubt about Hector, though. I steeled myself, knowing this would be uncomfortable. "You care about Hector."

He hesitated, then finally nodded, as if expressing affection for a family member was dangerous. It probably had been.

"I'm going to ask you something, and I need you to swear not to lie to me."

"I'm not going to lie to you." He sounded offended at the idea.

Promises were meaningless in Mistei, but Kallen had risked his life to save me, and he was currently standing weaponless in the heart of my territory. Trust had to start somewhere.

"Drustan said something once," I began haltingly. "About the ladies Hector preferred. I don't know if you remember me mentioning it . . ."

I saw the moment he realized what I was talking about. His eyes widened. "Shards," he said softly. "I'd forgotten he said that to you."

Back when I'd been Kallen's spy, he'd ordered me to find out what Drustan knew about Hector. In retrospect, he'd obviously been trying to figure out how much Drustan knew about Void's plans for an uprising. He'd likely been anticipating this thorny succession question of what would happen if Drustan were to strike Osric before Hector could. I'd come up with the flimsiest of excuses to speak with Drustan, claiming I was worried about Hector watching Lara, and Drustan had said something chilling in response.

He normally likes them a little less noble. A little more defenseless.

"Is it true?" I asked, pulse racing and stomach beginning to feel queasy. "Is he a rapist?"

"No," Kallen said vehemently. "Never." He gripped my arms and looked me in the eye. "Hector has done terrible things over the years, the way we all have, but that is something he would never, ever do. Please believe me."

Relief fluttered in my chest, though a paranoid voice in my head told me people could be blinded by family loyalty. "Then why did Drustan say that? Did he make it up?"

Sadness ghosted over his face. "Drustan wasn't making it up, though I have no idea if he actually believes it. There was a rumor that went around after . . . something happened. Something awful." I opened my mouth to ask for details, but he shook his head. "It's not my secret to share. I'll ask Hector if he'll allow it, but . . . this is a deep wound, Kenna."

It was hard to imagine anything wounding the snarling Void prince. "Why didn't Hector try to clear his name, then? Why let everyone think he's a monster?"

Kallen's mouth tightened, and he let go of me and stepped back.

"It's better for our enemies to believe us monsters than to know what we truly care for."

A chill raced down my spine. What an awful thing to believe—and how horrible that after only six months in Mistei, I understood why he believed it. "But to that extent? He needs to address that rumor if he wants to become king; otherwise, how can anyone support him?"

Kallen made a frustrated sound. "You are vastly overestimating how much the Fae care if their rulers are monstrous. Osric's level of evil was unprecedented, but our history is full of tyrants." Before I could argue that was no reason to continue the tradition, he kept speaking. "It's not a well-known rumor, at any rate. And there was more in play at the time than just Hector's reputation. If Osric had discovered what truly happened, he would have started asking questions, and that would have led to consequences."

This lack of clarity was maddening. "What sort of consequences?"

Complicated emotions shifted across Kallen's face. "You asked me what I couldn't live with. I do have my limits, and I made a choice many years ago for the sake of what I thought was right." He shook his head. "At first Hector told me it was a foolish, dangerous idea. That I was placing the entirety of Void House at risk. But I did it anyway."

Did what? I wanted to demand, but at least he was telling me something.

"When Hector realized I wasn't going to stop," Kallen continued, "he accepted it. What was done was done, and there was no point wishing it were otherwise. Since then, he's helped me protect this secret. That's part of why he didn't deny the rumor—because revealing the truth would have risked many lives."

The urge to know the secret was killing me. I bit the inside of my cheek, looking at him pleadingly.

Kallen sighed and rubbed a hand over his face. "You are incredibly hard to say no to."

"Then don't say no."

He let out a weary chuckle. "You'll get it out of me, don't worry. Not tonight, though. Tonight you need to rest—and because this secret isn't just mine, I need to speak with Hector and Una first."

Frustration warred with intense curiosity, but I nodded.

"Now go to bed, Kenna. Tomorrow's scheming will arrive sooner than you think."

He left after that. I sat on the settee, staring at the wall and focusing on the ripples in the house's magic as it marked his passing. He'd refused to let me walk him out, telling me it would negate the entire point of him carrying me upstairs.

The entrance door closed far below, and then he was gone, off to the next step of his tireless quest to shape Mistei's future. I modified the house's guest list, denying him access once more.

My room felt strangely empty without him.

16

W<small>E HELD AN EMERGENCY COUNCIL MEETING TO DISCUSS</small> the conflict with the Sun Soldiers. I wasn't eager for a repeat of the first time, when I'd felt like the odd one out in a room bitterly divided. Why should Hector and Drustan each get an extra guest while I had no one? So I invited Lara to come as my advisor, and though she was nervous, she agreed.

Hector had proposed a new location: a chamber one level above the human quarters, where Noble Fae were unlikely to congregate. I kept my magical senses open along the way, searching for the bodies of invisible eavesdroppers. I didn't find any, but the effort left me fatigued. This wasn't a skill I could use constantly. Part of the balance, I supposed, since it offered a major advantage against Illusion House.

The others had already arrived and were in discussion around a six-sided table when we entered the room. Hector was seated next to Kallen and Drustan beside Gweneira, with empty chairs separating the two factions. Each had a piece of paper and a quill and inkpot. Silence fell as the four faeries stared at us. Even Kallen, who seemed to know everything at all times, looked taken aback.

Drustan looked Lara up and down, and a scowl crossed his face. "No."

I'd expected some disapproval at my decision to invite an extra person, but the bluntness of the refusal was startling. He hadn't asked a single question or consulted the others before issuing it, as if his were the only voice that mattered.

Perhaps it wasn't that startling, after all.

"Please clarify what you mean by 'no,'" I said.

"I don't need to clarify." He turned that glare on me. "Send her away."

Lara had been expecting this, since magicless faeries were never given positions of power. She looked at Drustan with withering condescension, then turned her attention to me. "I thought you said this was a council of equals. Perhaps you meant a council of one?"

Hector's inhale was audible, and Drustan's hand formed a fist on the table.

Gweneira was looking at Lara with intense interest. She wore a white tunic embroidered in gold over matching trousers, with the same sparrow belt. "I believe what Prince Drustan means," she said, "is that however pleasant it is to see Lady Lara again, she was not invited to these council meetings."

"And you were?" Hector pushed back his chair and stood, bowing to me and Lara in succession. "Princess Kenna, Lady Lara, welcome. I will admit to some hesitation myself, but I invite you to explain."

A tendril of smoke rose from Drustan's clenched fist.

I resisted the urge to grin. Lara might have no political experience, but she was used to the slippery insults of the Fae court. With only a few words, she'd wounded Hector's pride and challenged Drustan's proclaimed intentions.

"Thank you, Prince Hector," Lara said, curtsying. "I appreciate your reasoned approach."

Drustan stood, smoothing his orange-and-red brocade tunic. "Lady Lara," he said, bowing stiffly, "I apologize for my abrupt manner, which stems from a deep love for this realm and concern for its future."

Hector snorted.

"I respect you both too much to lie," Drustan continued, ignoring Hector, "so I will tell you plainly that I question Princess Kenna's decision to invite a young, politically inexperienced outsider to this confidential meeting, especially without consulting the rest of the group."

"Both you and Hector invited a second person without consulting the rest of us," I said. "And I'm also young and politically inexperienced. Do I not belong here?" Truthfully, I doubted I did, but the Fae believed in the privileges of inherited power, and I would never refuse a weapon offered to me.

Drustan looked like he was grinding his teeth. "The Shards elevated you. You have a place here because they ordained it so."

"You acknowledge that the Shards trusted me with this authority."

Drustan eyed me like he suspected a trick in my words. "Yes."

"That means they trusted my character and judgment. My judgment says Lara will provide a valuable voice on this council as a formerly high-ranking member of Earth House. If Gweneira offers a unique perspective, so does she."

Though Drustan clearly didn't like that answer, Gweneira looked even more intrigued. She stroked the metal bird at her belt as she studied Lara.

Kallen was harder to read, but I was getting better at decoding his shifts in expression. There was a slight lift at one corner of his mouth—amusement. He studied the others, assessing the responses to my proclamation.

Kallen seemed to enjoy the unexpected. A faerie fascinated by the inner workings of things, like a clockmaker who found more beauty in the maneuvering of hidden gears than in the steady sweep of hands across the clock's face.

That dark blue gaze landed on me and lingered. "A new perspective could be valuable."

Hector swept out an arm. "Please, have a seat, Lady Lara."

"I have not agreed," Drustan said sharply.

"It's merely a conversation," Hector replied. "Unless there is no room for dissent in your proposed rule of Mistei? Osric wasn't fond of discussion, either."

The atmosphere in the room was already tense, but at those words, it became nearly unbearable.

"Very well," Drustan said, tone clipped. "I welcome your perspective, Lady Lara."

Lara moved towards the chair between Gweneira and Hector, which left me seated between Kallen and Drustan. Kallen bent his head towards me. "How are you feeling?" he asked softly.

I nodded at him. "Fully recovered, thank you."

Drustan was looking at Kallen with narrowed eyes. "Let's talk about Light House," he said. "Walk us through what happened last night."

I launched into the story I'd practiced. "Kallen and I decided to do a late-night survey to get a sense of any preparations Light House was making." I omitted *how* Kallen and I had been conducting that survey. "We followed six Sun Soldiers and saw them placing crystals in various places throughout Mistei."

"Did you know about this?" Hector asked Gweneira.

She shook her head. "Torin oversees the Sun Soldiers. They're supposed to serve the house impartially, but many of them are loyal to him first and foremost." She looked at Kallen. "Can you draw a map of where you saw them? I know of a few spots where ambushes can be laid, but Torin may have additional ones."

Kallen nodded and grabbed his piece of paper, then started scribbling.

"And why were you doing this survey with Kallen?" Drustan asked me, running a thumb over his golden ring.

I looked at him coolly. "Because I wanted to."

His jaw clenched. He didn't like that answer.

"When the soldiers got to Blood House," I continued, "they released a bonebreaker salamander. Kallen killed it, which led to a fight. Kallen obviously won."

Drustan eyed Kallen with obvious distaste. "Witnesses?"

"None," Kallen replied.

"And the bodies?"

"Gone," Hector interjected, planting his elbows on the table and leaning in. "We stripped that cursed armor off and sent what was left of them into the void."

"Good," Drustan said. "Then there's nothing to officially tie us to this—though I'm sure Torin and Rowena are aware Blood House was involved."

Was that a hint of judgment in his voice? "You think it was reckless," I said.

He shrugged. "They broke the peace first, and you retaliated. As much as I want to avoid public conflict this month, some things are unavoidable. Our hands just need to look clean."

They notably didn't need to *stay* clean.

"Torin and Rowena won't acknowledge it," Gweneira said. "That would invite questions about why Sun Soldiers were near Blood House to begin with." She traced her finger over the tabletop, a furrow between her brows. "Bestial magic is rare. I didn't realize we had anyone within Light House capable of it."

"Bestial magic?" I asked.

"The ability to influence living creatures like that salamander," she explained. "It's not an elemental power, but something that was rumored to originate with the Nasties, like shape-changing magic. It surfaces occasionally among the Noble Fae."

I made a face. "Wouldn't that require interbreeding with the Nasties?"

"There has been some of that. They are not all entirely monstrous—some can be quite beautiful, depending on what form they choose to wear."

"And some faeries prefer the monstrous," Hector said.

I thought of Queen Dallaida—woman on top, spider on bottom, with bloodred eyes and a taste for murder—and shivered. Was she from a line of faeries who had always looked like that, or was she the result of interbreeding? Her face had been as beautiful as a Noble Fae's, but I couldn't imagine whatever unholy union would have resulted in that combination of features.

The Nasties didn't belong to any of the houses, so I'd never really considered what magic they might have. I'd seen one of them shape-shift, though, hadn't I? One of the winged fiends who had pursued me had transformed into a hawk.

"Speaking of the Nasties," Drustan said, "I plan to meet with Dallaida soon."

I stiffened. "Why?"

"Because she's our ally, and she will be essential when it comes time for war. She may also be able to send her people to spy on Illusion and Light House."

"She tried to kill me once," I pointed out. "Won't that be an issue?" It certainly was for me.

"Really?" Gweneira asked, looking interested. "How did you even meet her?"

"I was . . ." I gave Lara a guilty glance. We'd already been outed as cheaters in the trials, but that didn't make this comfortable. "I was looking for information about something. She tried to take my dagger by force, and I ended up running for my life."

"And you killed some of her people," Drustan said.

I bristled. "In self-defense, yes."

"Dallaida is protective of her borders. It's as unacceptable for someone to visit the Nasties uninvited as it would be for them to come to the upper levels without permission. The one time I showed up without sending Dallaida a letter in advance, her creatures attacked me, too." He shook his head. "It wasn't personal. You violated a taboo, so she did what she felt she had to. I'll smooth it over."

My face was beginning to feel hot. "I didn't know there was a taboo." Another area of ignorance revealed.

Hector spoke up. "When no one teaches us, we learn by attempting."

It was strange to be offered comfort by the Void prince—if that matter-of-fact statement even counted as comfort. It made me think of what Kallen had said about him: that once something was done, it was done, and Hector saw no point in dwelling on what else could have happened.

"I do question whether Dallaida is trustworthy," Hector continued, switching his attention to Drustan.

"Why?" Drustan asked, crossing his arms. "Because she's my ally and not yours?"

Hector's smile was thin. "Because she's notoriously violent and unpredictable and has taken to calling herself a queen. The Nasties have been stewing in resentment for centuries. Don't you think they might enjoy a taste of fresh air again? Perhaps the taste of vengeance?"

I realized I had no idea why Dallaida had been helping Drustan, other than her hatred for Osric. "Did you promise Dallaida something in exchange for the use of her soldiers?" I asked.

Every eye in the room fixed on Drustan.

He sighed. "As you have intuited, she craves more freedom for her people. The opportunity to begin reintegrating into Fae society in some limited way, as well as access to the world above."

"Nasties roaming the corridors?" Lara sounded appalled.

The prospect was disturbing, but they had fought beside us in the throne room. I thought about the golden snake who had protected me and the uncovered corpses of the Nasties who had been killed trying to overthrow Osric. None of us were defined by the leaders we served, and their leader hadn't even led them in the battle she'd sent them to die in. "They deserve something," I said. "I just don't trust Dallaida."

"We can decide where and when they're allowed freedom." Drustan looked at me with a serious expression. "You should know she originally asked for ownership of Blood House. I obviously refused."

The revelation knocked the breath from me. "She wants my house? How would that even be possible?"

"If no magic-wielding Noble Fae are left in a house, the ruler of Mistei may petition the Shards to gift that house to another. It's an archaic law, one which has never been invoked. The one time it was applicable, Osric chose annihilation instead."

A chill raced over me. "She wants you to kill me, then give her the house." And they'd have to kill more than just me. Lara didn't have magic, but the five Earth House deserters did.

"I refused even before you became princess. The last thing we need is for the Nasties to gain a stronghold on our levels or access to whatever weapons or gold Blood House kept locked away." Drustan's gaze was unflinching, like he was willing me to see the truth in his eyes. "Blood House is not on the table, Kenna. I promise you that. At this point, we're negotiating for shared events, some free passage through Mistei on certain days, and possibly ownership of territory aboveground. Nothing more."

Drustan had lost my trust when he turned on Selwyn, but I actually believed him. Not just because he looked and sounded adamant, but because he'd brought the issue up to begin with. There was no strategic reason to do that if he meant to offer Blood House to Dallaida.

I pressed a hand over my fast-beating heart, then nodded. "All right."

Drustan returned my nod. "All right," he echoed quietly.

"That is a dangerous door to open, no matter what," Hector said.

"Yes," Drustan agreed. "But before Kenna gained her powers, I believed the Nasties were the only ones who could slay Osric." His gaze swept around the table. "If Dallaida refuses to accept any constraints on her power or movements once the war is done, I will take care of it. This may only be an alliance for a season."

He would use the Queen of the Nasties for her soldiers, then turn on her if she wanted more than he was willing to offer. It would be yet another betrayal to add to Drustan's list, but I couldn't fault him for this one—so long as he didn't treat all her people the same. "If you're thinking about her that way," I said, "she's probably thinking about you that way as well."

Kallen slid me an approving look. Perhaps I was getting better at politics.

Drustan chuckled. "Oh, she certainly is. Dallaida's appetite is endless. But I'm her best chance at breaking her creatures free, so she will entertain me for a while. Then it will be a matter of who is cleverest at forcing the outcome they want, and if that falls apart, it will come down to who is fastest and most determined to win." He met my eyes again. "Which will always be me."

"We needn't rely solely on her," Hector said. "Queen Briar is sending shipments of liquid fire, and she can likely be persuaded to send troops in exchange for more favorable tariffs and a mutual defense promise."

Drustan's fists clenched on the table. "You're negotiating with a foreign power without consulting us?" His voice lashed like a whip.

Hector leaned back in his chair, spreading his arms. "I'm consulting you now, aren't I? I brought Briar's latest terms for us to discuss." He reached into his black tunic, then pulled out a scroll and slapped it on the table.

"Who is Queen Briar?" I asked. Lara looked as lost as I was.

Kallen explained. "Elsmere's new monarch as of a month ago. Her father, King Godwin, grew tired of ruling and selected her over her older siblings. She's a controversial choice because of her age, but she's popular among the lesser nobles in particular, and she doesn't lack ambition. We were in negotiations with her father for years, but she has a much better appreciation of the urgency of our cause."

Elsmere was a faerie kingdom located in the country of Lindwic, to the west and south of Enterra—and Kallen had learned they were seeking new leadership from me after I'd eavesdropped on Drustan and Gweneira.

"Yes, you were whispering in Briar's ear at Beltane, weren't you?" Drustan asked, still looking irritated. "How did you learn of that power change before it happened?"

"One of my spies," Kallen said, not so much as glancing at me.

Gweneira cocked her head like an inquisitive bird. "I thought I was the only one who knew about it. The information didn't leave Godwin's inner circle until after Beltane."

"Then how did you learn it?" Kallen asked.

Her smile was small and secretive. "I have my sources, same as you have yours."

The meeting quickly veered into territory I couldn't understand. Tariffs, trade routes, agreements of mutual defense against places I'd never heard of. The only taxes I knew much about were the ones my mother and I had been forced to pay for the upkeep of Tumbledown's temple. I didn't know how countries traded with one another or arranged for military defense or . . . any of it.

Useless, I thought, hating myself for it. But Lara looked equally overwhelmed as she scribbled notes, and I would never call her useless, so I tried to reframe my thinking. Politics, warfare, and economics could be learned, like anything else.

Assuming I had time to learn. Our enemies were clearly targeting the weakest link in this alliance, and I didn't know when they might try to kill me again.

17

LATE THAT NIGHT, I FOLLOWED THE SHIVERS IN THE HOUSE'S magic to find Kallen standing beneath the Blood Tree. He was unarmed and dressed simply in a long-sleeved black shirt and matching trousers. "Ready to train?" he asked.

I looked over my shoulder, thinking longingly about my bed. We'd had our first house meal in a dining hall near the kitchen—an awkward affair, considering how many people from different backgrounds were in attendance—and I was emotionally wrung out from faking confidence. Worried, too, because Anya had refused to join and then refused to talk to me about it, instead sequestering herself in her room with a bottle of wine. All I wanted was to hide under the covers and pretend none of this was happening.

I had agreed to being trained, though, and over a hundred people were now depending on me to be strong. "Yes," I said, facing him again. "Let's do it."

His gaze traced over me as if assessing me for battle preparedness. Caedo was shaped like a necklace, and I was still wearing my dinner attire—a red dress secured by a black sash. "Should I dress more like you?" I asked.

"No, this is good. You should learn to fight in what you'll most often be wearing."

I fell into step beside Kallen. We turned right down the slope, heading in the direction of Void House. It was located the farthest underground, and I'd never been near it before. "What's the trap outside Void House?" I asked.

"Thinking about breaking in?"

"Trying to avoid dying if I come to see you."

He slid me a glance, as if surprised I would want to visit. "There's a pitch-black chamber before the door. In the middle of it is an abyss you have to walk across. If you belong to the house or are an invited guest, pavers will appear beneath your feet, creating the path. If not..."

The intruder would fall. A shiver skittered down my spine. "So stop outside the room is what you're saying."

"Stop within the first ten feet, at least."

We reached an intersection, and he pressed his hand to my lower back and guided me to the left. His hand lifted from my back as quickly as it had settled, but it returned again when the path split a second time.

I still wasn't used to these casual touches from him. Truthfully, he didn't seem used to them, either. There was a slight hesitation before each one, like he was weighing the risks. What those risks might be, I had no idea.

Each passage was narrower than the last, until we were moving single file through a damp hallway coated in moss. It was a mazelike warren of tunnels, and the slick moss and narrow passages made me think of...

I frowned. What did they make me think of? Somewhere I'd been with Lara once. Some dark, twisting place full of danger. It must have been during one of the trials, but I couldn't remember what the place had been or why we had been there.

Again I felt disoriented and disturbed. So far, I could remember most of the time leading up to each trial, as well as the immediate aftermath. Bits and pieces from the trials themselves, too, like camping in the woods or killing Garrick or holding Lara's hand in the dark, but nothing that revealed what trait had been tested or how it had been tested. My memory had been modified by a magic even older and more powerful than the Noble Fae, and I didn't like it one bit.

Kallen stopped at a plain wooden door and held it open. The chamber within had an unusual padded floor. Mirrors lined the walls to the right and left, and racks of weapons were bolted to the stone in front and back. The air was cool with a slight breeze, and I noticed a narrow ventilation shaft near the ceiling, no wider than the width of my palm. In one corner, a stuffed burlap sack dangled from chains. Intrigued, I pushed it with my hand, feeling the heavy resistance. "What is this for?"

"Practicing punching," Kallen replied, closing the door behind him. Shadows coiled at his feet, seeping out through the crack beneath the door to stand watch, and then he waved a hand and a ward descended over the entrance like a translucent black curtain.

"Can you teach me how to do that?" I asked.

Kallen nodded, then reversed the motion, making the magic vanish. "You can set this one."

I moved into position next to him and held my hand up, palm facing the door.

"Close your eyes," he said.

I hesitated, then obeyed. The air shifted as he moved behind me, and then his hand was curving around mine, positioning it more to his liking. He tilted my hand back on my wrist, curling my fingers like I was preparing to catch a ball.

"This is a piece of basic magic common to all the houses," he said. "It's not elemental in nature or overly complex, so most of the Noble Fae should be able to cast a ward with enough training—though the effectiveness varies."

"So it might make sound quieter, rather than blocking it entirely?"

"Exactly. But wards aren't just designed to block sound, though that's the most common kind. A minor one, like the shadows I cast here or at the entrance to Blood House back when we were . . ." He trailed off, and I wondered how he planned to finish that sentence. Back when we were in an uncomfortable blackmail arrangement? "Some function more like alarms," he said, apparently deciding not to open the door to a discussion of what we had been doing only a few days ago. "They let us know when a person crosses a threshold they aren't supposed to. And more powerful wards can delay someone from entering a room or stop them entirely. Those are rare, though—it's unusual for someone to be able to cast with that level of intensity, and especially on a large scale. Which is why no one before Osric was capable of turning Mistei into a prison. That level of power was unthinkable."

I shivered, thinking about the wards that had once bounded Mistei. Those hadn't just stopped faeries from leaving; they had killed anyone who tried. "The spell protecting him against the other houses—he called that a ward, too."

The spring equinox ritual had been the first time I'd realized how devastating Osric's grip on Mistei was. Before then, I'd imagined it would be possible for someone to chop his head off if they got close enough.

"It was a variant on this magic, yes," Kallen said. "A ward is a prohibition at its core, and though it's usually cast on a place, it can be cast on people, as well—so long as something of the person goes into the spell. My understanding is that the equinox ward only worked because the house heads participated."

I thought about the house heads dragging blades over their forearms. It was bitter to think of them choosing to chain their own people in suffering, but they'd probably seen no other choice. "Why did he use blood, though?"

"It strengthens wards. Osric told me he used his own blood to cast the ward bounding Mistei—and the blood of many others, too." His fingers twitched around mine, and I wondered why he was still holding on to me, now that he'd positioned my hand to his liking. I felt the tingling nearness of him at my back, one animal attuned to the presence of another. His hand finally fell away. "Stay like that. Imagine the door in your mind, and now imagine a curtain falling across it."

I imagined a velvet curtain, but that didn't seem quite right. Instead I tried to think what my own ward would look like to an outsider, settling on a gauzy veil of dark red. I painted it with a scarlet glimmer and imagined sparkling points of silver. "Is it working?" I asked.

"No." I heard amusement in his voice. "Because I haven't taught you the spell word yet."

My eyes popped open. "There's a word?" I turned my head to look at him over my shoulder. "I haven't needed words for the other things I do." I'd never heard Drustan speak a spell out loud, either.

There was a trace of a smile on his lips. "Magic is complex. The first thing young faeries learn about is the elemental power associated with each house. It takes practice, but it doesn't require any language because it's an innate ability."

I'd always thought of Kallen as a warrior first, but the scholarly side of him I'd been seeing lately intrigued me. I was greedy for more of these thoughtful, detailed lessons.

"That's not the only magic, though," he continued, "or why would bestial powers exist? Why would some of the Nasties be able to shape-shift? There are magical artifacts sprinkled throughout legend, too—a bone fiddle that can raise the dead, metal animals that repeat anything spoken in front of them, impossible weapons like your dagger. More than can be explained by house magic."

A fiddle that could raise the dead. I got goose bumps at the thought. "The dagger doesn't require a spell to work. Not a spoken one, anyway." It did need blood, though, and I supposed that was a type of ritual.

"The greatest rule of Faerie, wherever it can be found across the wild places of this world, is that every rule has an exception." His smile had grown; he was enjoying this. "Even things that look the same aren't. Hector and I are similar, but not identical in power or temperament. Una is . . ." He paused for a moment. "Different, too. She cannot cast wards, for instance, even though the rest of her magic is strong. The spell does not enjoy being spoken by her tongue."

Now *that* was interesting. "Do you know why?"

His face grew blank. "I have a suspicion."

"And that suspicion would be?"

"A private one."

Maddening faerie. He could be so detailed in some of his explanations and utterly cryptic with others. I sighed, then faced the door again. "Fine. Keep your secrets. What's the spell?"

"Close your eyes again. Think of the door and the curtain."

I closed my eyes, thinking of the door, but I was also thinking of him. Not being able to see made me more aware of how close he was standing. How he was likely watching me, picking up the small details of my posture or the flicker of my eyes behind my lids.

"Daemaria," he whispered, breath painting the shell of my ear.

A shiver raced over me. It wasn't just from his proximity, though that was certainly part of it—there was an inexplicable sort of magnetism that came with standing close to Kallen, like dancing on the edge of a cliff and wondering what it would be like to fall. But there was power in the air, too, the delicate vibration of an invisible string being plucked.

"Daemaria," I repeated breathlessly.

The word seemed to change in my mouth—as if the language were a living creature, too wild to be tamed. I felt a prickling over my skin, and then the sensation was gone and the air was still again.

"You can open your eyes," he said.

When I did, I gasped to see a curtain of magic hanging over the door, just as I had envisioned. Red and glimmering, dotted with spots of silver like tiny stars. I spun to face him, eyes wide. "I did it!"

He inclined his head. "A very fast learner, as expected."

"What language was that?" I asked, breathless with my success.

"We call it the old language. It's as old as memory. Maybe it came from the stars, too."

He hadn't backed away when I turned, and I was again aware of how close we were standing. There was just enough room between us for me to raise a hand and press it over his heart, and I felt an abrupt craving to do exactly that. To know the steady beat beneath black fabric.

I wrestled against the urge. Why was I thinking about touching him? Maybe it was a side effect of my new magic, making me more attuned to the bodies in my vicinity. Blood House was a house of the flesh and the senses, and touch was one of those senses.

Kallen's expression hadn't changed, but his chest was rising and falling more rapidly than the moment warranted.

I turned and took a few steps away, putting space between us as I battled a surge of flustered anxiety. This bizarre awareness that pinged between us . . . did he feel it, too? Did his skin also feel like it was coming alive whenever our bodies drew close? Why was this happening?

I closed my eyes, rejecting the answer my mind had started to whisper. "I don't hear other faeries speak when they cast wards," I said, grappling to get back to safer territory. We needed to return to a state of equilibrium, one where I didn't imagine the beat of his heart under my palm or wonder what else might make him breathe hard.

There was a pause, and my foolish brain was tempted to fill it with wild possibilities. But when he spoke, his words were even and practical. "You'll need to speak the spell out loud until you're used to it. But eventually you can say it in your head."

I nodded, then opened my eyes and strode towards a rack of spears, determined to ignore the odd direction my thoughts had taken. "So what now? You teach me to fight?"

I forced a smile and looked back at him, only to find him studying me with an intense expression. His words might have been practical, but that look was anything but, and I had the half-mad thought that something burned beneath Kallen's skin. Like a slow-smoldering bog fire, one of those rare blazes that burned along hidden paths when the peat caught after a lightning strike. Those buried flames were undetectable—until the heat grew too overwhelming to be contained, and the tinder at the surface came alight.

A moment later the look was gone, and he was back to being the same cold, contained Kallen I was used to.

Maybe I had imagined it.

Except a rising hysteria in my breast was whispering that maybe I hadn't.

"Yes, we can spar. Though not with that," he said when I wrapped my hand around the haft of a spear. "You'll need to work up to holding something that big."

I jerked my hand away, then cursed my addled brain for placing innuendo where none had been intended. Truly, I was a disaster tonight. "Then show me what I should start with," I said, voice too sharp. "Not the dagger, I presume, unless you feel like being sucked dry."

My face flushed hot. Shards, why did I say it like that?

Kallen paced closer, an assessing gleam in his eyes. "Why don't you show me what you can do first? Try to hit me."

I wasn't sure I should get anywhere close to touching him in this state, but I'd agreed to this, and pride would never let me back down. I pulled Caedo away from my neck, looking at the thick silver circlet and trying to decide where it would be least likely to hurt Kallen. I'd been feeding the dagger animal blood every night—courtesy of the ever-helpful kitchens in both Earth and Blood House—but it always craved more. "No drinking," I told the dagger before bending to place it around my ankle instead. "Even if he accidentally touches you."

Fine, Caedo said sulkily.

"I appreciate that." Kallen held out a hand, beckoning me forward. "Now come on. Hit me, Princess."

I lunged, swinging my right fist, but he dodged before I made contact. I stumbled past him before spinning, skirts swishing at my ankles.

He tossed the hair out of his eyes before gesturing for me to come at him. "Again."

I tried a series of punches this time, high and then low, but he moved so fast nothing landed. I tried to kick his knee, but he evaded that, too, shifting like liquid. He wasn't even holding his hands in a defensive position: they rested loose at his sides, as if it would be a waste of energy to raise them.

He wasn't even *trying*.

Humiliation mixed with anger at being made a fool of. "At least pretend I stand a chance," I snapped.

He smirked. "Only if you can do better than that."

I made an outraged noise, then charged him, feinting like I was going to punch him in the throat before ducking to ram my shoulder into his gut. A soft noise rushed out of him at the hit, and triumph filled me.

The triumph was short-lived, though, because he wrapped his arms around me and twisted, using my momentum to sweep me off my feet and down to the ground. My back hit the padded floor hard enough to startle a gasp out of me, and he followed me down, a hand on my throat and his knees squeezing my hips.

"A surprise attack is always good," he said as he hovered over me. "But do you know what you did wrong?"

My pulse fluttered against his fingers at the vulnerability of the position. His hand was firm around my neck, not rough but not entirely gentle, either, and I was excruciatingly aware of how easy it would be for him to crush my throat. I swallowed, knowing he could feel the ripple against his palm. "No."

His hair tumbled around his jaw, black and tousled, and his eyes seemed darker than normal. "You practically gave yourself to me," he said, a rough edge to his voice. "I'm larger than you, and you're untrained. That means you do not want to give me an opportunity to use brute strength. Once you're on the ground, it's hard to get back up."

A reckless exhilaration was ripping through me, some potent combination of fear and animal instinct. I shifted under his grip, then brought my knees up sharply to try to hit the backs of his legs. It didn't work, but while he was smirking down at me, I hammered a fist into his ribs.

He let out a soft grunt. "Good," he said. "If you do get pinned, try to get out of it as quickly as possible. There are some grappling techniques I can teach you. But the point of this lesson is that you let anger get the best of you. Your pride was wounded, so you did something risky."

I bared my teeth at him.

For some reason, that made him smile. "You can still be angry," he said. "Just not reckless. Not if you don't have to be." He shifted his grip, letting go of my throat to grab my wrists and pin them above my head. "What now, Kenna?" he asked, devilry glittering in his eyes.

I jerked my head up, snapping my teeth in the direction of his arm. I didn't make contact, but he let out a startled laugh. Then I bucked my hips up hard.

He grunted and lurched forward, letting go of my wrists to catch his weight on his palms.

Maybe it wasn't honorable, but I took the opportunity to reach around and smack my fist into his testicles from behind. Not too hard, but hard enough to make a point: *I could have made this hurt much worse.*

Kallen let out a strangled sound and released me, rolling away. I followed, straddling his hips and wrapping my hand around his throat this time. "At this point," I said, leaning in until a loose curl slid over my shoulder to brush his lips, "I would stab you."

"And I would deserve it," he said, wheezing slightly. His breath made the strands of my hair flutter. "But you should have gotten up and escaped after breaking my hold."

"This is more satisfying, though," I said, squeezing his throat.

"I won't argue that."

Wait, what did *that* mean?

Suddenly aware that our pelvises were almost in contact and his hands were hovering an inch above my hips, I scrambled upright and backed away.

He followed more slowly, wincing. "You've got a good grasp on the first skill you'll need. Fighting dirty."

"Too bad I apparently don't have a grasp on any of the other skills." Embarrassment still heated my skin, and it was hard to look at him without reliving the feel of him on top of me.

"You're just starting. And there's a lot to like about what you did." My eyes flew to his face, and his lips quirked. "You're fast, for one. That's going to be one of your greatest assets. You have good instincts, and you're both agile and aggressive. The technique can be taught."

Now I felt hot for different reasons. I wasn't used to being praised. "So where do I start on the technique?" I asked, rubbing a hand over my neck. My hair was falling from its pins, as it always did, and my nape was damp with sweat. "Are you going to show me how to grapple?"

If he did, would I survive the attempt? This sparring session was setting me off-kilter in ways I didn't want to think about.

"No, I'm going to start by teaching you how to punch. Show me again."

He had no idea how many fistfights I'd won in the Tumbledown schoolyard. "I know how to—"

"Humor me, Kenna."

I sighed, then tried to hit him again.

This time he stopped my fist with his hand. "I saw that coming. You pulled your elbow back, and you swung wide instead of punching straight. When you move your arm in an arc, your hits will be slower. You're going to be best served by fast, direct strikes."

He demonstrated, lashing his fist out to the side of me. The movement was so quick I jumped. If he'd actually been aiming for me, he would have knocked me to the ground.

"Let me show you again, slower this time."

He walked me through each component. The precise angle to hold my fist at, how the power should come from my legs and hips rather than the shoulder, and how it should explode out of me like a snake striking.

He showed me how to break a nose with the heel of my palm—something I had done before, thank you very much, and telling him so earned a grunt of approval—then taught me elbow strikes and a way of swinging my fist like a hammer that worked best against collarbones and other bony areas. There was more padding at the base of my fist than on my knuckles, he said, so it was a safer strike when aiming for some parts of the body. A fractured hand would heal quickly now that I was Fae, but even a second of hesitation could mean death when facing someone with more experience. Which was almost everyone in Mistei.

"The next thing you'll need to learn is anatomy," Kallen said after an hour of running me through strikes, both against him and the bag dangling from the ceiling. "For the Nasties in particular—they don't all have the same vulnerabilities we do. I can send over some books, but I imagine the Blood House library has plenty."

"I imagine so." Blood had been a house of healers, not just warriors, and both types had needed to know how other people were built.

My knuckles were sore from hitting the bag over and over, though the redness was quickly fading. I blotted my sweaty face on my sleeve. Even with my new Fae endurance, that had been a lot of exercise, and the neck, armpits, and back of my dress were damp. Kallen looked much more composed, of course, though his cheeks were lightly flushed from the exertion and his eyes were bright. He seemed to have truly enjoyed this.

I had, too, I realized. It was nice to get out of my head for an hour. Nice to learn something new. I'd been a disaster, but though Kallen had been blunt with his critiques, he'd also commented on what I was doing right. Hopefully I wouldn't need to use these lessons often—Caedo was still the first and best line of defense—but anything that made me stronger could only be a good thing.

"Thank you," I said, grinning at Kallen. "I liked that."

At my words, he smiled slightly. "Good. Same time tomorrow?"

I nibbled my lip, wondering if it was wise to make a frequent habit of this. It felt risky somehow, like an addiction waiting to happen.

Kallen's eyes briefly dropped to where my teeth dug into my lower lip.

Risky or not, all power was good power, and there was only one answer I was ever going to give. "Yes."

18

A FEW DAYS INTO THE ACCORD, IMOGEN HOSTED A SECOND silvered event. She was calling it a garden party, and it was going to be held on the same grassy hill where we'd celebrated the spring equinox and Beltane.

The most powerful faeries from each house had been invited. For the other houses, that meant approximately thirty guests each and their personal servants. For Blood House, it meant Lara and me, since the five Noble Fae from Earth House were too nervous to go public with their new allegiance, and two Earth Underfae who had offered to serve as our handmaidens. A dryad named Carys trailed my steps, while Lara was accompanied by an asrai named Besseta.

I eyed Carys as we climbed the stairs towards the surface. She was slender and pale, like the aspen trees her kind liked to sleep inside, with short, curling yellow hair. White bark grew at her hairline and over the backs of her hands. She'd been beaming all morning, thrilled by her new position, but I kept feeling the urge to apologize. Having a personal servant after recently being one myself was . . .

uncomfortable. But none of the Underfae wanted to rest or flee Mistei as the humans did; they wanted to serve a house.

"It's the Fae way," Lara had told me. "They aren't going to want the same things as the humans do because they aren't human."

At least I'd found the vaults where Blood House kept its gold so I could start paying my new servants. It had been a shock to look at those heaps of shining coins and know they were mine. Lara said we would need to select a treasurer to manage what went out and came in—not that any funds would be coming in until we had services to offer the rest of Mistei. Blood had once provided healing services and midwifery, but with only me wielding that power, we would need to find other ways to sustain ourselves.

At the top of the stairs, a door cut into the hillside had been flung open. The sunshine made my eyes water, and the breeze held the heady perfume of flowers. Planter boxes bursting with dahlias, lilies, geraniums, peonies, and more were laid out in rows ringing the hill, and between the rows were wooden tables topped with gauzy canopies. The tables were set for tea, and servants circulated with trays of wine.

The gown I'd chosen today was glittering silver with an intricately wrapped bodice, and a ruby-studded tiara perched atop my braided hair. Beside me, Lara looked like a flower herself in a rose-red gown layered with organza petals. Everywhere we walked, faeries watched and whispered.

Imogen presided over the gathering from beneath a lavender awning that matched her eyes. She wore pink again, the puffed sleeves bound with opalescent ribbons, and Osric's crown rested on her brow. Torin and Rowena sat with her, radiant in white. When Lara and I passed by, the three ceased their conversation. I nodded at them, trying to pretend I didn't feel like a deer being sized up by wolves, and it felt surreal when they nodded back.

"May I bring you anything, Princess Kenna?" Carys asked, practically skipping beside me.

"Why don't you rest in the shade?" I suggested. There were a few trees scattered over the hill, stragglers that had survived whatever long-ago clear-cutting had smoothed out the slope, and many of the servants were clustered beneath them.

Carys's eyes grew plaintive. "I wish to be useful, my princess."

I wasn't comfortable ordering her around, so I tried to think of something that would keep her busy. "Can you listen to the servant gossip? It would be helpful to know what's happening in the other houses."

Carys looked thrilled. "I will learn anything I can."

I watched her scurry away, wondering if I'd become like Oriana and Kallen. Was dispatching Carys as a spy truly better than letting her bring me strawberries or wine?

Lara looked at my face. "Where did you send her?"

"To listen in on the servant gossip."

"Oh, that's a good idea." She gave Besseta similar instructions, and the asrai curtsied before gliding away. Lara looped her arm through mine. "I see Imogen is inviting comparisons to Queen Brigitta again."

"How so?"

Lara gestured at a trellis wound with yellow and pink roses. "Her standard was a yellow unicorn on a pink field."

More symbolism implying Imogen would be a benevolent ruler. I wondered if anyone actually believed it.

We passed Lord Edric of Fire House, who was dressed in a gold tunic bright enough to rival the sun. My eyes quickly found Aidan nearby, watching his master with a smile. When he saw me, his grin widened.

I smiled back, though I felt the sting of unhappiness. If I failed to support Drustan, that friendship would likely snap like a thread pulled too tight.

Kallen's sister, Una, joined Edric in conversation. Her black linen dress was simpler than those worn by the other Noble Fae, and I remembered with an unpleasant jolt where I'd last seen her wearing this outfit. At a picnic celebrating the trials—one that had ended with the candidates Garrick and Markas tearing my dress open.

I rubbed my arm, feeling the bulge of Caedo beneath the fabric. There was a sting at my palm as Caedo cut through the sleeve. *He's here*, the dagger said darkly.

I was about to ask who was here when my focus caught on a familiar face. A redheaded faerie in a purple tunic watched me warily from a nearby table. Markas, the sole surviving Illusion candidate.

Anger swept through me, and crimson magic seeped out of my skin to wind around my fingers. Before I'd thought it through, I started stalking towards him, Caedo sliding into my hand.

Markas paled and lurched to his feet, knocking the table with his knee and tipping a glass over. Golden liquid puddled on the table before dripping onto the grass.

I stopped in front of him, dress swirling around my ankles. I hadn't had a speech planned, but as Markas's pupils swelled and sweat beaded his brow, a realization made the words burst out of me. "You're afraid of me now."

He swallowed. "Princess Kenna." Then he seemed to collect himself, because he shook his head, straightening his posture. "Afraid? Don't be ridiculous—"

I slammed Caedo into the wooden table point-first. Markas made an alarmed sound and stumbled back.

What a coward. Without Garrick to shape his cruelty, he didn't amount to much at all. "You're lucky this is a silvered event," I hissed under my breath. My smile showed teeth. "But we have an appointment."

"An—an appointment?" He looked nauseated.

I pulled the knife out of the table, then raised my hand, encouraging Caedo to take the form it had the first night in Blood House. Steel bones tipped with vicious claws. I clicked the claws together, reveling in his obvious terror. "You won't know when it's coming," I told him. "But I'm looking forward to it."

I turned and stalked away.

"How do you do that?" Lara asked, catching up to me. She looked breathlessly excited.

"Do what?" My own pulse was slow to calm. I was imagining Markas falling to his knees, begging for a mercy I would refuse to give him.

Yes, Caedo crooned, sharing its own imaginings of a pool of blood mixing with the spilled wine in the grass. *Vengeance is better.*

The fantasy should have disturbed me, but it didn't. Markas had nearly stripped me naked at that picnic. He probably would have assaulted me further if Kallen hadn't intervened.

"How do you say and do whatever you want?" Lara asked. "Everyone was watching, and you didn't even care."

They were still watching, I realized. Dozens of eyes fixed on me, dozens of mouths moving behind shielding hands. Still, better for them to think of me as a predator than remember me as a victim.

I encouraged Caedo to swirl into a thick bracelet now that the threat had been delivered. "They aren't going to respect me more if I'm well behaved."

"I need to be more like that," she said, a furrow between her brows. "No one's ever afraid I might hurt them."

"We can start by getting you a knife."

"I think I need to actually stab someone before anyone will believe I'm capable of it."

"Then we'll find someone for you to stab," I said distractedly, because I had spotted Drustan. He wore vermilion satin banded with gold, and his arms were folded as he gave me an unimpressed look. When he started walking over, I changed course, aiming for an empty table set for tea.

"How about Markas?" Lara asked, following me. "I should be the one to confront him, not you."

I grabbed a cup full of berry-hued liquid. "Why?"

"Because I didn't protect you the first time."

That got me to stop thinking about Drustan. There was a soft ache in my chest as I looked at Lara's guilty expression. She was remembering that picnic, too. "Would it make you feel better to hurt him?" I asked quietly.

She nodded, looking into her glass. "I want to be different. I should have started a long time ago."

A shadow fell across the table as Drustan arrived. "This is a silvered event, Kenna." He bent his head towards me, and my mind took that moment to remind me that the last time we'd been on this hill together, we'd been naked in a circle of fire.

"Did you see me break the peace?" I asked, raising the cup to my lips. The tea was cold and tasted like honey and raspberries.

"You threatened him."

"Maybe you don't remember what happened the last time I was at a party with Markas." I set my tea down hard enough that the saucer cracked and a fracture jagged up the side of the cup. Reddish-pink liquid beaded along that seam. "It makes sense you would forget," I said, venom spilling out of me, because who was he to judge? "You weren't the one to rescue me."

His lips compressed, and flames suddenly licked up his gray

irises. That comment had struck true, and I felt a dark delight at discovering a vulnerability.

"I wasn't there," he gritted out. "If I had been—"

"Do you think I care?" Talking over him gave me another thrill. Drustan was used to the ballet of diplomatic words, of being the one controlling the conversation. "You weren't there then, and you don't get a say over what I do now, either."

"The Accord," he started, trying again. "It's—"

"Still intact. If I had broken it, it would be very obvious." I looked away, shading my eyes. Then I recognized a tall figure making his way towards us, and a strange anticipation swooped in my belly. "Oh, here comes Kallen," I said casually, feeling a shiver of excitement as Drustan's expression darkened. "I know he remembers what happened with Markas. Do you suppose he's going to lecture me, too? Or do you think he'll understand why the Blood princess needs to threaten her enemies?"

I knew the answer.

"Princess Kenna," Kallen said, bowing to me. He straightened, looking at Drustan. "Prince Drustan. I trust you are enjoying the afternoon?"

Drustan's eyes still held the heat of magic. "Why are you here, Kallen?"

Kallen raised his brows, looking politely surprised. "I was invited."

"Not at the party. Why are you interrupting a private conversation?"

Kallen stared at Drustan for a long moment before switching his attention to me. "Forgive me, Kenna. I didn't realize you preferred privacy."

"I don't," I said. "We're allies, are we not? We shouldn't keep secrets from one another."

Except I was keeping secrets, and both Kallen and I knew it. His lashes flickered, and I wondered if he was thinking about our nighttime sparring sessions, too. It had only been a few days, but already those lessons felt essential. Mistei didn't seem so frightening when Kallen was teaching me how to carve my way through it.

"What an interesting policy for you to suddenly hold," Drustan said, enunciating the syllables precisely. "Those Sun Soldiers were dead long before I was informed you were doing a late-night *survey* with Kallen."

He was talking to me, but he was looking at Kallen as he said it. Kallen smirked slightly in response, and a muscle ticked in Drustan's jaw.

My pulse thumped at the growing tension. It made me feel reckless. There was an invisible blade poised between the three of us, and I wanted to know how sharp the edge was.

Maybe I was a hypocrite, as Drustan had pointed out. I was definitely using this conversation to lash out at Drustan because I was still angry with him and grieving what we'd once had. I should be more dignified than this.

But the taste of power was in my mouth, and it was addicting.

"Drustan was lecturing me about threatening Markas," I told Kallen. "He believes I shouldn't do or say anything objectionable in public during the Accord."

"Drustan has the luxury of a full house and a standing army," Kallen replied. "He can afford to be passive with his enemies if he wishes."

Lara was looking between the two faeries as if she were viewing a sporting match. My pulse tapped in my throat. I was feeling a more intense sort of interest than that.

"Afford to be passive?" Drustan snapped. "I'm playing politics, Kallen . . . but I suppose you wouldn't understand the more subtle applications of strength. A weapon doesn't know how to wield itself."

Drustan was smiling again, like he could never take the mask of the charmer off for long. And that was the problem, wasn't it? When he smiled at everything, it was impossible to tell what was real.

The anger peeking through now, though—that was real. Maybe I craved it for that exact reason.

"If Kenna wants to be a wise ruler," Drustan continued, "she should follow my example rather than yours."

"You should play politics on your own behalf rather than hers," Kallen replied.

"And you should stay out of matters you don't understand, you vile creature."

I gasped at the animosity in Drustan's voice. As disturbingly thrilling as I'd been finding this hostility, that had been a step too far. "Don't talk to him like that."

"Isn't this what you want, Kenna?" Drustan asked, not looking at me. "You provoked this. Maybe you wanted a reminder that I'm capable of passion on your behalf."

My cheeks grew hot, and an ugly feeling coiled in my gut. Because he wasn't wrong, not entirely. And that was the problem with Drustan, too. He was never completely wrong.

"You should treat him with respect," I said.

"I should treat him like what he is," Drustan replied. "Someone who has killed and killed again, and never for the right reasons."

"What do you know of my reasons?" Kallen asked softly.

"I know enough. And now what is he doing? Manipulating you, Kenna. Sinking his claws in and nearly getting you killed, because he can't touch anything without destroying it."

Kallen flinched almost imperceptibly.

I licked my suddenly dry lips. *He isn't trying to touch me*, I wanted to say. Or maybe, *You sank your claws into me first.*

But I didn't say anything.

The two of them stared each other down. I'd provoked this, but it was obvious the conflict between them had begun a long time ago. The day was alive with sunshine and the buzz of insects, but the air itself was changing from the force of their anger. Heat pressed against my skin from one side, biting cold from the other.

"How easily you condemn others for what you yourself have done, Drustan," Kallen said. His face was still, but there was danger in every taut inch of his body.

"Be very careful how you speak to me." Drustan's voice was just as quiet, each word edged like a blade. "I am no puppet to dance on your strings—and no innocent to die on your sword."

"Drustan," I tried again. "Stop." This no longer felt like my power to wield. It no longer felt good. And now I was aware of the watchers again, all the faeries staring as they fanned themselves or drank wine. Spectators to this little show I had started. They weren't close enough to hear the words, and Drustan was still smiling, but it had to be obvious this wasn't a friendly encounter. "Kallen," I said, switching my focus to him. "You don't have to—"

Kallen cut me off with a sharp slice of his hand. "No, Kenna. This is between the two of us." His jaw clenched, and he stared at his own outstretched hand for a long moment.

My skin prickled. The air seemed oppressive, heavy with the potential for violence. Like the moments before a storm broke.

Then Kallen untied the knot at his belt and drew his dagger, the slide of steel ringing through the air.

My heart lurched. "Kallen," I said, breath snatched away by a surge of fear. "You can't—"

"Here," Kallen said, flipping the dagger so the hilt was up. He held it out to Drustan in offer. "One of the blades that killed all those innocents. I've wiped it clean countless times, but perhaps some blood remains for you to comment on. Or maybe you can show me how you would wield it better."

The contrast between the two had never seemed so stark. Drustan gleamed in his reds and golds, long copper hair pulled back in a neat tail and arrogance dripping from his chiseled features. Kallen was a tense shadow in comparison: his long tunic was the color of ink, stretching from his chin to his polished boots, and his hair was tousled around his jaw as if he'd spent an uneasy night. He might rank lower than Drustan at court, but there was an edge of barely contained violence to his bearing that struck me as far deadlier.

"How many were there?" Drustan asked with a sneer, making no move to take the proffered weapon. "Hundreds? Thousands? They say you were nine years old when you first killed for Osric, and you haven't stopped since."

My breath caught. *Nine?*

"How much blood stains your hands?" Kallen shot back. "We all do what we must."

"You betrayed members of your own house. They were executed at your bidding."

I'd seen one of those executions, I thought sickly. At the first formal banquet I'd attended, when I'd watched prisoners be murdered in horrifying ways. One had been a faerie from Void House, ripped in two by Hector's magic . . . after Kallen had reported him for treasonous speech.

"I did," Kallen said, dipping his chin slightly. "Just as you sent Lady Edlyn to her death at the summer solstice. Sometimes sacrifices have to be made—especially when the reckless actions of a few put the entire cause at risk."

Drustan's laugh was wild-sounding. His cheeks were flushed, and a lick of flame danced across his teeth as he bared them at Kallen. "Do not ever compare the depth of your crimes to mine," he said, voice guttural. "You know very well you do not always kill for a cause."

Drustan hated Kallen, I realized with a lurch of my stomach. Not just as one rival hated another, not just as an enemy on the other side of a war. This was something deeper, something that craved blood.

Time seemed to pause as the two stared at each other with open animosity. Fire and night, light and shadow. The spark . . . and its potential extinguishing.

Then Kallen sheathed his dagger. His face was blank once more; he'd drawn back into himself, resuming the mantle of cold indifference. "No," he said. "I've killed for reasons you can't even imagine."

He turned his back on Drustan and strode to a nearby table, sitting next to Una and Edric. The abrupt de-escalation of the conflict made me nearly limp with relief. Drustan stared at the side of Kallen's head like he was contemplating lighting him on fire, but Kallen no longer seemed to care. The confrontation was over.

I was watching Kallen closely, though. A coil of night whispered over his exposed wrist. He adjusted the cuff of his sleeve, tugging it down until the shadow was obscured.

The Fae produced magic during moments of high emotion. Hints of smoke or shadow, the unfurling of a flower, a shimmering in the air. Kallen had shoved his feelings deep below the surface, but that didn't mean they were quiet.

His eyes flicked to mine, and I felt the impact of that look as if he'd touched me physically. My breathing stuttered, and my heart began a faster beat. It was hard to tell from here, but I didn't think there was any blue left in his eyes at all.

The back of my neck tingled, a race of cold-hot-cold that skittered down my arms. There were secrets in that gaze, and power, and something raw I couldn't put words to. Hate, maybe.

Except that didn't seem quite right. Or at least, it seemed too simple.

"I regret that you had to see that," Drustan said.

The words broke my focus on Kallen. "What?" I asked, turning to face the Fire prince. "Why?"

Drustan was reining in his rage. His gaze was cinder-cool once more, and his smile was self-deprecating. "I can hardly advocate for good public manners if I am incapable of them myself."

"At least you're self-aware."

His smile was too stiff, as if it had been painted in place. "There is bad blood between Kallen and me. An old animosity. I should not have let it poison this afternoon."

There was probably bad blood between Kallen and all of Mistei—and between Drustan and much of it, too. There was certainly bad blood between him and Lara, not that he seemed aware of the way she was eyeing him like she was imagining how nice his spine would look outside of his body. He had notably offered no apologies to her for the scene. I wondered if he'd even taken her presence into account—if he calculated her into any of his equations, or if she'd ceased to matter to him the moment she'd lost her position in Earth House.

"Will you let that old animosity poison our alliance?" I asked Drustan. "If you were to gain the throne, you would still need Void's support."

"I can stomach a great deal when it comes to saving Mistei. Even Kallen." He bowed his head to me. "I will endeavor not to lose my temper again. But I wonder if you understand the forces you're playing with, Kenna."

I didn't, and he probably knew it.

When I didn't reply, he nodded. "The game is intoxicating, isn't it? But Void plays by different rules than you or I do. Use Kallen to antagonize me if you wish . . . but don't imagine he will ever be a reliable ally."

"I don't need your lectures."

"When you're pretending to be friends with the King's Vengeance, clearly you do."

Now who was antagonizing who? "We aren't friends," I said, then wished I'd had a more clever retort.

But that was what Drustan did best, wasn't it? I wouldn't win a battle of words. I needed to play to the strengths that set me apart in the Fae court: my unpredictability and my bluntness. Faeries were good at spouting pretty phrases that meant everything and nothing. I was good at speaking the truth.

Something about the phrasing Drustan had used a few moments before was bothering me. *I regret that you had to see that.* I thought on it, trying to place when he had said that to me before, then remembered. It had been after the summer solstice, after I'd watched him publicly humiliate Edlyn before sending her to her death.

"You said you regret me seeing that confrontation with Kallen," I said, lifting my chin. "Why do you regret that, rather than doing it to begin with?"

He opened his mouth, then closed it again, clearly pausing to formulate the right answer. He didn't need to admit it, though. I knew why. He didn't regret doing it—not any of it.

I curtsied. "Enjoy the rest of the party, Prince Drustan."

19

"THAT WAS INTENSE," LARA SAID.

I tried to ignore the stares as we wandered between tables. "They hate each other, don't they?"

"Everyone hates Kallen."

"I don't."

She grimaced. "I'm aware. I just don't understand why."

"Do you not remember him saving my life?"

That got her to pause. "Fine. He did one good thing, and I'm grateful for it. He also blackmailed you."

"At least he didn't pretend it was anything other than what it was." He hadn't hurt me, though he easily could have. Hadn't seduced me to make me his ally. Hadn't taught me to hope before ripping it away from me.

"I think your standards are too low." Lara eyed my stubborn expression, then sighed. "I was rooting for him to gut Drustan, but that's as far as I'm willing to go with the Kallen support."

"Fair enough." I wasn't even sure how far *I* was willing to go when it came to supporting Kallen. I shaded my eyes, looking around. "Where should we go?"

Lara glanced over to where Oriana was seated with other members of Earth House, then quickly returned her attention to nearer tables. "Joining a Fire or Void group would make sense. We just have to decide which one."

Even here, at this party dedicated to imagining Mistei's peaceful future, most of the tables were segregated by house. Edric had gotten up as soon as Kallen sat down next to Una, instead choosing to speak with Drustan. Wherever Lara and I sat would be seen as a political statement, too, and either Fire or Void would benefit.

What would benefit Blood House? More members, mainly, but until that could happen, we needed a reputation that would make the others wary.

My strengths were in being bold and unexpected. An idea came to me, and though it made me nearly sick with nerves, it was the last thing Drustan, Hector, or anyone else would expect. "Let's get to know Imogen, Torin, and Rowena."

Lara looked at me askance. "Kenna!"

I tugged on her arm. "We're not going to win by behaving like every other house, right? We have to do things they don't expect."

"I don't want to talk to them," she complained, though she let me pull her along.

"I don't, either."

"They tried to kill you."

A huge part of why this was so terrifying—and also why I had to do it. "If I avoid them, it'll look like I'm afraid, and they'll feel even more emboldened." I shook my head. "I'm not going to sit back passively and let Drustan or Hector tell me what to do."

Lara grumbled under her breath but didn't argue further.

The tables closest to Imogen's were populated by Illusion and

Light faeries. As Lara and I passed, they watched us with a mixture of interest and disdain. Ulric, the Illusion lord who had delivered the message about the Accord, stood before the high table, speaking with the three faeries seated there. Imogen noticed me arriving, then nodded in my direction, and Ulric turned to look. His brows rose fractionally, and then he bowed—first to the faeries at the table, then to Lara and me—and backed away.

Imogen sat flanked by Torin and Rowena, with three empty seats opposite. The self-proclaimed queen was smiling, twirling a glass of sparkling wine lazily between her fingers, while Torin and Rowena were studying me with their heads cocked at matching angles, like hawks perched on a branch.

I took the empty seat across from Imogen. Lara made a barely audible sound of protest, then joined me. Her polished expression was firmly in place, but I could tell from the eloquent look in her eyes that I had broken protocol.

Which was the entire point.

"Princess Kenna," Imogen said. "And Lady Lara, too. How unexpected." She set the wine down, then laced her hands together on the table, showing off silver rings topped with chunks of amethyst. "Do take a seat."

"Princess Imogen," I replied, ignoring the sarcasm. "What a lovely party."

Her lips pursed. "My title is Queen, as we've discussed."

"I'm not going to call you that." *Be bold*, I reminded myself. *Be blunt.* If there was anything that put a silver-tongued faerie off guard, it was that.

Torin eyed me like I was an insect, but Rowena was beginning to look intrigued. The summer day suited her type of beauty—her pale gold hair shimmered, her eyes were reminiscent of the clear sky, and the warmth had brought a flush out on her cheeks. "How fascinating that you should choose to sit with us," she said in that girlishly high voice. "Shouldn't you be at the Fire prince's side?"

I worked to keep my expression neutral. "Why would I be?"

"My handmaiden said it looked like he got in an argument with Lord Kallen over you."

Torin sneered. "The two of them, quarreling over a human?"

"Not a human any longer," Imogen corrected. The Illusion princess leaned in, giving me a conspiratorial look. "Tell me, Kenna, what were they arguing about?"

I smiled sweetly. "None of your business, Imogen."

To my surprise, she laughed. Her lavender eyes sparkled, and the air shimmered with rainbow ripples. It was an illusion designed to enhance her beauty, and my skin crawled at the reminder of her power.

"You are disrespectful," Torin said, frowning at me.

Deciding to go even further, I planted my hands on the table and leaned in. "And you aren't? This is supposedly a peace period, yet Sun Soldiers released a bonebreaker salamander on my doorstep the other night."

Lara kicked me under the table.

The three faeries looked taken aback. Because I'd dared to bring it up?

"Oh dear," Rowena said, compressing her pink lips into a rosebud pout. "I don't know a thing about that. Are you sure you didn't imagine it?"

What nonsense. There was no way it had happened without Torin and Rowena's approval, and her patronizing tone confirmed it. "Don't imagine me to be weak because I used to be human," I said. "And don't imagine I'm going to rely on Fire or Void to fight my battles for me."

All three looked even more intensely interested. This was exactly what I wanted—to prove that I wasn't a pawn in their larger game, but a new and unpredictable player they should be wary of. I wasn't sure how to back that impression up with action if it came down to it, but perception shaped reality in Mistei, and I would take any armor I could get.

"There will be no publicly sanctioned acts of violence during the Accord," Imogen said.

Publicly sanctioned. I wasn't an expert in all the nuances of faerie conversation, but I interpreted that easily enough. Imogen was telling me exactly what Drustan and Kallen had—that though everything might look peaceful on the surface, we were in for a month of backstabbing.

"How wonderful to hear," I said. "I wouldn't dream of publicly sanctioning anything I might do in retaliation."

Lara kicked me again, but I ignored it. This was already worth it. I'd set them off-balance, and I was confronting the issue head-on, rather than waiting the way Drustan would want me to. I was doing this on my terms, not his.

"And what happened to these soldiers you imagine you saw?" Torin asked, running his finger over the rim of his goblet. Around and around, and I thought of the nymph he'd forced to dance on broken glass.

"In my imagination, it was gruesome." I smiled, tapping one of my canines with my tongue. "What a relief none of it was real."

He exchanged a glance with Rowena. They had been together for centuries—I wondered how much they could communicate in a single look. What could they do about it, though? If they pushed me for details, they would have to acknowledge dispatching those soldiers to begin with.

"Did you join us to exchange veiled threats?" Imogen asked. "This is more entertainment than I was expecting."

"No," I said, looking her in the eye. "I joined you because I don't believe in avoiding confrontation, and I want everyone to know I'm not going to willingly follow wherever I'm led. I'd also like to hear your plans for ruling Mistei."

Imogen's eyes widened, and her mouth dropped open. "How *enchanting* you are," she breathed. "Yes, let us talk." She stood, and when Torin and Rowena started to rise as well, she gestured for them to remain seated. "You may stay here and speak with Lady Lara."

Torin and Rowena shot displeased looks at each other, then gestured for Imogen to lean in and began whispering to her.

Lara tugged on my sleeve. "What am I supposed to say to them?" she hissed in my ear.

"Talk about the weather?" I cringed at Lara's damning look. "Maybe ask them about Gweneira or what their hopes for Mistei are. Or make polite conversation for a minute and then excuse yourself. You don't have to stay."

"I am going to murder you," she said, fixed society smile still in place.

I nudged her arm. "You can do this." Then I stood and made my way around the table towards Imogen.

"Do not forget who wears the crown," I heard her murmur to Torin.

Torin's posture grew stiff at that soft admonishment. Was there trouble in the Light-Illusion alliance?

Imogen finished the rest of her wine, then extended her hand to me, smiling. "Come, Princess Kenna. Let's get to know each other better."

We began walking side by side down the hill, and if I thought everyone had been staring before, it was nothing compared to now. Imogen and I were an odd pairing, and it didn't help when she hooked her arm through mine as if we were close friends.

I was now questioning the wisdom of my plan, because this was a different political statement than the one I'd intended to make. I was no longer just showing myself to be bold, unexpected, and unafraid of confronting my enemies. Imogen had taken my direct approach and shifted it in her favor. By inviting me for a walk where everyone could see, she was implying a potential alliance between our houses.

An impression wasn't forever, I told myself as I struggled with the urge to rip my arm out of her hold. And maybe this was good. Maybe everyone should be unsure of my real motivations.

Oriana watched us pass, face devoid of expression. I wondered what she thought I was doing and how harshly she judged me for it. At least I was doing something, though.

"Have you declared for Hector or Drustan yet?" Imogen asked me. "I hear that was the ultimatum Drustan gave in the throne room."

So we were going to discuss this immediately. Faeries did seem more willing to be direct in one-on-one conversations. "This is a very public venue for this discussion."

"Anyone who gets close enough will only hear us remarking on the weather."

"How—" Then I realized, and alarm jolted through me. "An illusion." She couldn't just manipulate what people saw—she could get in their heads and change what they heard or felt, too.

She fluttered her eyelashes prettily. "A small one."

This led to an even more unpleasant realization. "You could cast an illusion to make everyone believe the other house heads are swearing fealty to you." What was the point of this Accord when she could manipulate everyone into thinking peace had been decided her way?

"I could," she acknowledged. "It would be a large net to cast, affecting so many minds at once, but I'm capable of it at the scale of this party. Possibly even the scale of a state dinner—I've never extended my power that far, but I am of the blood of Ceridwen." She glanced at me. "But it would soon become clear those oaths were a lie. That would eradicate all public trust in me, which would defeat the purpose."

It was a small comfort, but Shards, I hated her power. At least being burned by mystical fire or ripped apart by shadows was tangible. I would see a death like that coming. With Imogen in my head, I might not see anything at all. "I will not react well if you use your magic on me," I told her.

"And I will not react well if you use yours on me," she returned. "Which is why we must rely on social niceties." She smiled, raising her hand to show off the thin chain crossing her palm. "For now."

This close, I was struck by how small she was compared to the impression she gave off. Not short—though she was on the smaller side for Mistei's faeries, a few inches shorter than Lara—but slight, with pointed features and delicate fingers. Her brown hair tumbled prettily over her shoulders, and she smelled like lavender and wine.

"How do you know about the conversation in the throne room?" I asked. "The Illusion soldiers were all dead or gone by then."

"One of the corpses wasn't quite dead." She shrugged. "I would have guessed at the outcome, anyway. A vacant throne must be filled quickly, and Hector would never allow Drustan to be the sole one to seize that opportunity. If they are against each other, Light is with me, and Earth is neutral, they each need the validation of the final house's support."

Maybe I could gain important information from her, or at least sow doubts that might help my faction. "Is Light House with you? Because that doesn't seem certain."

"Enough of it. Soon to be all of it." She gave me a sympathetic look. "I hope you haven't grown attached to Gweneira. Idealists tend not to do well in that house."

I barely knew Gweneira, but I was attached to the idea of her versus someone like Torin. "You must not be an idealist, either."

"Oh, I am," she said, guiding me farther down the slope. "As much as anyone who thinks the future can be better than the past is an idealist. Mistei will have its eternal spring again." She waved her hand, and the flowers in a nearby planter box transformed into jewel-bright birds before taking flight. There were murmurs of appreciation from the guests, which quickly turned to gasps of delight when the floral centerpiece on their table became a pile of precious jewels. "For you," Imogen called out. "Anything you desire, let me make it yours."

After we passed, I looked over my shoulder. The planter box was intact again, no birds in sight. The jewels, however, remained. They'd been disguised by magic all along.

She repeated the performance at the next table. Everywhere we went, fortunes sprouted, quickly scooped up by greedy hands. "You think to buy their allegiance," I said judgmentally.

She laughed. "There's the human in you. Yes, I will, because the Fae love nothing more than indulgence. Once I'm queen, we will sing and dance and make merry for a thousand years. We will remember what we once were."

I remembered those legends—of faeries who lured human musicians into their revelry with promises of gold and fame, then forced them to play for a single night that lasted a century. Lies mixed with truths: the faeries did love to dance, but even this twilight realm followed the rhythms of the sun. "But you're willing to kill to get there."

"Yes, because the Fae love that, too."

The straightforwardness with which she said that was disturbing. "And you consider that idealism?"

"Do not mistake me," she said, giving me a chiding look like I was the unreasonable one. "I do not personally enjoy killing the way Osric did. Most of the Fae would say they do not, either. But this is a cycle we find ourselves in again and again. If we did not love it, why would we keep doing it?" She shrugged, then gave me a blinding smile. "I do hope to accomplish this without too much bloodshed. But much like you wanted Torin and Rowena to know what you're capable of, I want you to know what I'm capable of."

Was it a threat? An honest confession from someone seeking to win me to her side? Both?

We were passing the Fire section now. I kept my eyes straight ahead as riches shimmered into existence on the tables. I could imagine the metaphorical holes Drustan's stare was burning in me as Imogen performed her latest mass act of bribery with our arms still linked together.

"And you think Light House wants to make merry with you for a thousand years?" I asked, having trouble believing it.

She giggled. "Oh, they are so joyless on the whole. No, Light House wants a firm hand and a firmer purpose. They crave being the keepers of order—so I must provide them with an order to preserve. What it consists of matters little, as you saw with Osric. Wouldn't you prefer a merry queen to that?"

She was making a disturbing type of sense. "Torin and Rowena are ambitious, though. Possibly even insane. Are you certain they won't turn on you?"

"Look how quickly you try to drive a wedge between us." She was still smiling as she shook her head. "Oh, I like this."

"Why?"

She reached out to snag a glass of wine from a passing servant's tray. "Have you tried this yet?" she asked instead of answering my question. "It's a special vintage. No one outside Illusion House has tasted it in centuries." She leaned in conspiratorially. "You could have a barrel of it every night if you wish."

"I'm not interested."

She pouted. "Oh, very well." She drained it in a few quick swallows, then flung the empty glass aside. It shattered against a planter box, and a servant immediately rushed to pick up the pieces. "Then tell me, Kenna. What is it you crave?"

My brows rose at both the question and her intemperance. How much alcohol had she consumed already? "For no more poisonous salamanders to be left on my doorstep, as a start."

She made a tsking sound. "You cannot blame them for moving to eliminate an enemy. Without the support of a secondary house, both Drustan and Hector's claims to the throne are weakened."

I was surprised she would admit it. "So you knew."

"I will deny it, of course."

"Then you must also know about the Illusion faerie who attacked me at Earth's entrance."

There was a delicate pause. "I will deny that, as well."

"Was it you?" I asked bluntly.

Her lashes swept down, and a dimple popped out on one cheek. "Queens usually delegate the more unsavory tasks."

I wondered which faerie it had been. Her advisor, Ulric? Markas? More likely an unimportant soldier, someone she wouldn't mind losing if they were caught. "Are you also delegating to eliminate Hector and Drustan?"

She shook her head. "That would cause more problems than it solved. No one would believe it was an accident, and once one party breaks the Accord, the others are free to follow."

"How would killing me be any different?"

"You are so new to this world, and accidents happen. How are you to know what's safe and what isn't when you've only been a faerie for a few days?"

A chill swept over me.

"And your house is so small," she continued. "Who would avenge you for a bit of clumsiness, or for touching something you shouldn't have? It would be a terrible tragedy, of course, but worth risking the entirety of Mistei over? I think not."

My vulnerability was excruciatingly obvious. A house was the root of all power, and I barely had one. I didn't have a fearsome reputation, either. If I touched a poisonous animal or tripped into a trap, the Fae who disdained humans would be quick to let that scorn color their thinking. My very nature would provide the alibi for my killers.

"It doesn't have to be like that, though," she said. "If you vow to support me after Lughnasa, I will ensure there are no more surprises left outside your door—and no more invisible assailants, either."

Another bribe. A barrel of wine every night, piles of jewels, the protection of the queen . . . If I pointed at the sun, she might promise to take it down from the sky, so long as it meant I abandoned my cause for hers. "My loyalty is not so easily won."

"Not even by Drustan, it seems." She glanced that way, and a laugh tumbled out of her. "Oh, he looks angry. Is that the reason you came to speak with me? To anger him?"

She was too close to a portion of the truth. "I told you why I came over."

"None of us are motivated by only one thing." She cocked her head, still studying him. "Normally he's much more charming than this. I wonder . . ." Then she shook her head and pulled me onward. "No matter. I'm beginning to sense threats aren't the best way to motivate you. Tell me what else you want. Wealth? Power? A company of soldiers to order around? The Fire prince in your bed?"

"No," I said vehemently.

Her lips curved, and I realized I had made a mistake. "Ah, but I see."

I wasn't going to ask what she saw. I wasn't—"What do you see?"

"Kallen rarely gets in public altercations unless he's executing someone. Drustan never gets in altercations at all. He's too political for that."

I felt the prickle of unease at the back of my neck. "Tempers are running high this week."

"My very favorite thing is learning what people want," Imogen said, bringing her head closer to mine as if confessing a scandalous secret. "Not just the desires they wear on the surface, but the real ones underneath. And then I like giving it to them." She pulled me to a stop, then gripped my hands in hers. Her fingers were cool, the nails long and sharp enough to press a warning into my skin. "Drustan would eat and breathe power if he could," she told me. "That is his obvious desire. And that's what you want, too, you pretty little thing, even if you won't tell me so. You want strength. You want respect. I can give that to you." Her eyes changed color, the purple spinning into a silver vortex. The scent of flowers on the air intensified, growing heady and intoxicating. "I can give you more, though," she whispered. "If you want one of them, or even both of them, I can help break them to your will. I can show them such imaginings, the kinds of dreams that haunt them during the day, too, until all they can think about is—"

"Stop it," I said, tearing my hands out of hers and backing away. My backside hit a table, and I heard the clatter of falling glassware.

The laughter and chatter at that table abruptly died. The guests seated there had probably only heard us talking about the weather, but there was no hiding my hostile posture as I faced Imogen with my fists clenched and my cheeks so blazing hot I knew they looked red.

"Come now," Imogen said softly, that canny smile still on her lips. "It's not a crime to want things."

I stalked towards her again. "I don't want anything created from a lie," I said, low and fierce. "You'll have to do better than that."

Then I hurried past her to find Lara, trying to ignore the stares that followed.

20

Lara, Anya, and I met that evening in Lara's chambers, during the lull between the house dinner and my sparring session with Kallen. Lara lounged on the sofa in a silky white robe embroidered with scarlet flowers, drinking wine, while I sat cross-legged on the floor next to a pile of books Gweneira had sent Lara. Anya was pacing, listening to the conversation.

Anya had been distant ever since the first group of faeries had joined Blood House, going out of her way to avoid them—which meant avoiding me, since I barely had a moment alone these days. It was as if, once the shock of seeing me nearly die had worn off, she'd retreated inside herself. She rarely answered my knocks or emerged from her room. I'd left flowers, books, blankets, and all her favorite foods outside her door, but she never acknowledged the offerings.

She was here now, though. Restless and mostly silent, but here. So I told them about my conversation with Imogen—leaving out what she'd begun to offer me at the end—hoping something would be enough to spark interest in Anya's closed-off gaze.

"Imogen doesn't sound too bad," Lara said when I was done. "She just wants us to dance, not die."

"I think she's willing to accept either."

She shrugged. "Still, better a frivolous queen than a cruel one."

"Don't tell me you're suddenly a supporter," I said, appalled.

Lara traced the embroidery on her robe. "At this point, I don't know if I care who rules Mistei. They're all bad options."

The words were jarring. I'd assumed Lara would want the rebel faction of Void, Fire, and Blood to win, even if the ruler we chose was an imperfect one. "I know you hate Drustan, but Mistei needs to change. You really think another Illusion ruler would be preferable to him or Hector?"

She shrugged again, still not looking at me. "I think you're being too optimistic about how drastic the change will be under any ruler."

Anya had stopped pacing. She turned to face us, arms crossed and face pensive. "Did Imogen support Osric?" she asked.

Lara looked surprised Anya had spoken. "I suppose. But we all had to, and Imogen more than most. She was part of his house."

"Had to," Anya echoed, picking at the sleeve of her gray shirt. She'd worn this same drab, baggy outfit yesterday, and the fabric was rumpled and sweat-stained.

"A house isn't just a place to live," Lara said. "It's our identity. It's our power. Who's in charge of each house doesn't matter in the long run—we can't abandon where we come from." Then she looked at me guiltily. "Except in extraordinary circumstances, I suppose."

An uneasy feeling tightened my throat. For the first time, I questioned whether Lara would go back to Earth House if she could. If Oriana extended a hand... would Lara take it?

Oriana wasn't going to extend a hand, though. I had, and Lara was here.

It still felt like I'd swallowed a thorn.

Anya was looking increasingly angry. She ran a hand over her shaved scalp, then turned abruptly to Lara's dressing table to grab the decanter of wine. Rather than filling one of the spare glasses, she tipped it to her lips, drinking deeply. And she didn't stop.

"Anya," I said, scrambling to my feet.

"No!" She slammed the decanter back down. "Stop treating me like a child."

The accusation stung. "I'm not. It's just . . ."

"Just what?" When I took too long to formulate a response, Anya looked up at the ceiling and let out a ragged laugh. "What a joke." Then she focused on Lara. "If it doesn't matter who rules, then what does anything matter? Or is the most important thing that you still get to wear jewels?" She sneered. "Apathy is so pretty when you're already rich."

Lara looked like she'd been slapped. "You know nothing about being Fae. You don't understand."

"Good. I don't want to." Anya grabbed the bottle by the neck, then stormed away, slamming the door behind her.

I got up to follow, but Lara's voice stopped me. "You think she wants you chasing after her?"

"She's my friend."

"And I'm not?" Lara sighed. "Go on. She'll be angry with you, and then you can come back."

I hurried away, not wanting to think about how right Lara probably was.

Stop treating me like a child.

I wasn't. I *wasn't*. But as I headed towards Anya's room, I thought how much I wanted to wrap her in a soft blanket, hand her a cup of tea, and tell her everything would be better in the morning.

I knocked on the door. Anya flung it open, bottle still in hand. A drop of wine trailed down her chin, and she wiped it away with the back of her hand. "What?"

"Do you want to talk?" I asked hesitantly.

Her eyes traveled over me, from the silver band securing my braid to the embroidered scarlet silk of my robe. "The princess wants to check in on her new subject?"

I flinched at the angry words. "It's not like that."

"Isn't it?" Her hazel eyes were reddened, and there were purple smudges under them. Her head looked vulnerable without her beautiful golden-brown hair, and the shiny pink mark on her cheek taunted me. She'd refused to let me use magic on her, so I'd tried erasing one of my own scars last night with no success—there were apparently limits to what I could accomplish once a wound had healed on its own.

"You're my friend," I said. "I'm worried about you."

"Worried," she repeated. "And yet you keep inviting faeries into the house. Why, if not to build a kingdom to rule?"

Pain arrowed into my heart. This acid tone, this cynicism—this wasn't Anya. She was hurt, though, and considering how she had suffered, it made sense she would be wary of the new faeries. "They needed a home, too," I told her softly.

Her expression twisted into something vicious. "This isn't a home." Then she slammed the door in my face.

I stood there for a while, feeling like tiny knives had been jammed between my ribs.

Then I turned and trudged back to Lara, who had known all along how this was going to go.

Lara was sorting through the books when I returned. "That was fast," she said.

I sagged against the wall, pressing the heels of my palms against my eyes. "She's so angry."

"You think she shouldn't be?"

"No!" I dropped my hands, glaring at her. "She has every right to be angry. Just not . . ."

"Not at you," Lara finished. "You, the Blood princess, who has all the power and magic she never will. You, who get to choose our new ruler." Her face was too still, like she was forcing her own emotions beneath a mask.

It was too much. My eyes welled with tears. "Do you hate me, too?" I whispered. "For having all of this when you have . . ."

Lara's lips pressed together. "I don't hate you."

"I didn't ask for this," I said, having the argument anyway.

"No, the Shards gave it to you. Because you were worthy. And I was not."

The tears spilled over, trailing down my cheeks. "I think you're worthy."

"No, you don't." She shook her head when I started to argue. "Or maybe I don't. The point is, it doesn't matter. We're here, aren't we? You're a princess, I'm a lady with no influence, and Anya wakes up screaming multiple times a night. And it's not any of our faults, but we can't hurt the people whose fault it is."

I sank to the floor, bringing my knees up and wrapping my arms around them, wishing I could weep for a whole night and get the fear and grief wholly out. But my tears were already drying, like my mind couldn't let me linger in the emotion. It was always forward, forward, forward, even though I had no idea how to navigate this new life.

If I'd never come to Mistei—if I'd tried harder to sell the dagger in Tumbledown before the solstice selection—none of this would have happened. Anya and I could be roaming Enterra with money in our pockets. Oriana wouldn't have decided a human servant would be perfect for helping Lara cheat, and Lara would have ended up passing the trials on her own, the way she'd always been capable of.

The Nasties would have killed Osric instead, or maybe Elsmere's soldiers would have done it at Samhain.

Selwyn might still be alive, too.

I leaned my head back against the wall, feeling the bite of shame. All my promises to be honest, and I was still keeping that secret because I was too weak to risk losing her.

"Maybe Anya's right," Lara said, pulling me from my thoughts. She grabbed a book off the stack, then curled up on the settee, opening it over her knee. "Maybe I am too apathetic about who rules Mistei."

I bit my lip. "Do you want me to answer that?"

She gave me a dark look. "No." There was a long pause. "Do you know what Torin and Rowena asked me at the garden party?"

I knew she'd left the conversation quickly, but not what it had entailed. "What?"

"If I imagined my existence to have any value."

"*What?*"

She nodded. "I tried to ask them about their plans for Light House, and Torin said they didn't speak with magicless outcasts. And then Rowena asked if I was embarrassed to show my face in public. And then Torin said . . . that."

I wanted to gut them. "I'm so sorry."

"What are you sorry for? It's their cruelty." Her face was composed, but her grip on the book was too tight. "We're surrounded by people who think we're nothing. It's hard not to feel that way, too." I saw her swallow. "You didn't do this to me, Kenna. You didn't do it to Anya, either, and she knows that. You just need to give her space."

I blinked back the burn in my eyes, then nodded.

Knowing something and truly believing it were two different things. Anya and I had spent most of our lives at each other's sides. She knew I loved her. But Osric had ripped away the part of her that truly *believed* in the goodness at the heart of all things, and I didn't know what it would take to restore it.

But if she needed space away from the faeries filling the house—and away from me—I would give her that. Even if it was the last thing I wanted to do.

IN THE SPARRING CHAMBER THAT NIGHT, KALLEN WAS QUIETER than normal. Not that he was ever boisterous, but I'd grown used to his thoughtful lectures about proper fighting form, how magic worked, and the complicated history of the Fae. This time he limited himself to brusque comments, and while last night he'd had no problem grabbing my arms, hands, or even hips to correct my form, he seemed to be going out of his way to avoid touching me.

We'd begun incorporating weapons into our exercises. When he reached out to shift my grip on the haft of a spear, then once again pulled back before making contact, I couldn't stand it any longer. "What is it?" I asked, resting the butt of the spear against the floor.

"What is what?"

"You're distant tonight."

I felt foolish even saying it. It wasn't like we were close. He was my blackmailer turned ally and tutor. He wasn't my friend or my . . .

I can show them such imaginings, the kinds of dreams that haunt them during the day, too.

I shoved the memory of that whispered promise out of my head. Imogen had been trying to get under my skin. She'd succeeded, because now I was thinking about things I shouldn't be. Imagining reasons Kallen might be interested in touching me, when that was the last thing I ought to want.

I *didn't* want it, I told myself, and neither did Kallen. Imogen had just gotten in my head.

Kallen was quiet, watching me. I felt the heat of embarrassment creep over my skin. I had gone too far, and now what must he think of me? Probably something similar to what Drustan had: that I was jealous of his time and his focus, just a silly little human craving attention.

"Never mind," I said. "You don't owe me anything." I raised the spear, leveling the point towards him. "Let's keep going."

"No, you're right," Kallen said, surprising me. "And I do owe you something." He sighed, looking away. "I'm on edge tonight. It's not your fault."

I wondered what he thought he owed me. His honesty? If so, it was a better gift than most. "What has you on edge?"

He tipped his chin at the spear. "Show me a thrust first."

He was having me work with a short spear because, like the dagger, it was a stabbing weapon. Both could be used for slashing if needed, but he wanted me to get in the practice of always choosing the fastest and most efficient strike, whether with a weapon or my bare hands.

I settled into position with one hand holding the butt of the spear near my hip and the other angling the tip towards his eyes. He grabbed his own spear, which had been resting on the floor while he'd been correcting my form, then stepped out of range and nodded at me to proceed. I thrust the weapon quickly towards him, bringing my back hand up to my breastbone before jerking it down to rest at my hip again.

"Good," he said, circling beside me. "Another."

"You said one thrust," I complained.

"Make it ten."

I grumbled but obeyed as he watched my form. I was on number five when he started speaking again.

"Imogen found me at the party after you left."

I hesitated with the spear extended, and he lashed out and smacked it out of my hands with the shaft of his own weapon. My palms stung from the impact, and I yelped as I scrambled to pick it up.

"Don't get distracted," he chastised me.

I glared at him before resuming the exercises. "What did she say to you?"

"She said if I told her what I wanted more than anything, she would help get it for me."

I snorted. "So she was trying that line on everyone." Inside, though, I was starting to feel an odd, quivering sort of suspense. "What did you say?"

"That she couldn't give me what I wanted." His eyes tracked my final jab. "Good. Your form is improving."

I turned to face him, resting the spear on the ground again, tip pointed towards the ceiling. "Does she imagine she can win you away from Hector's side? You wouldn't betray your own brother."

"She doesn't know me. All she sees is an assassin who turned on the king the moment he could. I served one master while planning to betray him, so now she's testing to see if that might hold true elsewhere."

So few people seemed to understand a thing about Kallen. I wasn't even sure I understood him, but I knew he wasn't going to betray Hector. "She'll be disappointed."

He nodded. "I'm unsurprised she's testing me, though. Fae rulers tend to take on one of two roles to seize power—either the tyrant or the seducer. She knows she cannot rule by force as Osric did, so she must make her subjects crave her control."

An unpleasant feeling jolted through me. "She tried to seduce you?"

"I—" He stepped back a pace, then seemed to remember himself and resumed his confident stance. "No. Not like that." He hesitated before confessing the rest. "But she started . . . speculating. About what I might want."

The feeling in my stomach grew heavier, like I'd swallowed rocks. "What did she offer you?"

He shook his head. "It's laughable, anyway. That I would think—" He bit off the words, then started again. "It doesn't matter. But if I'm distant tonight, it's because of that. I've grown used to watching others from the shadows. I do not like being the subject of someone else's scrutiny."

Maybe he could see the questions that hovered on my lips, because he moved swiftly to rerack his spear, then grabbed a sword instead. "Time for a new lesson," he said. "How to fight an opponent wielding a longer blade. Get your dagger out."

Still seething with a feeling I didn't like and didn't want to name, I followed his lead, racking the spear before reaching a hand up to my hair where Caedo had been curving as a headband. The dagger flowed liquidly into my grip and solidified. I felt the hum of its excitement through our mental bond. Caedo loved these lessons for the violence they promised, and I knew we would revisit them later in shared dreams of the battlefield.

"Imogen had the same conversation with you," Kallen said as if just recalling what I'd told him. "What did she offer you?"

I felt suddenly hot all over. Why hadn't I anticipated this question? "Power and respect, mainly."

I can give you more, though.

"Mainly?"

I didn't dare answer that.

He was looking at me too closely. "And what did you tell her?"

I could pretend I didn't know what Imogen had begun to offer at the end. She hadn't finished that sentence, after all. If she hadn't actually said the words, then I could pretend the images they had conjured in my mind didn't exist, either. "That I didn't want anything she could offer me."

The air felt thick with everything we were leaving unspoken. It was hard to draw a deep breath, but I kept my gaze steady, willing Kallen not to delve further into the topic.

He nodded, then retreated towards the center of the room. The echoes of him in the mirrors moved, too. Sometimes when we fought, it felt like we were in the middle of a dance floor. "She's going to keep trying to find vulnerabilities," he said. "We'll need to be careful—and we should find out if she's offered the others anything."

Relief swept over me as we moved on from the uncomfortable moment. "Drustan and Hector want to rule too badly to be bribed."

"If she demands their total fealty, then yes, that's true." He settled into a fighting stance, then beckoned for me to approach. "But if she's clever enough to guess at secret vulnerabilities, then she's clever enough to be thinking through a number of possibilities for the endgame."

"Such as?" I asked, advancing on him with my dagger in a guard position.

"I don't know yet. I don't know what pieces of her own power she's willing to cut off and offer as consolation prizes. But if she is willing to, and if the prize is sweet enough . . . that could change things."

A chill went over me. The strength of our alliance rested on knowing we were all serving the same goal, even if the ultimate outcome was up for debate. Either Drustan or Hector would rule, and once that was determined, all of us would abide by that decision and fight for our faction in the war to come.

But what if I chose Drustan, and Hector wasn't willing to accept that? What if I chose Hector, and Drustan decided he would seize power some other way? He might choose to support Imogen in the short term if it meant eliminating other challengers for the throne in the long run.

I could see him doing that. A sacrifice now for a later victory. His hatred of Void House certainly seemed to go deep enough.

And Gweneira, too. Was Imogen genuine in believing Torin and Rowena were the best options for Light House, or might she offer Gweneira that power instead? Gweneira knew all our plans. She knew the schedule of our patrols and the exact numbers of soldiers Fire and Void had to offer. She could do a lot of damage if she turned on us.

I didn't know Hector well enough to understand what might sway him. But if there was something there, and Imogen found it... Would Kallen go with him down that road?

Now that Kallen's comment had opened the door to those doubts, they were pouring in. Every member of our alliance had secondary goals, and few of them aligned. If we couldn't trust one another, how were we supposed to fight together?

"Come on, Kenna," Kallen said, gentling his voice. "Worrying about it tonight won't fix it."

"I can't stop worrying about everything that might go wrong just because you tell me to."

"No. But you can train so you're ready when it does."

I raised my brows, dismayed at that phrasing. "*When* it goes wrong?"

"Nothing will be perfect, even if we win. There is no way for every single person on our side to get everything they want. There will be losses." His eyes looked sad. "And some dreams are so impossible, it's best to forget them before you get close enough to break yourself on them."

My throat felt thick. I wanted to ask what dreams of his seemed impossible and what he thought was capable of breaking him. But before I could open my mouth, he raised his sword. "Let's spar," he said. "We can't control everything, but the wise prepare for all ends."

"The wise prepare for all ends," I echoed softly. Even the end where I would wind up fighting for my life. If I was ready when that fate came for me, maybe I could change it.

So I took a deep breath, centered myself, and leapt at him, blade flashing.

21

I MOGEN CONTINUED HER ONSLAUGHT OF CHARM AT EVENT AFter event. Concerts, extravagant meals, wine tastings that ended up more like wine guzzlings. The Fae's appetite for stimulation was vast, and she fed it with delight. Most were more intimate affairs than the garden party had been, but as a princess I was apparently expected to attend all of them. By the seventh day of the Accord, I never wanted to see Imogen—or another glass of wine—again.

It was a vain hope. A shipment of rare delicacies had arrived from Grimveld, delivered by faeries riding enormous winged bears, and she'd scheduled a party for that evening to enjoy the offerings.

Grimveld was a country northwest of Enterra, across the mountains called the Giants' Teeth. It was an icy, forbidding place, full of jagged peaks and glaciers, where night and day were rumored to last for six months at a time. The faeries who lived in its frozen north were the traditional allies of Illusion House, according to Kallen, and everyone on the council agreed the shipment likely concealed weapons, just as Queen Briar was planning to supply Void House.

"Elsmere and Grimveld are ancient enemies," Kallen explained to Lara and me as we headed to the party. He'd been waiting outside Blood House to escort us, and though Lara was clearly unenthused, I was glad of his presence. "They pretend to be cordial, but that political tension will explode into violence the moment Grimveld's king starts listening to the wrong advisors. Mistei's conflict makes for an ideal proxy war."

"Proxy war?" I asked, unfamiliar with the term.

"A battle fought between two powers at a distance and without actually participating in the fighting." We reached an intersection, and Kallen's hand ghosted over my back briefly, guiding me to the right. "Both kingdoms would benefit from a close alliance with Mistei now that we're abandoning Osric's isolationist policies, so they'll arm the side of their choosing, watch us kill each other, and hope the outcome allows them to reap the benefits."

That sounded like meddling cowardice to me. "Didn't Hector say Briar might send troops, though?"

"Yes, she's open to direct intervention. That would be ideal—her soldiers are excellent, and we need the numbers."

Lara was frowning. "If that happens, won't Grimveld commit their troops to Imogen?"

"Likely so," Kallen acknowledged. "Then it becomes a game of numbers and timing. Whose supporters arrive first, and in what amounts."

I wondered if Kallen's head ever ached from keeping track of so many different possibilities. It was intimidating to realize how many levels of strategy he had been considering leading up to this, from blackmailing servants to negotiating with foreign powers.

The party was held in the ballroom where the Illusion trial had occurred—not that I could remember the details of what that had involved. Tall tables had been scattered throughout the center of the room, where the dancing would normally be, and faeries stood around them, eating and drinking. Marble statues lined the perimeter, and the mirrored walls duplicated them and the extravagantly dressed Fae endlessly, giving the impression of a gathering many times the size.

My attention was drawn to seven transparent statues that had been erected at the front of the room. I startled when I realized one of them was me, with wild hair and a dagger clutched in its fist.

"Ice sculptures," Kallen said. "Created by Grimveld's master carvers and mystically enchanted not to melt. They were delivered this afternoon, along with quite a few barrels of wine."

I tried not to gape. "No one's even drawn a picture of me before."

"I wouldn't be so sure of that." Kallen glanced across the room, nodded at someone, and bowed to Lara and me. "Princess Kenna, Lady Lara, it's been a pleasure. I have business to attend to, but I hope you enjoy the party."

Lara watched him go with narrowed eyes. "I don't trust him when he's polite."

"Do you ever trust him?"

"No."

I laughed despite myself.

Lara's gaze moved past me, and her face brightened. "Gweneira's here already. I need to ask her about a book she sent me." She hurried away in a flutter of silver gauze and red ribbons.

Knowing it was only a matter of time before I was dragged unwillingly into social encounters I'd rather not have, I positioned myself at a table draped with blush-pink fabric. A bowl containing large, glistening red seeds had been placed in the center, and I studied it curiously. This must be one of the delicacies sent from Grimveld.

A servant appeared holding a lily-shaped glass containing a purple liquid. "Ice wine aged beneath a glacier, my princess," she said with a curtsy.

I accepted the offering and sipped curiously, then grimaced. If there was any wine in there, it was fortified with something, because though the beverage did taste vaguely of plums, it tasted more like cleaning products.

I reached for one of the seeds instead and was displeased to discover it was encased in a slimy membrane. Hoping the taste would make up for the appearance, I popped it in my mouth.

I immediately grabbed a napkin and spit it back out.

Hector chose that moment to appear at my left elbow. "Do you know how much that seed cost?" he asked.

"Too much, considering how it tastes." Downright rancid, made worse by the mucus-like exterior. I grimaced and drank some ice wine to wash the taste away. The spirit seemed ambrosial in comparison.

When Hector named the amount, I nearly choked. "What?" I gasped.

"The plant it comes from only fruits once a decade under the light of an aurora."

"A pity it's that frequent."

He chuckled, then popped a seed in his mouth. "Tastes like gold-plated shit."

I stared at the crumpled-up napkin, which was now worth more than the majority of houses in Tumbledown. "What a waste."

He grunted. "It's coming from the crown's funds, too. At this rate, she'll beggar the realm before I can take over."

I hadn't spent much time in one-on-one conversation with Hector, and I eyed him warily. His long black hair hung loose and his tunic was simple in cut, but closer inspection revealed a pattern of interlocking crowns worked in deepest gray across the fabric. "Why is she allowed to use those funds when she isn't officially queen yet?" I asked.

"Unfortunately, she is the queen, according to Mistei's laws. She's Osric's legal successor until she's replaced."

"And we can't depose her until after the Accord."

He nodded, narrowing his eyes in Imogen's direction. "It was a clever move for many reasons. We're in a gray area, and the longer she stretches it out, the more accustomed everyone grows to her rule."

As I watched Imogen raise her ice wine in a toast, I had the uneasy thought that by forcing us to postpone the war, she might already be winning it.

LATER THAT NIGHT, AFTER FAR TOO MANY CONVERSATIONS WITH faeries aiming to interrogate, insult, or ingratiate themselves to me under the guise of small talk, I finally had a quiet moment to study the ice sculptures up close. They were unsettlingly lifelike, and the chill emanating from them made me shiver.

Rowena approached, looking icelike herself in a crystal-encrusted gown. She stopped beside me, admiring her own frozen visage. "What a pleasure to see you, Princess Kenna. Did you know this ice has been enchanted to stay frozen for two months?" She gave me a simpering smile. "Which do you suppose will last longer—your statue or you?"

Ever since the garden party, she'd had plenty of small barbs for me. Entertaining a secret fantasy of punching her, I forced myself to return that smile. "You know, I don't think they got your statue quite right."

"No?" She looked at it again, lips pursed. "What did they miss?"

"They only carved one face, when you clearly have two."

She giggled. "I'll have to tell Torin that one."

She was so strange. She clearly wanted me dead, but like Imogen, she also seemed to find me entertaining. She hadn't tried to kill me again, as far as I knew, but presumably that would be coming. Unless Imogen had ordered the Light faeries to stand down so she could try to win me over?

I glanced across the room and found Torin frowning at us. They seemed like an odd couple, one cheerful and one dour, but clearly they found something to admire in each other. "How long have you been with Torin?" I asked.

"We were born on the same day," Rowena said dreamily, moving down the line to his statue and reaching up to cup its frozen cheek. "Our mothers were cousins and best friends, and my mother had the midwife delay her labor to ensure we came into the world together. Since then, we've rarely been apart."

That was . . . a bit disturbing. "Was it a Blood House midwife?"

"It was." She turned to face me again. Faerie lights floated overhead, striking glints off her gown and making her blond hair shine. "Will you begin offering those services yourself?"

"How can I, when you believe my statue will outlast me?"

"It doesn't have to be that way. Imogen rewards her allies well."

"Imogen certainly knows how to spend," I said, casting a critical look at the nearest table with its bowl of abominable seeds. "There's a human saying about people like that. Those who pour gold like water soon find themselves thirsty."

The smile vanished from Rowena's face, and something cold and hard looked out of her eyes. Then the happy, simpering mask was back, and she was giggling behind her hand. "How quaint. Do let us know if you feel like living longer, Princess Kenna."

She hurried to Torin's side, and I watched as she whispered in his ear, then tugged him into a quick kiss. I must have struck a nerve, because that had been the true Rowena looking at me for a moment. She didn't like how much Imogen was spending—or maybe what it was being spent on.

I watched them move arm in arm through the room. Rowena's belt had a silver flask hanging from it, which I eyed suspiciously. Light faeries often adorned their attire with crystals and glass lenses—the equivalent of wearing a sword, considering their powers—but this was a more unusual fashion choice, and one that didn't bode well, considering her reputation as a poison collector.

Torin and Rowena met Ulric by a table filled with flutes of ice wine. I'd learned he was Imogen's closest advisor, as well as the uncle of Karissa, the dead Illusion candidate. That resemblance was particularly strong tonight. The amethyst-tipped pins in Ulric's curling red hair sparkled, and his tunic was a mulberry shade Karissa had often preferred. His smile as he greeted Torin and Rowena was like hers, too—slightly simpering, slightly wicked.

I watched the three of them carefully. The Light and Illusion candidates had been allies during the trials, but animosity had risen between them behind closed doors. Did their relatives hold similar grudges?

Torin leaned in to say something to Ulric, and Ulric's smile grew. Then the Illusion lord bent over Rowena's hand, kissing it. When he dropped it, I saw the glint of something in his palm, which he quickly transferred to his pocket.

The Light faeries left, heading towards the food, and I realized the flask was missing from Rowena's belt.

Ulric picked up a glass of wine and began making the rounds. I followed him from a safe distance, keeping track of who he spoke to.

It took thirty minutes of watching, but my patience finally paid off. Ulric moved past a tall table where Gweneira was standing with Lara, and though he didn't pause to speak with them, his eyes lingered on the drink next to Gweneira's hand. He moved to a nearby table, took a few sips of his own drink to lower the level, then quickly reached into his pocket, uncapped the flask, and dumped the contents into the wine.

A moment later he retraced his steps. He faked a stumble and bumped into Gweneira and Lara's table, interrupting their conversation. He set his wine down next to Gweneira's, apologizing profusely for the clumsiness, and upon their assurance no damage had been done, picked up his glass before moving on.

Except he hadn't grabbed his glass. He'd picked up Gweneira's.

Gweneira said something quiet that made Lara laugh, then smiled and raised the wine to her lips.

A panicked surge of magic burst out of me, freezing her arm before she could tip the drink onto her tongue. Alarm flashed over her face. I felt her straining against my magical hold, but then the alarm was replaced by a look of realization, and she stopped fighting and swept her eyes over the room instead.

I pushed my way through the crowd. "Don't drink that," I said, releasing the hold on her arm.

She slowly lowered the glass to the table.

"Why not?" Lara asked, looking puzzled.

Gweneira looked like she already knew. "Who did you see?"

"Ulric. Rowena handed him a flask, and he poured it into his drink before switching the glasses."

Gweneira didn't react outwardly, other than a twitch of her fingers on the stem of her glass. "Doing it at a public event is bold."

Lara leaned in, lowering her voice. "Are you saying that's . . ."

"Poison." Gweneira frowned down at the purple alcohol. "Something with a delayed effect, presumably, since toppling over dead at a party would ruin the mood."

She was far too calm about this. "Have they tried this before?" I asked.

"Oh, we try to kill each other every chance we get. I sleep with guards in my room and only eat what I prepare with my own hands."

"It's not just their doing if Ulric is involved," I said.

"Imogen wants Light House united and subservient to her before the Accord ends." Her expression was thoughtful as she tapped her fingernail against the glass. "She promised to guarantee my safety if I vowed fealty to Torin and Rowena and stopped aiding Drustan. I told her she's naïve if she thinks she can control them to that extent. Apparently she's given up on me."

Another bribe from Imogen. "She offered to protect me from them, too. Drustan and Hector are too important to kill, but apparently you and I are fair game."

"Why would they be any more important than you?" Lara demanded.

"They have armies," I pointed out. "And she said it would be easy to make my death look like an accident, since I'm new to being Fae."

"None of the candidates for the throne can be seen starting this war during the Accord," Gweneira told Lara. "If I die, that can be framed as a Light House succession issue. If Kenna dies, there's enough plausible deniability for Imogen to get away with it. Any of the others?" She shook her head. "Imogen will try diplomacy first."

Lara was looking increasingly angry. "What are you going to do?"

"Do?"

"With the poison."

"See if an herbalist can identify what's in it," Gweneira said. "I'd like to know how they envision me dying."

"Why not slip it to Rowena instead?" Lara asked. "Torin will think Ulric turned on them."

Gweneira gave Lara an impressed look. "That would be an excellent idea . . . if Torin and Rowena hadn't been watching us this entire time."

Lara's eyes widened. She started to turn, but Gweneira stilled her with a palm on her hand. "Don't. They're just pretending to look at the sculptures." Her smile was wry. "I'm so used to them glaring at me that I didn't even think about it until Kenna stopped me from drinking. But they saw Ulric swap the glasses, which means we won't be able to frame him."

My skin crawled. I hadn't noticed them watching, either.

Lara looked down at where Gweneira was touching her. "It was a nice thought," she muttered.

"It was." Gweneira squeezed Lara's hand before letting go. "Exciting as this party has been, I believe I will retire early." She smiled at me, though there was tension around her eyes. "Thank you for the rescue, Kenna. This is the last party I'll be drinking at."

She left, glass in hand. I looked for Torin and Rowena and found them beside Imogen's ice sculpture, scowling as they watched Gweneira exit the ballroom. Rowena's gaze snapped back to me, and her eyes narrowed.

I smiled at her, raised my hand, and waggled my fingers. Then I turned my back, vowing not to drink any more wine at these events, either.

22

Hector hosted a party on the eighth night of the Accord. It was a surprise to receive the invitation, inked in silver on black paper. Void House didn't host many events, and Hector in particular had been absent from most of the more frivolous court functions. I couldn't imagine him presiding over the typical drinks mixed with poisonous small talk.

It turned out to be an intimate gathering, consisting of Lara and me, a handful of Void nobles, and several Earth faeries. The reception room was candlelit and opulent, with furniture upholstered in black-and-silver damask, a large crystalline globe containing decanters of alcohol, and shelves full of abstract sculptures. The obsidian walls reflected wavering pinpricks of flame, and shadowy mist drifted over the floor, coiling around our ankles.

One of the guests was Lady Rhiannon, a powerful Earth faerie and Talfryn's mother. She was regal-looking, with eloquent dark eyes and long black hair she wore in braids. Her green velvet gown was embroidered with three golden birds, and I remembered with a pang seeing Talfryn wearing a similar design the night he'd died.

"Lady Rhiannon," Lara said, squeezing her hands. "It's good to see you."

"You, as well." Rhiannon's expression grew shadowed. "Earth House has lost much."

Lara looked down at her feet. "I'm sorry. Talfryn was a good friend."

"The Shards can be cruel." Lady Rhiannon turned to me. "Princess Kenna. We have not officially met."

"I'm sorry for your loss," I said, feeling wretched for being evidence of what the Shards had chosen not to do for Talfryn. "Your son was always kind to me."

"Kindness is rarely rewarded." Her eyes glistened, and she quickly covered them with her hand. A moment later, she straightened, having composed herself once more.

It was monstrous how genuine emotions—like grief, like love—had become too dangerous to express in Mistei.

"Oriana is not coming tonight," Rhiannon told Lara.

Lara's posture grew stiff. "I assumed."

"She dishonors the title of mother, the way she dishonors the title of princess." Rhiannon's tone was suddenly vicious. "She did not want me to come, either, since it might shatter the illusion of neutrality to accept Void's hospitality."

"How can she say that when she attends Imogen's events?" I asked.

"Oriana believes in traditions. She will treat Imogen as Osric's successor until that is no longer the case."

Hector arrived at my elbow, looking elegant in black brocade worked with a pattern of iron-gray vines. "It won't be the case for long," he said. "And Oriana will learn what comes of disguising cowardice as tradition."

It was a shocking thing to say in front of one of the foremost ladies of Earth House. Rhiannon didn't seem horrified, though. She signaled a servant, grabbed a glass of red wine off their tray, and raised it. "To the end of tradition."

Hector didn't pick up a glass of his own, but he did bow briefly. "I'm glad you're here, Lady Rhiannon."

"I'm not glad of much these days, but this is better than staying in that cage Oriana calls a house." She sipped the wine, then grimaced and set it aside. "Wine is good for toasts, but it goes to my head too quickly."

"There's tea in the corner," Hector said. "Our servants would be happy to pour you some."

"I can pour my own tea, thank you." Rhiannon extended her arm to Lara. "Will you join me, Lady Lara?"

Lara nodded, then took Rhiannon's arm. They moved away together, shadows swirling in their wake.

"A party with Earth House," I told Hector. "How interesting." And Drustan, who was always dancing and flirting strategically with Earth ladies, was nowhere to be seen.

He grunted. "Surprised I know how to socialize?"

"You don't seem fond of it in general."

"It's the usual company, not the activity itself, that bothers me."

Una arrived then, clad in a midnight dress with feathers at the shoulders. "You don't like the activity much, either," she said, munching on a tiny chocolate cake.

"Remind me not to name you to any diplomatic positions," he replied. "You'll tell our allies I despise them, and then where will we be?"

His quick, dark wit still caught me off guard when it appeared. Hector looked ferocious normally, all sharp edges and frowns. He seemed more likely to stab someone than joke with them, no matter how caustic the humor.

Una smiled. "You don't despise Queen Briar."

"Because Briar is actually competent."

The mention of Elsmere's queen intrigued me. "How long have you been in communication with her?"

"Personally? Since Beltane. Kallen kept up a correspondence with her before that, though. He had a feeling King Godwin was growing weary of the responsibility, so he made connections with a few possible candidates. Briar seemed the least likely, but she was also the one with the biggest ideas. And then it happened faster than we imagined."

The mention of Kallen made me glance around the room, and I fought a surge of disappointment when I didn't see him. "How did he even communicate with her with the wards up?"

"Pigeons."

I snorted, but Hector was looking at me like it wasn't a joke. "Seriously?" I asked.

"Osric's wards were aimed at faeries and humans, not animals."

Messenger pigeons seemed so mundane for the Fae. But that must be precisely the point. The Fae disregarded everything they considered beneath them.

Hector was regarding me thoughtfully. "You're the reason we were ready when that transition happened."

I grimaced. "Kallen's blackmail, yes."

He shrugged. "It's effective." He didn't look sorry, but honestly, I liked that better than him pretending otherwise.

"I didn't know what I was telling Kallen at the time," I admitted. "I didn't even know what Elsmere was. I was just trying to make him go away."

Una raised a hand to her mouth, covering her smile. "You should tell him that."

"I'm sure he already knows." I watched Rhiannon and Lara begin a discussion with an imposing-looking Void lady over the tea tray. "Were Drustan and Gweneira invited?"

"They were," Hector confirmed. "But their invitations may have had a small error in the start time."

I bit the inside of my cheek. Hector was starting his politicking early. "Drustan won't like that."

"Drustan doesn't dictate my schedule or who I speak with. On that note," he said, reaching for a scroll tucked into the pouch at his belt, "I have something for you."

I accepted it, studying the black wax seal. "Another policy?" Like Drustan, he'd sent a few—scribbled promises about everything from border security to a more robust trial system—and I'd already received a letter from both of them today.

"Details on how I see our relationship with Elsmere progressing beyond the war. We've been isolated for so long that we're barely aware of what's happening in the larger world. We need a strong ally before our return to greater visibility."

I had no idea what was happening in the larger world, either. We hadn't been taught much in school other than the details of Enterra's history and a bit about our immediate neighbors. And that was only the human world we'd learned about—I knew nothing about faerie politics. I tucked the scroll into my skirt pocket. "I'll read it."

"How have you liked the others I've sent?" he asked, watching me closely.

I hesitated. "They all sound fine."

"Fine," he echoed, his habitual frown deepening.

"Good, even." Like Drustan, Hector wasn't just touching on trade and warfare—he was making promises about changelings and protections for servants and humans. The two of them were in agreement about a surprising number of things, considering how much they despised each other.

"But?" he pressed.

Nervousness fluttered through me. "But I don't know you. And..." I trailed off.

Hector watched me, waiting.

Kallen must have spoken to him by now. What was the best way to bring this up? "I heard a rumor," I settled on.

A violent expression tore across his face, and he looked away. "So I was told."

I swallowed, feeling even more anxious. "Kallen says it isn't true." And I trusted his word more than most, but...

"But?" Hector said, as if he had intuited my thoughts.

I took a deep breath, then squared my shoulders. "I need to hear what happened from you."

Drustan had been vague about the specifics, but Mistei was full of enough monsters that I'd filled in the gaps. *He likes them a little less noble. A little more defenseless.*

Fact and fiction blurred in Mistei, but this was a principle I would not bend on. If Hector was a predator as Drustan had implied—if he was anywhere close to it—I would choose Drustan as king. And if Kallen had lied to me on Hector's behalf, made excuses for a crime he knew had occurred, I would be done with him, too.

The silence felt heavy. Una was watching Hector, though I couldn't read her expression.

"You might as well ask me to cut my heart out of my chest," Hector said, low and fierce. He turned and stalked away.

Una looked after her brother, a crease between her brows, before her gaze snapped back to me. She did not look friendly. "Sit with me, Princess Kenna."

I nodded, nerves prickling with apprehension, and followed her to two chairs tucked into a corner.

She didn't waste time with small talk. "You ask much of him."

"He wants to be king. I won't ask less."

She tapped her fingers against her knees. Her dark brown eyes were fixed on me like she was trying to look beneath my skin. She hadn't lost any of the controlled intensity that had made her such a ferocious competitor during the trials, and it took effort not to squirm under that stare. "Kallen thinks he should tell you. I was shocked when he suggested it."

"Why?"

"Because Void is a house of secrets." She paused. "He thinks highly of you. It's . . . unusual."

"Kallen?" I felt far too pleased by the thought, though I wasn't sure what I'd done to deserve it. "Where is he tonight?"

"Spying on a musicale Rowena is hosting." She pulled her shiny black braid over her shoulder, toying with the end of it. "What do you think about Kallen?"

I had no idea how to even begin answering that question. "I respect him," I said, hoping she couldn't tell how flustered I was by this line of inquiry. "He's been . . ."

What had he been? Terrifying, at first. Controlling, violent, occasionally cruel. But those layers had gradually peeled away, and now I was left looking at someone I didn't quite know how to explain.

Una was still waiting for my answer, so I fumbled for words that might start to define the edges of whatever moved between Kallen and me. "He's honest with me when he doesn't need to be. He's killed to protect me. And . . . and I would kill for him, too."

How else to explain all of it? The uneasy fascination that drew me to him, the way he could hold my hand so gently while promising to destroy my enemies . . . And the sadness in him, that called to me, too. There was a loneliness in his eyes that felt familiar, though I suspected his was of a magnitude far greater than my own.

So, yes, I would kill for Kallen. Even if I didn't understand him yet. Even if sometimes I worried about what it would mean if I did.

Una angled her head slightly. "Do you fear him?"

"No." Privately, though, I acknowledged that wasn't quite true. Because something about him frightened me, but it wasn't what she was asking about. Una wanted to know how I felt about the notoriously violent King's Vengeance, and I was no longer afraid of that constructed monster.

When had that happened? While we were dancing, maybe. Or possibly even before that. It had been a gradual slip into a new way of thinking about him.

"Maybe that's why," Una said, tone contemplative.

"Why what?"

"Tell me what you want to do with Blood House," she said, switching the subject.

"I—"

"Your ethos. How you intend to move forward."

Una was testing me with this conversation; that much was clear. She felt protective of Hector and Void House's secrets, and she was trying to find out if I was worthy of them.

Would it be more clever to lie or dance around the issue? Maybe. But Kallen seemed to like my honesty, so maybe Una would, too. "Blood House will be a shelter," I told her. "A place where the survivors make our own rules and where we come from doesn't matter."

"You don't care about preserving the magic? Breeding for strength the way the other houses do?"

My laugh sounded wild. "I'm the only one with Blood magic. What am I going to do, repopulate the entire house myself?" That wasn't a role I'd been sure about wanting even before coming to Mistei, and though I could imagine having a child in some hazy, distant future, I couldn't imagine having one in Mistei as it was today—much less turning into a broodmare for the sake of preserving my new magic.

The Fae thought and acted on extremely long timelines, though.

I could conceivably have a few children with another Noble Fae, and without Osric to banish them as changelings, they could grow up safe in my house before finding partners and having more children. As the centuries passed, there would be more and more faeries who had inherited at least a fraction of Blood's power.

I could have more than a few children now that I was no longer human, I realized with an unpleasant shock. Fae births were rarer than human births, but I could still have dozens of children if I wanted them and lived long enough. Hundreds of them. An army, sprung entirely from my flesh.

The idea was viscerally disturbing. Surely that wasn't what the Shards had intended when they'd told me to restore the balance? If so, they were going to be disappointed.

I shook my head. "There's no point trying to be like the other houses. So we're going to be something else. Something better."

Una had been hard to read throughout this conversation—there was definitely an echo of Kallen in both her abrupt questions and the reserve she wore so well. To my surprise, though, she smiled after my last words. "I think I understand now." She tossed her braid over her shoulder and stood, smoothing her palms over her black skirt. "Enjoy your evening, Princess Kenna."

I sat in silence for a few minutes after she left, watching the movements of faeries through the crowd. Void faeries speaking with Earth faeries, Una whispering something in Lara's ear, Hector guiding Rhiannon towards an empty corner of the room. A party was never just a party, like a dance was never just a dance.

Something gold caught in my peripheral vision. I turned to see what it was, thinking Drustan had finally arrived in gleaming raiment, but the doorway was empty. Candlelight reflected off a framed mirror, though, and I saw the room doubled in it. Twice the scheming, and it would only intensify once he did arrive.

I rubbed my temples, suddenly exhausted. If Kallen were here, we could lurk in a corner debating philosophy, but he wasn't, and that wasn't what a princess should do, anyway. I should be making connections.

I was so tired, though.

Lara was visible in the mirror, a splash of red in the largely dark room. She caught my eyes in the reflection and beckoned. I sighed and stood up.

Princesses weren't allowed to be tired. And Mistei's schemes didn't stop for anyone.

23

THE HALLS OF BLOOD HOUSE FELT MELANCHOLY LATE AT night.

It was one of the nebulous hours before dawn when time seemed to stretch out impossibly long. Kallen had worked me into exhaustion during tonight's lesson, testing my defensive strikes until my arms and legs were trembling, but sleep had eluded me afterwards. As I walked the empty ground floor, the leather satchel at my side brushed softly against my skirt. It held scrolls from Hector and Drustan; if I had to be awake, I might as well make use of this time.

In Earth House, there would have been a few faeries around at this hour—some of the Noble Fae rose with the twilight and slept with the dawn—but most of my house members followed the schedule of servants. I would probably wake early with them, regardless of tonight's insomnia. That had happened frequently when I'd been serving Lara—up late for one of her parties, then rising early for my chores. I'd gotten too used to getting by on scraps of sleep.

At least being awake had one benefit. The last few nights, I'd listened for Anya's nightmares and was relieved when she seemed to be having fewer. She still looked exhausted, and she was still avoiding me, but Triana was keeping an eye on her, so I was trying my best to leave her alone.

For the most part. I stopped at the kitchen to grab a hunk of cheddar cheese, sliced it carefully before covering it with cloth and placing it on a silver tray, then detoured to a nearby study to grab a book I'd noticed the other day. It was a small illuminated manuscript filled with Fae poetry, with tiny, complex illustrations around each initial letter. Anya had dreamed of learning how to illuminate manuscripts; maybe this would remind her of that hope.

I returned upstairs to leave the tray outside her door. The blanket I'd left in the morning was still there, along with some sachets of bath herbs from the previous night's offering, though they were positioned haphazardly, as if she'd inspected them before tossing them aside. My heart ached as I nestled the cheese and book beside them. If she didn't want to talk to me or accept my gifts, at least she knew I was thinking about her.

I returned downstairs. The ceiling crystals provided a faint red illumination wherever I moved, dousing behind me. It made the violent colors of the tapestries look even more saturated, and the veins in the marble floor, which appeared garnet red during the day, seemed black as ink.

I finally heard signs of life—splashing and laughing, the delicate sound of a lyre. I followed the sounds to a bathing room I hadn't had a chance to linger in yet. The tiled floor was slick, and steam rose from three hot springs, thickening the air. Carved gargoyle heads poured water into the pools, and a curtain of blood cascaded down the back wall before disappearing into the hidden channels that circulated through the house.

An Illusion satyr was seated beside one pool, plucking a lyre for a dancing Light nymph who was splashing in and out of the water, the glow of her scantily clad body making the drops of water shine like diamonds. At the next pool, three people were soaking their feet. The first was our new head servant, Nadine. The chatelaine at the dryad's belt sparkled in the humidity, and with her skirt hiked up to her knees, I could see lines of brown bark swirling over her golden skin.

I was surprised to recognize Maude beside her, dressed in a voluminous nightdress like she'd been tempted from her bed for an after-midnight soak. Next to her was her friend Bruno, with his distinctive white beard and shiny bald head. They spoke in quick flickers of their fingers while Nadine watched with a smile on her face, laughing periodically at Bruno's jokes. Like many servants, the dryad had learned the language of the humans in order to work with them.

My melancholy eased. The five of them had come from different backgrounds, yet here they were, enjoying one another's company. Even Maude had softened, relaxing more with every day of rest and security. Seeing her with the Underfae was evidence of what I'd known about her since the day we'd met—that as wary as she was, she would still take a chance on a stranger.

The nymph saw me and squeaked, nearly toppling into the pool. The satyr abandoned his lyre to steady her, and then the three Underfae scrambled to their feet. Maude raised her brows and kept soaking, though Bruno made a brief attempt to rise before grunting and signing, "Damn my knees."

"Princess Kenna," Nadine said, curtsying deeply. "How may we serve you?"

I held up my hands, dismayed to have ruined the moment. "I was just walking by. Don't let me disrupt you."

"You must need something," Nadine said.

I forced a smile. "No, thank you. Please, return to what you were doing. I'm just heading to the library."

I turned and left before she could ask whatever question was hovering on her lips. *Will you need a drink in the library? Are you satisfied with the selection of books? May I bring you anything additional?*

A bruised feeling settled in my chest. I wasn't one of the servants anymore. I couldn't plop down next to them and soak my tired feet while we gossiped about the Noble Fae.

The library was a cozy one, with shelves taking up every inch of wall space and a seating area in the middle. I sat on a striped red-and-gray couch and pulled two scrolls out of the bag, then cracked the orange seal of the first letter and started reading.

I'd asked Drustan and Hector to be specific about their plans for the humans who lived in Mistei, as well as how they intended to interact with villages like Tumbledown now that the borders were open. Both had good policies, I was pleased to see. There would be no more forced servitude or mutilations, and the humans already in Mistei would be given the opportunity to return home laden with gold. Both offered assistance with the evacuation, so long as it was done quickly. Every faerie would be needed once the battle broke.

The humans could leave Mistei as soon as tomorrow, now that escort had been arranged. I wondered if Maude would decide to leave, after all. If Triana would, or if her kindness and perpetual desire to be useful would make her stay to help those still in need of shelter. There were humans in Mistei who hadn't defected to Blood House, people who would never believe anything a faerie said—even if that faerie offered escape.

Hector and Drustan anticipated that as well, and both proposed that any humans who remained be compensated for their continuing service. Drustan was of the opinion that each house should be responsible for sheltering and paying a portion of them, while Hector believed the humans should be housed separately, with their salaries paid by the crown.

I traced my fingers over the slanting lines of Hector's writing and the elegant curl of Drustan's, torn between the two points of view. Hector offered them a measure of independence, and I would fear for any human assigned to Light or Illusion House. But Drustan argued that each house should be actively involved in rectifying the damage they'd done. *So long as someone continues monitoring their welfare,* he wrote, *I believe accountability is the best path forward.*

Ultimately, I decided Hector's path was the wisest. Even with someone checking on the humans, the Fae were too cruel and duplicitous to be trusted. If someone like Torin was responsible for the upkeep of those servants . . . I shuddered to think what might happen to them.

The second half of each letter delved into their approach for building relations with humans outside our borders. Hector was open to reestablishing contact with the villages across the bog as soon as the upcoming civil war was over, but Drustan was more cautious, saying the patterns of abuse were so entrenched in Fae thinking that we needed time to address that before risking more lives. And in that instance, I found myself agreeing with Drustan.

Dismay crept over me. The answer to who I should choose as king hadn't come any clearer, and it had been this way with every policy I'd read so far. I tossed the paper aside, then rubbed the heels of my palms into my gritty eyes. "I'm not equipped for this," I muttered.

Caedo tightened affectionately around my arm. *It's boring.*

"Boring?" I laughed tiredly, dropping my hands. "I suppose you prefer other activities to reading."

There are better stories to be read in the spill of entrails.

I made a face. "I would prefer not to gut my allies." Then I sighed and leaned my head back against the couch. "Why can't I just choose?"

Because if I chose wrong, people would die. Our armies might fight differently, depending on who led them. Our alliance might splinter.

You are struggling with this role. This voice in my head was different, coming from a distance, and I twitched in surprise. The Blood Shard was usually maddeningly silent, answering occasional questions but mostly seeming content to let me fumble my way forward unaccompanied.

I hadn't been communicating actively with the Shard, and the reminder of exactly how powerful it was unsettled me. This was a sliver of a god. Even as an echo of something greater, it could peer inside my head and pull out my thoughts.

Oh, now you're interested in how I'm doing in this position? I asked mentally, feeling the sting of resentment.

I am always interested.

But now you're willing to intervene.

I don't intervene in Fae matters.

I ran my hands over my face again, dragging the skin under my eyes down with my fingertips. *I don't understand. You intervened in the trials.*

That was different.

Of course it was. Everything in Mistei had a condition and an exception.

You are the vessel for some of the goddess's power, the Shard said, apparently deciding to appease my frustration. *I helped gift it to you, and I can teach you some small things about using it, but everything must be done by your will.*

Sometimes I felt like I stood on the edge of a vast lake of knowledge and history, and everything I knew about the world existed in the ripple spreading from a single toe I'd dipped into it. The Shard, the tree, the house, and now me—all of us were fragments of something so large I couldn't imagine it. *What was the goddess's name?* I asked.

Things like that have no name as you would understand it.

My head was starting to pound, and I felt the foggy nausea that came from lack of sleep. *Why are you talking to me?*

You are conflicted, the Shard said. *I wish to know why. I want to know how you understand your truth.*

What was my truth? I stared at the bookshelves, trying to put words to the gnawing anxiety that had settled permanently in my gut. *I have all this power now*, I told the Shard, *but I'm still just . . . me. I'm not any wiser for it, or a better politician, or anything. I don't know how to restore the balance. You created me, and then . . .* I trailed off mentally, not sure if I should say the rest.

The Shard waited. I felt its attention as a soft throb at the front of my skull, like a small creature breathing in and out.

I sighed, shoulders slumping. *You brought me back from the dead, and then you just . . . left me. Like it doesn't matter to you if I fail.*

You are afraid, the Shard murmured.

The Shard had always encouraged me to be honest. Or the Blood Tree had, anyway, but they were part of the same thing, like individual mushrooms sprouting off the mother plant. Probably the nameless goddess had liked honesty, and that's why I was being asked the same question over and over in different forms: Do you regret it?

What was fear but regret about something that hadn't come to pass yet? The confession tumbled out of me. *What if I can't change Mistei for the better? What if more people die because of me? What if I'm not Fae enough for this role?*

You wish to be more like the Fae?

No, I said instinctively.

I was envious of them, though. They moved through the world like it owed them something. I wanted that certainty. I wanted confidence, and power, and revenge against my enemies—not just Imogen,

Torin, or Rowena, but all the Fae who would look better under a few shovelfuls of dirt. Everyone I hated already and the ones I would learn to hate in the future.

Imogen had told me the Fae loved revelry, but they loved death just as much.

Maybe I do want to be like them, I confessed.

Interesting, the Shard said.

The pressure in my head vanished. I was left alone in an empty room, no closer to answers than I had been before.

HUMANS FILLED THE INNER HALL OF BLOOD HOUSE. THEY WORE sturdy boots and traveling cloaks, and each had a leather bag filled with gold from my vaults. The fountain burbled in their midst, and though normally they would have given that crimson pool a wide berth, the atmosphere was so jovial that no one seemed to mind the spilling gore.

My eyelids were heavy and my head felt thick—I'd only managed a few hours of sleep—but it was impossible not to get caught up in that energy. A handful of soldiers from Fire and Void would be arriving shortly to escort the humans across the bog to their new lives, and the prospect of escape had made them giddy.

Triana approached me. Unlike the others, she wore a red housedress and slippers—because she wasn't leaving today. She wanted to stay for one more week, just after the midway point of the month, to convince as many humans as she could to believe in Blood House's promises. Drustan had told me he was willing to arrange for a second escort then, though that would be the last until after the war was done.

"Are any more coming?" I asked Triana.

She shook her head. "There are thirteen who don't feel certain yet. They worry the escorts will execute them."

I wasn't sure how to furnish the proof they needed that this evacuation would have a good outcome. Perhaps a letter from someone happily resettled? But if that wasn't enough and they wanted to stay indefinitely, Blood House would still be a home for them. "Maude?" I asked.

Triana made a face. "Insisting on staying with me."

It was unsurprising. I took a deep breath and asked the question I dreaded most. "And Anya?"

"She wouldn't open her door. I think she's still asleep."

I felt a shameful sense of relief. She hadn't answered my knock, either, which meant Anya was about to miss this opportunity to leave. Wanting her to stay was selfish, though, so I hurried upstairs to wake her and ask what she wanted to do.

The cheese and book had vanished at some point early this morning. I knocked on Anya's door, but there was no response, so I turned the knob and poked my head in. Her room was dark and smelled of sour wine and unwashed skin. The blankets were piled at the foot of the bed, but Anya wasn't in them—she was asleep at the desk, head planted on the open book.

I stepped forward, and something crunched beneath my boot. Shards of a shattered wineglass.

My chest felt tight with a too-familiar worry. "Anya?" I murmured.

She twitched, then started shaking. Her mouth opened around a silent scream.

"Anya," I repeated, louder.

She sat upright with a gasp, and the chair nearly toppled over. I rushed forward to steady it, and Anya made a guttural noise and leapt away, falling to the floor.

Horrified at having frightened her, I crouched, holding up my empty hands. "It's just me. It's just Kenna."

Her face was wet. She shook her head frantically. "I'm not asleep. I'm not."

"You're awake," I said soothingly. "You just woke up."

More tears spilled over. "How do I tell?"

I couldn't imagine not knowing the difference between sleep and waking, but she'd spent six months being tortured with illusions. How could I convince her she was safe?

"Do you remember when we were thirteen?" I asked. "We found blackberries in the forest south of town."

She sniffled, wiping her nose on the back of her hand. Her eyes were still overflowing, but she was listening.

"You were already tall enough to get the ones near the top if you stood on tiptoes," I continued. "I was annoyed because I wasn't growing nearly as much. So I rolled a log over and stood on top of it—and immediately fell straight into the bramble patch. My arms were scratched up, and after you pulled me out, you nearly fell over laughing."

It was funny which memories became dear with time. Tumbling into the blackberry brambles had been humiliating at thirteen, and I'd cried and shouted at Anya before we'd made up. But now I thought about warm sunshine, berry juice on my chin, and a friend who could laugh at me while wiping my scratches clean.

"You never did grow tall enough," Anya whispered.

I chuckled, the sound barely a breath, because there was an echo of the Anya I recognized. "I didn't," I confirmed. "You're awake, Anya."

She stood, and I followed. "I wasn't supposed to sleep at all," she said, bracing a hand on the desk.

"What do you mean?"

She shook her head. The skin under her eyes was exhaustion-bruised, and she was swaying. When she rubbed her forehead, her hand trembled. She looked like she might collapse.

She wasn't in any state to cross the bog. Again I felt selfish relief, because I wasn't ready to let her go yet. There would be another evacuation in a week—we could discuss it over the next few days and figure out which path would be best for her, whether that was staying under my protection in Mistei or trying to pick up the pieces of her old life back in Tumbledown.

"Why don't you lie down?" I suggested. "I can send up some warm milk."

She hugged her arms around herself. "Don't."

A ripple went through the house's magic and resonated in my head, as if a fly had flown into the edge of a sticky web and I was the spider sensing the vibrations. The soldiers from Void and Fire House had arrived to escort the humans to freedom.

Give her space, I reminded myself. "All right," I said, stepping backwards. "But you can send for anything you need. Please get some rest, Anya."

She didn't reply.

24

Imogen hosted a silvered ball near Illusion House to commemorate the tenth day of the Accord.

The halls were brighter here, flickering with candles and lined with an off-white marble veined with dusty green and pink. The tiles beneath my feet were the inverse, alternating pink and green squares with gold veins. Illusion was the house that most favored beauty, and there was more art here than I'd seen anywhere else in Mistei—tapestries, paintings, draperies, vases stuffed with flowers, alcoves full of statuary. Candelabra burned on decorative tables, and more candles floated overhead. Pixies flitted between those wax tapers, showering sweet-smelling golden dust on us as we processed towards the ballroom. The sheer volume of decoration should have made the area look cluttered, but instead it all fit perfectly together, drawing the eye from one attraction to the next seamlessly.

"Have you been here before?" I asked Lara.

"A few times," she said, fluttering her crimson fan, "but Illusion didn't host as many events as the other houses during Osric's time.

Normally a king would have named a new prince or princess to run the house, but he didn't trust anyone to step into his old position."

Paranoid even towards his own house members. "Did he stay here?"

She shook her head. "There's a royal wing behind the throne room. Not every ruler in Fae history used it, but most did."

Gweneira came up beside us. "So you have been reading my history books."

Lara's cheeks were already rouged, but I could have sworn they grew even rosier. "Just doing my best to make up for the years I spent dodging my tutors. You look lovely tonight, Gweneira."

Gweneira wore a formal dress rather than the tunic and trousers she normally preferred, and the glittering ice-white attire sparkled in the candlelight. A glass crown topped her short brown hair. "Never as lovely as you," she told Lara. "The bards will invent dozens of poetic titles for you when they tell the story of this era." She grinned quickly at me. "And for you, of course, Princess Kenna."

"No need to flatter me," I said dryly. There was no denying that Lara was far lovelier than most of the faeries in this corridor. With her shiny black hair held up by ruby combs and her voluptuous figure highlighted by a plunging scarlet gown, she'd been catching almost every passing eye.

My own garnet-hued dress was a style I'd come to favor, with sleeves that culminated in points over the backs of my hands and a flat neckline that knew better than to try to make much of my bust. The main drama was in the back of the dress, where a plunging cowl revealed the line of my spine to my waist. With my hair pinned up, everyone could see Caedo coiled as a snake around my throat, silver tail winding down my bared back. I felt as fine as I ever had.

Lara and Gweneira fell into conversation. I listened with half my attention, looking for familiar faces. The crowd grew closer as we funneled towards the entrance to the ballroom, and this was one of the moments when I regretted being shorter than the average Fae. The Shards had gifted me eternal life; could they truly not have offered me any extra height?

The pressure eased as we entered the ballroom, and I stifled a gasp at the beautiful sight. Thousands of candles floated above, their warm light bringing out golden tones in the parquet floor. Most walls in Mistei were stone, but these had been covered with wooden paneling painted with scenes from an airborne hunt. An orchestra played from a rainbow-shielded gallery overhead.

Faeries were already swirling in intricate patterns on the dance floor, while others gossiped and strolled along the edges. Heavily laden banquet tables lined one entire wall, while the opposite held deep-cushioned chairs for anyone who wearied of dancing. The air smelled of lilacs.

Imogen presided over the room from a glass throne, with Torin and Rowena flanking her and armed guards standing behind—because no event was without guards these days, despite the chains crossing our palms. She sipped from a goblet, surveying the room with obvious pride. The mood was exuberant, as always at Imogen's parties, and as I watched a laughing couple nearly careen off the dance floor, it was clear many faeries were already inebriated.

Only twenty days left in the Accord. We drank and danced our way towards destruction.

"You should smile," Lara said, tapping me lightly with her fan. "You look gloomy."

I forced a smile to my lips. "Better?"

She eyed me. "Not particularly."

Gweneira extended her hand. "Lady Lara, may I have the honor of your first dance?"

Lara curtsied. "I would be delighted." She accepted Gweneira's hand, and the two headed for the floor.

Lara would be dancing all night. Though her loss of magic had caused her to be ostracized by some faeries, the combination of her beauty and notoriety, the novelty of the situation, and the support of both the Blood princess and faeries like Gweneira had ensured her continuing popularity.

I spotted Drustan standing by the refreshment table, clad in apricot velvet with gold piping. I had promised not to let our history get in the way of the cause, so I reluctantly made my way over to him.

"You owe me more policies," I said as I scooped punch into my cup from a crystal bowl. Enough faeries had been drinking from it already that I assumed it wasn't poisoned.

He gave me a sardonic look. "Hello, Princess Kenna. How are you this evening?"

"Must we engage in empty pleasantries every time?" I asked, facing him fully. "We see each other often enough."

"Do we?" He raised his brows. "Not as frequently as we used to."

"I see you at all of Imogen's parties," I said, ignoring the implication.

"Then perhaps not as frequently as I'd like." His eyes grew heavy-lidded, and he lightly touched his tongue to his lower lip.

I scowled. "Don't play the flirt."

"It's a public event," he said, still smoldering away. "I have to play the flirt."

It was obnoxious how good he looked. How much time had he spent practicing that expression in a mirror? Had he deliberately pulled that small section of hair out of the neat tail he'd tied it back in? "And why is that?" I asked.

"Because I've been doing it for hundreds of years. Loyalty isn't won with swords alone."

"It's won by making people want to fuck you?"

"Sometimes."

I rolled my eyes, then sipped my punch, hoping the action disguised the stab of hurt at hearing him admit it so openly. The liquid was harsher than I'd expected—Imogen seemed determined to keep everyone nearly insensate this month. "Is there a reason you're admitting this strategy? It doesn't make me think better of you."

"Doesn't it?" That seductive expression dimmed. "You wanted me to be honest with you. My power has been built on making connections. Making others want something, whether that's freedom, revenge, a new world, revelry . . . or me."

I took another drink, even knowing I should be more like Kallen and keep my head clear. "That's what you did with me."

"Yes and no."

I hadn't expected him to admit it so readily. The *yes* stung, but that *no* was trying to dig its claws into the tender parts of my heart, too, the parts that wished some of what we'd shared—any of it—had been real. "You admit you seduced me for access to Earth House?"

"Yes," he said, gaze steady. "But I didn't need to take it as far as I did. I did that because I wanted to."

I looked away, watching the dancers as I processed the multifaceted pain of that admission. The swirling figures looked like flower petals caught in the wind. "It doesn't matter now."

"Maybe not. But as I told you, two things can be true. You wanted my honesty, so I'm telling you plainly that will always be the case with me. You might not like it, you might not think it's moral, but that's how it is."

It wasn't the answer I wanted to hear, and that in itself made me like it more. I looked back at him, begrudgingly appreciating that he was finally telling me who he was. Appreciating, too, with the lonely part of me that had been grieving this loss, that while our romance hadn't been entirely real . . . it hadn't been entirely false, either.

That still wasn't enough for me. I wanted to be someone's everything. I wanted them to be everything to me. But that small *yes and no* felt like a poultice applied to an inner wound.

I aimed for a lighter tone. "Then let me know when you're done seducing the room so we can talk about our shared cause."

"Why don't we talk while we dance?" he asked, extending a hand as his expression relaxed into a toothy smile.

"Why don't we talk sitting down?"

The smile faltered. *Got you*, I thought. Two things were always true at once with Drustan. He knew he'd made progress with me and was looking to press that advantage. It hadn't been honesty just for honesty's sake, or even just for my sake.

"Very well." He offered me his arm, and I set the punch down before taking it, letting him guide me to the vacant line of chairs. We sat, and he angled himself towards me. "I can't remember the last time I sat at a ball," he complained. "I assume you've checked for eavesdroppers?"

I hadn't, and I really needed to get into that habit. I opened my senses to check for heartbeats, breathing, or the twitch of muscles from an invisible spy. "There's no one nearby." I launched into it. "When are you sending more policies? Your last letter mentioned more details about Elsmere would be forthcoming."

He sighed. "I'll send you something detailing our most important relationships with foreign courts, but the main point of interest is that Queen Briar sent letters to both me and Hector today. She's decided to pledge her troops to our cause regardless of who leads our joint army. The soldiers are already on the march—they'll be here by the end of the month." He eyed me. "Is that what you wanted to hear?"

I was glad to know this would no longer be a proxy war for Elsmere, but there was also a dismayed tumbling in my stomach. If Briar had only promised to support Hector, the decision would have been made for me. "That's a good thing," I said, hoping he didn't see the conflict on my face. "And Grimveld's troops?"

"Also on the move, if Gweneira is correct. They must have spies in Briar's court."

Two armies marching towards us, five houses at odds and one abstaining... and only twenty days left. I needed to make my decision soon so our side could unite under one leader. "And Earth House?" I asked, trying not to panic. "I've noticed you spending more time with Rhiannon since Hector's party."

He tipped his head, making the golden powder dusting his copper hair glitter in the candlelight. The too-familiar scent of cinnamon and smoke wafted towards me. "Rhiannon is... receptive to my arguments."

That sounded like a euphemism. "Your arguments or your seduction?"

"Jealous?" he purred.

"Judgmental."

Again, my answer made his smile slip. "You sound like—" He shook his head, and his grin returned. "Rhiannon would rather shove me off a cliff than be seduced by me. At least in the sense that you mean it."

"And how do I mean it?"

He rolled his shoulders, sending more of that spicy scent my way. I despised the memories that rose with it—of hot skin and strong hands, of a curtain of fire and the soaring joy that had briefly made me believe in happy endings. "You imagine me constantly stripping off my clothes to achieve my ends, when that's the least part of it," he said. "Most of those I bring to our cause are seduced by other desires. Rhiannon wants Earth House to use its voice, and she wants vengeance for those she's lost, and she wants whatever power she can grab, because she imagines—rightly, in my opinion—that she'll wield it better than most."

Most of those I bring to our cause are seduced by other desires. Was there a path to his aims where I hadn't fallen for him? Or had he sensed the vulnerability in me immediately, the desperate desire to be cared for? "Do you think to entice her away from Hector's side?" I asked, feeling that split emotion again—the allure of his honesty, the pain of not liking the truth.

"A faerie like Rhiannon does not need to be enticed," he said. "Like Dallaida, she has specific goals to accomplish. It matters little who helps her accomplish them."

Dallaida, who had demanded Blood House as a prize—and I had to trust that Drustan would keep his word and never offer it to her. "Do you still have the Queen of the Nasties on a leash? She'll turn on you eventually."

"She'll turn on someone else first." He leaned forward to rest his elbows on his knees, eyes roving restlessly over the dance floor like he was imagining being in the spin of it. "Imogen has been making overtures to the Nasties because she's clever, but she isn't truly willing to give them free rein, and Dallaida knows it. I'm taking advantage of that."

Of course Imogen was trying to bribe the Nasties, too. She and Drustan were quite the pair, competing to seduce their way into the strongest position for the butchery to follow. "I doubt Dallaida believes you'll give the Nasties complete freedom, either."

Drustan returned his attention to me. "The goal isn't for me to fulfill all of Dallaida's dreams. It's to be her least objectionable ally—and therefore the last one standing. The best use of one enemy is to set them at another."

Like Kallen, it was intimidating how many schemes he was juggling at once. Drustan had a plan for Dallaida, for Briar, for Rhiannon, for everyone who might give him power, and those plans were flexible, depending on his needs and the shifting situation. No matter what, Drustan intended to come out on top.

"Well, you seem to have the situation in hand," I said, standing and shaking out my skirts. "I'll look for your next message."

He rose, too, and gave me a roguish smile. "Can I tempt you into one dance?"

He seemed relaxed, happy to have confided his scheming in someone. Pleased to be near me, even. Drustan was terrifyingly clever behind that carefree facade, though, and his ultimate goal was the crown.

He might want something else from me, I realized with an uncomfortable twist of my stomach as his gaze dropped to my lips and I registered the still-smoldering heat in his eyes. Maybe this flirtation wasn't just an act to win me to his side and shore up his reputation as a charmer. Maybe having me again was a secondary goal.

I wasn't willing to be anyone's second choice. But he was right: there were other ways to collect power than by baring my teeth at everyone, and desire was a powerful thing.

I pressed my hands to his shoulders and rose slightly on my toes. His eyes flared before his hands settled at my waist. When I licked my lips and leaned in, Drustan made a soft noise, grip tightening.

Oh, yes, he still wanted this.

Feeling a rush of power at the knowledge, I changed direction at the last moment, pressing my mouth near his ear instead. "No," I breathed. Then I backed away. "Enjoy the dancing, Prince Drustan."

I suppressed a smile at the sound of protest he made behind me.

I FOUND KALLEN LURKING IN A CORNER BESIDE A GLASS SCULPture of a unicorn. His arms were crossed, and he was brooding even more than usual. The silver chain glinted on his right hand, and his belt held a dagger tied in place with a ceremonial peace knot, rather than his usual sword.

When he saw me coming, his eyes narrowed. "Playing with fire?" he asked.

So he'd seen my display with Drustan. My face grew warm. "Not really. I was just—"

"Toying with him because he still wants you."

The blunt interruption took me aback. I hadn't believed Drustan's desire was genuine until tonight, but Kallen had apparently known all along. I thought over my reply carefully, not wanting to give the wrong impression. "He deserves to want something he can't have."

His midnight gaze was inscrutable. "You're punishing him."

"Yes," I admitted. "But it's not just that. He's used to being the seducer, the one pulling all the strings. If he's not controlling the situation, that gives me power over him." I shook my head. "I need any power I can get."

Any advantage that might keep me alive was good. If Drustan wanted me—if I was a goal to be pursued—it might make a difference later, even after my usefulness in declaring our faction's leader was over.

Kallen still hadn't uncrossed his arms. His jaw was tense. "How far will you let it go?"

Did he truly think I might fall into Drustan's bed again? "No further than what you saw. He's not getting a second chance." I scowled. "Do you really think I would let him touch me after everything he's done?"

Kallen looked away sharply. His throat bobbed. "It has never ceased to amaze me what Drustan can acquire merely by the act of wanting it."

He sounded almost . . . jealous. My pulse thumped too hard, and the floor felt like it was tilting. Nonsense, I told myself, struggling for breath. I was imagining stories that weren't true again. "Can you not have what you want?"

His mouth twisted in a sneer. "I don't deserve to have what I want." He looked back at me, and the hostility faded from his expression. "I apologize for sounding accusatory. I . . . mislike how he treated you."

I was still caught off guard by those words—*I don't deserve to have what I want*—and the vicious look that had accompanied them. "I don't like it, either," I murmured. "And I deserve better than to always come second to someone's lust for power."

His arms finally dropped to his sides. "You do."

I was watching his expression closely. "We all deserve that."

There it was—the clench of his jaw and the tightening of the muscles beside his eyes. What I'd said bothered him. "You needn't worry about my lonely heart, if that's what you're aiming at," he said, voice growing cold. "I have purpose enough."

He was putting on the persona of the King's Vengeance again. It crept over him, frosting his expression and making his posture even more rigid. Kallen was protecting himself. From me or from the implication that he deserved to be cared for?

From both?

"Did Drustan tell you anything of note?" Kallen asked, widening his stance and linking his hands behind his back like a soldier awaiting inspection. He was all sharp angles now, closed off.

It felt wrong to see him like this. He'd been relaxing around me this past week, letting me in. Smiling sometimes, even laughing when I startled him. I hadn't gotten to the core of Kallen yet, but I'd gotten further than most people ever had, and I didn't want to lose that progress. "Nothing you probably don't already know," I said, stomach starting to hurt. "Briar is our ally regardless of leader, Rhiannon has aspirations towards power, and Imogen is trying and failing to win the Nasties to her side."

Kallen nodded crisply. "I did know most of that, though I hadn't realized Imogen was actively trying to recruit the Nasties. It reeks of desperation, which is good for us."

"Drustan is hoping Dallaida will take care of Imogen for him. 'The enemy of my enemy' and all that." I couldn't focus on the issue of Dallaida, though. I was still thinking about Kallen's newly applied armor and how I could claw my way back beneath it.

"If only we could be so lucky. Unfortunately, I don't believe in luck." He began surveying the crowd again. "You should go dance. Make new allies."

Stung by the dismissal, I touched his arm. The muscles hardened beneath my fingers, and when I used a sliver of magic to chart that tension, I realized that despite how calm he looked, his heart was racing.

Kallen looked down at my hand, then up to my face, expression blank. That frantic pulse throbbed in his throat, just above the line of his black collar. What Kallen was on the surface and what he was beneath rarely matched.

It was suddenly imperative that I get him to smile again, that I loosen some of the brutal tension in his frame. His body had to hurt from how rigidly he always held himself. "I don't want to make new allies," I said.

"A princess should—"

"I don't care what a princess should do." I eased closer, and with my magical senses open, I felt the hitch in his breathing like it had seized my own lungs.

"You don't want to dance?"

"No." I smiled and squeezed his arm lightly. "Unless you want to dance with me?"

The cold expression finally broke, but it was replaced by a fleeting grimace of pain. "Don't use me, Kenna."

"Use you?" I asked, taken aback.

"To make Drustan jealous."

Was that what he believed? "That's not why I asked."

"Then why—" He shook his head. "I don't like dancing."

This wasn't about my motives. It was about him. "You enjoyed it at least one time."

His eyes traced over my face, my upswept hair, down to my neck. I wondered if he was reliving it, that heady midnight we'd spent spinning on a hidden balcony, taking our first steps into this strange not-quite friendship. "That was different."

Sensing a softening in him, I pressed my advantage with another smile, another squeeze of his arm. "Would you prefer I stay here, bothering you until you can't even spy properly?"

That finally pulled a reluctant twitch out of one corner of his mouth. "You don't bother me."

"Not yet, I don't." I leaned in conspiratorially. "I haven't truly tried yet. I promise I can be very annoying." I bit my lip, and his eyes followed the movement. "*If* you'd prefer that to dancing."

I didn't know why I wanted this so badly. He'd already said no, and I should respect that.

Except he hadn't said no, had he? He'd said, *Don't use me* and *I don't like dancing.* And I hadn't asked him to dance, either—I'd asked him if he *wanted* to dance.

He seemed torn, hesitating even though he was normally confident in his decisions, and I felt suddenly certain he did want to dance. He just didn't think he deserved it, the way he didn't think he deserved any other softness or kindness. So I gambled on that instinct and released his arm to hold out my hand. "Lord Kallen," I said with a curtsy. "Would you do me the honor of this dance?"

His lashes lowered as he looked at my outstretched palm. Then he sighed and placed his hand in mine. "Yes, Kenna."

The music was slowing and shifting into a new key as we walked towards the center of the ballroom. Some couples were still spinning while others were changing partners, and around the edges the Fae drank and schemed. Curious eyes followed our progress, and waving fans flicked up to cover gossiping mouths.

"They probably think I'm blackmailing or interrogating you," Kallen said grimly.

"Why?"

"That's normally why I dance with people."

He'd done that to me once, hadn't he? At the spring equinox, he'd asked me to dance—ordered me, more like—and spent nearly the entirety of it quizzing me about Drustan and Earth House. "No wonder you don't like it."

He grunted but didn't reply.

I let go of his hand once we reached a clear space at the edge of the floor, then turned to face him. This wasn't a patterned dance involving simultaneous choreography—the music was slow and aching, the kind of melting tune that demanded a closer touch. I raised my arms, and though Kallen had been reluctant to agree to this, he showed no hesitation as he pulled me into his hold. His right hand settled low on my bared back, just beneath the tip of Caedo's silver tail, and as the delicate chain crossing his palm pressed against my skin, I shivered.

No biting, I reminded Caedo.

Kallen led me into the first step, the tension in his arms both anchoring and guiding me. He moved as gracefully as he did while fighting.

Words hovered on my tongue. Should I make a quip about interrogating him instead? Ask how many of Elsmere's troops were on the move? Discuss what else he'd learned while spying lately?

I wanted him to actually enjoy the dancing for once, so I settled on a compliment. "You're very good at this," I said after he'd twirled me away and brought me spinning back.

"It's a tool like any other," he replied.

Dancing as an interrogation technique, dancing as a tool. How little joy he found in life. "When did you start learning?"

"I can't remember a time it wasn't part of my training. It was important to Osric that I master the courtly graces in addition to the martial ones."

The mention of Osric's name was like a discordant note fouling a perfect chord. "You trained with him, rather than at Void House?"

He deftly spun us out of the path of a drunkenly twirling couple, and my skirts briefly wrapped around his legs. "Most of my childhood was spent in his private wing."

"You *lived* with him?"

"Alongside his personal guard, yes. He delighted in the idea of raising a child into a weapon. Once he believed I was entirely his creature, he found it more advantageous to send me back to the house—and some Void faeries will never trust me because of that." Though Kallen was moving without missing a step, his gaze moved restlessly across the room, like he was even now searching for betrayers in the shadows. He never let himself relax into a moment.

I gripped his hand tighter. "Look at me," I ordered.

Kallen's focus returned to me. He raised his brows slightly.

"Let's not talk about Osric anymore," I said, running my thumb along the line between his shoulder and neck. "He doesn't get to have this dance, too."

A sigh left him. "No, this one is yours."

He pulled me closer, hand shifting across the small of my back until the tips of his fingers slid just beneath the edge of my dress. If I was supposed to be doing specific steps, I'd completely forgotten, but his lead was so good it didn't matter. His body asked questions that mine answered, and though that silent communication felt easy, the air between us was increasingly thick with tension.

The strings swelled, and Kallen twirled me out. Rather than spin me in again, he took two long strides in pursuit before snatching me up into his hold. I pressed my left hand to his chest, startled by the possessiveness of that sudden movement. The silky black fabric of his shirt was warm from his skin. I felt the strength of his muscles beneath and, below that, the urgent tap of his heart.

We were barely moving now, no longer executing complicated steps but turning in a slow circle. I twisted my fingers in his shirt, then fumbled up to cup the nape of his neck, beneath his dark hair.

Kallen's lips parted. His eyelids were heavy. His fingers flexed against the dip of my waist, just beneath the fabric of my dress.

Goose bumps raced over my skin. He had a warrior's hands, and with my back bared, I felt the scrape of those calluses in a way I never had before.

"Is this what you wanted?" he asked, voice low and rough.

I nodded, unable to summon words.

"Good." He lowered his mouth to my ear to whisper the next words. "You make me wish I was different."

I was starting to feel lightheaded. "I don't want you to be different."

He pulled back, gaze falling to my mouth.

A crash of cymbals broke through the music. I jumped as my pulse went skittering, and Kallen spun, shoving me behind him.

"What is it?" I asked, gripping his arm.

He relaxed, but only minutely. "Imogen."

The music had stopped. Everyone turned towards the dais, where Imogen stood between two cymbal-wielding Underfae. A beatific smile crossed her face as she raised her goblet high in the air. The liquid was the purple of ice wine. "My beloved subjects," she called out. "Isn't this ball wonderful?"

There were murmured agreements, but confusion was written on many faces.

"Osric's parties were so dull. Dancing, drinking, a few executions..." She made a face. "No variety."

"No *variety*?" I echoed under my breath. "That's her complaint?"

Kallen made a soft huffing sound. "I can think of a few more pressing concerns."

"This event could be better, though," Imogen continued. Her voice had a slightly messy quality, and I realized she was drunk. "I've been puzzling over it—how to make this ball a novelty for you."

Ulric was at the front of the crowd. He approached the dais and bowed, then beckoned for Imogen to bend closer. I didn't hear what he said, but she shook her head and scowled. "Nonsense," she said, straightening. "We're going to make this night special. Isn't that right?" She raised her drink again, and a cheer broke out. When she quaffed it, dozens of faeries mirrored her.

Ulric's expression grew grim as he retreated.

Torin rose from his chair, eyes narrowed. "My queen," he said, "we discussed the plans for this event in depth. My house even provided the musicians, the best we have to offer. Are you displeased with them?"

"Oh, the musicians are fine," she said, waving her free hand so the light glanced off her jeweled rings. "But I want *more*."

Torin exchanged a glance with Rowena. If they had helped plan this party, that had been a very public insult.

"One thing Queen Brigitta excelled at was offering herself to the people she ruled," Imogen continued. "In public audiences, private conversations—she even played the fiddle so that her people might dance."

"Do you have a fiddle?" Torin asked, an edge to his voice.

Imogen threw her head back and laughed. Too loud, too reckless. I wondered how many glasses she'd drunk. "Are we to be satisfied with music alone? No, I'm offering a new type of entertainment tonight. One performed by the house heads."

My worry grew. Where was this leading?

"Queen Imogen," Torin said through gritted teeth. "Perhaps you might like to sit down?"

Her head snapped towards him. "I beg your pardon?"

"There is more to ruling than drinking and making merry," he said coldly. "I wonder if this speech—whatever you intend to accomplish with it—might be better saved for a more sober moment."

A ripple of sound went through the ballroom at the outright disrespect.

Imogen's eyes glittered with pinpricks of light, and her dress whipped in an illusionary wind. "My *dear* friend," she said, tone turning just as icy, "have I not given you enough cause to believe in me? Let me remedy that." She touched her crown, as if checking it was sitting straight, then faced the crowd. "Your house heads have grown lazy," she called out. "They rely on their titles, forgetting that power must be continuously won. So for the next event in this month of revelry, I propose something no one has seen before."

The crowd waited in breathless anticipation.

Imogen grinned. "A melee battle of your leaders, with only one left standing."

25

THE ROOM EXPLODED IN A BUZZ OF SHOCK AND EXCITEment. My stomach dropped like a stone.

"House head against house head," Imogen said, looking smug as a cat with bird feathers sticking from its mouth. "The victor gains one boon from the crown."

Kallen's face remained impassive, but he shifted closer to me.

"This is unnecessary," Torin argued.

"Are you afraid?" Imogen taunted, eyes still sparkling. "Perhaps you would like Rowena to fight on behalf of Light House instead?"

Rowena looked like she wouldn't mind. Her eyes threw daggers at Imogen.

Torin's jaw clenched. "No. But you cannot think to make us butcher each other for your amusement."

"There will be no butchery. This is still a silvered event." She paused, tapping her finger to her lips. "Contestants will be disqualified at first blood. Magic will be allowed, but nothing that will cause serious injury or death." Her smile grew. "And I will be fighting, as Osric was always too much of a coward to do."

The uproar that met that was deafening. I faced Kallen, breath coming shallowly and cold sweat breaking out over my body. "What do I do?"

"Three deep breaths," he told me, modeling them with one long inhale of his own. "Focus on the ground beneath your feet. Get the fear off your face."

I sucked in a ragged breath, trying to focus on my balance. *Out of the head, into the body*, he'd told me more than once when I'd grown frustrated during training. Spiraling thoughts led to sloppy actions. I flexed my toes, then used his own calm expression as my template.

"Good." He lowered his head, speaking even more quietly. "She cannot allow any of you to be killed. It would destabilize the realm. This is merely a clever bit of pageantry."

A bit of pageantry that would end with blood, but the true price the losers would pay was worse than that. Reputation was everything in the Fae court. "The weakest house heads will be humiliated."

"Yes, which is why it's clever. She'll attack Drustan or Hector first, since a loss would be a blow to their images. It will shake any support they're cultivating outside their houses."

My heart raced. I'd been focusing on the danger to me, but this was significant on so many levels. "She's drunk, though."

"Yes, but she's a habitual drunk, so I wouldn't count on that impacting her abilities. She may even be exaggerating her impairment. Imagine the story if she wins—even after a few bottles of wine, Imogen was able to best all five of the house heads." He shook his head. "The Fae will adore that."

Another chill raced over me. "She must be confident she can win."

"I've never seen her fight, but Illusion House trains their nobles brutally."

It was hard to imagine Imogen competing physically with the tall, muscular princes, but she also had a terrifying type of magic. "I'm going to lose," I said, despair threatening to swamp me.

"Do not say that," Kallen said sharply, composure slipping. "Many battles are won or lost before anyone touches a weapon, and this is a fight well suited to your skills."

I couldn't help but make a face. "I've been training for less than two weeks."

"It's not just about the training or the weapons. Being underestimated is a strength, and your magic is going to be your greatest asset."

I hadn't been thinking about that, only my ability to wield a sword. I closed my eyes, focusing on the liquid heat filling my chest and veins. When I thought about slowing my racing heart, the magic leapt to help with the task.

What could I do that wouldn't violate the rules? I could slow my attackers down, as I had during the revolution, or cause cramps or other physical distractions. I could freeze someone's arm to avoid being stabbed.

I focused on the steady expansion and contraction of my lungs. I was the weakest house head. It was possible someone would try to eliminate me immediately to clear the floor of a distraction . . . but it was more likely the deadliest faeries would turn on one another first, leaving me for later.

I didn't have to win. I just couldn't be the first to lose.

I opened my eyes, met Kallen's searching gaze, then nodded.

His smile was tight. "Go show them who you are, Kenna."

As I turned away, his fingers brushed mine.

I joined the others at the center of the ballroom. Oriana was having a quiet argument with Imogen, and I could guess what that was about—whether or not this counted as breaking neutrality. Torin and Rowena were consulting with each other, while Drustan was accepting a sword from a bowing Illusion servant. Another servant rushed up to me, presenting a matching blade.

"I already have a dagger," I said, touching my deadly necklace.

The Underfae bowed. "Forgive me, my princess, but our queen wishes for this to be an equal fight. You must wield the same weapons."

I begrudgingly nodded and accepted the blade, gripping the leather-wrapped hilt. The silver peace chain pressed into my palm. Kallen had spent a few nights on swordplay, and I recognized this as a side sword—light enough to wield one-handed but with sharp edges that made it ideal for slicing as well as stabbing. It was the same type of sword he carried most days.

Caedo thrummed with disappointment as I took a few experimental slashes. *I know*, I told the dagger. *I don't like it, either.*

Another servant handed me a red tunic and shirt, and then four sylphs flew overhead, carrying a bolt of purple fabric. They circled me, then dropped it, creating a curtain. A portable changing room, apparently. I stripped off the dress and replaced it with the sparring clothes. A pixie zoomed down from above to tug at my bootlaces. Taking the hint, I kicked the shoes and socks off and flexed my toes against the cool wooden floor. *Out of the head, into the body.*

When the curtain was whisked away, I saw the same had happened to the others. Even Oriana was scowling with a pile of green fabric in her arms as the sylphs dropped a curtain around her; she'd apparently lost that argument.

Hector was frowning at his sword. It was strange to see him in bare feet with his long hair tied back. I approached him, making my first move of the match. "I propose an agreement," I said quietly.

The Void prince didn't look at me, still inspecting his blade. "I'm listening."

"Spare each other at the start so we can focus on our mutual enemies."

His brows raised. "I wasn't going to attack you first."

"I figured. But I like to be clear about such things."

He nodded. "A truce, then. But it will have to break at some point."

"I'll try not to hurt you too badly when it does."

He chuckled, glancing at me. "What a turn this evening has taken."

"Are you upset about it?"

"Not at all." His smile was as sharp as a blade. "I much prefer this."

I slipped to Drustan's side next, making the same offer.

He nodded, embers smoldering in his eyes. "Imogen and Torin are my priority," he said in a clipped voice. "I'll be keeping them busy, if you'd like to practice your magic while they're distracted."

"You didn't expect her to do something like this," I said, guessing at the source of his pique. He liked being the one in control, but this had shocked him.

"Did Kallen expect it?" he snapped.

"What?" My forehead furrowed. "No, why would he?"

He shook his head. "Never mind." He turned that seething look on the spectators. "Look at the crowd. They adore her for this."

Faeries were packed in around the edges of the dance floor, and more were pouring in through the doors. Word must have spread that the house heads were putting on a show. The atmosphere was festive, with drinks and plates of food circulating.

"I suppose we could have refused," I said.

"No, we couldn't have. It would be seen as cowardice." His scowl deepened. "The people crave a spectacle, so she's giving it to them—and she'll seem even more of a queen because she set the terms."

Illusion House's favored virtue was cunning. Seeing those excited faces and hearing the buzz of conversation, I begrudgingly admired Imogen's bold choice. She was not only entertaining her subjects but proving her mettle, and the rest of us were forced to go along. If she won, unlikely as it seemed, that would support her claim to the throne.

It was a gamble . . . but big wins required big risks.

"Keep an eye on Torin," Drustan said. "Imogen did not endear herself to him just now, so he might let me take my chances with her and focus on collecting easy wins instead."

And I was the easiest win of all.

Imogen sauntered forward in a simple purple sparring set. Diamonds still sparkled at her neck and wrists, but she'd removed her heavy crown. "The rules," she said, ticking the points off on her fingers. "If even a drop of your blood spills, you will leave the floor immediately. No grievous maiming, no amputations, no killing. Slicing is preferred, but any stabbing must avoid major organs. Magic may be used but is subject to the same constraints, and all blood must be spilled by sword to count."

What made a maiming *grievous*? Panic started to squeeze my chest again.

"This is an absurdity," Oriana said through gritted teeth. "You demean us by making us entertainment."

"I think we have all forgotten that we do not just rule our people," Imogen said. "We serve them, and we cannot demand blind obedience without proving ourselves in return."

More than a tad hypocritical, since she was demanding Mistei's blind obedience when it came to her reign, but this was exactly the sort of partly true, partly false, and entirely self-serving argument the Noble Fae excelled at, so I ignored it. I was too busy looking from opponent to opponent, trying to predict what they would do.

"When the horn blows, we fight." Imogen grinned. "Are you ready?"

I wasn't, but I nodded anyway.

In the last moments before the battle began, I looked for Kallen.

He was standing at the front of the crowd, and as we locked eyes, a small amount of relief mixed with the terror. I wasn't alone.

Then a horn sounded, and all hell broke loose.

Drustan lunged towards Imogen in a flash of orange. She sidestepped, and suddenly there were two of her darting around him. When Drustan lashed out at one, his sword met empty air. A third Imogen appeared, circling behind him, and Drustan turned just in time to meet this one's blade with his own. The clash of metal was met by cheers.

A swirl of black smoke rushed across the floor, coalescing into Hector's shape before he stabbed towards Imogen's side. She had vanished again, though, and there was nothing left for his weapon to find. He immediately ducked, and a lock of his tied-back hair fluttered to the ground, chopped off by an invisible weapon.

Nearby, Torin was advancing on Oriana, hacking his sword in vicious arcs—apparently he had decided to target the Earth princess rather than me. Oriana evaded him with surprising quickness, then launched a counterattack.

I stood frozen, shocked at the speed and viciousness with which everyone else had leapt into action. My feet felt like lead.

Oriana was an adept fighter, but Torin was clearly about to overpower her. She spun fluidly out of the way, water spilling from her free hand and slithering towards Torin's feet. She didn't even glance my way as she retreated past me.

That was how little the others feared me. And that was likely why Torin hadn't attacked me first—he thought I would be easy prey whenever he got around to it.

Move! I silently screamed at myself. This was the only advantage I would get.

I reached for my magic, sensing the web of life filling each of the faeries on the floor. The two Imogens darting around Drustan felt like nothing at all, but a blank spot of air near Hector had a beating heart, so I focused on the contours of that invisible body and forced her to stop moving. Imogen turned visible again, looking startled. Hector surged towards her, but she was too strong to be held by my magic for long—or else I was still too new to using it—and she broke free in time to intercept his attack.

Next I imagined a knot forming in Torin's calf. It barely had an impact, considering his innate resistance to magic, but the slight hesitation in his gait was all the encouragement Oriana needed. Her sword slashed towards his shoulder, and Torin threw himself to the side.

Oriana pressed her advantage as the water reached Torin's boots, but he was too fast. Light glinted off his sword, and a second later he had sliced open Oriana's bicep.

The crowd roared. Oriana spat out a curse, then stormed away, dripping blood.

Torin's back was still turned; this might be the best chance I got to eliminate him.

Heart hammering, I sprinted towards Torin, preparing to stab him in the leg. Something must have alerted him—a cry from the crowd or maybe a shift of the air—and he spun, intercepting my sword with his. The blades shrieked, then caught at the hilts with a painfully jarring impact. As my arm briefly went numb, I tried to freeze him with my magic, but the effect lasted less than a second, giving me just enough time to disengage and skip back before his blade flashed an inch from my face.

"Gut her!" someone called out. The crowd screamed in excitement.

Torin snarled at me. A light blazed from his upraised hand, sending sparks scattering across my vision. I instinctively lunged to the left, feeling the breeze as his weapon passed by. Still half blinded, I sent more freezing magic his way, desperately hoping it would give my vision time to recover. My foot hit a puddle of Oriana's magically cast water, and I slipped, crashing to the floor with tailbone-bruising force.

My eyes watered with pain. The pounding of blood in my ears was a drumbeat. With my senses opened, I heard Torin's heart, too, and sensed the swing of his arm through the air. My power looped around his wrist, slowing the movement enough for me to roll away before his sword crashed into the floor next to my head. Chips of wood flew where the edge of the blade gouged into the parquet.

A shocked cry rose from the crowd, while others cheered.

That blow wouldn't have just cut me—it could have killed me.

"The rules," I gasped, scrambling away and trying desperately to get my feet under me.

He sneered down at me. "Not my fault you're so clumsy with magic that it affected my aim."

So that was the lie he would use. The reckless human, not yet in control of her powers, inadvertently bringing about her own death.

A surge of hot wind ripped my hair out of its pins. Torin stumbled back, bracing an arm in front of his eyes. Licks of flame rode the air currents, setting his clothing alight, and I realized who had come to my aid.

I jumped to my feet, shooting a grateful glance towards Drustan. He was still busy with Imogen, blasting each apparition of her with bursts of wind and flame to drive the real one away. Hector was swirling in and out of shadow nearby, using his sword to accomplish the same.

Rage surged through me as I faced my would-be murderer. Torin was slapping at his clothes, trying to put out the fire. Drustan was limited to the less deadly aspects of his magic, so this wasn't the type of fire that burned hot enough to turn bones to ash. A pity.

Gritting my teeth, I lunged towards Torin, lashing out in a fast, direct strike. He pivoted to avoid being skewered, but my magic was wound around him now, and I yanked him towards the sharp edge of the blade.

I only had a moment of control over his body, but it was enough. My sword met his side, sinking in. Blood bloomed over the white fabric.

Shocked cries echoed through the room, and the Light faeries instantly stopped cheering. Torin looked down at the growing red stain like he couldn't believe it. When his gaze snapped up to mine, I'd never seen such hatred on anyone's face before.

"You'll get what's coming to you," he hissed.

Triumph spilled through me, hot and addictive. I showed him my middle finger before running towards the three faeries still battling for supremacy.

There were four of Imogen now, whirling around the floor in swirls of steel. Hector ducked the swing of one sword, then cursed when his counterattack breezed through empty air. Drustan swept up one version of Imogen in a fire-kissed cyclone before stabbing towards her.

A line of red lanced across Drustan's arm, bisecting the swell of his muscle. Blood dripped to the floor, and Imogen reappeared at Drustan's side, looking smug as she held her sword aloft. "The Fire prince falls," she called out.

Drustan had been eliminated.

I met his furious gaze. It wasn't a fair fight when one participant could cast countless decoys and vanish at will.

Imogen winked out of existence just in time to avoid an attack from Hector. I extended my magical senses, feeling her progress in the patter of her heart. Then I reached an invisible hand inside her ribs, wrapped it around her lungs, and squeezed.

Imogen coughed, staggering. She tried to suck in a breath, but I didn't let her lungs expand.

The room spun around me. I stumbled, dizzy, then cried out when Imogen suddenly appeared in front of me, stabbing for the center of my chest. I barely got my sword up in time to parry, but there was no contact, and then she was gone.

An illusion. And in my distraction, I'd loosened my grip on the real Imogen. She was moving like a whirlwind towards Hector, steel blade a blur.

Behind Hector, Torin lunged back into the makeshift arena, his side saturated with blood and eyes filled with hate. He swung his sword . . . and cut Hector's head off.

Horror swamped me as the severed head toppled to the ground. The rictus grimace, the wide-open eyes, the spraying blood . . . My sword sagged, and my ears buzzed as screams filled the air.

"Kenna!" It was Kallen's voice, slicing through the tumult. "Move!"

Operating on panicked instinct, I threw myself to the side. Something whooshed past me, and then Imogen was there, teeth bared. It was the real one this time, fully visible and with her heart pumping an aggressive beat. She performed an artistic twirl of her wrist, and despite the elegance of the movement, her sword met mine hard enough to knock me back several feet. I grabbed her arm with my magic, stilling it, and the screams around me stuttered, too, laughter breaking through in jagged, eerie bursts. Hector was whole again for a blink of an eye, snarling as he sprinted towards us through a sea of illusory Imogens, and then his headless corpse was lying on the floor in a pool of blood while Kallen knelt over it, screaming.

My head pounded, and my throat felt so tight from terror I might choke. I seized Imogen's throat with my magic instead, willing it to hurt. The world flickered between one reality and another—a ballroom where Hector was coming to my aid, then one where he lay dead in Kallen's arms.

I reached for Kallen instinctively, my magic surging towards the carnage. His heart wasn't beating.

That wasn't him. There was no one there at all.

I forced Imogen's legs to buckle, dropping her to the floor. The illusion broke, and I could see the truth again. Hector was alive and bearing down on us, grinning wildly. "Keep her there," he called.

Imogen bared her teeth, then flung her sword away. It spun through the air before the edge bit into Hector's thigh. The crowd cheered as the Void prince's blood sprayed.

He cursed and lowered his weapon. Defeated—and no longer coming to my aid.

The shock of his elimination caused my magical hold on Imogen to slip. My Blood powers were weakening—as small as these attacks had been, they added up, and my head was spinning from the sustained effort of fighting while using magic. When a second Imogen appeared in my peripheral vision, my instinctive flinch shattered the last fraction of control I had over her body, and she lunged to retrieve her sword.

I imagined pain lancing over her body like lightning, and she grimaced. She was strong, though, pushing forward despite my efforts, and a moment later she had knocked my sword aside with a vicious blow. She followed it with a kick to the center of my chest that sent me flying. The breath rushed out of me as my back hit the ballroom floor, and the pain of a fractured rib stabbed through me.

The room went dark and silent.

Every candle had been extinguished at once, and the only illumination came from the moonlight that filtered through a new crack in the ceiling. The crowd was gone. Cobwebs draped over the light fixtures and furnishings, and the air smelled of dust and decay.

Imogen stood before me in silver armor and a purple half cloak, the crown of state on her brow. "This is how it ends," she said.

Behind her, the tables of food were covered with mounds of flies, glittering like black jewels. The insects crawled over shapes at the edges of the room, too, a living carpet that shimmered and parted briefly to reveal a bloody, familiar face. Lara, I realized with a sick surge of horror. That was Lara lying in a broken heap, eyes blank and mouth open on an eternal scream, and next to her was a corpse with familiar copper hair, and face-down in a spreading pool of blood was one who had held me in his arms on the dance floor less than an hour ago.

"You will lose everything," Imogen said. Her lavender eyes shone like some nocturnal creature's. "You will be sacrificed on the altar of power, and you will watch everyone you love die."

"No," I whispered. My chest hurt unbearably, the pain worsening by the moment.

A dark crimson tide crept towards me. I wondered if it was deep enough to drown in.

"It's not too late," Imogen said, sounding sad. "I will still welcome you with open arms. And unlike those you call friends, I do not betray my allies."

"They won't betr—" I choked out, but I couldn't manage more than that. Something snapped in my chest, and I coughed up frothy liquid.

Imogen smiled gently. "Oh, Kenna. They already have."

The light came back all at once, so bright it stung my eyes. Imogen's boot was on my chest, grinding down on my broken ribs, and her sword was leveled at my throat.

I wheezed, blood bubbling at my lips from where my rib had punctured my lung.

"You did so well," Imogen whispered.

Then she cut my throat—the lightest, most delicate slice, just enough to break the skin.

The crowd cheered.

Imogen had won.

WINE WAS POURED, THE MUSIC STARTED AGAIN, AND FAERIES began dancing, their silk slippers tracking the blood of their leaders across the floor. Imogen left without a backwards glance, reclaiming her spot on the throne. She sat with the sword balanced across her knees and a smile curling her lips as she accepted the praise of her sycophants.

Lara and Kallen reached my side at the same time, eyeing each other warily before helping me to my feet. "You were incredible," Lara gushed, pulling me into a hug. When I made a pained noise, she released me, "Sorry, do you need medicine?"

I shook my head, pressing a hand to my breastbone. My ribs were already healing. "I'll be fine," I wheezed. At least the ordeal was over, but what would the ramifications be? The Fae were already spinning onward into the next dance, the next plot, the next alliance or betrayal. "Can you go talk to people, listen in? Find out what this might have changed?"

Lara eyed me worriedly. "You need to rest."

My knees were shaking with fatigue and the terror that hadn't caught up to me fully yet. "But Blood House can't rest."

Her jaw firmed. She looked at Kallen. "You had better take care of her," she said, a threat in her voice. Then she floated away, all beauty and smiles as she joined a group of gossiping ladies.

Kallen's eyes were worried as he guided me away from the dance floor. "She's right," he murmured as he helped me sit by the wall. "You performed extraordinarily well."

I grimaced. It didn't feel like it, since I'd mostly relied on my opponents eliminating one another. My martial skills weren't anywhere near theirs; I had only survived as long as I had because my magic gave me an advantage in combat. "Shouldn't you be with Hector?"

"Hector already left," he said, sitting beside me. "He had no desire to watch Imogen gloat."

Shards, what a mess. Drustan, Hector, and I had all been eliminated, and Imogen was preening on her throne, having vanquished everyone. "At least Torin didn't win."

"That was satisfying."

I nodded agreement, then regretted it when my head spun and my stomach threatened to revolt. I sagged back in the chair. "I feel sick."

"Battle does that when you're not used to it. Sometimes even when you are used to it."

I started to tell him I didn't want to get used to it, but the words didn't come out. Even now, I was imagining being the one standing over Imogen, slitting her throat as everyone cheered. The truth was, I didn't want to get used to *losing*. "It's the magic, too," I settled on. "Using it still exhausts me."

"That will get better with time, but even Hector was tired after shifting into shadow so many times. Our power takes its due."

Imogen didn't look tired. She looked vibrant and merry, laughing as she accepted a cup of wine. She was related to Osric, though, however distant the connection. Maybe she drew from a deeper well than the rest of us.

She was alone on the dais now. Torin was storming towards the exit, Rowena trailing behind him. An Illusion nymph, nude body partially shielded by layers of shifting rainbow mist, stepped into his path carrying a tray. He cuffed her so hard she collapsed, glasses shattering and wine spraying.

I wanted to get up to help her, but my head was still spinning. "That bastard," I spat.

Una was in the crowd nearby. Her expression darkened, and she hurried over to join a few servants in helping the nymph up.

"You've made a real enemy of Torin," Kallen said.

I grimaced. "Just what I need."

"It's a good thing. He's a high-profile enemy to have."

"And that's good?" My brows rose incredulously.

"Everyone knows to take you seriously now. You started the battle by attacking one of the strongest fighters on the floor, one who is not well loved even within his own house." He smiled slightly. "And then you won."

"Barely."

"Barely still counts."

I sighed. "I wish I'd made it hurt more."

"There will be time for that."

Only Drustan and Oriana were still present in the wake of their defeat, undoubtedly playing politics to recover any ground they'd lost. The thought of doing the same made my headache worsen, and I grimaced.

"Let me bring you water," Kallen said, starting to rise.

I shook my head. "Don't coddle me."

He hesitated, then settled back into the chair. "It's not coddling. It's practical."

Maybe it was. But it felt weak to want anything, even if my throat was dry, and I didn't like the idea of being alone. "What happened tonight will change things."

"Yes," Kallen said. "But not entirely in Imogen's favor." He moved his hand as if to touch mine, then curled his fingers and rested the fist on his thigh instead. "You showed them, Kenna."

My throat had healed almost immediately, but I still felt the tingling echo of that injury. I rubbed my hand over the invisible line, thinking that Imogen had shown me something tonight, too. That cut had been a promise, the same way the vision she'd forced on me had been a promise.

This is how it ends.

Imogen was a liar, the way all faeries were liars. But now I remembered her other promise, and the words stuck in my brain like thorns.

Oh, Kenna. They already have.

26

My entrance hall was filled with faeries the next morning.

I stopped in the doorway, gaping at the unexpected congregation. There were Earth faeries in greens and blues, Light faeries wearing white, Illusion faeries in dramatic rainbow attire, and a handful wearing dull gray clothing that marked them as outcasts. Unlike the groups of refugees I'd greeted in recent days, the majority of this crowd—some fifty or so—looked to be Noble Fae.

Someone bowed when they saw me, and the movement spread through the gathering like a rippling wave. Near the front was the Illusion nymph I'd seen Torin punch. She threw herself on the floor, hands clasped in front of her. "Princess Kenna," she called out, "please accept this humble servant in your household."

"Princess Kenna," someone else shouted, "I offer my service—"

More voices overlapped. "Princess Kenna!"

"Please—"

"Princess, I seek shelter—"

"My princess, I beg you—"

Awe filled me. Kallen had been right. The melee last night—even if it had ended with my throat slit—had enhanced my reputation. It wasn't enough for a leader to be kind; the Fae needed their rulers to be strong.

I raised my hand for silence. The chatter instantly cut off.

How surreal. There was power in the smallest flick of my fingers now. "I'm honored you chose to come to Blood House today," I told the gathering. "We are a safe haven for anyone in need of shelter, regardless of prior house affiliation—so long as you are willing to renounce your previous ties and swear allegiance to me."

I recognized some of the faces from Earth House as minor nobles, and I'd wager the Fae from Light and Illusion House were, too. The highest-ranking faeries stayed close to the center of power, and I couldn't offer them the same influence they already enjoyed. Those with less power had less to lose, though, and if they were already discontented in their houses, this was a rare opportunity. A new house, a new princess, and a chance for a new rank in the Fae's strict hierarchy.

It was early in the morning, and I'd just been planning on a quick walk to get my blood pumping and my mind working before facing a new day and new obligations—among them a meeting with Hector, which he'd requested late last night. I needed help to process these new house members, so I formed a thought and sent it into the house's web of magic. *Wake Lady Lara.*

The house hummed in my mind. The message would already be speeding to her on invisible threads, and hopefully those quivering vibrations would rouse her from sleep.

"I also need to meet with each of you individually," I told the faeries. "We're different from the other houses, and I must be certain you're a good fit—and that you'll treat the humans and Underfae here with respect."

That earned a few startled looks. Well, best for them to learn this now, while they still had a chance to back out.

Caedo was curled into a thick cuff at my wrist. I willed the dagger to shift into its favorite form, then raised the weapon. The jewel in the hilt shone the saturated red of the last slice of sunset. "Do not mistake my policy of welcome for weakness," I called out. "We will not be used or abused by the other houses, and we will not use or abuse each other for that same reason. Just as I will punish any outsiders who think to harm a member of Blood House, I will not hesitate to retaliate against any of you who do the same."

There were scattered nods at that. The nymph still kneeling on the floor looked at me worshipfully.

I heard footsteps and turned to see Lara, who must have already been getting breakfast, given the speed of her arrival. She looked sleepy and annoyed—until she set eyes on the gathering. Then her posture straightened and her chin raised into a regal angle.

I faced the crowd once more. "Let the interviews begin."

WE WERE AT IT FOR HOURS. MANY OF THE FAERIES WERE NERvous about being seen in case word made it back to their houses and their leaders decided to retaliate before they had gained my protection, so I opened a few rooms off the ramp leading to Blood House for them to wait in. Then I sent messages to Void and Fire House requesting assistance.

Drustan sent Edric, who positioned himself at the top of the slope leading towards Fire House and cast a wall of flame so no one could pass through or spy on what we were doing. Kallen himself came from Void House and did the same at the lower end of the ramp, erecting a barrier of cold shadow.

With the ramp sealed off, the faeries relaxed and opened up more, though they were still obviously nervous. The Underfae all had stories I'd heard before—abuse by Osric, Roland, Rowena, or Torin; family members lost to draconian punishments; fear that Imogen might become the same sort of monster Osric had been. Word was spreading among the servants that Blood House was a safe haven, and after seeing me cut Torin last night, these ones finally felt brave enough to take a chance on me.

Many of the Noble Fae had similar tales of despair, fury, and loss. The first interview was with a Light lord whose consort had been beheaded by Roland after he'd been overheard complaining about the king's wards. Seeing that Torin was cut from the same cruel cloth, he'd decided it was time to give up on the dream of justice Light House promised.

After that, we spoke with an Earth faerie I recognized but knew little about. His name was Wilkin, and he'd been a quiet figure around the house, spending most of his time tending a garden filled with white blossoms. He'd been in love with a Light lady centuries ago, he told us with tears in his eyes; when their child had been discovered and torn away from them, they'd both been publicly flogged. Prince Roland had followed up with his own punishment, but he'd gone too far, and the lady hadn't survived. Wilkin had planted the garden in her memory the next day.

Oriana had told him he was lucky not to be punished worse for siring a changeling—and that he was never to let his heart lead him astray again. Then she'd complimented his beautiful white flowers and ordered him to cut a handful for her.

Lara nearly cried with him. I knew she was thinking of her brother Leo and the tragic end he had come to. When Wilkin hesitantly opened his bag to reveal a small rosebush, the roots packed with dirt, she told him we would find the perfect spot for his new garden.

Another heartbreaking interview was with an Illusion lady who had been raped by Osric. She told me with bitter fury that every time she walked past the music room where it had happened, she swore she could smell his perfume, and she was tired of living with his ghost. Tired of living with the memories, too, of how her family had seen the abuse as an opportunity to gain influence. When the story was done, I gripped her hand and told her there were other survivors in Blood House who knew that pain, and she wasn't alone.

Not all the Noble Fae had suffered. One young Illusion lord told me he was tired of being ignored by higher-ranking faeries and wanted a chance to prove himself to a new leader. A scholarly Light lady wanted to devote herself to medicine, rather than her family's business in training executioners. And a pregnant Earth faerie and her partner told us they had already been disillusioned with Oriana's commitment to neutrality and had decided after the melee that the Earth princess wasn't strong enough to protect her people.

Soon, Blood House had nearly seventy new members. Nadine and Lara began showing the new arrivals to their rooms, and the kitchen servants moved quickly to prepare food for a grand luncheon. Looking at the quantity of ingredients piled on the worktables, I felt a twinge of worry about the house continuing to manufacture so much out of its reserves. The infusion of new magic we'd gotten would help, but we needed to start supplementing with actual meat and crops. There were empty livestock stalls near the grain stores, as well as chambers that glowed with the light of a mystical sun, but we needed cows and sheep, seeds to plant, and fresh soil to add to the packed earth floors.

Triana had been chopping vegetables—she still insisted on staying busy—but when she noticed my frown, she set down the knife and came over. "What is it?" she signed.

I shared my thoughts, signing since I wanted to limit who might overhear any concerns.

She shook her head. "Always a new worry. You should delegate that to Nadine."

"Nadine has plenty to do." The dryad was always on the move, setting a structure and schedule for the growing ranks of servants.

"If she's too busy, she'll know who can help." Triana eyed me worriedly. "You work too hard. You need to rest sometimes."

That got a tired laugh out of me. "Maybe when I'm dead."

Nadine popped her head around the door. "You have a delivery, my princess."

I swore under my breath as I hurried outside. What now? At this rate, I'd be busy with unexpected visitors all day long, and Hector would never see me.

My irritation faded when I saw Aidan waiting beneath the Blood Tree with an enormous basket of sunset-hued flowers at his feet. "Wait a moment," he said, holding up a finger when I would have run over to him. "It's going to do something."

I looked down at the offering, baffled. The flowers smelled like cinnamon and citrus, and they were nestled in a bed of jagged orange crystals, each of which had a tiny flame burning at its heart. Aidan pulled a stone out of his pocket, bent over to smack it against one of the crystals, then stepped back.

The crystal had cracked from the blow, and a tiny tongue of fire licked out. Sparks suddenly launched out of it, bursting in a radiant halo overhead. I shrieked in surprise, and the crow in the Blood Tree let out a matching squawk before winging away. The flame raced around the basket, causing more crystals to break, until the air was filled with dancing specks of light. The flower petals turned a deep red in the heat, edged with glowing embers.

When the display was done and the sparks had winked out into tiny fragments of ash, Aidan pulled a scroll from his belt and presented it with a flourish. "For you."

I took it, feeling both awe and trepidation. That display had been beautiful, but there was only one person this could be from. Sure enough, the paper was filled with Drustan's handwriting.

Dearest Kenna,

Congratulations on your performance last night. I regret I didn't speak with you afterwards—I needed to assure my supporters that our alliance is strong and Imogen's piece of pageantry was no more than that. She knows how to perform, but I know how to lead. One skirmish means little compared to the scope of the war ahead, and when the battle breaks, I will lead our side to a glorious victory.

I hope you, too, know that I am capable of leading us.

Was that what he was aiming for with this gift? A bribe to win my support?

I've been thinking on your anger since the uprising. How to work around it, how to change your mind and convince you to abandon your rage and support me once more. Last night I realized that trying to redirect that anger is fruitless, because it's a symptom of a larger issue—that you do not trust me.

That is fair. So I offer this gift with my vow to be honest with you, no matter what. You deserve that.

My eyes teared up, and I looked down, blinking away the sign of emotion. Why couldn't anything be easy? Why couldn't the heroes and villains be obvious and pure in their intentions, for good or ill? I was done with Drustan romantically, but there was a painful longing that came with hearing the right words a little too late.

I know you dislike my scheming at times, but it is a strength I hope you will learn to appreciate. A ruler must be powerful, but they must also be loved. I am no tyrant to assume my infallibility, though. I make mistakes, despite my best intentions. A tempering voice—yours—would be a gift to have at my side, if you would be open to sharing your insight and your trust once more. Perhaps someday you would be willing to share something sweeter with me again, too.

So scheme with me, Kenna. See who I cultivate and how. Ask me for whatever you want, and I will provide. My sword, my soldiers, my honesty, my touch . . . Anything you desire can be yours. You must merely ask.

—Drustan

I pressed a hand to my mouth. This hadn't just been a plea for support. It was a request to reopen that closed door between us. To take him back into my arms, my bed, and my heart.

Teasing him last night had been too effective, or else he'd seen it as an opening to achieve several goals at once. Knowing Drustan, it was both. Because he clearly did want me, but he'd also begun this proposition by telling me what an incredible king he would be. Those two desires would be tied together so long as I could place a crown on his head.

"Do you like it?" Aidan asked hesitantly.

The flowers smelled like the spices dropped into mulled wine, and the red petals were still lined with glittering embers. Tiny flames wavered from the cracked stones like blades of grass in the wind. Did I like it? Yes, because it was beautiful, and the promises in that letter were beautiful, too. A Drustan who was always honest with me, who included me in his schemes and admitted he made mistakes—that was a version of Drustan I didn't know yet, and I wanted to.

Imogen had also offered me anything I desired, though. She also showered her subjects with gifts. Some faeries were seducers by nature, and other than the letter, this had been a fairly impersonal offering. Drustan still didn't understand me well enough to realize that the gifts I valued most were intangible.

I thought about Kallen's hand on mine, shaping my grip on a sword. The throat he'd ripped out to protect me. The time and work he'd put into strengthening me so I could stand on my own.

"Why didn't Drustan come here to tell me this himself?" I asked Aidan.

He looked dismayed I wasn't tripping over myself to praise the basket. "He said you would need time to think about it."

"And he's in a meeting," I guessed.

Aidan's silence was answer enough.

I stared at the gently smoldering flowers, wondering what to do. Would accepting them make Drustan think he'd won my support or the right to my bed? Flowers weren't enough to win me over, but admitting he was a fallible person who made mistakes . . . I appreciated that more than any promises about glorious victory. It would make him a better king than someone who believed himself incapable of error.

The familiar panic of indecision fluttered in my chest, and not just over how to reply to the flowers. Time was running out.

Maybe Hector would say all the wrong things today, and the decision would become easy.

Maybe Torin and Rowena would try to kill me again, and I wouldn't even be alive to make it.

"I'll take the crystals," I told Aidan. "He can keep the flowers."

His forehead furrowed. "You don't want the flowers?"

I wanted the flowers more than the crystals, to be honest, but they were a romantic gift, and I couldn't give Drustan an enthusiastic yes or an enthusiastic no. It benefited me to have him invested in my well-being, and the things that tempted him most were the ones just out of reach.

"I appreciate the gift," I said, smiling gently at Aidan and missing the days when he was just my friend and not the Fire prince's messenger. "And it's wonderful to see you, but I unfortunately can't stay. I'm on my way to a meeting."

Aidan deflated a little. "I'll let him know." He shook his head, looking down at the flowers with a half smile. "This is going to drive him mad." When his eyes flicked up, they burned with the fire of a sprite's gift. "You need to figure out what you want soon, though."

I swallowed, worried about how deeply he could see into my muddled desires. "Are you going to tell him I don't know what I want?"

He shook his head. "I think you do know. You're just not able to admit it yet."

"And what is it you think I want?"

He shrugged. "If I was a mind reader, they'd pay me a lot more." The magic flickered out, and his eyes returned to their usual black. "I don't envy you this position, Kenna," he said with the rare seriousness he saved for private moments. "No matter what you choose, people will be hurt. One of the princes—and their entire house—will be furious with you. That can't be easy."

"No," I admitted. "It's not."

He was looking at me with compassion now. "But I can feel your desire to do the right thing and make the choice that saves the most lives. So I would counsel you—as your friend, not as a member of Fire House—to not lose sight of that. If you can't live with a decision, don't make it just because someone else thinks you should." His smile was lopsided and wry. "Even if that someone is me."

Touched, I pulled him into a hug. He made a startled noise, said something garbled into my shoulder about princesses not giving out hugs to servants willy-nilly, then squeezed me back.

"I hope Hector gives you uglier flowers," he muttered when I finally released him.

That got me to laugh. "I doubt Hector will send me any flowers."

But I was curious to find out what the Void prince was going to offer instead.

27

HECTOR WAS WAITING FOR ME AT VOID HOUSE, TENDRILS of shadow curling around his boots. He stood beneath an archway wide enough for six horses to walk through, beyond which was a blackness so complete it made my head hurt. Cold air wafted out from the room, and an answering shiver danced over my skin at the thought of the death that awaited.

"Kallen says your house grew again," Hector said. He rarely opened conversations with bland pleasantries, just leapt into them like they'd already begun.

"It did."

"It's amazing how persuasive violence can be." He grimaced. "My manners are abysmal. I should have begun by congratulating you on the fight—and on lasting longer than I did."

"It wasn't a fair fight."

"There's no such thing. If life was fair, we wouldn't need to fight about it."

"You sound like Kallen."

He grunted. "Only in my wiser moments." His hands were laced behind his back, and his toe tapped as he studied me. "Kallen says you can be trusted." Hector didn't seem entirely certain of that, though—there was tension in the tightening skin beside his eyes and the hard slash of his mouth.

"I would hope you already believe that," I said, feeling flustered by the mention of Kallen's good opinion, which I still wasn't entirely sure how I'd earned. "Since we're both on the council."

"So is Drustan, and he can only be trusted while our goals are in alignment with his." He tilted his head, as if conceding to an unspoken argument. "Though I suppose we all fight for our own ends first and everything else last. He's just particularly annoying about it."

"So long as his goal is the good of the realm, that isn't the worst trait for a ruler to have."

"It's the secondary goals he doesn't talk about that worry me." He shook his head. "I wish you'd consider being more petty. You're far too noble for the likes of the Fae. Some of that goodness might rub off, and then where will we be?"

Too noble for the Noble Fae—what a contradiction. I raised my brows, amused despite myself. "You don't want to convince me of your own nobility?"

"Not like Drustan does. I want to convince you of my courage, my strength, and my fitness to be king. I don't need you to compose heroic ballads about me."

I looked down, hiding my smile. "I'm sure Drustan would love a ballad."

It was rare to have a chance to speak alone with Hector, and I took a moment to study him. He was as tall as Kallen but sturdier, though not as classically handsome. He always seemed a moment away from leaping into action; even here in the quiet outside his own house he was shifting his weight, narrowed eyes skating over the surroundings as if searching for opponents hidden in the stonework. That, too, reminded me of Kallen.

"So, why are we meeting?" I asked him.

"Because you asked me for something."

My breath caught. He was finally giving me what I wanted—an explanation of the crimes Drustan had alluded to. The secret Kallen said he had risked everything for, the great unspoken tragedy of Hector's past. "Very well," I said, smoothing my hands down the front of my scarlet dress. "What would you like to show me?"

"It's a short walk down the slope."

"Let's go." I picked up my skirts and turned in that direction.

He fell into step beside me. "Drustan would've asked at least ten follow-up questions before allowing me to take him to an unknown location."

"Yes, well, Drustan also has reason to distrust you. I have no desire for the crown, and since I'm the one who can give it to you, I suspect my safety isn't in question."

He made a huffing sound. "You're right about that."

"In fact," I said as we headed down the ramp, "you're probably in more danger than I am. If I had already decided to support Drustan, you might be at risk of an assassination."

Perhaps it was foolish to say something like that, even in jest. But he laughed, sounding nearly as startled as Kallen did whenever I made him laugh. "Trust me, if you had already chosen Drustan, I would've heard by now. He would have sent trumpeters to my front door to alert me." He smirked. "I suspect you're holding a grudge against him, no matter how noble you're determined to be."

"Maybe." Definitely. "But in the end, I do want what's best for Mistei. Whatever my personal feelings may be about Drustan—or anyone else."

"And that is ultimately the argument Kallen made. You want to do the right thing, not the easy thing."

I felt warm all over. That was one of the nicest things anyone had ever said about me. Why would Kallen tell him that? Why would Kallen even believe it? Our odd connection—because I wasn't sure how else to term the way we sought each other out, the stares across rooms, and the sparring lessons that left me breathless and unsettled—had begun with Kallen blackmailing me because he'd caught me cheating. It hadn't started because either of us were pure of heart.

The corridors here were more dimly lit than elsewhere in Mistei. Rather than torches burning in sconces, illumination was provided by candles flickering in wall alcoves, both single black tapers and clusters of them in ornate candelabra. The lighting allowed for more—and deeper—shadows, but it was oddly soothing. Like midnights spent reading by candlelight, a golden glimmer barely keeping the night at bay.

Some of the metal candelabra were jagged and nonsensical, but others formed stunningly realistic shapes. We passed one that resembled a miniature silver tree, with candles on every branch and a golden bird hidden in the leaves. Looking at the knots in the wood and the delicate curl of the bird's talons, I thought that Mistei's greatest beauty was often found in its smallest details.

The path curved, then branched. Hector looked around, then raised his hand, sending shadows coiling around us. The darkness swept out in all directions before solidifying, blocking off the routes to this intersection. It was like being in a cocoon.

He clearly wanted to conceal our direction from any prying eyes. I reached out with my own magic, listening for heartbeats. "I don't sense anyone," I said.

He grunted. "It's impossible to be too careful." Instead of taking the left- or right-hand path, he turned towards the wall and pressed his hand against it. There was a clicking sound, and a door I hadn't noticed swung open, revealing another candlelit hallway. It was a short servants' passage, lined with closets. There were spots like this all over Mistei, concealed by doors that had been painted gray or covered with a thin layer of stonework—places for servants to grab cleaning supplies, spare linens, or cutlery and glassware for impromptu events.

Once we were inside and his shadows had come rushing back through the crack below the door, Hector pulled a key out of his pocket and unlocked a closet. There were no shelves inside; instead, a staircase spiraled steeply down.

Where was he taking me? Curious and nervous, I followed him down the steps. The air clung heavy and damp to my skin, and the banister was carved with runes and rough faces.

"Is there a less steep way to get here?" I asked when we reached the bottom. The descent would have left my legs weary as a human.

"There's a ramp, but it would have taken forever, and we're both busy people."

We were in a long, low room with a vaulted roof. It reminded me of the cellars that had once stored grain below Blood House. Shadowed alcoves lined the walls, some of which were empty and others of which held burlap bags, crates, or sheet-covered furniture.

Hector led me to an alcove where the shadows seemed deeper than normal. When he waved his hand, they parted like clouds after the rain, revealing a door with a ring knocker. He stared at it for a long moment, then looked at me, as if second-guessing the decision to bring me here.

Then he sighed, gripped the knocker, and rapped it five times.

"I need you to know how serious this is," he said as we waited. His hand twitched like he was imagining gripping the hilt of his sword. "We're trusting you with a matter of life and death."

A shiver worked down my spine. "Who is we? You and Kallen?"

His jaw clenched. "And Una. Her most of all."

What did that mean? The mystery was killing me.

The door opened, revealing a Void sprite. His skin was reminiscent of the velvet dark of midnight, and his eyes were pure black, too, with no whites to be seen. When he saw Hector, stars sparkled to life in that dark gaze. He bowed. "My prince." Uncertainty flashed across his features as he looked at me. "You have brought a guest?"

"Yes," Hector said. "A guest who knows better than to speak a word of what she sees here." He gave me a hard look.

I was feeling even more nervous now. What could possibly be behind that door? "I won't. I promise."

The sprite studied me, eyes still sparkling. I wondered if he was reading my hidden desires, the way Aidan could. Not the exact direction of my thoughts, but the shape of my wishes and intentions. Then he bowed to me, eyes growing smooth as obsidian once more. "Princess Kenna. Welcome."

We entered a corridor, and the door clanged shut behind us. The sprite resumed his position in a small guard room off the entrance.

Hector led me down the hallway. The stone blocks that formed the walls had been set together so precisely there was no mortar securing them. Torches tilted out from wall brackets, and tapestries hung between them. Unlike the ones in Blood House, which showed scenes of faeries dancing, fighting, or romancing one another, the patterns stitched into the black fabric were unrecognizable. There were more runes and roughly sketched faces mixed with swirls leading to sharp corners, and the designs seemed to shift before the eye, as if the geography of those shapes made two types of sense at once. All of it was worked in shimmering thread that made me think of a rainbow viewed through black glass. Ink-dark reds, greens found in the depths of untouched forests, purples reminiscent of a bruise. Threads of gold and silver shimmered throughout, like lightning bolts crossing a midnight thunderstorm.

Each house had their own favored colors and designs. Void's had always seemed so simple—black on black, or black with some other dark color. As opaque and forbidding as the faeries themselves. These tapestries weren't for public viewing, though, and I wondered if this reflected Void House's true idea of beauty. Something private, something dark yet vibrant that puzzled the eyes and intrigued the soul.

I was drawn to a spiral stitched in rich, drowning blue. Then I realized it was the precise shade of Kallen's eyes and hurriedly looked away.

Hector stopped before one of the black tapestries. It didn't look like the others; there was no embroidery, and it rippled as if barely restraining itself from flying away. It was a sheet of Void magic, I realized, fringed in tendrils of night.

"What is this place?" I asked Hector, awed and alarmed.

He shook his head and reached towards that black curtain, which parted around his fingers. Then he held his other hand out to me.

I took a deep breath and slid my hand into his.

"Be kind to them," he said roughly. Then he turned and walked into the magic, taking me with him.

My vision went black. The darkness bit at my skin, deadly cold, and my bones vibrated like someone had made tuning forks out of them. I shuddered, feeling an awful dizziness, as if I had been plucked out of this world and set in the midst of a vast, empty space that stretched on forever.

Then my feet carried me to the other side, and the world came back. It had been less than a second, yet it had felt much longer than that. As if the darkness hadn't wanted to let me go.

I released Hector's hand and rubbed my arms, shivering. "Would

I have died if I tried to walk through that on my own?" It had felt like a cold that would kill.

"No," he said. "You would not have been able to pass through it alone, though, and it would not have been a pleasant wait for someone to come find you."

This corridor was vastly different from the hall outside. That had been orderly and smooth, directing the eye in an obvious direction. This one was crooked: the flagstones, the brick, even the ceiling tilted at a slight angle. Spots of shadow floated through the air like dandelion seeds on a breeze. We weren't inside Void House itself, but we were close, and I wondered if the same darkness drifted through those hallways.

A faint melody shivered through the air, too—a delicate, achingly lonely song played on an instrument I couldn't name. When I tried to listen more closely, it disappeared. "What was that music?" I asked, pressing a hand over my heart. It had made me want to weep.

Hector grunted. "We call that the song between the stars. An echo of the old world still drifting through ours. It comes and goes, especially near Void House."

The old world. He meant the place the Shards had come from, a world once inhabited by gods before they'd killed one another. That music was a memory, the way the old language and the Shards were memories. Alive and yet not.

It seemed impossible that gods could die, but I supposed everything did eventually. If they couldn't come to a natural end, they tore themselves apart.

A more tangible sound split the air: a woman's laughter.

Be kind to them, he'd said. Who was down here?

Hector abruptly turned to face me. "It was not always a crime to love someone from another house."

I looked at him, surprised by the abrupt change of topic.

"So the legends say, anyway." He shrugged, though his shoulders were tense. "I don't know how true anything we tell ourselves about the past is. But a long time ago, the houses mingled and faeries could move freely between them. An Illusion faerie could become a member of Void House if they felt more kinship there, and couples from opposing houses could live together. Maybe the magic was even mingled then, not as strictly separated."

Drustan had told me something like this, too. Some thought the magic had been separated into those six categories from the start, but he thought the Fae had bred for specialized power.

The laughter was followed by the murmur of voices. A haunted look crossed Hector's face. "I once thought it would take an eternity to return to that," he said. "But you've already begun."

"Hector," I said softly, wondering what was causing that tortured expression. "Where are we?"

He started walking. "Come."

We turned down a hallway lined with doors, and he opened the first one to reveal a large common area—a combined library and sitting room, full of bookshelves and comfortable couches. There were six faeries in the room, all dressed in black. A Noble Fae lady with coiled dark hair was picking through books, while a sylph scribbled at a writing desk positioned beneath a stained glass window. The window was lit from behind by flickering candles, casting jagged shards of color over his filmy black wings and blond hair. Nearby, two children were playing with dolls on the floor, laughing as they enacted some drama. One looked to be five or six years old, while the other was maybe ten.

Una and another faerie were seated on a couch, conversing while they watched the children. Una's hair was loose for once, the strands crinkled as if she'd recently taken out her long braid. She wore wide-legged trousers and a gauzy shirt, and her smile was relaxed in a way

I hadn't seen before. A Void asrai sat next to her, one with night-dark eyes and sable hair flecked with starlight. Both of them looked up at our entrance.

Una nodded to me, then murmured something to her companion. The asrai eyed me warily. "If you're sure," she said.

Una said something else too quietly for me to make out, then stood and walked over to us, ruffling the hair of one of the children as she passed.

The littlest girl grabbed Una's leg to stop her, then held her doll up. "Ria lit it on fire," she complained, pouting. And indeed, the doll was smoking, flame licking up its thread hair.

My brow furrowed as I looked at the doll. That had to be Fire magic, but what would a Fire child be doing in a secret location this close to Void House? They weren't hostages, were they? Leverage Hector was holding over Drustan?

"I'm sure it was an accident," Una said, smiling down at the older girl. "Can you put it out, too?"

The older girl—Ria—made a face. "Probably not."

"Come on," Una urged. "Try for me."

The girl sighed, then narrowed her eyes at the doll and raised her cupped hand above it. I expected the flames to wink out of existence, but instead she tipped her hand and poured out a stream of water. The flames hissed and extinguished.

I gasped, realizing all at once who Hector had brought me to see.

28

CHANGELINGS.

All this security—the hidden doors, the magic, the guard—was to protect this secret. These children of two houses, somehow growing up near Void House rather than being kidnapped and thrown into the human world.

These children weren't hostages—they were in hiding.

The littlest girl clapped her hands in delight after Ria extinguished the smoking doll, and a rainbow sprouted above the new puddle on the floor. Illusion magic. "Again, again!"

Una smiled at them. "Just make sure there's always an adult around when you're trying to light fires."

"No more fires today," the lady at the bookshelf said, carrying over a pile of books. "It's time for lessons."

The sylph at the desk rose, too, grinning at the children's protests. "Reading or meditation first?" he asked.

Ria scrunched up her face. "Reading, I guess."

"I'll make some snacks," the asrai said, rising from the couch.

Una nodded at the faeries, then continued towards us. "Let's find a place to talk," she said quietly.

We relocated to a smaller study down the hall. I sat on a couch, mind spinning from the revelation. "How?" I asked. "Why?"

"It started with Kallen," Hector said. He looked grim, and though Una sat next to me, he was pacing the room like a caged wolf. "He can tell you why and how it started. But we've been saving who we can for more than two and a half centuries."

Centuries? How was it possible they'd avoided detection that long?

"We teach them to control their powers," Una explained. "If they're part Void, we raise them in the house so they can undertake the trials without anyone realizing they're different. So long as they never let anyone see the other half of their magic, no one has to find out."

"And if they're not from Void?" Ria was clearly born of Fire and Earth—she couldn't pretend to be a Void faerie when the trials demanded the use of her magic.

"It depends on the parents and how the children came here," she said. "There's a whisper network among some of the Underfae midwives. If the parents can be trusted, and if they want to keep their children, we work with them to help control the children's magic so they can grow up in a house. It's a dangerous option, though—the parents must be reliable, and the children must be exceptional at magical control. The slightest error, and they'll be taken away and the parents punished for concealing the secret."

"The parents bring them to you?" I asked, shocked again. That would require collaboration between Void and the other houses, and Mistei's faeries rarely trusted one another or worked together.

"Sometimes." Sadness crossed Una's features. "Or sometimes the parents are so terrified they abandon the babies and we find them in the hallways. Or the parents are killed. Or the parents give them to a midwife and say they never want to see the baby again."

How awful. "What happens to the children who can't grow up in a house?"

"They don't go through the trials. Instead, they join one of the colonies of exiled Fae. They grow old and die, but at least they do it in Mistei, rather than being traded for a human."

"How many have there been?" I whispered.

"Forty-six," Una said. "Not as many as we would like, but Kallen wasn't always able to learn about them or make deals with the parents in time."

I pressed my lips together, overcome by a surge of emotion. Forty-six faeries saved from exile. Forty-six human lives spared, too—babies who hadn't been stolen from their mothers or had their tongues cut out before being forced into servitude. While Mistei's glittering court of fiends had danced through year after year of cruelty, Hector, Una, and Kallen had been quietly saving lives.

"I didn't realize there were so many changelings," I said, voice choked. Fae births were rare, and this kind of birth was a crime. But it had been happening anyway.

"Osric could make all the laws he wanted," Hector said, a bitter look still on his face. "But love does not answer to laws, and our remedies for unwanted pregnancies are not as successful as they are for humans—not without Blood House to assist. For every child we took in, two more were sent away."

Kallen had told me he'd done something that could put Void House in grave danger, and though Hector had thought it foolish at first, he'd accepted it. He'd clearly done far more than accept it—he'd created a safe space for the changelings, ensured they were trained to control their magic, then claimed the ones he could for Void House, even knowing that should they slip up with their magic in the public areas, the secret would be out.

Over two hundred and fifty years... But Hector had only been prince for a quarter century. "Your father, Prince Dryx—he was part of this, too?"

Una sucked in a breath.

Hector stilled in his pacing. Shadows suddenly coiled at his feet like snakes, winding up his legs, and when he looked at me, his eyes were blacker than night. The air grew cold. "My father would have torn them apart with his bare hands," he said, each word sharp as a knife. "Not that he had the time or attention to notice what we were doing. He was too busy drinking his failures away and beating my mother."

"Oh." The word left me like a whimper. "Forgive me. I didn't know."

There was frost forming on his sleeves. "I do not want to speak of this again after today."

I shuddered at the fury in his voice. "Of course. I promise not to tell anyone about the children—"

Una reached over and gripped my hand, squeezing hard. She shook her head. "He's not talking about them."

Confused, I closed my mouth.

Hector paced away again, shadows swirling in his wake. "Decades ago, Kallen brought an Illusion lady here to give birth," he said, staring at the door. "That was often the deal—a safe place to give birth, a new life for the child, and in exchange, the mothers would become his informants. They would often direct other expecting mothers to us, the ones who were desperate for a solution but hadn't wanted to or been able to end the pregnancy themselves."

He slammed his fist into the door suddenly, making me flinch. "Fuck," he snapped. "I hate this."

"You don't have to," Una said. "I can tell her."

"No. Kallen was right." He looked at me over his shoulder, eyes narrowed. "You want proof that I mean to help the people no one else does. So I'm not writing you an essay. I'm cutting out my heart to show you. You understand?"

I didn't, but I nodded anyway, throat thick with apprehension.

"That lady brought a maid with her. An asrai named Eluna." It sounded like he had to force her name out. "She was clever and sweet and pretty as a winter's night. She had the most incredible eyes—black and infinite, like she saw everything, but when she was happy, they shimmered with an aurora."

Realization filled me. This Illusion Underfae . . . she had meant something to Hector.

The pained tilt of his lips deepened. "She was *good*, in a way I could never hope to be. She believed in things like justice and gentleness and an afterlife beyond the stars where everyone would be equal in the end." He swallowed, throat bobbing. "Where everyone would be happy—and what was astounding was that she truly thought they deserved to be."

The way he spoke about her—*gods*. Even though whatever story this was had concluded years ago, I still felt the swell of fear.

Una's dark eyes shone with welling tears as she watched Hector. She already knew the ending, and even she looked afraid to hear it.

"The Illusion lady left and pretended it never happened," Hector said, "but Eluna came back to us over and over. She wanted to help teach the children. She didn't have Noble Fae magic, but she read to them. And I—"

He broke off, making a rough noise. Then he strode towards a bookshelf and grabbed a book at random, as if he needed something to hold, to look at, while saying this.

"I loved her," he said, fingers tightening on the cover until they went bone white. "As I have never loved before and never will again."

My heart ached for him. This forbidding, rough, restless prince had once loved a servant. And not just any servant—one from the king's own house.

"We had fifty years together," he said, staring at the book in his hand. "Fifty years that were as terrible as they were wonderful, because this love we had discovered, this thing that was . . . that was *divine* beyond any gods or magic, beyond anything I had ever known how to believe in—no one could ever find out about it."

Una was crying openly now, tears slipping silently down her cheeks.

My own eyes prickled. "You couldn't—" I broke off, clearing my throat. "You couldn't claim her for Void House, the way you claimed the changelings?"

He shook his head. "There's no way to tell which house a Noble Fae belongs to by looking at them. Eluna's eyes, though, and the rainbows—" His voice broke, and he cursed harshly before starting again. "The rainbows that followed where she went, she couldn't hide those. My father might have been blinded by drink and hate, but he would have noticed an Illusion asrai in the house, or someone would have told him about it. And she wanted to stay, anyway. To be a resource for the Illusion faeries who needed help." He looked at the book in his hands, then roughly shoved it back on the shelf. "Talking about this makes me want to break something," he snarled.

"Then break something," Una said.

He shook his head. "I've set enough bad examples for you over the years."

She looked around, then stood and crossed to a writing desk topped with a row of vases holding dried thistles. She picked through the papers and pens on the desk, then grabbed a paperweight made of swirling black glass. "Here," she said, offering it to Hector.

He scoffed but accepted it. "Always encouraging violence. This is what comes from being raised by me."

Because their father, Prince Dryx, had been murdered. What about Una's mother, though? Had she not been around?

I'd never heard her talked about, I realized. Never seen her at court, either, as far as I knew, just as I'd never seen or heard of Kallen and Hector's mother. If Dryx had been the type to raise his fists . . . Shards, were either of them still alive?

Hector closed his eyes. "Sit down so I can finish this."

Una patted his sleeve, then returned to sit on the couch.

Hector leaned against the bookcase, crossing his arms and tapping the paperweight against his bicep. "You may be able to guess what happened," he told me. "We were careful for fifty years, but nothing is foolproof, and she fell pregnant. We were terrified, but also . . . excited. We'd been saving other people's children for a long time, and this wasn't the first baby who was half-Underfae." He shook his head. "And somehow she'd taught me to believe that good things could and did happen."

A child born of a Noble Fae from Void House and an asrai from Illusion House. I tried to imagine it. Asrai were slim, tall, and graceful, with elongated fingers and narrow faces, and they always showed an elemental affinity. Alodie's blue hair constantly shifted like she was underwater, Fire asrai crackled with electricity . . . and rainbows had followed Eluna wherever she went.

"What were you going to do?" I asked. "The child presumably wouldn't have looked purely Noble Fae or purely Underfae."

"There you're wrong," he said. "In unions like that, the child usually takes strongly after one parent or the other. We worked out a plan: if she took after me and could pass as Noble Fae, the child would join Void House. If the babe took after Eluna, she would be raised in Illusion House."

She. Hector had had a daughter.

He sighed, looking down at the paperweight. "She was born on a summer night, screaming like she was going to tear the entire city down." He smiled, and it was the first break in the mask of pain he'd been wearing since we'd arrived. "She looked like Eluna, but her proportions were Noble Fae, and as soon as I felt the magic in her, I knew. She was going to be a Void faerie, like me."

I was entranced by the story despite the creeping horror that lay beneath it. There had clearly been no happy ending for Hector, Eluna, and their baby.

"It was hard for Eluna," he continued, "not being able to raise our daughter in her own chambers. Hard for me, too. But she often came to visit us here. And one day as she was leaving, I walked her out—and a servant saw us."

Una wiped fresh tears away. Hector glanced at her, and his eyes began to glisten, too. "The servant told my father I appeared to be enamored with an Illusion Underfae. And so Dryx roused from his drink and decided I needed to learn a lesson."

"What lesson?" I whispered, dreading the answer.

"That trying to change the world always ends in failure." He squeezed the paperweight, then tossed it from hand to hand. "After the rebellion, after he lost his first consort and all of his children, Dryx decided he didn't believe in love or dreams anymore." His voice grew quieter but no less cutting. "So he wrapped his hands around anything that might tempt him to care again, and he choked the life out of it. Starting with his next consort, my mother, and ending..."

He caught the paperweight, stared at it, then flung it with a sudden, violent motion. It crashed through the bottles lining the desk, and I flinched as glass shards and broken thistle stems scattered everywhere.

"He told me to kill her," Hector said, looking like he was barely restraining himself from picking up every object in the room and dashing it to pieces. "When I refused, he had me chained with iron... and then he strangled her in front of me with his bare hands."

Horror swelled, clinging to my insides like tar. What sick, relentless evil. "I'm so sorry," I whispered.

Hector's eyes glittered with grief and a hatred so virulent, I didn't think I'd ever seen its like. "Dryx didn't want anything to pollute the house's purity. Not even Eluna's body buried beneath our soil or sent to the void. He ordered the same servant who had betrayed her to toss her to the Nasties so they could destroy the evidence. But they were noticed along the way, and when word made it to the king that Void House was disposing of the corpse of an Illusion Underfae, Dryx was summoned to court to explain."

My hands were clasped to my mouth now. This was one of the worst things I'd ever heard, and somehow it still wasn't done.

"He took me with him," Hector said. He looked like he was in another time, another place, feeling the agony of a newly inflicted wound. "He told me it was better to be a monster than to love—one was strength, the other weakness. And if I couldn't manage to kill the part of me that felt love, then the second-best outcome was for everyone else to *believe* it was dead."

Kallen had said something like that, too. *It's better for our enemies to believe us monsters than to know what we truly care for.* I wondered if Kallen, too, had had that lesson forced on him.

The past was always sinking its claws into the present, eager to draw blood. How many of the words we spoke today were echoes of words from centuries ago?

"Osric was angry," Hector said. "Not about Eluna herself, but because it was an insult to his house. So Dryx told Osric something he knew the king would understand." He took a deep breath. "That I'd seen something pretty and decided to take it, but had accidentally destroyed her in the process. And to make up for the error, we would gift the king with one of our own servants to destroy in exchange."

"No," I said, voice breaking. My heart broke for him, too, just as it broke for Eluna and the baby and the servant Dryx had sacrificed to Osric. For the brutal end of a love story that should have spanned centuries.

"The king laughed," Hector said, still seeming like his mind was far from this room. "He laughed and laughed, and then he accepted Dryx's generous offer, and the scales were even between our houses once more."

The scales could never be even, though. Not between Void and Illusion, not between Hector and his father, and not between any of us and the evil that poisoned our lives and twisted our hearts until they could no longer love properly.

"Hector," Una said softly.

Her voice seemed to wake him from a trance. He shook his head, then looked at me again. "That's when a rumor started among the house heads that I liked to seize my pleasures by force—a rumor that hasn't spread beyond them, as far as I know, though clearly Drustan told you."

I nodded, sick at both the lie and the atrocities it had covered.

Hector sneered. "He's never bothered to ask me the truth."

"Would you have told him if he had?"

Hector was quiet for a few moments. "Not back then. If the king found out I actually loved Eluna, he would have started digging, trying to find out when the affair started and why, and there was more than my reputation at stake."

The children of two houses. This secret, safe place where those children could learn to control their magic until they found a place to belong.

"And now?" I asked. "I think he hates you for that."

"Does he?" Hector raised his brows. "I assumed it fell low on his priority list. He's perfectly willing to ally with me—so long as I know my place eventually."

"He also allies with Dallaida," Una pointed out, wiping away the last of her tears. "I don't anticipate that lasting long."

"True. But I don't think Drustan deserves to know this." His jaw clenched. "Or rather, I don't know if I can bear to give it to him."

I looked at Hector then, really looked. The perpetual sneer, the eyes filled with darkness, the restlessness that kept him pacing as if he saw the bars of his cage and was desperate to claw his way out . . . He wasn't just the arrogant, volatile Prince of Void. He was a faerie who had suffered deeply and would never escape the misery inflicted by his own father.

His father, who had been gutted in his bed. Yet another rumor had claimed Hector was responsible, and I was now certain that one was true. "This is why you killed Dryx. It wasn't just to seize power."

"Yes." He said it with relish, and his lips curved in something that wasn't a smile. "I didn't do it right away, though. He would have been wary of that, and there were schemes Kallen and I needed to put in motion first. So I let him believe me broken beneath his boot."

I imagined Kallen and Hector, heads bent together at the edge of a room as they often were, quietly discussing patricide. "I don't know if I would have been strong enough to wait," I admitted. "I don't know how you were able to pretend."

"Yes, well, that was mostly Kallen. I was ready to crush our father's skull that very night, but Kallen likes to play longer games." He eyed me. "That's why I'm trusting you with this, you understand? Not just because I need you to think well of me."

"Because Kallen told you to?"

Hector nodded. "He sees something in you. And for all he's done for me—for us—over the years, I am going to honor that."

It was a breathtaking, terrifying amount of trust. There were still children here learning to hone and hide their magic, and until Mistei's laws changed, they didn't have anywhere safe to go.

My lips parted. There *was* one place they could go. My house, where they would be as welcome as every other outcast. I could make acceptance of changelings a condition for anyone to join Blood House. And later, once the war was won, our alliance could force the rest of Mistei to follow.

But the groundwork had to be laid and power secured first—and Hector had brought me here anyway. Right to the heart of Void House's secret.

I wasn't sure if I should ask the next question. "And . . . your baby?"

To my surprise, Hector smiled. "I waited three months before killing my father. During that time, Kallen planted rumors that Dryx had impregnated one of the minor ladies of the house and a new heir was imminent. Dryx was drunk most of the time and volatile the rest of it—no one would dream of asking him for details. We even celebrated the night of the supposed birth, though my father wasn't invited." His smile grew. "That night, I ripped his guts out before strangling him to death. And once that was done—and it took a *very* long time, I promise you—Kallen framed the servant who had betrayed Eluna for the murder, and I declared that I would honor my father's memory by raising his daughter in his stead."

It took a moment for my brain to catch up. Then I gasped, snapping my head to look at Una.

She smiled, too, though her eyes were still reddened from crying. "That would be me."

Hector's daughter, not his sister. A beauty like a winter's night, who had inherited Hector's magic and could pass for Noble Fae. She'd passed the trials, too, gaining immortality and the full strength of her Void magic.

"So now you know," Una said. "Who I am and who Hector is."

"And what we plan to do next," he said, not looking away from me. "I'm not going to rest until we're allowed to love who we please. Until this world can be made safe for everyone—not just the ones like Una, who are lucky enough to hide their true natures." His mouth twisted. "I'm not going to pretend I'm a noble person or even a particularly good one. I'm not going to pretend you will like all of my policies or that all of them will be wise. But I swear to you, Kenna—I am in this for the right reasons. The rest can be sorted out."

And looking at him, at Una, in this place he and Kallen had created to shelter the vulnerable . . . I believed him.

29

AFTER THE CONVERSATION WITH HECTOR, I WAS DESPERate to speak with Kallen. I sent a note asking him to go spying with me, rather than sparring, and he replied, saying he'd heard a rumor that construction was happening late at night in the cavern where state dinners were held, and he wanted to know what Imogen was up to.

I'd hoped to bring up the changelings, but once we were in the catacombs, he launched straight into a discussion of military matters: how Fire and Void were running drills together, which young faeries he thought showed the most potential—Edric had apparently impressed everyone enough to gain leadership of a squadron—and which of my new house members might be able to fight in our combined army. He was rarely this talkative, and I wondered if he was nervous about the conversation he must know was coming.

"The Illusion army is also training heavily," Kallen said as we walked side by side. "Imogen tasked Ulric with getting them up to standard. I heard he's brought Torin in to consult."

I grimaced. "That doesn't bode well. Doesn't he oversee the Sun Soldiers?"

"Yes, but he's not going to overcome hundreds of years of benign neglect in a month. And Torin's expertise is tailored to what the Sun Soldiers are best at, which is ambushes and targeted strikes. He'll make the Illusion troops stronger and more disciplined, but he's not an expert in pitched warfare."

The corridor narrowed, and the floor grew uneven. I braced one hand against the damp wall, stepping carefully. "I assume the Light army also started training?"

He gave me an ironic look. "They never stopped."

"I worry Gweneira is losing ground in Light House," I admitted. "Lara says they nearly poisoned her a second time." We'd learned the poison in her drink paralyzed the heart and lungs. It had a slow onset, but after the first symptoms appeared—a lagging heartbeat, labored breaths—death would follow within thirty minutes.

Kallen's arm brushed mine as the narrowing passage pushed us closer together. "She's not going to win," he said bluntly. "It was a nice thought, but she still only has the loyalty of a third of the house, and the Accord is ending in just over two weeks. It's only a matter of time before one of their assassination attempts succeeds."

I had come to like Gweneira. More importantly, Lara liked her, even though she supported Drustan. I rarely saw her so engaged as when she was discussing Gweneira's books or Gweneira's insights or some conversation they'd had at a party.

I frowned, a sudden suspicion forming. Lara talked about Gweneira a *lot*.

My toes caught the edge of an uneven paver. I lurched forward, but Kallen's arm was already wrapping around my waist, yanking me back against his chest. It took a few moments to get my feet under me again.

"All right?" he whispered.

I was pressed against him so closely I felt the rise and fall of his breathing. I gripped the forearm banding my waist, then nodded. "Fine. Thank you."

I didn't let go of his arm, though. He didn't move, either.

The seconds stretched out, and the silence between us began to feel heavy. I was too aware of the muscles beneath my fingers and the subtle, delicious scent that clung to him.

It felt far too good to be held by him.

He abruptly let me go. "Careful with your footing. It's uneven up ahead, too."

He could see in the dark, I remembered. My perception was limited to the pool of light cast by the key, but he could look into the deepest black of the catacombs.

I used the treacherous footing as an excuse to keep my head down in case I was blushing. "So, the cavern," I said, changing the subject with as little grace as I'd exhibited walking. "Do you think Imogen's doing something nefarious? She might just be redecorating it to her taste."

Kallen didn't seem flustered by the interlude that had passed between us, but he rarely seemed flustered by anything. "I worry what her taste involves," he said, falling into step beside me as if we'd never stopped.

"She likes pink."

"So long as she doesn't like boiling oil to go with it."

That got me to look at him again. The key's light bounced off his features, highlighting his cheekbone and the sharp edge of his jaw. He didn't look like he was joking, but it was hard to tell with Kallen. "Boiling oil?"

"An old defensive technique. It's hard to mount a frontal assault when that's pouring down on you." He angled his face towards me so the light caught the rest of it, and I was struck once again by how beautiful he was. The lines of his features were so precise they were nearly severe, but his eyes seemed deep enough to drown in.

Stop it, I told myself. *Stop thinking like that.*

"Don't humans do that, too?" he asked.

"Do what?" I'd lost track of the conversation.

"Boiling oil. I've heard of it being used in castles under siege."

He was talking about murdering people, and I was thinking about how pretty his eyes looked. "I didn't live in a castle," I said, forcing myself to focus. "I lived in a one-room hut, selling peat bricks and bog trash for a living."

Despite the harsh words, wistfulness drifted through me for that lost place. I could picture it so clearly: the dried herbs hanging from the rafters, the scarred wooden table, the sunlight spilling through warped window glass.

"Will you tell me about it?" he asked.

I laughed uncomfortably. "About my hut? It was hardly up to the standards of the Fae."

"About where you came from. What you miss."

It was a melancholy question, and I wondered at the shift to discussing something so personal. Maybe it had something to do with the conversation we both knew was coming. A vulnerability for a vulnerability, a piece of me for a piece of him.

"I was not well loved in my village," I said. "It was an unkind place a lot of the time. Small-minded people who didn't like a girl wearing trousers, devout people who cared more about the distant Fae than their own neighbors. Most of us lived one meal to the next, and a single bad harvest or a single illness could spell ruin."

I was starting this all wrong. He'd asked what I missed, and here I was telling him everything I didn't. But it was possible to hate something and love it, too. Maybe that was required of the places where we grew up. We had to point at something and say, "That's where I used to be," to tell ourselves why the place we were now was so much better.

"It was pretty, though, in its rough way," I continued. "Everything was a little crooked—the houses, the market stalls, the chimneys. Like some giant had picked the whole town up and set it down too hard." I smiled, thinking of those rows of tilted chimneys coiling smoke into the dawn sky. "And the area around it was beautiful. There were moors to the east and a forest to the south and mountains lining the horizon to the west. And to the north was the bog." Wistfulness caught in my throat. "I loved that bog, awful as it was. It stank in places, and it was dangerous, and one of the worst nights of my life happened there, but there was also so much wonder to it. We lived at the edge, and I used to go fishing there at dawn, pulling up trinkets people dropped a long time ago."

"We," he said, eyes steady on my face. "You said *we* lived at the edge."

Our steps had slowed, but he didn't seem to feel the need to rush, and neither did I anymore. I was caught up in memories: summer sunshine on my face and icy winter rain splatting against the flagstones, the scent of peat smoke, the pink-and-gold slice of sunrise across the horizon. Warm, calloused hands holding mine, blue eyes smiling down at me.

"My mother and I." My throat felt even thicker now. "She was an herbworker, and her fingers were always stained yellow and green. She had the nicest laugh, but she always covered it with her hand like she was embarrassed. And she fought so hard." For us, for her health, for the dreams that had turned to ash before she'd had much time to dream them at all.

The pathway branched ahead. The right turning would take us to Earth House, the left in the direction of the cavern. "Turn left," I said, grateful for a moment to compose myself.

I was chewing over words, wondering what else to tell him, when Kallen spoke. "I like hearing about your past."

"You do?"

"It's nice to imagine the world through your eyes."

"I can't imagine why."

"Maybe not." He looked sad now. "What happened to your mother?"

My breath felt sharp in my chest. "She died. She got sick, and it took a long time." There was no reason to tell him the rest of it, but I found myself confessing anyway. "She begged the Fae for mercy in her last moments."

Kallen was quiet for a while. "I'm sorry, Kenna."

The simple statement nestled quietly into my heart. He wasn't offering me philosophy or comfort or clever words. Kallen was sorry she was dead and sorry for how and sorry that the Fae hadn't helped.

"Thank you," I said, fighting back tears. "I don't think anyone's said that to me in a long time."

THE SPY HOLES OVERLOOKING THE CAVERN WERE NARROW cracks in the rock, just wide enough to fit the head of an arrow through. I squinted at the Illusion and Light servants bustling around below. Some were erecting lattices covered in pink and yellow flowers on either side of the dais, while others used long poles to hang banners from hooks screwed into the walls. The violet fabric held a sigil I was unfamiliar with but could guess the significance of: a silver crown over a rearing unicorn, surrounded by flowers. The fringe at the bottom was the color of a blushing rose.

"Pink," I whispered to Kallen, stepping back to let him take a turn. "Not boiling oil."

He bent slightly to peer through the gap. "Not yet, anyway."

There were other places I could stand and look, but I was reluctant to move away. Kallen had always had a strange magnetism—I'd felt it even when I shouldn't have, even back when I'd hated him—but now that I knew his secret, it was so much worse.

He'd been Mistei's villain, but now I knew he'd been a hero, too.

Don't look at what people do when everyone is watching, my mother had told me. *Pay attention to what happens the rest of the time.*

More than two hundred years. Forty-six lives saved—ninety-two, counting the humans who had been spared. No accolades.

He'd undoubtedly ended far more than ninety-two lives during that time, too. It was impossible to separate Kallen the savior from Kallen the blackmailer or Kallen the killer, because he was all those things. There would be murders that weren't justified, bad choices and selfish choices and crimes I would have condemned as a human and might still condemn now. But the thing about Kallen that called to me on some deep level was that he didn't pretend otherwise.

When it was my turn to look again, I saw faeries bringing in ladders so they could string silk ribbons between stalactites. Others were setting up tables and placing vases full of feathers atop them, while more Underfae bustled in and out of the servants' entrances with crates of glassware and barrels of wine. "Gweneira says Imogen is hosting a masquerade ball here in a few days," I said. "Apparently the last ball wasn't enough excitement for her." That information had come courtesy of Lara, who had learned it while dancing with Gweneira, and now that the suspicion had settled into place, I couldn't believe I hadn't noticed what was going on between them earlier.

Kallen made a dissatisfied noise. "Gweneira knows too many things."

I pulled back to give him an amused look. "Does it bother you that you're not the only spymaster?"

"Yes," he said peevishly, and I pressed a hand to my mouth to cover my chuckle. "It makes sense Drustan had a spy on his side. I just don't know how she gets her information. I've never heard of her blackmailing anyone."

"There are other techniques besides threatening and blackmailing people."

He looked discomfited. "Probably true."

"You could have tried befriending people instead," I said, half jesting. "Charming them into giving you information."

A pained expression crossed his face. "No, I couldn't have."

I instantly felt remorse for teasing him. Not sure what to say to make it better, I focused on the room again.

Thirty minutes later, the most nefarious thing we'd seen was a faerie polishing the torch sconces too aggressively. "I think Imogen really is just redecorating for the masquerade," I said, yawning so widely my jaw cracked.

Kallen smiled slightly as he looked at me. "You look exhausted."

"Can we say this was a dead end?" My eyelids were heavy, and I felt the queasy lightheadedness that came from needing sleep. "Or should we keep watching?"

"We can stop."

"We should have trained instead."

He shook his head. "This is part of being a spy. You watch and listen to everything, and sometimes it's important, and sometimes it's not. Only with a large enough volume of information do the patterns start becoming clear."

"And what patterns do you see thus far?" I asked as we headed away from the cavern.

"Did you notice the feathers on the tables?"

"Yes." Glittering scarlet flights edged with gold, from no bird I'd ever seen before.

"Those are phoenix feathers. They're so expensive you wouldn't believe it. She's paying more than they're worth, too, because she's importing them from Elsmere, and Briar is canny enough to recognize an opportunity."

I'd only heard of phoenixes in stories, but I'd dreamed of seeing one in the wild, burning as it fell out of the sky before resurrecting from the ash. "More reckless spending," I said.

He nodded. "She can't keep this up forever, and I've heard rumblings her advisors are trying to get her to slow down. She risks tipping her reputation from merry to wasteful—and there are those, especially in Earth House, who have concerns about how the feathers are sometimes harvested, since not everyone is content to wait for the birds to molt. Even if these were collected ethically, it's a miscalculation, because it could spark rumors she procured them from illegal poachers."

It was hard to believe the Fae valued any form of life that much, but the birds inside Earth House had been well loved. Perhaps the Fae found it easier to care for creatures they had no need to empathize with. "Will you be the one spreading those rumors?" I asked.

His smile was quick and sly. "I've already started."

We had reached the intersection leading towards Earth House. Kallen abruptly flung an arm in front of me, stopping my progress as he stared down that blackened corridor.

"What is it?" I asked nervously.

"Brambles. They weren't there before."

"What?" I ducked under his arm, then hurried forward. The light of the key caught on a tangle of dense, thorny vines at the end of the hallway, just before it turned at a sharp angle. They formed a bristling wall from floor to ceiling. "Oriana blocked it off," I breathed.

Kallen joined me. "That route leads to Earth House?"

"Eventually. It makes sense she would block off the house, knowing I'm still using the catacombs, but this is . . . aggressive." Had she realized we were here and decided to send a message? I cast my magic out, searching for a hint of her in the distance, and found nothing.

The stems were thick, with needlelike thorns. Branches clung to the walls and ceiling in a way that made me think of the tendrils of a drowned woman's hair. As I watched, the vines moved, stretching their tips a few inches farther.

"They're growing," I said, fear rising in my throat.

Oriana hadn't created this wall tonight. She was using her magic to consume these tunnels bit by bit, ensuring I wouldn't be able to use the tools of Earth House for a war she wanted no part of.

If you enter the catacombs again, you will not enjoy what you find there.

I'd dismissed the threat as an empty one because Oriana's neutrality would prevent her from trying to kill me. But it hadn't been empty at all. "I can't lose this," I told Kallen, breath coming faster.

He unsheathed his sword, studying the vines. "This probably won't work." He swung the blade down hard on a protruding branch. There was a sound like metal striking stone, and he grimaced as the weapon stopped dead.

A green tendril shot out and wrapped around the hilt of the sword, then yanked it out of his grip. The weapon vanished into the wall of thorns.

I pressed my hands to my mouth. "Your sword!"

He frowned at the plants, shaking out his hand. "I have others. It was worth testing." Then he grimaced, rubbing the place where his neck and shoulder met. "Shards, that hurt."

I moved towards him. "Are you all right?"

"I'll be fine." He dug his fingers in harder.

Kallen always assumed his own pain didn't matter. I wrestled with myself for a moment, then gave in to the impulse. "Turn around."

His eyes flicked between mine as if he was trying to figure out what I was thinking. Then he slowly turned.

I took a deep breath before placing my hands on his shoulders. He twitched. When he didn't protest, I started rubbing the tense muscles more gently than he had.

Kallen groaned, a sound so rough it raised goose bumps on my skin. "That's good," he breathed.

I slipped my magic lightly beneath his skin to assess the pain in his sword arm, from the aggravated knots in his muscles to the tips of his fingers. His hand had gone partially numb from the jarring blow and was prickling as it regained sensation. I imagined the numbness receding faster and sensed the discomfort ease.

Kallen sighed. "Thank you."

"You're welcome," I whispered.

I could have relaxed the knots in his shoulders with nothing but my magic, too. But I didn't.

We were quiet—him standing with his head bowed, me exploring his muscles with my thumbs, the plants creeping forward. Fear for the future crept through me just as insidiously. What would I do without my greatest advantage?

"You will find other weapons," Kallen said at last, intuiting the direction of my thoughts. "Use this one as long as you can, but even after Oriana takes it from you, know there will always be other avenues to explore. Nothing is set."

Things felt very set in Mistei—the hierarchies, the history, the roles we were all expected to play. Sometimes I felt like an audience member who had stumbled onstage during a drama, briefly interrupting the plot. The Fae repeated their performance in an endless cycle: the pursuit of power, the attainment of it, the loss of it. A new show night after night, but the same old lines.

Except I wasn't the only one who had disrupted a cycle, was I? Kallen had, too.

I'd been wanting to discuss this with him all night. The intimacy of the moment loosened my tongue. "I met with Hector. But you already knew that."

Kallen hesitated before answering. "Yes."

I rubbed a thumb against the side of his neck. "How did it start?"

"The children?"

"Yes." I slid my hands down his back, digging into the tight muscles beside his spine.

Kallen tensed, then sighed and relaxed. "I was young and dangerously reckless, that's how."

"You don't consider yourself reckless now?"

He gave a half laugh. "Now I'm old and slightly less reckless." He rolled his head on his neck, then let it droop. "I had been sworn to Osric for thirty years when everything started. It was—unbearable."

His magic wisped out to join the shadows surrounding us. The darkness pressed in, threatening to swallow the light of the key. The weight of history felt as oppressive as the blackness and the brambles stretching into the distance.

"He'd realized my potential as a spy, not just an assassin," Kallen continued, "and he expected a constant flow of information. Who was speaking about him, who was exhibiting less respect than they should, who was breaking the rules he'd set. I walked as careful a line as I could, but . . . sacrifices had to be made."

I kept working the knots out, gradually increasing the pressure and aiding my touch with the slightest brush of magic. "What do you mean, sacrifices?"

For a while I thought he wouldn't answer. "If I didn't bring enough information, he tortured me."

I gasped. "Kallen!"

"It's fine. That part, anyway. I had already learned to tolerate it."

He spoke about it so matter-of-factly. Tortured. And not just once—he had *already learned to tolerate it*. That was far from fine.

"It frustrated him that he couldn't get the reactions he wanted out of me anymore," Kallen said. "Then he learned that torturing others in front of me was a better incentive."

I stroked my hands over his shoulders to his upper arms. "I'm sorry," I whispered.

"It is what it is." His muscles flickered, like he was tempted to tear out of my grasp. "So I played the game as strategically as I could. Targeted faeries I knew were cruel or ones I anticipated getting in my way. I even framed a few of his closest advisors. The more isolated he got, the easier he would be to kill one day." He shook his head. "Or so I thought. Instead, it made him more volatile."

The fear over losing the catacombs was receding. What a small price to pay, when Kallen had paid far worse over the years and was still fighting. I trailed my fingers down to his forearms before digging my thumbs in there, feeling the strength hidden beneath the fabric of his shirt. Another soft exhalation left him.

"There were innocents, too," he said. "Before you get the wrong idea. Faeries I betrayed because I was panicking and needed to say something, or because I suspected someone else had the same information and I wanted to act first to secure Osric's trust." He paused. "Sometimes I was wrong about that and had them killed for nothing."

It was unimaginable. First taken hostage in exchange for his house's safety, then tortured into compliance, knowing that no matter what he chose, someone would suffer.

"And there were dark periods when everything felt cold and nothing mattered. I obeyed him then because it seemed pointless to do anything else. I imagined a vast scale teetering between us, and I told myself that so long as it eventually tipped in my favor, anything was acceptable."

I had stilled, no longer massaging him, just holding his forearms in a grip that was growing too tight. "You were still a victim."

"That doesn't excuse it." He looked over his shoulder at me, eyes dark with echoes of the past. "There's truth to what Drustan says about me, Kenna. I have always been a monster, and not always an unwilling one."

"You're more than that."

"Am I?" He shook his head, then faced forward again. "The point I'm working up to is that for a span of decades, I told myself my heart had no use anymore. I—" He broke off, then cleared his throat. "I had already killed it, or tried to. But then one day the king ordered me to go to Earth House and retrieve a pregnant faerie for him."

I stroked my thumbs over his wrists. I didn't know why I was still holding him like this. It was almost an embrace—my arms wrapped around him, my front nearly pressed against his back.

He seemed to find it easier to confess without looking at me, too, because the words tumbled out of him. "After I brought her to Osric, I found out the child's father was from Illusion House and had told the king about the baby in exchange for a lesser punishment. And that's when I realized my heart wasn't entirely dead, after all."

"Did you save that one?" I asked, my own heart aching.

He shook his head.

"But you started finding the pregnant faeries after that, didn't you? You offered to help them."

"In exchange for information," he said bitterly. "Those motives weren't all pure, either. I wanted to know what went on behind house walls—and there are plenty of bodies in the ground because of those deals, believe me."

He was so determined to condemn himself. "You still risked a lot to save them. If the king had found out..."

"That's why it was reckless." His back expanded on an inhale, and he blew it out between pursed lips. "Hector objected at first, but he soon grew even more passionate about the cause than I did. During the years I felt too broken to go on with any of it, he convinced me to keep trying. Even if it never came close to balancing out the evil I'd done."

He leaned back slightly, and our bodies pressed together. I stilled, clutching his forearms. Small tremors raced through Kallen's body and into mine.

We were balanced on the edge of something. Every time we touched, we tested that balance, seeing what would finally be enough to push us over. I closed my eyes, inhaling his now familiar scent. Like cold midnights and rare spices and rarer flowers. "You're too hard on yourself," I whispered.

He ripped out of my hold so violently it startled a cry from my throat. He spun, then clutched my shoulders to hold me at arm's length. His skin had gone cold—it was like being gripped by an ice sculpture. "No, Kenna," he gritted out. His nostrils were flared, and his lip was curled in an expression of scorn. "Do not make me out to be some tragic, misunderstood hero. I could not possibly be hard enough on myself."

My chest rose and fell rapidly. That scorn wasn't directed at me; it was directed internally. Kallen hated himself. "So you made some terrible choices," I said, voice shaky. "You also made good ones. Do those not matter?"

His expression was full of such horrible pain. Shadows wound around his neck and down his arms as his irises swirled black.

I'd once thought of his eyes as the openings to a deep pit where unspeakable crimes roamed like monsters and every kind instinct was shackled like a prisoner. There was more to him, though, and the more I saw of the person behind the mask, the more I wanted to uncover.

"I think they matter," I said when he didn't respond. I raised my hands to clasp his cold cheeks, and freezing tendrils of magic started curling around my wrists. "You're not going to convince me to judge you, Kallen. Unless you plan to judge me for what I've done?"

"What you've—" He broke off, and his fingers tightened on my shoulders, like he was desperate to keep me away. "What are your sins, Kenna? You give of yourself endlessly, no matter how much danger it puts you in. You *freed* us, when all I did was cause centuries of suffering. And you make me—" An anguished sound left his lips. "It kills me. Everything you are. I can't bear it."

I blinked rapidly. "You can't— What are you saying?"

My heart was pounding so hard I felt faint. I leaned forward, pressing against his hold, wanting to know why he was looking at me like it was agony, but he couldn't stop.

He released me abruptly and backed away. I lurched forward, and he reached out as if to steady me before cursing and snatching his hand back.

We stared at each other, breathing hard.

"I have to go," he said.

"Kallen—"

He shook his head. "Not tonight, Kenna. Just let me . . . not tonight."

My heart ached at the pain in his voice. I wanted to demand he stay and tell me more about his past and what he thought he couldn't bear, but that wouldn't be fair. He was a private person who had torn open his wounds for me, and he wanted to retreat to lick them in peace.

"All right," I whispered.

I guided him back down the passage, away from the brambles and towards the nearest hidden door. I peered through a peephole and extended my magic to make sure no one was nearby, then opened it to reveal an empty hallway.

Kallen lingered, still watching me with that tormented expression. He raised his hand slowly to my face, running his thumb over my cheekbone.

Then his fingers slipped away, and the door closed behind him, leaving me alone in the dark.

30

I SAT CROSS-LEGGED ON MY BED THE NEXT AFTERNOON, SURrounded by scrolls. At my request, Drustan and Hector had delivered thoughts on what to do with the aboveground territory now that Osric's wards were down, and since the day was unusually calm, I was using the time to compare everything they'd sent.

Calm was a relative term, of course. Getting to know my new house members and setting expectations for our collective behavior had taken priority this morning, but none of the outside events were major, so I'd declined those invitations. Tomorrow would have more than enough activity—a party in one of the libraries followed by the masquerade ball.

The ball marked the thirteenth night of the Accord, and I was determined to name a king by the end of the week. My indecision had lasted for far too long. I read and reread the letters, grappling with the magnitude of this responsibility.

Drustan was in favor of splitting the territory aboveground into equal segments by house, with areas of free passage between. Hector was in favor of keeping the entire surface unaligned territory. *We do not need to break the entire world into pieces*, he'd written in his scrawling hand, and I was inclined to agree. Drustan made a good point, though, that providing a structure and setting expectations wherever we could would help the tradition-bound Fae navigate this period of regime change.

It had been like this on every issue. Each made good points. Each said mostly the right things. If they were genuine in their promises, either would make a decent king. And that was the major question: Would they live up to those promises? If they tried and met resistance, which one would push through to force the needed change to happen? Sometimes the right thing was also the unpopular thing, and of the two of them, I knew which one most enjoyed his popularity.

Another question was who would be a better figurehead when it came to gathering public support. That was almost certainly Drustan, since Hector had spent less time at court and had a reputation for being unpredictable, reclusive, and occasionally violent. The violent reputation wasn't as much of a liability as one would think in Mistei, though, and Drustan had been losing ground when it came to public opinion. My new house members told me he'd enraged much of Earth House by soliciting their support before betraying Selwyn.

Both wanted to end the barbaric changeling practice, but Hector had been actively working to save those lives for a long time, and that was heavily weighting my decision. But there were thousands of lives at stake—would the larger populace trust him, especially if other faeries had heard the rumor about him being a predator?

There were personal questions that haunted me, too. If I chose Hector, would Lara's budding romance with Gweneira come to an end? If I chose Drustan, would Kallen no longer want to train me?

I closed my eyes, cursing myself, because it wasn't just his training I would miss.

There was an urgent knock at the door. "Come in," I called, welcoming the distraction.

Triana nearly ran inside. "You have to come," she signed, expression frantic.

Scrolls tumbled to the floor as I leapt out of bed. "What's wrong?"

"Anya. She's gone mad."

Panic swept through me as I raced after Triana into the corridor and down the spiraling stairs to the fourth floor. The bedrooms on this level had been claimed by a mixed group of Noble Fae who were clustered in the hallway, staring at an open door.

"She barged into my room," I heard Wilkin, the Earth faerie with the white flowering garden, tell someone. "Raving about the princess inviting faeries into the house."

I heard a familiar shout, then the sound of something shattering. Cursing under my breath, I pushed past the gawkers.

The bedroom was decorated in shades of dove gray and burgundy. A scarlet-petaled rose lay in a puddle near the entrance, surrounded by the shards of the vase that had once housed it. Ornamental weapons hung on the walls, and the air smelled of fragrant woodsmoke.

Anya stood before the lit fireplace, yanking at the handle of an axe mounted above it.

"Anya!" I exclaimed. "What are you doing?"

The axe was bracketed to the wall, and she made a frustrated sound before letting go. "Get them out," she snarled.

"Get who out?" I asked, heart pounding. "What's wrong?"

"The faeries. There are faeries here."

She didn't sound entirely awake. Her eyes were reddened and lost-looking, and as she turned to face me, she staggered like she was about to fall over.

"The faeries here are good ones," I said, trying to keep my voice calm despite the fear that hummed through me. "You've seen them before. Don't you remember them arriving?"

She hadn't attended last night's dinner, which had been held in a banquet hall large enough to accommodate everyone, but I'd spotted her lurking in the doorway and listening as the new arrivals had introduced themselves and their hopes for the future. Though she'd locked herself in her bedroom afterwards and ignored the pot of hot chocolate I'd placed outside her door, I'd taken it as a sign of progress—that if I left her alone like she clearly wanted me to, she would gradually begin opening up on her own terms.

"This is Wilkin's room," I said when she didn't answer. "Do you remember him talking about planting a garden?"

Anya stared at me like she couldn't comprehend the words. I wasn't even sure if she was seeing me, or if her mind was somewhere far away. She swayed like a birch sapling caught in a strong wind, and her eyes drifted back to the axe.

"Were you sleepwalking?" I asked, taking a step closer. She'd done that a few times as a child.

She jerked her gaze away from the weapon, then looked down at her shaking hands. "I don't remember sleeping."

"When's the last time you remember sleeping?"

"I can't sleep. If I sleep, I dream. I can't dream. It's all drowning and fire and *he's* there."

She sounded delirious. The skin below her eyes was puffy and purpled—she looked more tired than I'd ever seen her. More tired than I'd ever seen anyone except my mother during the final brutal nights of her illness.

Guilt swamped me. I hadn't been hearing her nightmares lately, and I'd thought it was because they'd been getting better. Now it was clear she'd been staying awake to avoid them.

There was a purple stain down the front of her shapeless gray dress. "Were you drinking?" I asked. The servants said she hadn't taken wine upstairs with her dinner trays these past few nights, so I'd thought that issue was improving, too. But maybe she'd found an abandoned wine cellar, or maybe the house was providing her with alcohol—it was as Fae as anything down here, and the Fae didn't deny even their most destructive cravings.

"If I drink, I don't dream," she said, words slurring.

So she'd been staying awake to avoid nightmares of Osric, and because her body would always eventually give in, she'd tried to drug her mind until it couldn't produce dreams. And this was the result—Anya rampaging delirious and drunk into someone's bedroom, trying to pull an axe off the wall.

"What were you going to do with that axe?" I asked, dreading the answer.

"He needs to die."

Prickles raced down my arms. "Anya, you know Osric isn't here, right?"

"You invited them in," she said, sounding like a lost child. "My mother says you should never invite the faeries in. If you let them in, they'll steal everything you love."

My heart felt like it had been wrapped in the same brambles that were consuming Mistei's catacombs. Osric had broken Anya. He'd twisted her mind until she couldn't tell what was real and what wasn't, and even in death, he was stealing her sleep and her sanity. And I'd let her fall deeper into this hole, so consumed by my myriad responsibilities that I hadn't realized how bad it had gotten.

I'd thought giving her space would help, but I'd given her enough space to get lost in.

Anya made an anguished sound, then smacked her head with her palms again and again, like she was trying to knock something out of her mind.

"Stop hurting yourself!" When she didn't, I ran forward and grabbed her wrists.

"Don't touch me!" she shrieked. She threw her weight into me, knocking me backwards. My heel struck the low stone ledge in front of the fireplace, and my skull cracked hard against the mantelpiece. I collapsed, planting one hand in the flaming logs in an attempt to catch myself. Burning pain ripped across my palm, and heat licked up my sleeve as the gauzy fabric went up in flames.

Wilkin sprinted into the room, then dragged me up and away from the fire. He summoned water and poured it over my sleeve, and the flames sizzled and went out. "Are you all right?" he asked, gripping my shoulders when I staggered and nearly fell again.

No, I wasn't.

The smell of burnt fabric filled the air. I held my seared hand against my stomach like a wounded animal, gaping at Anya. Her hands were clapped to her mouth, and her eyes were wide with horror.

"Leave her," Wilkin was telling me. "We need to get you somewhere safe."

But Anya had always been my safe place.

Faeries gawked from the doorway. I couldn't imagine what they thought. Attacking the Blood princess . . . in any other house, that would likely be a death sentence.

"Thank you," I told Wilkin. My voice was shaking. "That won't be necessary. Please leave and close the door behind you. I'll send word when you can return to your room."

He hesitated. "Someone should stay nearby."

Because Anya might hurt me. She *had* hurt me, regardless of whether she'd meant to, because she was no longer in control of herself. "Very well," I murmured. "But keep the door closed, and please ask everyone else to leave."

He bowed and left, shutting the door behind him.

The crackle of the fire was the only sound as I stared at Anya.

She looked sick with regret, but also more alert, as if the violence had shaken her out of her delirium. "Kenna, I'm so sorry—I didn't mean to—"

"I know you didn't." The words tasted bitter. The burns on my palm and the pain in my skull were already gone, but there was an aching wound inside me that couldn't be fixed by magic or immortality.

"I dream about fire," Anya said, eyes beginning to glisten. "I drown, and I burn, and I die, over and over, and then you burn and die, too." Her voice rose in pitch. "And now I did burn you, like he showed me I would."

There was only one *he* she could be speaking of. "What do you mean, he showed you?"

"I saw you die a hundred times," she whispered. "Most of them my fault. And he was right, because look what I just did." Tears slipped down her cheeks. "I'm so sorry," she sobbed.

I wanted to kill Osric over and over again, every day for the rest of my life. He'd seen us running through the bog together; he'd either guessed or learned what I meant to her and used it as a weapon. Crimson magic flickered at my fingertips and wound around my forearms, and I closed my eyes, grappling with the flare of rage.

I wasn't just furious with Osric, if I was being honest with myself. I was angry with Anya. For refusing to sleep, for drinking too much, for going on a rampage, for hurting me. For hurting herself most of all. But shame rode with the feeling, because she didn't deserve that anger.

I just didn't know what to do with this hate now that Osric was dead.

I breathed deeply, willing the magic back beneath my skin, then looked at her again. She might not deserve my anger, but she couldn't continue like this. No more giving Anya space. I needed to take control of this situation, and that started with summoning the right words to get us from this moment to the next. Second by second, breath by breath, because some destinations had to be crawled to.

"Osric lied," I told her firmly. "You aren't going to kill me." She started to say something, but I talked over her. "Whatever he showed you, it didn't happen just now, and it's not going to happen. I'm fine. See?" I held out my arms, willing her to see the physical reality in front of her. "And now we're going to go upstairs, and you *have* to get some sleep, Anya."

"I don't—"

"No," I said, raising my voice. "No arguments. You're a danger to yourself in this state." A danger to others, too. The nightmares would come, but they were coming no matter what.

She wrapped her arms around herself, shoulders curving inward like a vulnerable creature protecting its belly. I ached with the urge to hug her, but she didn't like being touched anymore, so I clenched my fists and waited.

Finally, she nodded.

We passed Wilkin on the way out, though the rest of the hallway had thankfully been cleared. He seemed surprised to see Anya walking beside me. I dipped my chin as we passed, and he bowed in response.

Upstairs, Anya's room had been recently cleaned. It smelled like gardenias rather than body odor and spilled wine, and the bedding piled on the floor was fresh. I walked Anya to her nest of blankets, standing over her with my arms crossed until she crawled into them. A volatile mix of grief and fury still roiled inside me, threatening to send magic spilling out of my fingertips, but I kept it tightly contained. She needed me to be strong.

"I'm sorry," she whispered again, fingers digging into the pillow.

"I know," I said, crouching beside her.

"What if it's worse next time?"

"There won't be a next time, because you're going to sleep. I'll find out if there's anything that can help with the dreams—something that isn't wine. A tonic."

She was silent, staring at the far wall.

"Close your eyes," I ordered in the same firm tone that had gotten results thus far.

She did, though the frown remained etched between her brows. Her fingers were white-knuckled where they gripped the pillow.

She would hate what I was about to do, but I didn't see much of a choice after what had happened—and what could have happened if she'd managed to get that axe off the wall. I closed my eyes, matching my breathing to hers. Then I imagined my Blood power drifting gently between us and sinking behind her eyes.

Her brain felt unfathomable and terrifyingly complex. I could understand the heart because it beat and the lungs because they filled and emptied, but I couldn't understand the processes of that dense, complicated organ inside her skull. Intention seemed to matter most when it came to my powers, though, so I focused carefully on one goal. *Sleep*, I whispered mentally, imagining a gentle tide carrying her out to sea. *Sleep.*

Anya's breathing shifted into a slower rhythm as exhaustion took her. I pulled my magic back carefully and waited for a few minutes to make sure she stayed asleep.

I was going to fall apart soon. The pressure was building, like water behind a dam. It couldn't happen where anyone might see, though, because princesses didn't break down: they did what needed to be done.

I walked downstairs in a haze and found Nadine to tell her I was attending a meeting and Lara was in charge. Then I walked out of Blood House, found a door to the catacombs, and let myself inside. Cocooned in the dark, I sank to the floor and finally let myself weep.

31

I WANDERED THE EARTH TUNNELS FOR A LONG TIME.

The brambles had advanced. I saw them down side passages, coiling dark and angry at the edge of the key's light. How long before they overtook everything? How long before this haven was added to the list of everything that had been lost with time?

What else—and *who* else—would I need to mourn before this war was over?

Anya wasn't dead, but the way I'd wept over her had felt like mourning. It wasn't supposed to be like this. She was supposed to heal in Blood House. She was supposed to rediscover what safety and hope felt like, and I was supposed to help her along that path. The two of us, making our way forward together the way we always had.

Supposed to. A selfish thought. Anya wasn't a tarnished candlestick that needed to be scrubbed until she shone again, then set back into the neat space she'd always occupied in my life. She didn't need me telling myself stories about her recovery.

I needed to take a more active role in protecting her, though. I'd been tiptoeing around, obeying her orders to leave her alone, letting her isolate herself with disastrous results. But if I stopped letting her tell me no, would that do more harm than good considering the nature of her trauma?

My mind churned over the problem, finding no easy solutions.

I reached a familiar turning and hesitated. That twisting corridor would lead to the brothel eventually, and I felt a sudden, sick need to revisit the place where Anya had suffered. My feet carried me forward before I was conscious of making the choice.

Moans echoed off the stone as I approached, and my skin crawled. A quarter of the workers—fifteen humans and Underfae—were being forced, which meant there could be atrocities happening tonight. Some of the new Blood faeries had fighting experience, which meant I could finally liberate the unwilling victims here. I just needed to come up with a way to do it without anyone knowing it was me. Since Imogen had inherited this brothel and its employees from Osric, I wasn't sure if that would count as attacking another house during the Accord.

I climbed to the crawl space above the scarlet-draped rooms, both dreading and needing to see what was happening within.

Every bed was occupied, but the scenes thankfully seemed pleasure-focused and consensual, though it was impossible to know for sure. A few couples were cuddling, whispering to each other affectionately as I'd seen on previous visits. Now I understood why some of the Fae might have a fantasy like that—and why they might need to pay for it.

Despite not seeing anything obviously horrific, my apprehension increased the closer I got to the last and largest room. The king's bedchamber, where Osric had destroyed the women he'd called his "pets." That room was seared in my memory: white walls carved with carnal scenes, opalescent gossamer hangings, a low purple couch. A fire banked low and candles flickering in a parody of romance. And in the center of it all, an enormous bed topped with violet sheets.

The room would likely be empty, unless Imogen frequented the brothel, but the thought of seeing it again made me want to vomit. At the same time, I felt compelled to—as if by seeing the place where Anya had suffered, I could take some of that suffering into myself. It wasn't a rational thought, but nothing about my life felt rational anymore.

At last, I reached the grate overlooking the king's bedchamber. Below was the purple-and-white room of nightmares, illuminated by wavering candles and a crackling blaze in the fireplace.

It wasn't empty, though. Torin and Rowena were inside with an Underfae.

I froze, shocked at the sight of Mistei's most famously devoted couple in a pleasure-house. Rowena sat on the settee in a translucent nightgown, sipping a glass of red wine, and Torin was playing the flute while an Illusion sylph with pretty iridescent wings danced barefoot. He was fully dressed in leather armor and a sword, face flushed and bronze hair damp with sweat, and I wondered if he'd just returned from training the Illusion army. The evil bed taking up the center of the chamber was perfectly made—either they'd just begun, or they had no intention of using it.

The sylph pirouetted, wings fluttering and gauzy skirt flaring out. Rowena smiled into her wine. "Lovely," she said. "You are so light on your feet."

The sylph giggled. "Thank you, my princess."

"It's all so . . ." Rowena paused, dabbing her tongue to her lower lip. "Predictable, though. I was told you were the best dancer here."

Torin lowered the flute, cutting off the tune mid-measure.

Worry spiked in my chest. I recognized that look on Torin's face—the promise of retribution. Because of a dance? No, I thought as he switched his expectant focus to Rowena. Because the sylph had displeased her.

The dancer's smile faded at the abrupt shift in mood. "Forgive me, my princess," she said, curtsying. "I can do another dance."

"Yes," Rowena said. "You will." She turned an adoring smile on Torin. "Would you be so kind, darling?"

He set the flute on the bed. "Anything for you, my love." Then he paced to the fire, grabbed a set of tongs, and shoved them into the flames to adjust the logs.

The sylph looked even more uneasy. "Is it not warm enough, my prince? Do we need more wood? I would be happy to retrieve some."

Torin prodded at something in the fireplace. It didn't look like wood, but an oblong shape that burned red hot.

Anxiety squeezed my chest. What *was* that?

"Restrain her," Torin said.

I stifled a gasp as Rowena stood and grabbed the Underfae, twisting her arms behind her back. "Don't scream yet," Rowena said when the sylph let out a high-pitched sound and started to struggle. "I don't want you to scream until it's real. Until you feel it."

What awful thing was about to happen? Could I stop it? My Blood power surged liquidly to my fingers, fueled by my rising panic.

Frantic thoughts tumbled through my head. If I did stop this, what would the consequences be? The Accord was at risk if I attacked Torin and Rowena. If they knew it was me—and they certainly would if I used the magic of the body to freeze or injure them—they would tell everyone, and then I would be the one who broke the peace early. Imogen would be able to retaliate with impunity. Our side would lose popular support. Worse, we would likely lose the war. Queen Briar's troops were still on the march, and our side still had no leader because of my indecision.

I could kill Torin and Rowena—but how, without implicating myself? Immortals didn't drop dead for no reason, and there was only one faerie in Mistei with my abilities. And the sylph belonged to Illusion House—if she witnessed them dying, I couldn't trust that she wouldn't report back to Imogen.

I knelt with my fingers curled in the grate, frozen by the enormity of the consequences I'd be risking.

Torin pulled the object out of the fire. He carried it over with the tongs, then set it before the Underfae. It was a shoe, I realized with a surge of sick horror. A glowing-hot metal shoe.

He grabbed the sylph's ankle and shoved her foot in.

A raw, animal scream ripped out of her. She thrashed, but Rowena held her still.

"One more," Rowena said, a dreamy smile on her face. "And then you can dance for me again."

Torin grabbed the second shoe and put it on her just as brutally. My ears rang from her agonized cries, and I bit my lip so hard I tasted blood. My stomach threatened to revolt. When Rowena released her, the sylph collapsed and tried to crawl away.

I needed to save her.

And the war that will start in response? my conscience whispered. *And the house you've been building that will fail if they kill you in retaliation?* There were humans like Triana and Maude who still needed to evacuate. There were faeries who had placed their trust in me, risking everything because they believed Blood House was a safe haven. There was Anya, a breath away from succumbing to her nightmares. I might stop one faerie's suffering, but at what cost?

"Up," Torin said, kicking the sylph's ribs. "My consort wants to watch you dance."

The sylph wept as she tried to drag herself upright. She managed to get one foot beneath her before falling again.

I could smell her burning. I could hear it, too, between her desperate cries. A sizzling as her flesh and muscle charred away.

Still, I didn't move.

"You can't get up?" Rowena asked. "Just one spin for me and it'll be done. We'll take them off."

The sylph's wings twitched. She managed to drag herself off the ground, flapping until she was mostly upright, metal-booted feet dangling. She didn't put weight on them, but the tips scraped over the stone as she fluttered her wings, turning in an unsteady circle. Sobs ripped out of her throat.

Tears streaked down my cheeks. I could heal her. Once they were done with her, I would find her and heal her.

I could help her *now*, I realized, horrified at the oversight. Magic roiled in my chest, and I imagined numbness spreading through the sylph's body so she didn't feel the burning. Her eyes widened, and her wings fluttered faster as she veered towards the door, feet dragging.

"I was hoping this would work better," Rowena told Torin, frowning.

"It was worth trying."

The sylph sobbed as she fumbled at the doorknob. *Please*, I thought, sending strength to her wings. *Get out of here. Fly far away.*

Torin stalked after her. As the door started to open, he unsheathed his sword, then cut her head off with one brutal stroke.

The sobbing cut off instantly. Her head tumbled away as her body sagged, and the weight of her corpse pushed the door shut once more.

I clenched my jaw against the scream that tried to rip out of me, digging my fingers into the tiny holes of the grate separating me from Torin and Rowena. These monsters. These horrible, cruel, evil creatures.

Rowena's gauzy gown was splattered with blood. Her hair had come loose, a coil of gold unfurling over her shoulder. She stood on her toes and kissed Torin softly. "Thank you," she said. "We haven't done something like this in too long."

Torin was frowning down at the corpse like it was an inconvenience. "We'll try a different metal next time," he said. "Or we won't leave it in the fire quite as long."

Rowena smiled, then wrapped her arms around him, kissing him more passionately.

Torin's sword tumbled to the ground as he pulled her into his embrace.

The desire to kill them burned through me. I saw it in my mind's eye—crushing Torin's feet and ankles in an echo of what he'd done to the sylph, then squeezing his skull until his brain became pulp. Choking Rowena a little at a time, making her die in small increments next to her lover's bloody corpse. Forcing her to watch the ruin I'd made of him, the way she'd watched this atrocity.

I didn't do it, though.

My tears splatted onto the grate, and I fumbled to wipe away the drops before they could fall into the room. Then I crawled backwards an inch at a time, sick and shaking.

After I finally made it down the ladder, I sagged against the wall, sobbing into my hands. Caedo raced up my arm to coil around my neck, settling the red jewel that was its heart over my own. *Soon*, the dagger said. *Cut them, bleed them, drink them soon.*

The moment the Accord was over, Torin and Rowena were dead. I would do it slowly, and I would enjoy it.

The sylph's screams echoed in my head as I stumbled away from the brothel.

32

Kallen found me in our sparring chamber late that night. I was punching the bag over and over, my knuckles bruising and healing in turn. "Go away," I said, voice hoarse.

He didn't reply, just closed the door and stood in front of it, arms crossed. He wore a long black coat that covered him from neck to ankle, and I wondered where he was coming from and why he was here, since I'd sent a note canceling our lesson.

I moved around the bag to put my back to him, then furtively swiped my wrist over my eyes, hoping he didn't see the residual tears. This was weak. *I* was weak. And because a princess didn't have the luxury of fragility, I'd stopped at Blood House to change into sparring clothes and pen a note for Kallen, then come here to let the pain out where no one could see.

Even without looking at Kallen, I was uncomfortably aware of his presence. It was as if the air shaped itself differently around him. I glanced at the mirror and found him watching me with a furrow between his brows and a brooding angle to his lips. "What happened?" he asked.

I gritted my teeth and slammed my fist into the bag harder. My knuckles throbbed, and the pain reverberated into my arm. "Don't you already know? You always know everything."

"Was there a problem in your house?"

I stopped hitting long enough to press the heels of my palms against my eyes. Yes, that was how this horror of a night had started. An ugly suspicion formed, and I spun on him. "Do you have a spy in my house?" I demanded.

His eyes narrowed. "No."

I let out a rough laugh. "How am I supposed to believe that?" And how had I not considered this before? He had spies everywhere.

Kallen took one step closer. His coat was clasped with silver, and the fabric whispered around his boots with the movement. "Have I given you reason to doubt my word, Kenna?"

Anger felt better than sorrow or the gnawing worry in my gut that never left. I glared at him, notching my chin into a more confrontational angle. "Then tell me why you think there were problems in my house."

A muscle flexed in his jaw. "If you're this upset, it's because you saw someone else suffering. Since I haven't heard of anything happening, an issue at home was the most logical conclusion."

It's because you saw someone else suffering. Why would he say that? Why would he *know* that? But the first conversation I'd ever had with Kallen was when I'd been weeping over King Osric's executions. Maybe he'd understood me from the start.

My skin prickled under his unrelenting focus. Sometimes I hated how Kallen looked at me. Like he was noting every detail of my appearance—the mess of my hair, my reddened eyes, the fading purple on my knuckles—and could read the emotions and thoughts beneath the surface, too.

I wasn't ready to talk about Anya yet, and that wasn't what had sent me here to batter my knuckles bloody, anyway. "I went to the brothel."

"Ah." His lashes flickered. "Thinking about helping them escape?"

"Now how the fuck would you know that?" The question exploded out of me.

"Because I know *you*."

A small sound caught in my throat, a scoff that couldn't pick up the required level of disbelief. "Do you?" I turned my face away and wrapped my arms around myself as the last traces of soreness in my hand vanished. I'd fractured a knuckle an hour before, and even that lightning crack of pain hadn't lasted long.

I was too aware of my own body these days. Too aware of everything—my failings and fears, the vast gulf that separated me from the other Noble Fae. All this power, and I'd still watched helplessly as a faerie was tortured and murdered.

"Kenna." The way he said my name drew my attention again. But I always wanted to look at Kallen, and that was another thing I was far too aware of. "Do you not want that?"

"To be known by you?"

He nodded.

"I'm not sure I want to be known by anyone." It wasn't true, though, and that made me even more anxious. There was something endlessly hungry in me, endlessly lonely, and it stirred whenever Kallen was around. I sniffled and wiped my eyes again. "Have you seen what happens in the brothel?"

Sorrow crossed his face. "I know what happens there, but I've never been inside. Osric warded it against me."

"Why?"

"He didn't want me at risk of forming any . . . connections."

What did that mean? Love, sex, companionship, all of the above?

"I wouldn't have gone for that reason," he said quietly. "But I would have been tempted to try to save them." He paused. "I sometimes wonder if Osric suspected there was a part of me he hadn't been able to corrupt yet."

More likely he'd wanted Kallen completely isolated. No friends, no allies, no lovers. A weapon didn't require anything but the hand wielding it.

"Talk to me," Kallen said, stepping closer. "Tell me what happened."

I shook my head, but it was a useless denial. It was only a matter of time before I confessed my failings to him.

"Kenna. Why were you crying?"

"Can't you just leave it?"

"No."

Of course he couldn't. Kallen was dogged in his pursuit of whatever he wanted to know.

I turned to slam my fist into the bag one more time. The skin over my knuckles split, releasing ruby drops.

He was walking towards me now. Quickly, purposefully. My heart raced with sudden panic, and I backed away. Realizing how cowardly it made me look, I hurried towards a rack of weapons, yanking a spear out like that was what I'd meant to do all along.

"Tell me," Kallen ordered. "Tell me why you're hurting yourself."

I squeezed the haft of the spear in my sore hand. "I watched Torin and Rowena force a sylph to dance in red-hot metal shoes," I said, the confession ripping out of me. "I was in the catacombs, and I watched as they tortured and killed her, and I didn't do anything to stop it."

He was still coming, not seeming to care that I was armed and he wasn't. Why would he, though? I was useless. "Why didn't you do anything?"

The answers tumbled out. "Because of the Accord. Because everyone would realize it was me if I killed them with magic. Because it would have started a war before we were ready, and I have people I'm responsible for now." My throat felt painfully tight. I could hear the sylph in my head, screaming as her skin burned down to the bone. "And none of those—*none of those*—seem like good enough reasons right now."

He was within arm's reach. I halfheartedly angled the spear towards him, but he grabbed it in one hand, wrenched it out of my grip, and tossed it away. It clattered against the floor.

"Aren't you sick of me by now?" I asked, grief and self-reproach welling up until my eyes stung. "I'm weak."

"No." He gripped my shoulders. "Let it out."

Tears were streaking down my cheeks now. I choked out the question that was haunting me. "What is the point of all this power when I'm still failing to save people?"

I had watched Osric torture Anya and done nothing. Tonight I'd watched the same thing happen again, except this time I had magic and immortality and a deadly weapon on my side and there had been no wards stopping me from attacking Torin and Rowena, and I'd still done nothing. I hadn't saved the sylph. I wasn't saving Anya, either, and no matter how many people I brought to Blood House, it didn't make up for that.

Kallen's jaw worked, and his fingers flexed on my arms. "You didn't fail. You chose the long game. And you saved lives by not rushing us rashly into war."

"Not that life," I whispered.

"No," he said. "Not that one."

It was blunt and matter-of-fact. Free of judgment and forgiveness both. I envied him his certainty—how he could look straight at a situation like that, understand my decision, and quantify the loss without diminishing it.

This was precisely the type of calculation Kallen was best at, though. Weighing lives against other lives. Weighing crimes. Trying and sometimes failing to fight the sense of futility that permeated our lives down here. History ate itself like a snake swallowing its own tail as the Fae continued their unending battle for power . . . but that didn't mean we should give up.

Even if our victories had a steep price. Even if we lost.

I closed my eyes, breathing in his scent. I felt wrung out and exhausted, but confessing had been a relief. It felt like poison had been building up inside me, and I'd finally bled some of it out.

"Sometimes we have to pick the least awful of two bad choices," he said quietly.

I nodded, letting the words sink in. It wasn't absolution, because no one could offer that. But it was perspective.

I kept breathing, letting the messy emotions settle into a gentler ache. Kallen didn't try to fill the silence. He held me by the shoulders, waiting.

"How do you do it?" I finally asked.

"Do what?"

"Survive this."

He took a moment to answer. "Well, sometimes I hit things late at night where no one can see."

"You guessed I'd be here?" I opened my eyes again, unable to resist looking at him for long.

"No. I set a few shadows in the corridor outside."

Irritation sparked again, but it was a relief to feel something besides guilt and grief. "Why didn't I see them?"

His lips quirked up on one side, but it wasn't really a smile. "I've been doing this a long time, Kenna. I know how to make them blend in."

The dark stone of the corridor, the shadows between torches—yes, I could see how a few tendrils of darkness could escape my notice.

I shifted out of his grip, turning to look at the rack of weapons. "I wanted to be alone."

"Do you still want that?"

I gripped another spear haft, considering the question. Speaking to him had made me feel better. Still ashamed of my failure, still angry and grieving, but . . . a little better.

I wanted to be alone when it came to everyone *but* him.

Kallen had gotten inside me somehow, in the form of an ache in my chest and an urgent need I'd been trying and failing to ignore. The tension growing between us was unbearable—I both craved and feared what would happen when it finally snapped. Because where had a feeling like this led me last time? Straight to someone who had seen my naivete and passion as useful tools. Who had seen *me* as a tool. Selwyn was dead because of that feeling.

There were so many reasons why I should tell him to leave, rather than give him any more pieces of me. We were on the brink of war. Everyone in Mistei feared him. And I . . .

"I want to hit things," I said. An answer and not an answer, because it was too dangerous to confess what I was really thinking.

"Then hit me."

My breath caught. Such a blunt, simple offer. *Hit me. Use me. Take out your anger on me.* "As if I'd be able to land a punch."

"Maybe I'll let you tonight."

The challenge in that annoyed me as much as it intrigued me. A restless energy began to collect in my limbs, an urge for movement. I seized that feeling like a thirsty traveler reaching for water and let it push aside the lingering fog of tonight's nightmare. I didn't want to be wrung out and hollow anymore. I wanted to fill that emptiness with something that made me feel alive.

I let go of the spear and faced him. "Weapons?"

"No." He crossed his arms. "Think you can take me, Kenna?"

The taunting note in his voice made my skin flush hot. "Oh, I know I can take you."

"You want a fight."

The echo of a memory shivered through the room. *Are you looking for a fight?*

I had been looking for a fight that time, and I was again now. The difference was that this time I was willing to admit it. I licked my lips. "Yes."

"You'll get one." His eyes held mine for a long moment, and then he raised his hands to his throat and unhooked the first silver clasp that held his black coat together.

My breathing grew unsteady.

He undid the next and the next, never looking away from me.

The hairs on my arms rose. "What are you doing?"

"Getting ready." He shucked the coat off, revealing a sleeveless black tunic. The muscles of his arms rippled, and my eyes were helplessly drawn to the exposed skin.

I'd never seen his bare arms before, I realized with a jolt in my stomach. He was usually covered from neck to wrist, wrapped in a dark formality that made him seem intimidating and aloof. Now I couldn't stop staring at this new part of himself he'd revealed. His forearms were corded with veins, and his biceps swelled beneath pale skin.

Scarred skin, I realized. The marks curved in a familiar way—not as elaborate or as numerous as Anya's, but it was immediately obvious who had caused them.

A sound caught in my throat—the start of a useless protest or a question that had no pleasant answers. Considering what it took for faeries to scar, either this had happened when he was very young or the king had wanted Kallen to carry a permanent reminder of his torture.

He kicked off his shoes and socks to match my barefooted state, then raked a hand through his loose hair. "We go until you tell me to stop."

"You can tell me to stop, too."

He shook his head, eyelids lowering. "I won't."

The promise made me shiver. We hadn't even begun, and already this felt too intense.

Seeing his bared arms made me overly aware of my own attire. My trousers were made of a soft fabric that clung to my hips and fluttered around my ankles, and my sleeveless tunic displayed more skin than I was used to. Caedo spiraled around my upper arm, pulsing with restless energy. It wanted a battle, too.

No drinking from him, I reminded the dagger.

Caedo grumbled but didn't argue. I stroked it, encouraging the circlet to grow tiny teeth to nip me with.

"Are you going to make me bleed?" Kallen asked.

"Not with this." I looked at the pad of my finger, watching the cut heal over. There was a single drop of blood left, and I smudged it over the metal, letting Caedo absorb the last taste. "Though I suppose you'll have to take my word for that."

He nodded, as if trusting me were easy, when it had to be anything but. "You can make me bleed other ways, if you want. Bruise me. Break my bones. There are no limits, Kenna." He backed away to stand in the middle of the floor.

No limits. Did he truly mean that? He looked like he might even *welcome* me breaking his bones. It was a terrifying level of permission for him to give—and even more terrifying for me to have.

The ceiling crystals brightened as they adapted to our intentions. The light caught on Kallen's dark hair, the angle of his cheekbones, the curl of his scars. It was almost too much, seeing him illuminated so starkly. I'd be raising bruises on those bared arms and shoulders if I could get close enough. He would probably grab me, and there would be nothing to blunt the touch. My skin would know his in ways it hadn't before.

A pulse started between my legs. Terrifying, terrifying, all this terrifying, but I wanted it so badly. I *needed* it.

He looked like a predator, focused and expectant, waiting for his prey to come to him. But as my breath came faster and my pulse tapped an intoxicating rhythm, I wondered if I might be a predator, too.

I stepped forward.

Kallen smiled, small and tight. His eyes didn't leave my face.

Another step.

He shifted his weight, sliding his right foot back, knees bent in preparation. He raised his hands—not in fists, but in the loose position that would allow him to hit, block, or grab with ease. Kallen was always so tense, like there was an invisible leash he'd wrapped around himself and couldn't help straining against, but he never seemed so relaxed as when he was ready for a fight.

Only his body, though. His eyes burned in a way that raised goose bumps across my skin. I knew how quickly that relaxation could shift into brutal, mesmerizing power.

"Hurry up, Princess," he murmured. "Or are you afraid?"

I bared my teeth as exhilaration rushed through me. Then I charged at him, ready to force those words back into his beautiful, taunting mouth.

My fist breezed past his cheekbone as he jerked to the side. My other hit his stomach, but he twisted away quickly. I spun and launched myself at him again.

He parried my blows, smacking my hands aside, blocking the hits with his forearms before launching a counterattack. He was pulling his punches—we both knew that—but he wasn't letting me off easy. I blocked hit after hit, and then one landed on my ribs, and the sweet sting of pain made me gasp.

"Too much?" he asked, shoving his hair back from his face as he paced around me.

"Not enough," I snapped. That bright spark of sensation had been far too brief.

His lashes flickered. "I'm not going to really hurt you. You know that?"

"I know." Because he was Kallen, and even though he'd said there were no limits tonight, and even though he probably meant it when it came to hurting him, he was considerate beneath those layers of cold menace. Considerate to me, anyway, and maybe only to me, and some greedy, dark thing inside me liked it that way. "But you can hurt me a little."

His smile was subtle. "Maybe a little."

He lunged and grabbed my wrist, yanking me towards him. I let out a startled cry as I smacked into his chest, and then he flipped me around, one arm banded tight around my waist and one crossing my torso so his forearm dug in between my breasts. His chest was hard against my back, and with his shoulders curving around mine, there was no denying how much bigger than me he was. Not bulky, but tall and leanly muscled. That body was a weapon, and feeling it pressed against me made me dizzy.

He lowered his head so his breath puffed hot against my cheek. We stayed like that for a long, tense moment, and then he shifted and caught the lobe of my ear between his teeth. A ragged noise tore from my throat.

"Try again," he whispered.

Fury and joy swept through me at the challenge. I rested in his hold, relishing the feel of his arms encircling me, knowing he could crush my ribs if he wanted to, but never would. Then I jerked my head back, cracking his nose with my skull.

He shouted and let go. When I turned, blood was pouring from his nose. Had I actually broken it? Remorse instantly filled me. I'd meant the hit to hurt, but I was so much stronger now than I'd ever been. "I'm sorry—" I started.

"No," he said vehemently. "I told you. No limits." He adjusted his nose, then swiped the blood away with the back of his hand. The flow stopped as his body healed, but a smear was left across his lips and chin. When he grinned at me, red slicked his teeth. "Do it again."

A shudder raced through me. That rough, dark note to his voice was new. This wasn't the contained, controlled Kallen anymore. He paced a circle around me like a wolf ready to pounce, and the burning excitement in his eyes matched the feeling sizzling inside me.

Was this wrong? It didn't feel wrong. And that frightened me, but it was a fear I couldn't get enough of. I wanted to drink this feeling down. I wanted to drown from it.

My eyes fell to his chest, to his waist. To the bulge pressing against the fabric at his crotch.

Kallen was hard.

I'd broken his nose, and he was hard.

The breath left me, and fresh slickness pooled between my thighs. I'd already been wet from the thrill of the fight and the way he looked like he was barely restraining himself from some explosive action that would change everything, but this need was growing dangerously fast, and I didn't know if it would ever stop.

No limits.

He was looking at me like he meant it. Like he wanted to taste his own blood.

I wanted to taste it, too. I wanted to lick the blood from his lips and the sweat from his skin. I wanted my hand around his throat as he cried out my name.

"Kenna," he said, demand and plea. "Don't stop. Take what you need."

The sigh that left me was half moan. This was madness.

I leapt at him again, aiming a punch towards his throat that he blocked with his forearm. Undeterred, I swung my leg up, trying to hit him in the crotch with my shin. He was ready, though, his hips angled to deny me the target, and he slapped my leg aside as he dodged. So fast. Always so, so fast. He punched me in the side again, finding his way beneath my guard in a way he would probably lecture me about later.

I danced back, biting my lip to hold in a startled cry. Not of pain—or if there was pain, it was a pain I wanted. Kallen's control was precise. He knew exactly how hard to hit to make his point without causing actual damage. But he wasn't treating me like I was helpless or breakable, either. He was treating me like a real and worthy opponent.

The feeling was addictive.

I pressed my hand against the exquisite ache that bloomed over my ribs, curving my shoulders and grimacing as if he'd actually injured me. His expression shifted into a look of alarm, and he stepped towards me with his hand outstretched. "Are you—"

I backhanded him so hard his head snapped to the side.

He grunted, cupping his face, then laughed. "Fuck," he said, working his jaw back and forth. "Should have known. You always fight dirty."

We grinned at each other, and the same madness that filled me was echoed in his exultant expression.

He retaliated for my trick, moving faster than it seemed possible to grab my shoulders. He shoved me, and I realized too late that he'd hooked my ankle. My balance gone, I fell, landing on my back on the mats. The impact rattled my rib cage, and I sucked in a greedy breath as I tried to roll to the side.

Kallen was there, though. He landed on top of me, grabbing my wrists to pin them over my head, one thigh pressed between my legs. He'd done this once before, but this time the way he pinned me wasn't anywhere near a true grappling hold. He lay half sprawled over me, our bodies hovering inches apart.

He was breathing hard, and it wasn't from the exertion.

No limits.

The air tore out of my lungs, too. I felt every place we touched, from his fingers gripping my wrists to the hard press of his thigh against my sex to my bare foot sliding against his calf. His face was so close to mine, and his eyes were so very dark, the blue just a sliver around the swell of his pupils.

This was always going to happen. I knew it then, the way religious devotees knew scripture. It was written somewhere beyond time.

I surged up and kissed him.

The first touch of our lips sent heat racing over my skin. He tasted like blood, like night, like no one else in the world possibly could.

Like *mine*.

Kallen made a raw, desperate sound. Then he was kissing me back, furious and frantic. The blood in his kiss, coppery and electric, only made me wilder. I moaned and pressed up against him, tugging at my trapped wrists. When he let go, I wrapped my arms around him, trying to bring him even closer.

I pulled his lower lip between my teeth and bit down. He bit me back, matching my aggression. Our mouths parted and merged, and the breaths that passed between us were ragged with want.

Finally.

I shoved his shoulder in an attempt to flip him over. He went willingly, and then it was his back against the mats, his body laid out beneath mine. As I straddled him, he gripped my hips and looked up at me with a lust so potent I felt it against every inch of skin. I wrapped my hand around his throat and leaned down to kiss him again, rejoicing in the needy noise that vibrated against my palm and spilled into my mouth.

I rocked over his lap, rubbing myself against his erection. His pulse hammered beneath my fingers as he ground up against me in rhythmic surges, taking my movements and giving them structure. When I licked into his mouth, hungry for the taste, he met me just as fervently.

This was more than lust. It was filthy, desperate greed.

I squeezed his throat harder. Bit him again. Snapped my hips like the friction between us was a punishment.

Kallen groaned. He grabbed my ass with one hand as the other slid up my back to tunnel into my hair. Then he made a fist, pulling tightly enough to sting my scalp. He used that grip to angle my head to the side, baring the line of my neck. His lips stroked over my pulse, and the swipe of his tongue made me moan.

"Yes," I said, the word breaking on the way out.

Kallen snarled against my skin, then flipped me over again. He settled fully between my thighs, and I gasped, raising my knees around his hips as his cock pressed hard against my core. Then we were kissing again, bodies moving in desperate tandem. His hair was soft and slightly damp at the roots from the fight, and when I made fists in those silky strands, giving him exactly what he'd given me, he made a guttural sound that reverberated down to my toes.

He pulled back, panting, and I caught a glimpse of his wild eyes before he pressed his mouth to the line of my jaw. "You . . ." he exhaled against my skin. The movement of his lips when he spoke was soft, like the brush of butterfly wings, but then he moved lower and sucked hard on a sensitive spot that made me jerk against him. "You're the end of me, Kenna."

I didn't understand what he meant, but there was no room to think about it as he strung hot open-mouthed kisses down my throat. One of his hands dropped to my breast, squeezing roughly.

This wasn't the practiced touch of a seducer. This was raw, overwhelming passion. Kallen was coming undone.

I seized the pleasure hungrily, gasping as he sank his teeth into the spot between my neck and shoulder, crying out when he ground against me. My hips surged in response, and I grabbed his hair and forced his face up so I could taste his lips again.

You, I thought deliriously as his tongue slid into my mouth. *It's you, it's you. It was always you.*

Maybe he would be the end of me, too.

"Tell me what you want," I said against his lips.

He groaned. *"Everything."* He took my ragged whimper into his mouth. "Every inch of skin, every touch, every sound you make."

He slid his hand under my shirt, and his calloused fingers coasted up my quivering belly to my bound breast. He made a dissatisfied noise, then worked his fingers under that fabric, too, shoving it up until his palm met my nipple. A spark of pleasure shot between my legs, and I moaned loudly, spine curving.

Kallen matched the sound with one of his own. He rolled his palm, kneading my breast in time with the flex of his hips. His cock was a hard bar between my legs, pressing insistently against my clitoris, and my feet slid over the floor as the sensations overwhelmed me. My body wasn't big enough to contain this want.

"I've imagined this," he gasped, resting his forehead against mine as his hand and hips worked me into a delirious state. "So much. So many nights alone, dreaming of the impossible. Hating myself, and hating everyone you've ever smiled at and everyone who's ever hurt you. You'll never understand the depth of it."

There was a faint buzzing in my ears. "The depth of what?" I panted, squirming against him.

"The need." He pulled back enough to look at me, and there was more than just desire in his eyes. The only word I could think of to describe it was *torment*. "I would tear the world apart for you, Kenna. And I don't deserve this, not a second of it, but I'm too greedy to stop."

"I—I—" I couldn't think. The pressure between my legs was making my stomach tighten and shivers race up and down my limbs. I clenched internally, imagining him filling me. An orgasm was building so quickly it was almost frightening.

The buzzing was back, louder this time. Something gold flashed in my peripheral vision.

Kallen abruptly swore and scrambled off me.

"Wait—" I pushed myself up clumsily. My legs were still sprawled, the space between them far too empty.

He ran to grab the discarded spear off the floor, then threw it. The tip clattered into the wall—right below a golden bird that had darted out of the way. The bird released a metallic chirp, then flew into the ventilation shaft.

My entire body was shaking. "What was that?"

"Someone's spy," he said grimly. He ran a trembling hand over his kiss-reddened mouth. I'd made a mess of him—his hair was tangled, his cheeks were flushed, and his chest heaved with desperate breaths, like he'd been running for miles.

My own breathing was just as uneven, and my head spun with lust and confusion. I stood, legs quivering and anxiety tightening my chest. "What do you mean, a spy?"

"It was metal. Which means enchanted."

All at once, I remembered something he'd told me. Caedo wasn't the only Fae artifact with unusual powers. There were fiddles that could raise the dead . . . and metal animals that repeated anything said in front of them.

My stomach dropped, and mortification swept through me. "Who would have sent it?"

"I don't know, but I'll find out." Kallen paced to the spear, then picked it up. His jaw clenched as he looked at it. "Fuck!" he snapped.

I wanted to scream the expletive. Our first kiss, the first step over that invisible line, and someone had ripped the moment away. It would have been another first if we hadn't been interrupted, because now that I knew I could touch Kallen, I didn't want to stop.

No. I refused to let anyone take this from us. I smoothed my shaking hands over my thighs. "Who cares if someone finds out? We can do what we want."

I knew better, though. I was the undecided princess, and he was the heir to Void House. Everything we did became political.

There was the strangest look on Kallen's face, like he was only half in the room. "They'll know how I feel about you," he said, voice hollow.

"Kallen," I said, worry rising. I stepped forward. "Are you—"

He stumbled back.

I broke off mid-sentence. He was still breathing too fast, but something had changed. His shoulders were stiff, his posture too rigid. His eyes darted, and I saw the whites around them.

"What is it?" I whispered. Kallen was always strategic, always pragmatic about turning a disadvantage into a strength, but right now he looked like his world was ending.

"I—" He made a broken sound, then shook his head. "I'm so sorry."

He turned, scooped up his coat and shoes, and nearly ran out of the room. His body was already starting to wisp into shadow when he crossed the threshold.

And then I was alone, with no idea what had just happened.

33

D AWN WAS A CRUEL CREATURE.
The lights in my room were still doused when I opened my eyes, but I knew what hour it was. That was what came of a lifelong habit. And once my consciousness drifted to the surface, the worries it found there ensured I wouldn't be getting back to sleep.

Why had Kallen left?

My thoughts weren't any clearer this morning. Someone had been spying on us, which made my skin crawl, but Kallen's reaction had gone far beyond that. He'd looked like he was *afraid* of me.

I sighed and sat up, rubbing my bleary eyes. Then I shuffled to the bathroom to start preparing for the day, because there would be no sorting through that mystery until I was more alert.

I heard Carys moving around in my room while I took a bath, and she was waiting with a cup of herbal tea when I emerged. "This should help wake you up," the dryad said as she handed it over. Her expression was sympathetic. "Meeting ran late?"

She must have heard me come in last night. I nodded, not trusting myself to invent any lies about that particular "meeting."

I sipped the tea as she combed and oiled my wet hair. It was bitter, but it did make me feel better. Once the moisture was mostly blotted out of my curls, Carys bound them in a scarf to continue drying, then moved to the wardrobe to select a dress. "What events do you have today?"

"A library party in a few hours." I made a face. "Not that I know what that means." Trust Imogen to turn reading into a spectacle. "And then the masquerade tonight."

She nodded, then selected a short silk dress with a tight bodice and flaring skirt for the first event. The fabric shimmered between crimson and a red so dark it was nearly black, and the sharp collar went all the way up to my chin. As she tied the laces at the back, I looked at myself in the mirror, grateful for the coverage—not because I could still see the marks Kallen had sucked into my neck, but because I could still feel them. My body was alive with the memory of his.

"Have you seen Anya this morning?" I asked.

She shook her head. "Triana checked on her an hour ago. She was sleeping well."

Relief mixed with fresh guilt. She'd needed the rest, but I'd also forced it on her—though her body wouldn't have been able to continue much longer without breaking down.

Once Carys finished doing my hair and applying my makeup, I went to Anya's room. I opened the door a crack, expecting to see her curled up in her nest of blankets.

She wasn't there.

Worry arrowed through me. I closed my eyes, mentally reaching for the connection with the house. The web quivered as I sent a question into it. *Where is Anya?*

There was a vibration at the edge of my awareness, somewhere to the left. I started walking, following it to the servants' staircase, then down. The Underfae already at work looked startled to see me. They bowed as I passed, and again I felt the pinch of no longer fitting into my old life.

The mystical tug guided me to the level below the kitchens, and I emerged from the stairwell into a corridor lined with rough blocks of stone. Dust carpeted the floor, and the air smelled stale. Blood House might be coming to life, but the vast majority of it still lay quiet and abandoned. I stepped over a sluggish stream of blood and noticed a set of footprints in the dust.

Torches sputtered weakly to life to mark my passing, and the snap of flame struggled against the heavy silence. Arched entranceways opened on either side, and I recognized where I was—the abandoned grain stores. The grain had long since rotted or been reabsorbed into the house's magic, and the vaulted rooms stood empty. The house and the footprints guided me into one of those chambers.

"Anya?" I called out, unease clinging to me like spiderwebs.

My voice bounced back. It felt like I'd shouted in a tomb. I could imagine all the servants who had once flitted back and forth here, milling grain into flour and bringing supplies to the kitchens above.

I continued into a corridor lined with storage closets. At the end of the hallway was a heavy-looking door with a silver wolf's head snarling from the lintel. It was cracked open, and the hinges creaked when I pushed, revealing a grimy stairwell spiraling down. The footprints descended those stairs.

"Anya?" I called again as I followed those phantom tracks. The air was musty with decay, but there was something else in the scent that clung to my nostrils unsettlingly.

The staircase ended at a door. I stepped through and found myself in another vast, vaulted chamber. This one wasn't empty, though.

It was piled high with bones.

I stared at the white mounds, heart in my throat. Some of them reached nearly to the ceiling, and though they hadn't been arranged in an orderly manner, there was a logic to the way the skeletons lay. Overlapping femurs, arms sprawled akimbo, and everything slumping as time dragged its heavy hand over them. The bodies had been thrown one atop the other until the piles grew too tall, and then they must have been dropped from above by creatures with wings.

I reached for my Blood power, but the bones didn't feel like much when my magic brushed them. Just an echo of something long gone.

There weren't hundreds of skeletons in here. There were thousands. And branching across the floor between them were narrow tributaries of blood, whispering liquidly.

Anya stood before one of the heaps, her silhouette stark against the white.

"Anya," I said, softer this time.

She flinched and turned to face me. "Kenna? What are you doing here?"

Her voice was hoarse, but at least she sounded lucid. The dim torchlight emphasized the hungry hollows of her face, and the scar on her cheek made me think of a coiling snake.

A shiver passed over me. I wanted to get her out of this place—this *tomb*—as quickly as possible. "I was trying to find you."

Anya tipped her head back, looking at the top of the nearest pyramid. "I found this place a few days after we got here," she said. "I come here sometimes after my nightmares. This is all of them, isn't it? Everyone Osric killed?"

"It must be," I said, throat thick. Their blood ran endlessly through the walls, kept liquid and restless thanks to the house's magic, but their bones had been here all along. "The soldiers must have dragged them down here before sealing the house off."

"There's a carving by the door."

I turned to look. Scratched into the stone were two simple words:
I'M SORRY.

My skin prickled. Who had carved that? Some reluctant soldier, regretting their part in the massacre?

When I looked back at Anya, she held a skull in her hands. I hurried forward, wanting to rip it away from her. "Anya, put that down."

She stared at the skull, chest rising and falling with slow breaths. "This one died from a blow to the head," she said, sounding calmer than she had in days. She turned to show me the jagged hole. "See?"

Anya belonged in sun-warmed kitchens and fields of flowers, not dusty rooms full of corpses. "We should go back upstairs."

"There are others who were cut with swords," she said, ignoring me. "I wonder if they were killed by the soldiers, or if he made them do it to each other. I wonder what he made them see."

I hadn't considered that. But she was right—Osric would have made the Blood faeries turn on one another. He'd enjoyed that sort of sadism.

I felt cold and sick. I'd known the carnage had happened on a shocking scale, but seeing them all piled here together, their bones marked with the cuts and fractures of battle, was worse than I could have imagined.

Anya let out a shuddering breath and closed her eyes. "How did he get into the house? I want to know the details."

"He's gone, Anya. It won't happen again."

"He's not gone," she snarled. She shifted the skull to rest in one hand, then touched her own forehead with two fingers. "I need to know how he got in."

I didn't understand, but I'd tell her whatever she needed to hear. "The secret back entrances aren't protected the same way the front entrances are. When Princess Cordelia tried to help everyone escape, he killed them and forced his way inside. But it's blocked off now. No one can get in."

Anya swayed slightly, still rubbing her forehead. "Who has his body?"

"Osric's?" My brows rose. "Illusion House, I imagine."

"I want it," she said, voice growing savage. "I want to crack him open to see what's inside. I want to sleep next to his bones. I want to take them with me everywhere so I always know exactly where he is."

Chills raced over me. Desperately worried, I closed the last distance between us. I reached out to gently touch her shoulder, then dropped my hand before making contact. "Let's go upstairs. Want to soak in the hot springs? Or maybe we can listen to music—"

Anya's eyes flew open. "You got to kill him," she spat. "I didn't. I don't want to soak in a tub or listen to some sweet fucking song while you're off playing the heroine."

"That's not—"

"I don't want to *be* this anymore, Kenna." Her voice cracked, and she tossed the skull back onto the pile before wrapping her arms around her waist, eyes sheened with tears. "I don't want to be who I was yesterday, and I don't want him in my head anymore. I don't want to be like them."

"Like who?"

She jerked her head towards the piles of the dead. "His victims."

My chest hurt horribly. I finally understood, though. Anya came here after her nightmares because she felt some kinship with these scarred remains. But unlike them, she was still living, still breathing. She couldn't kill Osric... but maybe she could take power back some other way.

A revelation came to me, the answer to the question of how to protect her when she refused to accept my concern. I'd been coddling her—offering warm milk to help her sleep, asking if she was all right when the answer was obvious, shoving presents at her like that would somehow fix this horrible wound. She'd always been the soft one of the two of us, so I'd thought she needed soft things.

Anya didn't want to be coddled, though. She wanted to rip something apart.

"Do you want to learn to fight?" I asked her. "We have a whole armory. You can have your own weapons."

She looked at me, eyes still wet. Her lips trembled . . . and she nodded.

My answering smile was wobbly. This wasn't the same Anya I'd known. None of us were the same, though. Time wore over us like a river, smoothing some areas and sharpening others, twisting us into shapes we'd never imagined. "All right," I said. "I have some books about fighting techniques, and I can show you what I've been learning. There are some former soldiers in the house who can probably help, too." Though she would have to choose between her hatred of faeries and her desire to get stronger.

Anya's eyes were drying. Her arms loosened and fell to her sides. "I want that," she breathed. "I want to know how to hurt them."

"Only our enemies," I told her, feeling the prick of anxiety. "Not the people here, not like yesterday."

"I know." Regret washed over her face. "Yesterday doesn't feel real. I woke up today, and I couldn't understand it."

"Because you slept." She probably wouldn't like this next part, but it was a mandatory condition for her training. "You have to keep sleeping, even if it scares you. You have to stop drinking so much. But if you can do that, you can have whatever weapons you want, and I'll teach you how to kill."

Once upon a time, Anya would have been horrified at the idea of hurting anyone. Now she looked like a drowning person who had been thrown a rope. "I can do it," she said. "I'll do anything if it means I won't be that helpless again."

An electric energy hummed through my veins. Now that I knew

what Anya wanted, I could help her seize it. Who cared if she looked as excited about murder as she once had about pretty dresses or village festivals? Whatever got her from this moment to the next was what we needed to do. Whatever made her feel better, stronger, and more powerful. "You won't be. I promise."

Anya's hazel eyes were so bright I could imagine a fire burning behind them. The flames of renewed purpose. She had finally found something to look forward to, so she would have it, no matter the cost. And when I raided the brothel, I would hack apart the king's bed and drag the mattress here for target practice.

Maybe she would still decide to return to Tumbledown in a few days. We hadn't had that conversation yet. But maybe . . . maybe she would choose to stay with me instead.

"When do we start?" she asked.

I smiled, throat tight. "One more night of sleep, and then we can begin first thing in the morning."

34

THE LIBRARY PARTY WAS ALREADY UNDERWAY WHEN LARA and I arrived. Faeries laughed, snacked, and drank—of course—as they examined curiosities in display cases. A small cheer went up when we entered. I stopped, startled by the sound.

"The Princess of Blood," Imogen announced, hurrying over. I flinched, but she gripped my hands in hers like we were bosom friends. Her cheeks were flushed, and her eyes sparkled. "We were discussing the melee. What a remarkable performance."

It was my first time seeing her since the battle. "Thank you," I said, words clipped. "What an interesting show you decided to put on." I looked beyond her, wondering whose benefit this conversation was for, and found a small cluster of faeries watching, Torin and Rowena among them.

Hate whipped through me, and I imagined letting Caedo slither into my hand and stabbing them both repeatedly. Then I smiled at them, because that was the nature of this war for the next seventeen days.

Rowena simpered in response, but Torin's cold expression didn't change. He raised his glass of wine, hesitated with it just before his mouth, then tipped it towards me. It felt more like a threat than a toast.

Imogen was still prattling on about the melee. "Funny, isn't it? Some think mirth and merriment can't coexist with strength. But the most notorious warrior was one of the first to fall, and here I stand, the victor. How embarrassing for everyone else." She laughed, and most faeries nearby laughed with her.

Rowena narrowed her eyes at Imogen, then gripped Torin's arm and pulled him close to murmur in his ear. His jaw clenched, and he nodded.

Imogen asked me the next question in a stage whisper. "Is Drustan as upset about losing as Torin is? These princes have such fragile feelings."

Imogen clearly hadn't forgiven Torin for publicly chastising her, though I wondered if alcohol was once again to blame for her antagonizing him—she had that look. "I wouldn't presume to know anything about Drustan's feelings," I said coolly.

It wasn't a joke, but Imogen giggled. "That's wise of you," she said, squeezing my hands. Then she released me, gesturing for a servant who immediately offered both of us wine. "To the Princess of Blood," she said, raising her fresh glass, "who has proven herself to be truly one of the Fae."

"One of the Fae," the crowd echoed.

My skin crawled, but I pretended to sip with them before setting the wine aside.

Imogen drained half of the glass, then blinked, looking surprised. "Shards, this is strong."

"It should be, for how expensive it was," Rowena said. She was smiling, but her blue eyes were icy. "You should experiment with pleasures you don't have to pay for."

What a hypocrite. How much gold had Rowena paid last night for the right to destroy that sylph?

"You should thank me for providing such expensive pleasures," Imogen said. "You're borrowing my good taste." She was slurring her words now, and even her sycophants looked taken aback. A merry queen was one thing, but it wasn't even noon. Ulric watched with his arms crossed and lips pursed. Even her most loyal supporter seemed to be questioning this reckless indulgence.

Imogen passed a hand over her forehead, frowning. "I tire of this." She snapped her fingers—badly—and a servant appeared with a tray. She set the glass down clumsily. "I'm going to bed." Then she swept away, the train of her fuchsia dress hissing behind her as the crowd parted to let her through.

The buzz of gossip immediately started. I looked after Imogen, a crinkle between my brows. Then I studied Rowena, who looked far more cheerful now.

Was Imogen drunk, or had Rowena slipped something into the wine? What reason would she possibly have for doing that?

"How embarrassing," Rowena told Torin, just loud enough to be overheard. "I hope she sleeps off some of that mirth and merriment before tonight."

And there was the reason. Imogen had publicly humiliated Torin, so Rowena was humiliating her in return.

There were deep fractures in the relationship between Illusion and Light. Would we be able to take advantage of that? My first impulse was to ask Kallen what he thought.

That would mean facing Kallen again, though. Which would mean thinking about his body surging against mine. I did a quick survey of the room and was both relieved and dismayed when I didn't see him.

I tugged on Lara's arm, and we moved deeper into the library. It was enormous, with shelves extending twenty feet overhead and far into the distance. Golden ladders rolled on tracks, pausing next to the faeries perusing the collection as if offering their services. Most of the activity was in the main reading area, which had been cleared of desks to allow for mingling, but I spotted a few figures wandering between the labyrinthine shelves.

"That was tense," Lara said.

"Hmm." A black-clad figure down one aisle caught my eye, but it wasn't anyone I recognized, and disappointment shot through me.

Kallen was supposed to be here today. Was he avoiding me?

"You're being odd," Lara commented.

My attention snapped back to her. "What? I'm not being odd."

She pursed her lips. "So you are listening to me. You've been frowning and staring into space all morning, and you keep blushing."

"No, I don't," I said reflexively, even as my cheeks started to heat again.

"Does it have something to do with you coming home late last night?"

I covered my face with my hands. "No."

"Well, that's certainly convincing."

I peeked at her from between my fingers. "How did you know I was out late?"

"My room is across the hall from yours." She narrowed her eyes. "Who were you with?"

"Who says I was with someone?"

Her brows rose.

My face was probably bright red. "It's not important."

"Was it Drustan?"

The question took me aback. Did she think... "No! Drustan and I are done."

"Good. Flowers are not enough." She still looked suspicious. "Who was it, then?"

"No one. I was just nervous about seeing Torin and Rowena after . . . you know." We'd talked about what had happened at the brothel over a breakfast I'd barely been able to eat. A breakfast at which, apparently, I'd been blushing whenever my mind drifted to what had happened with Kallen afterwards.

"You're lying to me."

"No, I'm omitting."

She gave me an unimpressed look. "You've spent too much time with the Fae if you think that's a good argument."

I rubbed my face, taking care to avoid the gold shadow Carys had applied to my eyelids. "Can we talk about this later? It's . . . complicated."

One of the most dangerous faeries in Mistei had his tongue in my mouth last night. I was ready to fuck him on the floor, but he ran away from me. Now we're at a party that includes my former lover, multiple political factions who want to kill each other, and two faeries who want to kill me, specifically, and all I can think about is why he isn't here yet.

Lara sighed. "Fine. You will tell me the truth soon, though, won't you?"

"I will," I promised. Though she would probably question my sanity.

The library doors opened again, and I turned to see who the newest arrivals were. Una, Hector . . . and Kallen.

There was a tumbling sensation in my belly. I turned swiftly to look at a display case at the end of one row. When I realized the case held a mummified cat, I grimaced and moved to the next one. This was better: a palm-sized illuminated manuscript open to a page calligraphed in what must be the old language, with art depicting a dragon soaring beneath falling stars.

"This is interesting," Lara said, bending to inspect the next case over. "A flute carved from a giant's finger bone."

"Giants are real?" I asked, startled. The flute looked like any other, except for being pure white.

"Who knows? Could be someone's arm." She tapped a nail against the glass. "Bone instruments are supposed to have mystical powers."

That made me think of other objects in Mistei that had power. Who had sent that bird last night? I wished it were here so I could snatch it out of the air and crush it under my boot.

The back of my neck prickled. When I glanced over my shoulder, I found Kallen staring at me.

The sound of chatter grew fuzzy as everything else receded. I was vaguely aware of Una beside him, pointing at a gilt-edged book on a plinth, but the library might as well have been empty otherwise. My entire focus was taken up by midnight eyes and slightly parted lips.

Those lips had been on me last night. Goose bumps erupted at the memory.

Lara looped her arm through mine. "I want to find Gweneira to ask about the flute," she said. "If anyone knows if it's real, she will."

The mention of Gweneira jarred me out of my stupor. I forced a smile, then placed one foot in front of the other, letting Lara guide me. It didn't feel like I was properly in my body. Half of me was still in a brilliantly lit sparring chamber, wanting desperately and wondering how it had all gone wrong.

Gweneira was on the opposite side of the room, which meant we would have to walk past Kallen to get to her. I focused on his pitch-black tunic rather than his face. That was quickly revealed to be a mistake, because it made me think about the scarred skin beneath and the ripple of muscles as he'd caged me in.

I tore my eyes away. The refreshment table. That was a good thing to look at. Mounds of grapes, plates of cheese, bread that was somehow still steaming from the oven. "Bread," I said, pointing it out to Lara. The rest of that brilliant thought vanished, because Kallen was moving to intercept us.

Lara gave me a sidelong glance. "Bread?"

How was I supposed to behave normally? I focused on Gweneira instead. She was in conversation with a serious-looking Light faerie with an impressive pair of slashing brows. General Murdoch, the faerie in charge of their portion of the house army. Gweneira glanced towards us, and her expression turned grim. She touched Murdoch's elbow, and the two of them turned and walked away.

"Oh," Lara said, steps faltering.

Kallen moved into our path, and every thought flew out of my mind. "Kenna," he said, voice slightly raspy. He cleared his throat. "It's good to see you."

All I could manage in response was a high-pitched "Hmm."

Lara seemed baffled, but I could tell the moment she figured it out. Her eyebrows jerked upward, and she shot me a swift, incredulous look. "Lord Kallen," she said, switching her attention to him. "What a surprise."

Paranoia itched at my shoulder blades, and the room felt far too hot. "Yes," I said, aiming for a composed demeanor. "Good morning, Kallen. I hope you . . . slept well. Last night."

I can't believe you, Lara's narrowed eyes said.

"I was wondering if I might have a moment of your time," Kallen said. "In private."

Lara released my arm like it was on fire. "I have somewhere else to be, anyway."

"You do?" I asked, torn between relief and nervousness.

"I have some very important drinking to do." She stalked towards the refreshment table.

Kallen watched her go, face carefully blank. "Does she—"

"She figured it out."

"Ah." There was a weighty pause. "She does not seem pleased."

"Where should we have this private discussion?" I asked. *A bed?* He jerked his head towards the shelves.

I walked beside him, struggling to breathe. Faeries watched and whispered as we passed, and though that was normal at these events, paranoia told me it was because everyone knew what we had done.

Kallen led me halfway down an aisle. "I'm sorry," he murmured, crossing his arms and leaning back against the shelf.

He'd apologized last night, too. "For what?"

"For being reckless. For being careless with your safety." He shook his head, looking bitterly disappointed in himself. "For not realizing sooner that we weren't alone."

I realized belatedly that we might not be alone right now and checked for heartbeats, finding none close by. "The bird might not have been there for long," I said, face flaming. "And if it was listening for conversations, we weren't really . . . talking."

His fingers flexed on his bicep. "There was enough."

I would tear this world apart for you, Kenna. And I don't deserve this, not a second of it, but I'm too greedy to stop.

I felt dizzy remembering the press of his body against mine. It felt like there was a thread knotted below my navel, tugging me towards him. I wanted his tongue in my mouth and his hands bruising my skin. I wanted to collect more of those harsh, desperate noises he'd made against my lips. I wanted to know how he would feel moving inside me.

"I wish I knew who was responsible," I said, hating them bitterly for stopping me from finding out.

His jaw worked. "I think it was Gweneira."

"Gweneira?" I asked, astounded. "Why?"

"Her belt."

All at once, I remembered one of the Light lady's favorite accessories: a golden belt with a metal sparrow perched on it. "Shards," I breathed. "I should have realized sooner." That explained her frosty stare today.

"I should have, too." Kallen's voice was laced with judgment. "She's made a study of Fae history and artifacts, and she always knows more than she should."

I tried to find something positive in the situation. "At least it's better than Imogen finding out. Gweneira won't try to use this against us."

"If you declare for Hector, she might. She could argue you're easily swayed and Void House manipulated the outcome."

I shook my head. "She promised to abide by the same agreement the rest of us did. Whoever ends up leading, we'll overcome our differences to support them."

His mouth was pressed into a tight line. "I don't know if I believe that."

I didn't know if I believed it, either. "What's done is done. We'll tell the others we're involved, but it won't affect my decision—"

"No."

The interruption startled me. "No? What do you mean, no?"

Kallen straightened and dropped his hands to his sides. "You weren't thinking clearly last night. I took advantage of your distress."

My jaw dropped. "Excuse me?"

"It was a mistake," he said in a cold voice. "You don't want this."

I flinched. It wasn't just the voice; all of him was becoming ice before my eyes. Flat stare, rigid jaw, military posture. The King's Vengeance.

Anger and humiliation mixed. "Don't you dare presume to tell me what I want."

"I'm a monster, Kenna," he said, each syllable precise and dagger sharp. "And last night I did something unforgivable."

"Why are you talking about it like something you alone did?" I snapped. "I kissed you because I wanted to."

There was a crack in his cold expression, a fleeting look of agony. "You shouldn't have wanted to."

I knew what this was. This was the same self-hatred Kallen always flogged himself with, except this time it was hurting me, too. Furious, I gripped the front of his tunic. "You don't get to decide that. All you get to decide is what you want. Do you no longer want me, Kallen?"

His throat bobbed. He didn't reply.

I wanted to shake him. He did want me. He'd just decided it was impossible or that he was a bad person for wanting me or that I deserved someone better. All three, probably. But he was acting like he'd somehow forced this on me, and that was unacceptable.

"Tell me," I said, lips growing numb. "Tell me you don't want me." I shifted closer, until my skirts brushed his shins. "You never lie to me. So look me in the face and tell me the truth."

We were both breathing hard. He leaned closer, breath puffing across my lips, and my eyes drifted half shut.

"Everything I touch dies," Kallen whispered.

Then he was pulling away from me, dissolving from beneath my hold. My fingers clenched on shadow and empty air. The patch of darkness lingered for a moment before swirling away, leaving me alone and aching for the second time.

I STRUGGLED TO KEEP MY FACE IMPASSIVE AS I RETURNED TO the party. A few onlookers eyed me curiously, but what would they have seen if they'd been looking? Just a quiet argument between two faeries.

Kallen had run away from me. Again.

"Coward," I muttered bitterly.

He was probably telling himself he was protecting me from the complications of a romance. Or maybe he planned to deny both of us unless I supported Hector. I considered the idea as I glowered at an embroidery display, then swiftly rejected it. Kallen played politics, but not like that. He didn't use seduction as a tool.

So why was he determined not to let himself have even a scrap of joy? He'd looked nearly panicked last night after that bird had flown away.

Everything I touch dies.

I closed my eyes, allowing the words to sink past the lingering heartache. Kallen was always honest with me, which meant he believed what he'd said. He was afraid of losing me.

No, more than that. He was afraid of *causing* my death.

I breathed out, letting go of some of my anger. Why did he believe that touching me—loving me—would kill me?

"Kenna."

My stomach sank. I opened my eyes to find Drustan at my side. He was dressed particularly kingly today, in cloth of gold that matched the golden stars dotted through his hair. He was smiling, but his eyes were flat.

"Drustan," I said, feeling queasy. Because if Gweneira knew what Kallen and I had done . . .

"Walk with me," he ordered, turning on his heel.

I bristled at the order, but I wasn't going to cause a scene. It was better to resolve this now, rather than stewing in anxiety. "We're leaving?" I asked as he led me towards the exit.

"Unless you'd prefer to take me into the stacks?" he asked sharply. "You'll earn a reputation if you do that too often."

"Oh, please," I said, seething. "As if my reputation could ever come near yours."

He shot me a nasty look but didn't reply. Instead he bowed and held the door open like the perfect gentleman he wasn't.

Faeries strolled up and down the corridor outside—nobles not important enough to be invited to the party, but wanting to be near the center of power. Drustan's scowl instantly transitioned into a grin. "A bit dull, don't you think?" he asked, offering me his arm. "Imogen's losing her touch. But no matter—you simply must sample a new wine I had imported from Elsmere."

I returned the smile, annoyed nearly beyond bearing. "Do I have a choice?"

"You always have a choice, Kenna." He leaned in to murmur the rest near my ear. "I wish you'd make wiser ones, though."

"Are we going to talk about this in private, or are you trying to goad me into stabbing you right here?"

His eyes narrowed. "Come, then."

The library was located between Fire and Earth territory, and I felt a twinge of alarm when he started leading me up the ramp towards Fire House. He stopped outside a familiar door and held it open.

I took a deep breath, then entered the room.

The study where we'd conducted our affair was smaller than I remembered. The bookshelves, the desk with its decanter of wine, the red-and-yellow-striped couch. What a grand passion I'd thought I'd discovered here, and the entire world had seemed bigger because of it.

I took a wide path around the couch towards the desk, gripping the back of the accompanying chair as nerves rioted through me.

Drustan warded the door with fiery orange magic, then spun to face me. The cheerful mask instantly dropped. "You're choosing Hector," he snarled.

The vehemence was startling. I'd expected him to be angry about my entanglement with Kallen, considering our history, but this was what he truly cared about. "I haven't decided yet."

He advanced on me, and though I was tempted to back away, I held my ground. "You sold yourself to Void House, and you didn't have the fucking decency to tell me your mind was already made up."

I raised my chin, glaring at him. "I told you, I haven't made my mind up."

His laugh was disbelieving. "Oh, please. You had a private meeting with Hector."

Gweneira's bird again, presumably. Shards, I'd seen it, hadn't I? It had been perched on a candelabrum shaped like a tree. At least Hector's shadows had disguised our path, so it hadn't followed to eavesdrop. "And I'm meeting with you now. That's what allies do. What they *don't* do is send spies after each other."

"You lecture me about spies when you're spending your nights with Kallen?" His lip curled in a sneer. "How do you even stomach it? Do you scrub your skin raw afterwards, telling yourself it'll all be worth it in the end? That if you lift your skirts for him often enough, even a monster can be convinced to eat out of your hand?"

The blast of rage I felt was so powerful the edges of my vision darkened. I let go of the chair and slapped him.

His head snapped to the side. He stared at the far wall, cheek reddening. The lines of my fingers were imprinted over his cheekbone.

My hand stung from the force of that blow. I was so angry that if I opened my mouth to speak, I might scream.

Drustan swallowed. "I deserved that."

"Yes, you did," I bit out. "Shaming me, when you've whored

yourself for your cause for centuries? That's not why I'm with him, anyway."

"With him," he echoed. When he looked at me again, his irises were wholly overtaken by flame. "He's evil, Kenna."

"He's not evil."

"He was Osric's right hand!"

"Not by choice."

He laughed again, even wilder. "What nonsense has he filled your head with? He betrayed countless people to Osric, including Lara's own brother. Is it acceptable when he does it, but not me?"

I blinked rapidly. "What are you talking about?"

"How do you think Osric found out about Leo and Mildritha? Kallen spoke with her mere minutes before she was arrested." Grief joined the fury on his face. "He found out who fathered her child, and she's dead because of it."

My breath caught. This was why Drustan hated Kallen so virulently, even more than he seemed to hate Hector. Not just because of the years with Osric—because he thought Kallen was responsible for the death of his closest friend, the lady he'd grown up loving with hopeless dedication even knowing she didn't return his feelings.

Looking at that expression of furious sorrow, I knew with even more certainty that his passion for me only went so deep. Despite the countless lovers he'd taken, despite the years of charming and seducing to build his power, Drustan's heart was locked away. It belonged to a pile of ashes.

"That's not what happened," I said, trying to keep my voice steady. Kallen would have tried to save that child. Someone else had betrayed them to Osric.

He paced away, jamming his hands into his copper hair. "How would you know what happened?"

"Because I know Kallen. Have you ever actually asked him about it? Maybe you should speak to both him and Hector like the allies you claim they are." I wasn't going to betray the secret of Void House's changelings, but something needed to change soon, because our alliance couldn't survive with a poison like this eating away at its core.

He shook his head. "First her, now you. He's going to destroy you." He stormed back to me. "When are you going to declare Hector king? Since you know so much about Void House now."

We were back to this. Back to the anger and demands, because as I knew, it was easier to hold hate than pain. "I told you—"

"That crown is mine, Kenna. Mine by right. I *will* have it."

Drustan's fervent eyes flickered orange and then a pale, scorching blue I'd never seen before. The air wavered around him, warped by the heat coming off his body. It was painful to stand this close—sweat poured down my face, and my skin felt so tight it might split.

Fear pulsed through me. That was the face of a fanatic.

There were moments when everything came clear at once. Weeks of indecision, hours spent reading measured words and promises about a better future, and it came down to a single, shattering realization. The crown was Drustan's faith, and I was the obstacle in his path.

"You told me you valued a tempering voice," I said, trembling. I reached for my magic, readying to use it. He could burn me alive if he wanted to, and though I'd never believed Drustan capable of doing something like that, I'd never seen him in a state like this, either. "I am telling you right now that I have not declared for Hector yet, and Kallen doesn't decide my politics for me." I swallowed, knowing my next words were dangerous but unwilling to soften them to appease him. That wasn't the deal I'd made with the Shards or with myself. "But if you think the crown is your *right*, not a privilege or an honor or a responsibility, then you don't deserve it."

Flames shimmered at the corners of his eyes. They were tears, I was shocked to realize. Burning tears that he wiped away, flinging aside in drops that singed holes in the upholstery of the couch.

I'd never seen Drustan cry before.

My Blood magic was woven through his chest now. I held his heart in an invisible grip, waiting for his response. It pulsed beneath the cage of my power, the paired beats counting out the fragments of a moment that felt infinite. Such a fragile thing, that heart.

My magic followed the expanding of his lungs as he took a deep breath, then another. The flames in his stare extinguished, and his irises turned gray as ash. His hands dropped to his sides, loose and open.

"You're right," he said, sounding distant, and I got the sense he was wrestling with himself, shoving the fire and rage back down into whatever dark hole he usually hid them in. "This is not the ruler I want to be. I'm sorry, Kenna."

My knees went weak with the relief of a confrontation averted, and I braced myself against the back of the chair. "You mean that?"

He closed his eyes, taking more deep breaths. One, then three, then ten. When he finally looked at me again, his expression was full of remorse. "You've seen a different side of me today. One I do not particularly like and try hard to keep under control." He grimaced, rubbing his temples. His fingers were trembling. "I hope you will forgive me."

What was forgiveness? Was it an action? A feeling? A dream that the future could be different if only we knew how to let go of the past? I wasn't sure any of us knew.

"It's all tangled up," he whispered when I didn't respond. "Her and you and all of it. Centuries of pain, and I've been fighting so hard to fix it, but I don't—I don't always know where the lines are anymore. Or if I've become exactly what she would have hated."

I gently released his heart, feeling a swell of bitter pity. I thought of Hector shattering a line of glass bottles over his lost love. Kallen telling himself—and me—that he didn't deserve anything bright or beautiful. We were all eaten up by fury and regret, and those feelings festered when none of us were allowed to show them openly.

Every demon broke free eventually. Even Drustan's.

"I think asking yourself that question is a good start," I said.

His hand was still shielding his eyes. I watched the ripple of his swallow. "You should go."

This confrontation felt incomplete. Everything between us felt incomplete, but maybe it always would. We'd crossed a line today, one that couldn't be uncrossed.

Of all the feelings I'd thought I'd experience when my decision became clear, I hadn't realized grief would be the greatest part.

"Kenna," Drustan said quietly. "Please. Let me have my dignity."

There was moisture on his cheeks. Real tears this time, not flaming ones. For Mildritha? For me, lost to the arms of his enemy? Or for his aspirations, which he must surely know he'd damned?

The reasons were impossible to separate, probably.

I slipped out of the study, leaving him alone with his regrets.

35

Lara and I dismissed our handmaidens and prepared for the masquerade together. I did her hair before she did mine, and we talked about impossible choices.

"How do you feel now that it's done?" she asked as she tucked a ruby-tipped pin into the bundle of braids at the back of my head. She'd secured the top half of my hair, leaving the rest to hang free.

"It's not done yet," I said, staring at myself in the mirror. We were both still wearing dressing robes, and my face was clean of makeup, since I'd be reapplying it to match my ball gown. There were fatigued shadows under my eyes, and I had the feeling of being two people in one body—the princess and the peasant. "It won't be done until after midnight."

I'd sent letters to Drustan, Hector, and Gweneira, calling a meeting of our alliance after the masquerade ball. Five hours from now, I would tell them Hector would be our new king, and we would all find out how good our word was.

"The decision is made, though," she said. "It has to be a relief."

"It is. But I'm afraid, too, because I don't know how Drustan and

Gweneira will react." I'd seen a new side to Drustan today. He'd shown me something real, something ugly, and there was a bitter irony in his truth—the one thing I'd wanted from him—being what finally drove me away.

I comforted myself with the thought of Hector's changelings and his promise that I might not always agree with him and he might not always be wise, but his reasons were good, and we could figure out the rest together. That was a foundation a future could be built on.

Mine by right wasn't.

"Do you worry about Gweneira's reaction?" I asked softly, meeting Lara's eyes in the mirror.

Her lips pressed together. "If she doesn't accept this, she isn't who I thought she was."

It was the closest we'd gotten to speaking about her feelings for Gweneira. We'd talked about Kallen—Lara did, in fact, question my sanity, though she said that was hardly new, and what she cared about most was how he treated me—but although I'd left her openings to confess her own romantic hopes, she'd stayed quiet. Maybe she wasn't willing to acknowledge the possibility until she knew it wouldn't be snatched away.

"For what it's worth," Lara said, "I think you made the right choice."

There was a lump in my throat. "Because of Selwyn?"

She was quiet as she slid another ruby pin into the coiled braids. The glittering drops made me think of a rainstorm at sunset—like the clouds had briefly parted so the sun could saturate everything in its dying red glow.

"Mostly because of him," Lara finally said. "But also because you're right. Drustan wants the throne for the wrong reasons, not just the right ones."

"I'm sure that's true of Hector, too."

She grimaced. "I'm sure it is. But neither of them were ever going to be perfect."

I hadn't even told her about the changelings yet—it wasn't my secret to share—and she still thought this was the right choice. "You aren't worried that Hector is less popular than Drustan?"

"Most people are less popular than Drustan, and none of you are going to be well loved after you start commanding armies." Her brown eyes were serious as they met mine in the mirror. "It's going to be war, Kenna, and you're one of the ones starting it. You can't worry about popularity when you're doing something like that."

Thousands of lives on the line . . . and I would be one of the leaders sending them off to die.

I stroked Caedo, who was curled around my wrist. The dagger had drunk a pitcher of pig's blood tonight, but it stirred hungrily at the touch. I supposed once something started craving blood, it could never be entirely satisfied. "If we can kill Imogen quickly, it doesn't need to be a long war."

Lara shrugged one shoulder. "Depends on her successor. It won't end until there are people in power who value peace more than glory—or until there's no one left to fight."

The house shivered, a tremor in the web of magic that made both of us stiffen. There was urgency in the invisible currents that eddied around us. Someone was here, and the house wanted us to hurry.

We raced downstairs in our robes. The entrance door slid open, revealing General Murdoch of Light House with Gweneira cradled limply in his arms. She wore a white ball gown only a few shades paler than her ashen face. Her eyes were closed, and her mouth sagged open.

Lara cried out and rushed forward. "What happened?"

"Poison," Murdoch said grimly. "Rowena finally got to her. She collapsed after dinner."

I'd been furious with Gweneira for spying, but sudden fear overtook everything. I placed my hand on her chest, trying to sense the extent of the damage. Her heart was struggling sluggishly, and her lungs were barely filling. "Antidote?"

"I don't know. But I thought your magic—"

"Does anyone know you brought her here?"

"No. But when Rowena discovers there's no corpse, she'll send soldiers looking."

"Inside," I ordered, hastily modifying the house restrictions to allow these two access to the ground floor.

Murdoch hesitated, looking at the spikes lining the metal door.

"We can't do it out here," I said. "Not if soldiers will be coming."

He nodded and stepped forward. As he came into the path of the spikes, he flinched. When nothing happened, he began striding forward quickly, Lara and I at his side.

Gweneira was fading rapidly. "Put her there," I ordered, pointing at one of the couches in the inner hall.

Murdoch laid Gweneira down. She looked so still I would have believed she was dead if not for the faint echo of her heartbeat pressing against my magic. Her gown spilled over the crimson cushions, and I spotted the golden sparrow clinging to her white satin belt.

"This has to be the poison they tried before," Lara said, twisting her fingers together. "The one that paralyzes the heart and lungs. She said—" She broke off, making a raw noise of anguish. "She said she'd die in thirty minutes."

We had to be close to that, considering how long it had likely taken Murdoch to get here. I knelt and pressed my palm to Gweneira's chest, closing my eyes and imagining my magic wrapping around her heart like a fist. The organ gave one faint beat—then stopped entirely.

I squeezed lightly with my magic. There was a moment of resistance, and then the muscle moved under my command and blood surged through her arteries. "Get an empty bowl," I ordered Lara, feeling a swell of relief. "And Nadine or Triana, someone we can trust to be calm in a crisis."

Lara's footsteps pattered away. I kept my eyes closed, breathing through the rising panic as I kept pumping her heart. I'd never done anything like this before. If I squeezed too hard, she could die. If I got the rhythm wrong, she could die. And she might die anyway because my magic was unpracticed and easily exhausted and I knew nothing about poisons.

"What's happening at Light House?" I asked Murdoch to distract myself from the fear.

"Torin took over the house using the Sun Soldiers. I would be there fighting, but this was the only thing I could think of that might save her."

"What will happen to her supporters?"

"They're rounding them up," he said, grief breaking through his controlled tone. "Most will fall in line, but there are a few who would rather die. I hope they run instead. Better a retreat than a total defeat."

"Do they have somewhere to run to?"

"Some may come here."

Which meant we needed to be ready to accept them.

I squeezed Gweneira's heart again and again, then forced her lungs to expand. It was a wobbling, unpracticed rhythm, but I sensed her blood freshening as air filled her. My head was already starting to ache, though, and it took all my concentration to keep the magic flowing. The power didn't spill out of my fingers easily—it felt like moving underwater. Because Gweneira was a Light faerie, I realized. Her resistance to magic was affecting my ability to heal her—likely part of Mistei's complex system of balance—which meant this would be harder and exhaust me faster than if I was working on anyone else.

Lara's footsteps returned. "Here's the bowl," she said breathlessly. "Maude and Triana are coming."

I opened my eyes. "I need you outside. There may be refugees from Light House."

Lara made a noise of protest. "But I want—"

"It has to be you," I told her firmly. "You're the only one who can add them to the house. Murdoch, go with her so you can tell her who's trustworthy. We don't know who Torin and Rowena might send if they realize she's here."

Murdoch was already on his way out the door. Lara hesitated, looking at Gweneira with desperate longing, then swore and hurried after him. A moment later, Triana and Maude arrived, and I ordered them to roll Gweneira onto her side so she could vomit. Maude held Gweneira in place while Triana knelt before her with the empty bowl.

I didn't know how much poison she'd swallowed or if I'd be able to get enough of it out. I barely knew what I was doing at all—reading anatomy textbooks wasn't a substitute for holding someone's actual organs in my grip. My control of Gweneira's heart and lungs faltered as I explored her stomach. It felt similarly paralyzed, but waves of pain burned her from the inside out. I took a deep breath, then willed her to vomit in a rippling surge.

The mess poured out of her, splashing into the bowl. Triana flinched but didn't move. I did it again and again until Gweneira's stomach was empty. Then we rolled her onto her back again so I could keep working her stone-stiff heart and lungs.

Sweat beaded my brow, and I wrestled down fresh panic as my magic dwindled. If I couldn't get her body working again soon . . .

A minute later, I finally felt a softening in Gweneira's organs as the poison relaxed its grip. My head spun from the prolonged effort, but I kept going. When her heart struggled back to life, I nearly wept. "It's working," I gasped.

Her lungs recovered next, pulling in desperate breaths. Gweneira's eyes flew open, though her gaze was unfocused.

"You're all right," I said as Triana stroked her brow. "You're safe."

I pulled my magic out of her, then dropped my sweaty forehead against the arm of the couch as fatigue swept over me. Black spots drifted at the edges of my vision, and the pool of power in my chest was nearly empty.

Gweneira blinked rapidly, and awareness came back into her gaze. She sat up, then coughed, pressing a hand to her throat. "What—" she wheezed.

"Poison," I said. "Murdoch brought you here."

Shock washed over her delicate features. "You saved me."

I nodded.

"Thank you." She looked around, and I saw the moment she realized where she was and what the implications were. Shock shifted into horror. "Did I lose Light House?"

There was no point softening the truth. "Yes."

She closed her eyes, making an anguished sound. "My supporters?"

"Murdoch said Torin and Rowena are rounding them up. The ones who surrender, at least." Gweneira undoubtedly knew what would happen to the rest.

She stood and started to pace. Her dress was rumpled and vomit-streaked, her hair was damp with sweat, and she still had a sickly pallor, but her eyes blazed with hatred. "I will destroy them," she spat. "No matter what it takes. I will *end* them."

The house door rumbled in the distance. Moments later, a handful of blood-spattered Light faeries staggered into the hall. Gweneira gasped, then ran towards them. They held an urgent discussion, and then two more refugees arrived, and then three more. Triana and Maude went to retrieve Nadine, and soon the hall buzzed with activity as the servants took care of the new arrivals. I watched from the floor, certain that if I stood, I'd faint.

Nearly a hundred Light faeries arrived at Blood House over the next few minutes—wounded and weeping, ashen-faced and devastated. The commotion alerted more of my house members, who leapt into action to escort the Light faeries upstairs.

Finally, Lara and Murdoch returned. When Lara spotted Gweneira, she made a relieved noise and rushed forward. The two clasped hands as they exchanged quiet words, and then all three faeries joined me at the couch.

"There are no more coming," Murdoch told me grimly. "The doors to Light House are barred."

I managed to get to my feet, knees shaking. "At least this many escaped."

Grief shone in Gweneira's eyes. "Thank you for taking them in," she said, looking at me and then Lara. "Most wouldn't."

"They can stay so long as they agree to follow my rules." I was still angry with her over that bird at her belt, so the next words came reluctantly. "You can stay, too."

She was still, face frozen like a statue's. "Thank you for that as well."

We both knew it was a bitter gift. "It's not forever," I said, offering that small comfort. Maybe it was a lie, but if a lie got us through the worst times, it was enough. "You'll regain the house."

"May your words grow wings." She turned to Murdoch. "Do Torin and Rowena know where everyone escaped to?"

"I'm hoping not, since the Sun Soldiers were too occupied with the last pockets of resistance to pursue them. Princess Kenna is known for taking in refugees, though."

Gweneira rubbed her forehead. "We need to seed rumors quickly. Someone saw our people fleeing to an outcast colony, someone else saw them heading aboveground. Confuse the narrative in case there were any witnesses."

"And you?" Lara asked, eyes wide and hands clasped at her chest.

"I'm dead," Gweneira said bluntly. "My corpse went missing, but I'm sure we can come up with a convincing fabrication."

Murdoch nodded. "I wanted to give you a secret burial. I took you with me when I ran."

"Plausible, since Rowena would have strung me up in the entrance hall." Gweneira sighed, shoulders slumping. "Let's get our best remaining minds together and start strategizing."

"I'll stay here tonight," I told her.

"No," she said instantly. "You have to go to the masquerade."

"Why?"

"Because if you don't, they'll definitely know the Light faeries came here." Her expression grew more determined with each second. "Let them think us defeated. Let them believe me buried and my people scattered. If they think they've won, they won't be prepared when we strike back."

The last thing I wanted was to drink and dance among enemies after our alliance had been dealt such a brutal blow. We'd needed Gweneira's soldiers, but we'd also needed the hope she provided. She'd been proof that rebellion could grow even in Light House's strict walls.

But if my attendance helped lay the groundwork for revenge against Torin and Rowena, I would dance all night. "All right," I said. "I'll go."

Though there was someone I needed to see first.

36

This small study between Blood and Void House was beautiful in a dark, inviting way, but it didn't provide nearly enough room for pacing. I did my best, though, striding from bookshelf to desk and back, listening to the tap of my boots and the rustle of my skirts.

Like many rooms in Mistei, this one combined elements of the two nearest houses. Tapered candles the hue of fresh blood cast a soft glow over reddish-brown rosewood furnishings. The curving legs and polished surface of the desk were inlaid with jet, and the top held pens, baskets of blank paper, and a single red-black rose in a glass vase. Two armchairs upholstered in ebony velvet flanked a red-tiled fireplace, and a sinfully soft black fur rug stretched before the crackling hearth.

My reflection moved in the mirror over the fireplace. I hadn't been thinking about dressing to reflect my new alignment with Void House, but perhaps the choice had been subconscious. The bloodred satin was topped with a black pattern that resembled ornate metalwork. Small ruby pendants hung at the tip of each dark curlicue, hooked into the fabric so they trembled with every movement. My mask was silver to match Caedo at my wrist.

The other silver piece of my attire—the whisper-thin chain promising peace—was in my pocket. Considering the faeries wishing for my death, I didn't like wrapping it around my hand until I absolutely had to.

The door to the sitting room opened. I spun, raising my fists instinctively, but the figure that slipped inside was familiar, and my pulse accelerated for a different reason.

Kallen looked decadent in his masquerade outfit. His long-sleeved tunic was silk damask, soft and shining, with dark gray swirls and stars shimmering across the black background. A more structured fabric lined the front and extended into stiff shoulders, and engraved silver buttons held the garment together. He wasn't wearing his sword, since tonight was a silvered event, but his belt held two ornamental daggers tied into their sheaths.

His black enamel half mask was the one part of his attire I didn't like. He was good enough at concealing his emotions without anything assisting in the task.

Kallen cast a shadowy ward over the door, and I saw he wasn't wearing his chain yet, either. "I'm sorry to keep you waiting," he said. "Hector and I were strategizing."

I'd sent a messenger to tell the others what had happened at Light House, then asked Kallen to meet me here. We needed to discuss the choice I would be making later tonight.

His eyes wandered from my ruby-dotted hair to the hem of my dress, and I was painfully aware that we were alone in a small room with a ward blocking any sound that might escape. "You look beautiful," he said.

I cleared my throat. "As do you."

He shook his head slowly. "Not like that."

The heat in his gaze made my stomach clench. "Take the mask off," I said, unlacing my own and sliding it into the deep pocket of my dress.

He hesitated, then raised his hands to tug at the ties behind his head before setting the mask aside.

"Much better," I whispered.

He closed his eyes and breathed in deeply. When he looked at me again, his face was impassive. "So Light House fell at last."

"As you expected."

"Yes, though you claimed an unexpected victory by taking in those who escaped."

The approval in his voice went to my head faster than any wine. Needing something to occupy my hands, I reached for the rose displayed on the desk, toying with the thorny stem and velvety petals. "What will happen tonight?"

"Nothing, I imagine." When I glanced his way, I found his focus on my fingers. I paused, then lowered my hand to stroke the vase from base to rim. He made a soft, inarticulate noise, then looked away. "Torin and Rowena are unlikely to announce their victory," he said, addressing the fireplace. "Better to pretend the threat was never serious."

I hadn't summoned him here to discuss Light House. "I want to tell you something," I said, taking a step towards him.

His shoulders stiffened before he faced me. His expression was icily composed, but I wasn't fooled. "Oh?"

My pulse was tapping too quickly. I straightened my spine and raised my chin, knowing I was about to set Mistei on an irreversible course. "I'm choosing Hector as king."

His lips parted. Shock and then relief swept over his face, wiping away the ever-present tension. "Kenna, I—" He broke off, then strode towards me, and I gasped when he hauled me into his arms, hugging me tightly. His lips found my forehead as he rocked me back and forth. "Thank you," he murmured against my skin. *"Thank you."*

I melted into his hold. When I wrapped my arms around his waist, a shudder raced through him. He pulled away, gripping my shoulders to hold me at arm's length. "What made you finally decide?" he asked, eyes flicking between mine.

He was trying to put distance between us again. I curled my hands around his forearms, wishing I had claws to sink into him. "Drustan did. We had a . . . conversation."

I told him about the confrontation in the study. Kallen was deathly quiet throughout, but by the end, the blue of his irises had swirled into Void black. "You were afraid," he said.

"Yes," I admitted. "I don't think he would have actually hurt me, but at the time . . . I wasn't sure."

"Someday Drustan will learn what real fear feels like," Kallen said with such chilling fury it sent a shiver down my spine.

I liked that a bit too much, but where would hatred lead us? Back into the same cycle of destruction. "He's damaged, too," I told Kallen. "He lost someone he loved, just like Hector. Doesn't that change everyone?"

When people died, they took pieces of us with them. Our dreams, the stories we told ourselves about the future, the best parts of our hearts. The illusion of who we were shattered, too, because we'd relied on that love to give shape to our existence. Without it, what was left?

Drustan had used his grief to fuel a rebellion, as Hector had. That was the good—the *purpose*—that could come from loss. But now that he'd tasted power, I worried that Drustan would crave more and more, because nothing else had come close to filling the hollowness inside.

"I do understand him," Kallen bit out. "But I will not accept anyone treating you like that, no matter what losses they have experienced."

And there it was. The emotion at the core of everything, the one I was still trying to understand in all its vastness and complexity. The real reason I'd summoned him here, if I was being honest with myself. "Why, Kallen?" I asked softly. "Tell me why you won't accept it."

A muscle in his jaw ticked, but he didn't answer. He released my arms and stepped back.

"No," I said, moving forward to close the distance. "You don't get to run away again." I grabbed his tunic, snagging my fingers in the gap between two buttons. "Tell me why you're angry with Drustan."

"You know why," he gritted out, eyes still black as night.

"Because you care about me."

"It's more than that."

My heart was racing. "Then tell me what it is. Don't be a coward."

He made a pained sound. Then his hand shot out to curve around the nape of my neck, beneath my loose hair. "Do you have any idea what you do to me?" he demanded. "What I would do for you, how many people I would kill? I wake up thinking about you, and I fall asleep thinking about you, and on the rare nights the universe offers me some mercy, I dream about you, too. I'm *sick* with this wanting, and it just gets worse and worse. There's no end to it."

I was shaken by the fury in his voice, the depth of his need. "Why deny it? Why deny *us* when I want you, too?"

"Because I don't know how to do this!" The words exploded out of him. "The kindest thing I could possibly do for you is stay away, and that's the one thing I can't manage. You should be running from me. I don't understand why you're not."

"I'm not going to run," I told him, pulse hammering. "Why would I?"

His groan was anguished. "Because you deserve so much better.

Someone with cleaner hands who deserves to touch you. Someone who won't hurt you."

"You do deserve to touch me. I *want* you to touch me. And you won't hurt me."

"I've only kissed one other person, and then I killed her!"

It took a moment to process the horror of what he'd said. Then I gasped. "What?"

Naked pain filled his expression. "That's who I am, Kenna. I've spent my entire life learning how to break people. I'll break you, too, even if I don't mean to, and I won't be able to bear it."

"No," I said firmly, reaching up to cup his face, my fingers sliding into his soft hair. "You won't break me." Whatever gruesome story was in his past, I knew Kallen. He wanted to punish Drustan for frightening me—he would be even harsher on himself.

"You can't know that." His eyes were still pitch dark with suffering, but he wasn't pulling away. "Were you even listening? I killed someone I cared for. Only the worst kind of monster would be capable of that."

That was fear pulling his expression into agonized lines, not just self-hatred. He was trying to drive me away because life had taught him to be terrified of loving anything, lest he watch it be destroyed. "I'm not leaving," I told him stubbornly. "Tell me what happened."

He was quiet for a while, breathing through parted lips and staring at me like I was both poison and antidote. "A long time ago," he finally said, "I met a girl from Illusion House."

"How long ago?"

"We were both teenagers."

I made a soft noise of protest. "You were just children."

"I told you, I don't think I was ever that."

Because Osric had forced him to kill starting at age nine. Even if he didn't believe he'd been an innocent child, worthy of care, I did.

"Did you love her?" I asked, keeping my voice gentle.

He shook his head. "No. Or maybe, I suppose, in the simple way that the very young think of love." He took a deep breath. "We shared kisses and held hands, and we were just old enough to begin toying with more. But she asked me to tell her my secrets first, as a gesture of my devotion." He paused. "So I did."

"Oh no," I whispered, starting to sense the path this particular tragedy had taken.

"I told her I was afraid of Osric and afraid Void House would be destroyed if I made a mistake. That I hated killing people and despised the role I'd been born into, and I was afraid someday I wouldn't have any kind of heart left at all. I said I dreamed of running away, and maybe we could run away together." He recited it flatly, like he was confessing a list of crimes.

"What did she say?" I asked, briefly lifting my hand from his cheek to tuck a lock of hair behind his ear.

He turned his face into the touch, and his lips brushed my wrist. "She thanked me for being honest with her. And then she went to tell Osric everything I had said."

My stomach dropped.

"He summoned me," Kallen continued, "and I'll never forget seeing her standing by his side, grinning."

"He probably forced her to do it," I said, scrambling for any poultice to apply to this ancient, awful hurt.

"You think I don't know that?" His voice grew sharp, but then he closed his eyes, inhaling deeply. "But she meant it, too. She'd always told me she wanted to be a great lady. Feared and respected, with influence in the flick of her fingers. And Osric was the one who could give that to her."

A child betraying another child for the sake of power. I couldn't imagine how that had felt to live through. "Did he hurt you?" I whispered.

His eyes flew open as he made a raw sound. "Of course he did. And then he handed me a dagger and told me to kill my heart, because he never wanted to hear about it burdening me ever again."

"Kallen." His name was knocked out of me on a horrified exhalation.

"She begged and cried," he said, gaze gone distant. "But Osric didn't need another great lady in his court. He needed a weapon. So I did as he commanded, and then I stopped trying to have a heart."

Forced to kill his first love. Someone just as young and vulnerable as him, too, because as much as I wanted to hate that girl for what she had done, I refused to hate a child for the choices forced on them by the environment they grew up in.

Kallen had dedicated his later life to saving children. I wondered if he even recognized that parallel.

"So you see," he said, grief written over his face, "I destroy everything, and I always have. And the only thing I want more than you . . . is for you to be safe."

It was the sweetest thing anyone had ever said to me—and one of the saddest, too. I moved my hands to his chest, curving my palm over the beat of his heart like I could protect it. "It wasn't your fault," I told him. "What you did to her—there was no other choice."

He shook his head. "That's the excuse I've given again and again over my long life. That all my evil is either justified or something I'm helpless against. But there's always a choice."

"And what choice did you have back then? Or any other time Osric ordered you to commit an atrocity?"

"To die." He said it like it was indisputable: the sun rose in the east and set in the west, time moved forward no matter how we might wish it to stop, and the answer to every wrong was for Kallen to die. "If I'd had the courage to end it at the beginning, how many lives would have been saved?"

"None," I snapped, furious at the idea. "Or some would have been saved and others would be dead, because that's who Osric was. He would have found another weapon, and that one wouldn't have been a reluctant one."

There was a drowning look in his eyes, desperate for the shore. "You don't know that," he whispered.

"I do," I said fiercely. "And what would Osric have done to Void House if you'd killed yourself? What would have happened to the changelings? What would have happened to *me*?" The Princess of Blood would have had a very short reign without his protection or his lessons.

He didn't reply, but his lips were parted around ragged breaths as he stared at me like I was that distant shore.

"So, no," I said, stepping even closer to him, my full skirts rustling against his legs. "I'm not going to run away. I'm not going to judge you for killing that girl. Because I know you, and you aren't going to hurt me, and you're far more than what you've been forced to do." He started to protest, so I barreled on. "I know there will be crimes in your past that aren't as clear-cut. I *know*. I'm here anyway, and I'm not leaving, because you—" My breath hitched. "You're wonderful, Kallen. You're thoughtful and protective and you *fight*, long past when most people would have given up. I refuse to let you go."

There. I'd laid my heart out in offer, and he just needed to be brave enough to accept it.

Candlelight flickered around us. The silence felt thick. I waited, looking up at him with mingled hope and terror.

Kallen blinked, a slow sweep of lashes. Then he shuddered all over, as if shaking off some awful creature that had been clinging to him.

And then he grabbed my waist, leaned down, and kissed me.

Radiant sparks burst inside me at the press of his lips. I wrapped my arms around his neck and kissed him back, overwhelmed by both joy and sorrow. Sorrow for what he had suffered; joy because this embrace was a promise. Kallen was done running from me.

Our first kiss had been frantic, an explosion of need so intense it had become nearly violent. This was different. No less intense, but deeper, slower, *more*. Kallen kissed me like he wanted to consume me. His tongue slipped inside my mouth, and he groaned when I met him with a stroke of my own.

He backed me up, and my hips hit the writing desk, making pens rattle. Without breaking the kiss, Kallen swept the surface clean. The vase holding the rose shattered, and glass crunched underfoot as he picked me up and set me on the desk. I fumbled with his buckle, and his belt and knives thumped to the floor. I spread my thighs wider as he crowded into me, and as our bodies pressed together, we let out matching moans.

"Kenna," he panted, burying his face in my neck. "I don't—"

"Don't what?" I asked, near delirious with desire as he kissed up my throat.

"I don't know how anything can feel this good," he said against my fluttering pulse. "I don't know how to survive it."

I plunged my hands into his hair again, pulling him back to my mouth. My hips rocked, and he slapped a hand on the desk, wrapping his other arm around me and leaning in until my spine arched.

I began undoing the buttons of his tunic, desperate to feel his skin. Kallen made a noise of animal want, then released me only to start gathering my skirts up, tugging the fabric past my knees. The ball gown bunched between us, and he slid his hands under the satin to grip my bare thighs.

"The things I've dreamed of doing with you," he said. "The things I've dreamed of doing *to* you. You can't imagine."

I'd gotten two of his buttons undone, but it was hard to focus when his hands were gliding up my legs. "Tell me," I said, starting on the third.

"I've imagined taking you in shadowed alcoves where anyone might stumble across us." He followed the words with the stroke of his lips beneath my ear. "My hand on your mouth, keeping you quiet, because what I'm doing feels so good you can't help but cry out. I dream of your red-painted lips leaving streaks on my cock as you look up at me with those beautiful fucking eyes, and I dream of going to my knees for you multiple times a day, whenever and wherever I can catch you alone, because I don't just *want* you, Kenna. I'm starving for you."

"Oh!" I gasped as he sucked my neck. "Kallen—"

His fingers met the scalloped edge of my silk undergarments, and he dragged them down and flung them aside. Then he threaded his left hand into my hair and slid his right hand up my leg until his thumb stroked the sensitive crease where my thigh met my body. He bit down on my neck, a gentle sting of teeth. "I've imagined helping you put on an outrageously complicated dress like this before a ball," he said. "Tightening each string myself, then ruining it because I can't help but put my hands all over you. Cutting it off you, then bending you over in front of a mirror so I can watch your face as I fill you. And then dancing with you at the ball afterwards, knowing you're still wet from me." His sigh ghosted over my pulse as he kept teasing me with his thumb, each sweeping touch coming closer to my core. Then he drew back to look me in the eye again, his expression fervent with want. "But that's what I dream of most. Dancing with you, watching you smile, listening to you laugh, never letting you go. Being with you—not just in the shadows but openly, in the light."

The words were breathtaking. To know he spent his free hours dreaming of more than just sex, that he dreamed of dancing with me and standing proudly by my side... It filled a hollow place inside me, one that had been empty for a long time. My whole life, maybe, because I'd learned early and often that there was little about me that might entice someone to stay.

Kallen didn't think he was worthy of it, but he wanted to stay.

Like called to like, I thought, looking at his yearning expression. He'd been far lonelier than I had for far longer.

"I want all of that," I told him, pausing my work on his buttons to run my fingers through his mussed hair. His lips were reddened from more than the kiss: the stain on my lips was a sturdy one, best removed with oil, but even it couldn't withstand this passion, and the streak of crimson at one corner of his mouth made me feel possessive. "I want to make love with you. I want to dance with you. I want everyone in Mistei to know I've chosen you, and I will keep choosing you."

From my earliest days collecting in the bog, I'd always valued the treasures found in unexpected places. I wasn't going to let go of this one.

Kallen made a rough sound and seized my lips in a fierce kiss again. His thumb finally moved that last inch inward, stroking through my core, parting the outer lips to get to the softness within. I whimpered when he brushed my clitoris.

"Wet," he said, sounding awed. "So fucking wet. All for me."

"For you," I agreed, spreading my fingers over the slice of chest I'd managed to bare. His heart raced beneath my touch.

He rubbed the sensitive nub, keeping up a steady rhythm until my hips were rocking for more, then rotated his wrist to press his middle finger against my opening. "Is this what you like?" he asked, sinking it inside me.

"Yes!" I gasped, clenching around his finger.

He tightened his other fist in my hair to tip my head to the side, then brought his lips to my ear. "I need to put my mouth on you. Let me taste you, Kenna. Please."

He stroked me deep inside, his palm rubbing against my clit, and a whimper left me at the feeling and the mental image of Kallen on his knees. Then I thought of what he'd confessed. "Are you— Have you done that before?"

"No," he murmured. "But I've been spying for centuries. I'm very familiar with how it's done."

Kallen was truly a virgin. It was shocking considering how long faeries lived, but it also made sense in the context of what he'd experienced. He had learned the worst, most brutal lessons when he was young: that openly valuing something was the fastest way to have it stolen, that betrayal was inevitable, and that love made an excellent weapon. He'd never trusted anyone enough to let them get close.

He trusted me, though, and the swell of emotion that came with that thought was nearly painful.

"Is that a problem?" he asked, pulling back to look at me. His eyes weren't the furious black of Void anymore, but his pupils were wide within their ring of midnight.

"No!" I hurried to say. "Not at all. I just want it to be good for you."

He kissed me swiftly, hand still working between my thighs. "I've been imagining the taste of you for months now. There's no way it's going to be less than earth-shattering."

I gasped as his palm pressed harder against my clit. "Months?"

His sigh wafted over my lips. "This isn't new for me, Kenna. I've been obsessed with you from the start, even if I was in denial about the nature of that obsession for a while."

The way he looked at me was all-consuming. Thinking of that focus dedicated to the task of making me orgasm, I shuddered. "Please taste me."

He grinned, fast and feral, then slid his hand out from between my thighs and picked me up. He carried me to the fireplace and laid me down on the fur rug, then settled between my legs, kissing me again. Deep, endless, devouring kisses, like he could spend the entire night at my lips and still never get enough.

He finally broke away, gasping. "I want to cut this dress off you."

"I like this dress," I protested.

"I do, too, which is the only reason it's being spared." He rolled me to my stomach and started working on the laces at my back. I listened to the hiss of them sliding out of their grommets and the crackle of the fireplace, curling my fingers in the soft rug. When the dress was loosened enough, Kallen dragged it off me with the chemise and underskirts, and I was left bare except for Caedo at my wrist.

A shuddering exhalation left him. I looked over my shoulder and found him staring at me with heavy-lidded eyes. He trailed one hand down my back, raising goose bumps, then stroked over my bottom and squeezed. "Lovely," he breathed.

It wasn't fair I was the only naked one. I turned over, then struggled to my knees and started ripping at the remaining buttons of his tunic. The fabric parted beneath my fingers, and I shoved it off to reveal his muscled chest.

Shards, he was beautiful. Thick slabs of pectoral muscle, a rippled abdomen, and two cut ridges arrowing into his trousers. The signs of his suffering were here, too, though. In addition to the scars on his arms, a large one curled over his ribs, another arced across his abdomen, and a third wound down from his clavicle. I ran my hands over him, feeling the slightly raised skin of those scars, then leaned in to kiss the mark at his collarbone.

His muscles flickered beneath my touch. I kissed his neck as he had kissed mine, loving the sigh that fell from his lips as my hands stroked slowly down his torso. When my fingers reached his waistband, he snapped, surging forward to toss me to my back on the rug. He bent his head to my chest and opened his mouth over one nipple, licking and then sucking as he kneaded my other breast.

I gasped at the damp heat of his mouth and the calloused rub of his palm. My back arched as he worked his way from one breast to the other. He gave a strong suck that made my toes curl, then gripped my thighs, pushing them even wider. "Need to taste how wet you are."

"Do it," I said, feet flexing against the rug. I was soaked and aching, eager to feel that clever mouth moving between my thighs. "*Please*, Kallen. I need it so badly, please."

"I like hearing you beg." His voice was guttural. "And I'm going to earn it."

Kallen didn't seduce—he *overwhelmed*. Every word, every touch, every taste had a desperate edge, like he was afraid it would be the last.

He looked up, gave me a quick, heart-stopping smile, then shifted down my body, settling his shoulders between my legs and curling his hands around my thighs. He just looked at me for a moment, breath puffing hot against my wet skin, before dragging his tongue over my center.

We groaned simultaneously. "Fuck," he said, squeezing his eyes shut in what looked like ecstasy. Then he set in with hot, ravenous kisses, like he was starving for me.

My hands flew to his head, and I jerked against him, moaning. When he sucked my clit, my cry was loud enough to make the magic guarding the door ripple.

Kallen's eyes opened, and I saw the flash of his smirk between kisses. "That's it," he told me, voice rumbling against sensitive skin. "Let me hear it. I want to know exactly what I do to you."

Kallen had a filthy mouth. I could hardly believe this was what he'd been hiding beneath those layers of cold reserve. I was drowning in the intensity, losing control of my body and voice as I gripped his hair and rocked against his face. "Please," I begged deliriously. "More, please..."

He gave me more, his lips and tongue thorough and relentless. He watched me while his mouth worked, and I could tell he was cataloging every reaction, because whenever a flick of his tongue got a moan or twitch out of me, he repeated it with more intensity. The pressure was almost too much, right on the edge of what I could handle, and it was sending me towards the peak faster than anything ever had. Shivers raced over my skin as tension coiled in my belly. The sensations were so overwhelming that my legs instinctively tried to snap shut, but his shoulders kept them spread wide. He released my thighs to plant one hand on my stomach, moving the other to stroke at my entrance before sliding his finger inside me.

"Kallen, *gods—*"

A second finger joined the first. The pressure, the stretch, was exquisite. Crimson magic began glimmering at my fingertips, and my feet slid over the floor while my hips churned. He made a snarling sound, and when he sucked my clit again, the escalating passion finally broke. Waves of heat swept over me, and I cried out as my body clenched in rhythmic pulses. My abdomen flexed as I curled upward, clutching his hair like it was the only thing keeping me tethered to earth. Stars burst at the edges of my vision, and I tumbled into a bliss so intense it was nearly terrifying.

He didn't let up, and each flick of his tongue was followed by a short, sharp groan. "Never enough," I heard him say, distant through the haze of pleasure. "I'll never get enough."

The orgasm stretched out impossibly long as he kept working me. When it was finally done, I was a wet, quivering mess. My limbs were heavy, and my hand shook as I pushed on his forehead. He licked me one last time, then slid his fingers out of me and knelt up between my legs. He looked so smug I let out a delirious laugh.

The sound made his smile soften. "I could listen to that forever." Then he lifted his fingers to his lips and sucked them clean.

A shudder raced through me. I felt wrung out, but looking at his flushed cheeks, slick lips, and passion-bright eyes, I felt an overwhelming urge to take him apart just as thoroughly. I struggled upright, then planted my hands on his chest and shoved him onto his back. He laughed, sounding surprised, and I wanted to hoard that sound with all the others, a greedy dragon collecting treasure.

I ripped at the fastening to his trousers, and a button went flying. Kallen's chuckle instantly turned into a gasp as my hand slid into the fabric and wrapped around him. I pulled his cock out, and for a moment all I could do was stare in awe at how beautiful he was here, too. Long and thick against my palm, with veins I wanted to trace with my tongue, and beneath the soft skin was a core like stone. I tightened my fingers before stroking up and down, and Kallen grunted as his hips jerked.

I gave him a wicked smile, then bent to take him into my mouth.

Kallen made an animalistic sound and surged half upright before collapsing. His fingers speared into my hair, sending pins flying. "Kenna," he gasped.

I lowered my head, taking more and more. A slow, delicious slide. I took as much of him as I could, then wrapped my hand around the base. I closed my eyes, breathing through my nose, absorbing the perfection of the moment.

I drew my head back up just as slowly, and Kallen barked out a curse. At the top, I swirled my tongue around the crown, tasting the drops that leaked out of him. I repeated the motion again and again, bobbing my head, licking him, sliding my hand up and down his slick shaft.

Kallen's entire body was twitching, like he was determined to stay still but couldn't quite manage it. Stuttered noises spilled from his lips. I glanced up and found him staring down at me with wide, dazed eyes. Shadows coiled around his arms, wisps of darkness signifying his loss of control. When I moaned around him, he bared his teeth, and his eyes flooded pure black.

A thrill shot through me, and I worked him harder, cupping his testicles with my other hand. He thrust upward at the touch, and the tip of him nudged the back of my throat. "Sorry," he gasped, but he didn't need to apologize. I took the feeling greedily, like I would always take all of him. The pleasure and the pain, the violence of a need vaster than the night sky. There could never be enough.

"You're ruining me," he gritted out.

The shadows started curling around me, cold against my bared skin. I burned, though, consumed by the triumph of taking him apart. He swelled even harder against my palm, and as his groans grew louder, I moved my head faster.

"Going to—" He broke off, then shouted, back bowing and fingers tightening almost painfully in my hair. His orgasm flooded my mouth, and I drank every drop, reveling in the taste. I kept sucking through his twitches and stuttered groans, until he gasped and finally nudged me away.

He hauled me up his body, wrapping his arms around me and pressing his lips to the top of my head. I lay with my ear over his thundering heart, basking in a deep contentment. When I looked up at him, I was shocked to see tears glistening in his eyes. "Thank you," he said, looking at me like I was the entirety of his universe.

I smiled as a beautiful feeling unfurled inside me like a flower. "Thank *you*."

I laced my hands together on his chest and rested my chin on them. We were quiet for a while, just staring at each other.

"No more running?" I finally whispered.

He shook his head, dark lashes sweeping down. "No more running."

"Good." I kissed the scar over his collarbone again. "I wish we could stay here all night."

We couldn't, though. I answered to more than just myself these days. The masquerade was underway, and I needed to get there soon so Torin and Rowena wouldn't grow suspicious. Then came the council meeting, when I would finally set us on the course I'd delayed long enough committing to. We couldn't let our personal desires outweigh everything else that was at stake.

It would be sweet, though.

A matching regret filled his eyes. "We have obligations. But afterwards, will you come back to Void House with me?"

I smiled, knowing what that meant. Kallen's home . . . and Kallen's bed. "I would love to."

37

After a detour to fix my hair and makeup, I headed to the masquerade. The vast cavern was filled with faeries and looked even more magnificent than when Kallen and I had watched it being decorated—the stalagmites were wrapped in purple silk, and Grimveldian ice sculptures were scattered between them, depicting dragons, phoenixes, and enormous bears. Faerie lights drifted overhead, and pixies danced in floating iridescent bubbles while an invisible orchestra played.

For the first time, Blood House was represented by more than two people. Lara had stayed at the house with Gweneira, but I was accompanied by two dozen faeries wearing red and silver: some of the Noble Fae who had defected from Earth, Light, or Illusion House going public with their new allegiance. Jaws dropped as we passed, and pride filled me. Blood House had been building quietly, but here we were, stepping into the light.

An eerie flute melody shivered into the space between notes, and a primal drumbeat started, the cadence matching my footfalls. It was a song for me, I realized with a sense of unreality. Just as Imogen had a tune that announced her arrival at events, someone had composed one for the Princess of Blood. That was the sort of thing that happened for mythical heroes and villains, not poor girls from Tumbledown, but which did the composer see me as?

My entourage split off to join the revelry, and I stopped to assess the layout. The dance floor was at the center, with tables ringing it for those who wanted to eat or talk. Long refreshment tables along the walls were piled high with platters of grapes and cheese, skewers of glistening meat, and thin peels of vegetables shaped to look like flowers. Large wooden sculptures of unicorn heads shielded the servants' entrances, and a steady stream of wine-bearing Underfae appeared from doors hidden in the unicorns' necks.

The servants and guards in attendance were a mix of Light and Illusion faeries, and I wondered how the Light faeries felt being here after what had happened. They'd likely had no choice, though. Wherever house leadership went, they followed.

Everyone in attendance wore a mask, though most were thin scraps of fabric, concealing little—the Fae were too vain of their beauty to obscure it. I looked for the most important players. Imogen was seated on the dais, of course, overlooking the dance floor. Like Osric, she had a throne for every occasion, and this one had been carved from an enormous piece of smoky quartz. Drustan was spinning Rhiannon across the dance floor, while Torin and Rowena spoke with Ulric at the refreshment table. Hate spiked inside my breast at the sight of them. Rowena's smile was so sweet, no one would ever guess the evil she was capable of.

Rowena spotted me and nudged Torin. When all three faeries turned to stare, I nodded politely, hoping they wouldn't read anything amiss in my expression.

I turned to look for Hector but found Oriana instead—who was unfortunately moving in my direction. Her chestnut gown was covered with embroidered gold vines, and her mask was metallic green. She looked as serene and perfectly put together as always, but as she took up position beside me, she struck me as somehow smaller. Stretched thin.

"Look how greedy they all are," she said. "Gluttons who don't care that the famine is coming."

The chatter and laughter did seem too loud, the dancing too exuberant. Faeries guzzled alcohol and tore into roast duck legs as if they were starving. There was a wild edge to the night; the end of this Accord was coming quickly, and the Fae were sinking their teeth into whatever they could.

I eyed Oriana with distaste. "Come to gloat?"

Her blond brows rose. "About the catacombs? I'm better than that."

I laughed incredulously. "No, you're not. You're not better than any of this." I tipped my chin towards the dancers. "Who are you to judge how they behave, anyway? It makes no difference to you."

She gave me a frosty look. "Do you imagine I don't care about Mistei?"

"It doesn't matter if you care. You'll spend your time the same regardless: trapped behind your walls of thorns, telling yourself it's wisdom."

"Wisdom means looking into the distance rather than being caught up in the passions of the moment. Maybe you'll live long enough to learn that lesson."

How she enjoyed lecturing me from her pedestal. "That so-called wisdom lost you everyone you claimed to love."

She shook her head. "My sons would still be alive if they'd followed my example."

She wasn't even thinking about Lara. Or else she didn't want to admit that she could have made different choices to save her. Lara was thriving in Blood House because I cared about her more than I cared about the cruel traditions of the Fae court. Because of my influence, she was still part of this world she wanted so desperately to belong to, and my influence was a fraction of what Oriana wielded.

There were so many ways I wanted to hurt her, so I chose the one that seemed like it might cut deepest. "If Selwyn and Leo were alive, they would be ashamed of you."

Oriana flinched. "Don't talk about them like you knew them."

"I know they died for their ideals."

"They still *died*." The word ripped out of her, and Oriana pressed her fingers to her lips as if startled by her own vehemence.

I was done with her. It was a sudden, final feeling, like a blade coming down. Of all the people I could spend my time on tonight, our conversations would matter the least, because how could I negotiate with someone who wasn't even honest with herself? She was never going to be the mother Lara deserved or the princess Mistei deserved.

"Good luck living with yourself," I told her, then walked away.

It took a few moments to wrestle down my temper. Caedo gently bit my wrist, and I used both the slight pain and the pleasure the dagger took from that taste to ground myself. *We could destroy her*, it whispered.

She isn't worth the effort.

Hungry, it complained.

You already had dinner.

I want more. Caedo shared a mental image of dead bodies piled around the tables and blood streaking the dance floor. *You could drink, too*, it whispered dreamily. *Taste your vengeance and then spill more.*

The notion was disturbing, and I was reminded that although we were connected, the dagger was an entirely alien creature. Magic made tangible, thirst personified. It had a limited moral code, but if

I didn't provide strict rules for both of us, it would stray to far darker places than I was comfortable going.

At least there were still places I was unwilling to go.

Seventeen more days, I told it, *and then you'll drink more than your fill.*

More faeries were trickling in late, and my attention was caught by a group of Void faeries led by Hector, Una, and Kallen. His eyes found me quickly, and desire coiled in my belly. I jerked my head to the side, then walked towards a sparsely populated corner of the cavern. I stopped beside an ice sculpture shaped like a dragon and waited.

The Void faeries joined me soon after. All three looked dangerously elegant: Hector's mask was black leather, and his dark tunic was studded with small points of steel, while Una wore a gown layered with black feathers and a matching mask. I'd already seen Kallen's outfit, of course. He was perfectly groomed again, tunic buttoned and hair no longer mussed, but all I could think about was his mouth moving between my thighs.

I curtsied, hoping I wasn't blushing. "It's a pleasure to see you tonight."

What a pleasure, indeed, Kallen's smile said as he joined the others in returning the bow.

Hector straightened, flicking his long hair over his shoulders. "I hear we are to have an eventful evening."

I'd told Kallen to prepare Hector so we could make the most of what little time we had before the meeting, and as usual, the Void prince was getting straight to the point. His toe tapped with restless energy.

"A decisive one, certainly," I said.

Hector looked around. "I would love to speak freely. Can you confirm no one's working Illusion magic nearby?"

Cursing myself for still not being in the habit of performing those sweeps, I reached out with my Blood powers, searching for any living bodies. "There are faeries behind that servants' entrance," I said, pointing to one of the unicorn heads some twenty feet away. "No one closer than that."

"Good." Hector's expression grew serious. "I want to start by thanking you. This can't have been an easy decision."

"I wish it had come clear sooner."

He shook his head. "It doesn't matter how we got here. We're here now, and we need to discuss how to approach the conversation later tonight. Will Gweneira be recovered enough to attend?"

"I'm sure she'll be at the meeting even if she doesn't feel recovered. She's not going to miss discussing what happened at Light House—especially if she suspects I'm also choosing a king."

"Do you believe she suspects?" Una asked.

"If Drustan told her about our argument, then yes. He must know that tipped the scales." The thought made me queasy. It was a relief to have finally chosen, but now I had to actually declare that choice to my former lover, who had spent decades preparing for a different outcome.

"Once you declare for Hector, Drustan will have to make some rapid decisions," Kallen said, and despite the topic, the sound of his voice sent a pleasurable shiver over my skin. "What does your gut tell you he'll do?"

I grimaced. "That only Drustan knows what he's doing." I paused, considering. "His goal is the throne, but he doesn't want to lose popular support. My guess is he'll accept my choice, play the selfless hero, then see what happens. If Hector dies in battle, our side will still need a leader." I glanced at Hector. "Obviously we hope that won't happen."

"Don't worry," the Void prince said. "If I die, it won't be in battle. It will be in *glorious* battle, worthy of an epic poem. Three thousand stanzas, minimum."

No one laughed at the dry attempt at humor. Una scowled at her father. "Drustan will probably arrange your glorious death if you aren't careful."

"Not if I arrange his death first."

"I would prefer if none of us arranged each other's deaths," I interjected.

Hector held up his hands. "That's entirely up to him."

Kallen tilted his head slightly, and my eyes were drawn to the fall of his dark hair. My fingers twitched with the memory of gripping it. "I suspect you're right," he told me. "Drustan hasn't gotten this far by prioritizing short-term gratification over long-term gain. He won't like it, but he'll accept it—at least to our faces. The danger lies in what other schemes he may have been spinning in the interim."

"Such as?" Una asked.

"The Nasties remain in play. He called on them once—he might do so again, if he's been making promises to Dallaida. The worst-case scenario is that Imogen found something to tempt him with, and he's prepared to shift his allegiance to her."

"He wouldn't," I said instantly. "It would undo everything he's been working towards."

"Not right away. But if the war looks to be on its way to lost?" Kallen shrugged. "Drustan thinks on long timelines."

And Imogen had implied my allies were already turning on me. Had that been a ploy to weaken our alliance... or a genuine warning?

Wisdom means looking into the distance rather than being caught up in the passions of the moment, Oriana had told me. Everyone else thought far into the future, while I was still struggling to think past the next two weeks. This war might go on for years, I realized with a drop of my stomach. And Drustan might be planning for outcomes that would come to pass far later than that.

"I still think it's possible he might do something unexpected to shift the balance of power," Hector said. "This is a vulnerable time; he may deem the risk worth the reward."

"Or perhaps he will honor his word," Una pointed out. "If you enter this alliance assuming betrayal, you'll look for it everywhere—and likely invent it where it doesn't exist."

Hector narrowed his eyes. "Don't start sounding wise in front of your elders."

"I'm as wary as you are, believe me," she said. "But we can't afford to manufacture our own enemies. Stay alert and plan for the worst, but remember that sometimes good outcomes do happen."

Kallen opened his mouth, then closed it again, looking at me. I could imagine what he was thinking. He and Hector had been shaped by centuries of violence and betrayals, while Una was a young faerie who had grown up believing that the three of them were creating a better world, one changeling at a time. It was the contrast between hope and bitter experience.

But tonight Kallen had also confronted his fears—that he'd hurt me, or else that I'd take his offered heart and use it to destroy him—and discovered one of the rare good outcomes.

"All right," Hector said, expression softening as he looked at Una. "We'll plan for the worst but give Drustan the opportunity to prove himself."

If I'd needed it, that was more evidence I'd made the right choice.

"I need to make the rounds," Hector said, switching his attention to me. "Check in with Lady Rhiannon about the mood in Earth House, talk to a few other prospects who have indicated an openness to Void leadership." He settled his hand on my shoulder. "Thank you, Kenna. Tonight is when everything starts."

Una smiled at me as the two of them moved away.

Kallen offered his arm. "May I escort you?"

I took it, curving my fingers around his bicep. "Are you nervous about the meeting?" I asked as we strolled slowly towards the dancing.

"No. Whatever happens, we'll navigate it."

I would love to be so confident. "At least there's something to look forward to afterwards."

He slid me a scorching look. "Are you sure you won't be too tired? It'll be after midnight when the meeting concludes, and I plan to be . . . thorough."

I shivered from head to toe, and when Kallen gave another of his sly smiles, I knew he'd felt it. "I'm more worried about you," I murmured, looking up at him through my lashes. "Are you sure you can keep up?"

He leaned closer. "Trust me, I have no trouble keeping it up for you."

Shocked by the raunchy joke coming from Kallen, I burst out laughing. Heads swiveled, fixing us with curious or hostile stares, and I wrestled my face back into a composed expression. "You make an excellent point, Lord Kallen."

We had reached the edge of the crowd. Though Kallen looked deadly solemn once more, a silent yearning stretched between us as we lingered in the moment.

"Save me a dance later?" I asked, finally releasing his arm.

His lashes swept down, and I saw the tiny tug at the corner of his lips. "Always."

Then he was gone, moving through the crowd to watch and listen for whatever plots were brewing in Mistei tonight.

I turned to do the same—and found myself facing Imogen. "I was wondering which way that was going," the Illusion princess said, sipping a glass of sparkling wine as her eyes followed Kallen. "An unusual choice, but you do have a tendency towards the unexpected."

I refused to give her any satisfaction. "I'm surprised to see you on the floor. Do you tire of your throne already?"

"Never." She grinned, showing perfect white teeth. "But it's good for a queen to spend time among her people, don't you think?"

"I wouldn't know. I've never met a queen."

She laughed, a rich and beautiful sound. "Walk with me, Princess Kenna."

It was the second time she'd ordered me to do so. Unable to come up with an excuse not to, I fell into step beside her, though this time I pulled away before she could loop our arms together like we were friends. "Are you planning on offering me another bribe?" I asked.

"At a certain point, one must accept that some outcomes cannot be bought, only forced."

I eyed her, disliking that phrasing. She looked as carefree and exquisitely beautiful as always, her eyes shining with magic behind a silver filigree mask shaped like a butterfly. Her mahogany hair was pulled into two braided bunches that looped over her shoulders, and her dress was a froth of pale pink gauze trimmed with indigo ribbons. Sweet and delicate-looking—but she also wore Osric's heavy crown, and I'd experienced firsthand her capacity for brutality. "We still have over two weeks left in the Accord," I said. "It's early to be threatening force."

"Tell me, how is Drustan feeling about your alliance?"

My skin prickled. "Why don't you ask him?"

"I have." She flashed those pearly teeth again, and her canines looked sharper than they had before. "I merely wonder if you have, as well. And which of us he's being honest with."

A chill swept over me. "You're trying to sow discord."

"You're sowing plenty of that yourself. Unless you think no one noticed you speaking with Hector just now? Drustan does have eyes and the ability to use them, even while dancing."

"I had a brief conversation with my allies at a public event. That is hardly unusual."

She hummed. "No, but we must always be cognizant of appearances."

I stopped walking and faced her. "What is the point of this interaction?"

There were sparkles in her lavender irises as she leaned in with the air of someone about to confess a secret. "Did you know Torin is in favor of killing you and framing one of the others? I told him it's against the principle of the Accord, but he would prefer to be done with that early so we can get started on the butchery. And it would be best if your side were seen breaking the peace."

My heart started to race. I looked around to see who might have overheard, but no one reacted. She must be concealing our conversation. "No one would believe it," I said.

She shrugged. "If you're seen cozying up to Hector while spurning Drustan, they might."

"Why warn me?" I asked as dread crept into my gut. "Doesn't it benefit you for our side to break the Accord?"

"Call this your last chance to consider the merits of my protection. You might not appreciate gold, but you do appreciate honesty, and I can offer that as well." The sparkles in her eyes dimmed. "And, yes, it would benefit me," she said more quietly, "but I believe our traditions have purpose, so I have ordered Torin to wait. He's marked you for an ugly death, though. At that point, I will be the only one who can save you."

"Are you sure Torin will follow your orders? He didn't hesitate to butcher his own house members tonight. His loyalty may have limits."

There was a long pause while she stared at me. "What do you mean?"

Did she truly not know? "I overheard the servants gossiping. They said Torin seized control of Light House."

"Ah. So he was finally able to kill Gweneira. That explains why I haven't seen her tonight." There was tension in the set of Imogen's mouth, though—she hadn't been informed of this development, and she didn't like finding out this way.

There was still a weakness to exploit here, a crack in the bond between Illusion and Light. I imagined sliding a knife into it and twisting, the same way she had been trying to carve holes in my own alliance. "I have conversations with my allies at events because we trust each other enough to share information. Your side should consider implementing the same policy."

She looked at the dance floor, and I followed her gaze to where Torin and Rowena were spinning in each other's arms. "And so the Blood princess delivers her own warning," she said softly. "Perhaps our negotiations have not ended, after all." Then she returned her attention to me. "I will not extend my hand to you indefinitely. Think on it. The next move is yours."

She sauntered towards the dais. I watched as she retook her seat on the throne, wondering if my refusal to accept that extended hand would guarantee my own death.

38

Torin and Rowena were dancing to a slow song, arms wrapped around each other with a level of intimacy no one else on the floor exhibited. They were watching me in the wake of my conversation with Imogen, their blue eyes hostile behind matching gold masks. The attire they'd chosen was halfway to armor—Torin's white tunic was fronted with a circular plate of gold, while the bodice of Rowena's snowy gown was covered with a metal chest piece that resembled a rib cage.

"Do you like to dance, Princess Kenna?" Rowena called out as I passed by.

I slowed, wondering what unpleasantness this would be. "In general, yes."

She smiled. "You require a lot of practice, but I think you have the potential to be quite entertaining."

I felt a bone-deep chill as I remembered the sort of "entertainment" Rowena enjoyed. "I don't care what you think."

Her smile expanded into a bright grin. "It's a shame—things could have turned out differently for you."

"Humans love lost causes," Torin told her. "They run towards death so enthusiastically."

"Indeed they do." Rowena's grin was wiped away as if it had never been. "I hope you enjoy your evening, Princess Kenna. Drink some wine. Think of the cost."

They whirled away, gold and white disappearing into the sea of bodies.

The cost of what? Not the wine, though the ice wine Imogen had imported from Grimveld was certainly expensive. The cost of making enemies of the two of them, probably. I comforted myself with the knowledge that in just over two weeks, I would be free to kill them.

I politely declined a few offers to dance, feeling too unsettled to converse with strangers. Instead, I did what I had been dreading all night and sought out Drustan.

He was dancing, light-footed and athletic, drawing the usual admiring glances. He shone in head-to-toe copper that was only outmatched by the gleam of his hair falling loose down his back. In the light of the drifting faerie orbs, he was so radiant it nearly hurt my eyes.

Sorrow filled me as I watched him. The Prince of Fire, who shone brighter than anyone. Drustan's schemes, his dreams, had brought us here, but I couldn't follow him any further down that road.

He spun his partner into someone else's arms, then turned towards me and held out his hand. His expression was inscrutable beneath his copper mask.

I took a steadying breath, then slipped my fingers into his hold, letting him pull me into the current of the dance.

We turned in a circle, hands linked. Then he brought me close, one hand at my waist. "You look lovely," he murmured into my hair. "But then you always do."

Another soft wave of grief moved through me. I forced myself to smile, because it seemed like something a princess should do in the arms of her ally, but the weight of that persona felt so heavy that my feet couldn't quite keep up with the music. "You don't need my compliments to know the same."

"No, but I never tire of hearing them." He gave me a rakish grin, but the mirth didn't reach his eyes. "Thank you for what you did tonight. It's always a risk to open house doors."

"It was the right thing to do."

"Not everyone cares about right or wrong." His gaze tracked over the crowd. "Will our mutual friend be attending later?"

It was too risky to say Gweneira's name out loud this close to others, even speaking as quietly as we were. "I imagine so. There are plans to be made."

"There always are. Plans and schemes, webs to weave, victories to seize from defeat. And so on and on we go, repeating our paths like constellations in the sky." His smile had faded. Maybe the persona of the prince had grown too heavy for him, too. When I missed a step, he slowed his movements, taking us out of time with the music. "I wish this had gone differently."

What good was a wish? The village girls had made wishes in the bog, tossing coins in and asking for their dreams to be given to them. The result was always an empty purse. I understood, though. A wish was a type of regret, and I had plenty of those. "We can't change what happened tonight," I told Drustan. "We just need to regroup and find a new path forward."

His eyes seemed silver in this light, like his entire being was composed of rare metals. "You've always embraced the difficult paths."

"Were any of them going to be easy?"

He inclined his head. "Probably not."

We were silent for a while, moving through the steps. A drunken couple careened past, laughing raucously, and he spun me out of the way.

"Choosing Kallen is a more difficult path than most," he finally said.

The unexpected tangent surprised me. "I thought we were talking about what happened tonight."

"Isn't everything connected?" His eyes were sad. "You laugh with him the way you used to laugh with me."

So he had been watching earlier. I didn't know what to say to that.

He sighed, bowing his head closer to mine. "You could have been my queen, Kenna. You could *still* be my queen, if you wanted it. Think of the world we could build together."

I stumbled, and he quickly picked me up, swinging me in a circle before setting me back down. "Don't say things like that," I told him when I'd gotten my footing and my breath again. Anger buzzed beneath my skin. "Don't try to win me over with false promises. You don't love me, and you never will, because I'm not Mildritha."

He was quiet for a few moments. "Love isn't a requirement."

"For me it is." I shook my head. "It should be for you, too."

There were unfamiliar lines carved around his mouth. "Sometimes I wonder if I'm still capable of it."

"Love?"

He nodded.

Some of my anger slipped away in the face of his honesty. "I can't answer that for you. But I think people who have loved once can love again. They just have to be willing to give without the expectation of getting anything in return." I raised my brows. "You should try that in other areas of your life first."

He grimaced. "Perhaps it's for the best. I wouldn't have enjoyed a lifetime of your lectures."

We completed a few more steps in silence, watching each other, and I wondered if he was formulating new arguments that might win me to his side in the final moments of this dance. Because this wasn't just about our doomed romance—everything with Drustan came back to the crown.

"Does he love you, then?" he asked quietly. "Truly?"

That was what he wanted to know? Not what might convince me to give him another chance, but whether Kallen loved me? "That's between us." The first time I put words to that possibility would not be in Drustan's arms.

His lashes flickered. "I have a hard time believing him capable of it, but I do believe you're too stubborn to accept anything less."

The music was shifting into a new tune, calling for new partners, but he didn't let go of me. "I should find someone strategic to talk to," I said, struggling to know what to say when he was looking at me with that mix of longing and resignation. "Is there anyone you'd recommend?"

He shook his head. "Let's just dance, Kenna. Let me pretend for a few minutes that I don't know what's coming."

There was a lump in my throat. "One more dance, then."

We moved in silence, the weight of my unspoken decision hanging over us. He knew I was choosing Hector. And though he'd seemed honest tonight, Drustan's truths often turned out to be lies, and I didn't know what he was going to do in the end.

When it was over, Drustan bowed and pressed a lingering kiss to my hand. Then he left the floor to consult with Rhiannon and her entourage of Earth faeries, a charming smile back on his face as he resumed his politicking.

I retreated to the shadow of a stalagmite and was unsurprised when Kallen appeared at my side. "How was that?" he asked softly.

"He seems melancholy tonight," I murmured just as quietly. "We didn't discuss it, but he knows I'm choosing Hector." I bit my lip, knowing he wouldn't like the next bit. "He did offer to make me his queen."

Darkness flooded the blue of his irises. "That's bold of him."

"It was a halfhearted attempt at best, and I obviously refused."

"He's delusional if he thought you'd say yes."

Kallen looked ready to untie the knots holding his daggers in place and throw a blade into Drustan's heart. Guilt swelled at his obvious jealousy. "Are you upset I danced with him?"

He shook his head. "Drustan upsets me by existing, but I'm not going to dictate who you dance with. That's just politics."

"I'd rather be dancing with you."

The black faded from his eyes. "I'd prefer that, too," he said, voice gentling. His hand nudged mine. "Later, when everyone's too drunk for scheming and I can stop listening in."

"Later," I agreed. "So what have you noticed tonight?"

Kallen tipped his head to one side. "Ulric has been avoiding Imogen."

I looked in the direction he'd indicated and saw the Illusion lord having a conversation near the refreshment table. "You think that's significant?"

"Maybe, maybe not. But I overheard him make a disparaging comment about her drinking. He believes queens ought to exhibit a certain level of decorum in public." I gave him an incredulous look, and his lips quirked. "A rare opinion among the Fae, but there are a few who hold their rulers to higher standards."

So Ulric would prefer a more temperate leader. "If he's having doubts, it's possible there's an opportunity to gain his support for Hector."

He looked pleased. "My thoughts exactly. It's highly unlikely he'll turn, but we should be chipping away at Imogen's support wherever we can. A second's hesitation can shift the tide of a battle."

Ulric was alone now, perusing the cheese. "Maybe I should get to know him better."

"I'll keep circulating." He leaned closer, raising his hand like he was whispering something to me, then used the cover of it to gently nip my earlobe. "And then I'll be coming to claim that dance, Princess."

After Kallen left, I made my way towards Ulric, who was frowning into his wine. A red feather edged in gold had been placed inside the glass—a phoenix feather, like the ones gathered in vases on the tables. Nearby, a servant was offering a similar drink to another high-ranking faerie.

"Princess Kenna," Ulric said when I stopped beside him. "What an honor to be graced by your presence." He held out the glass. "What do you think of this garnish?"

"Lord Ulric," I said, remembering his appreciation for etiquette. "The honor is mine. And that looks inconvenient to drink around."

"The entire point of phoenix feathers is to watch them go up in flames. But if I lit it, the alcohol would burn off." He tapped his lips. "A conundrum."

His tone was light, but I thought about what Kallen had overheard. "Imogen will certainly never light hers, if that's the consequence."

Ulric pulled the feather out of the drink and tucked it into his pocket. I raised my brows at the act of thievery, and he shrugged. "She shouldn't offer what she can't afford to have taken."

His blue eyes were bright in contrast to his mulberry-hued mask, and those extravagantly lashed eyes and his curling red hair reminded me so much of Karissa. Maybe that connection was the key to building rapport with him. "You're Karissa's uncle, aren't you?" I asked.

"I was."

"I'm sorry for what happened to her—"

"I'm not," he said without changing expression. "The weak have no place in Mistei."

The callous words took me aback. "You don't care that your niece was killed?"

"She was the one responsible for that, so no." He sipped his wine, watching me. "Anyone who makes a display of their weaknesses is responsible for the consequences. No matter how important they imagine themselves to be."

My skin prickled. That had felt oddly like a threat. "Does that apply to Imogen?"

"It applies to queens most of all." His mouth tugged into a sudden grin, and he hailed the servant with the tray of feather-garnished drinks. "You, there. Princess Kenna requires wine."

The Illusion sprite hurried over. "Anything for the Blood princess," he said fervently, holding out a glass.

"No, thank you," I said. "I don't feel like drinking."

"But I wish to be of service." The sprite's shimmering lilac eyes held adoration, and I wondered if he knew the servants who had taken shelter in my house.

"Look at the poor thing," Ulric said with a laugh. "So desperate to please. You're supposed to be a champion of the servants—it would be kind to indulge him."

"I appreciate the offer," I told the sprite gently, "but—"

"It's much easier without the feather," Ulric said, whisking it out of the drink and slipping it into his other pocket. "Drink up, Princess Kenna. Our queen expects nothing less than utter debauchery."

He was making me uneasy, but the bitter note in his voice signaled an opportunity. "I prefer being sober at these events," I said, holding out a hand to keep the hopeful-looking sprite at bay. "As Imogen should consider doing on occasion."

"Come now," Ulric said. "Everything will be easier if you do."

My head snapped towards him, and I was in the middle of drawing breath to ask what would be easier when the sprite grabbed my neck and poured the wine into my mouth.

I choked, trying to spit it out, but the liquid was scalding its way down my throat, half going to my stomach and half to my lungs. I coughed, eyes stinging and throat burning.

"There." Ulric clapped my shoulder with a smile. "Enjoy the party, Princess Kenna."

He left while I was still bent over coughing. When I straightened, my vision spun, and I staggered sideways into the table. The plates rattled, and vegetable flowers fell to the floor.

Violent euphoria swept over me as the world tilted. I wanted to dance until my feet bled and drink until my stomach burst. I wanted to light the faeries in this room on fire and warm myself by the blaze.

Kill, kill, kill, Caedo was chanting, furious it hadn't moved fast enough to drain the sprite dry. For a vicious, dizzy moment, I agreed, and magic leapt to my fingertips, promising retribution. I would tear that Underfae apart one bone at a time, and I would laugh while doing it.

A shard of panic pierced the delirium. These weren't my thoughts. There had been something in that wine.

I stumbled away from the table, dodging drunkenly careening faeries. Someone's shoulder slammed into mine, and I spun, barely staying upright. My mask had been knocked askew, and I unlaced it with clumsy fingers before flinging it aside. My magic felt loose and liquid, no longer bound by its normal constraints. It surged through me, trying to battle whatever poison I'd been dosed with. Excess power seeped out of my skin in bloody crimson spots, and I couldn't seem to pull it back in.

"Help," I gasped. "Kallen, help!"

I staggered in the direction he'd gone. I was too short, though, and as the crowd pressed in around me, I couldn't see my way out. Rage roared through me like a forest fire. "Get out of my way!" I shouted, shoving someone to the ground. She convulsed, clutching her chest, and the nearest faeries recoiled.

Something was wrong, something bad had just happened, but I couldn't think past the mix of fury and buzzing panic. As the crowd parted, I finally saw Kallen speaking with Hector beside a silk-wrapped stalagmite. "Help," I gasped, reaching out a hand as I staggered towards him.

The two Void faeries turned to face me. My vision blurred, and when it cleared, I realized there were three people there, not two. Kallen, Hector . . . and a copper-haired faerie leaping out from behind the stalagmite with bared teeth and a raised knife.

Drustan plunged the knife into Kallen's back.

I screamed as Kallen cried out and fell to his knees. He coughed, blood spraying. Drustan raised the knife again, face twisted in an expression of hatred.

"No!" Magic shot from my fingertips, wrapping around Drustan's throat. His neck snapped, and he collapsed, the dagger falling from his lax fingers.

I fell to my knees, too, dizziness overwhelming me.

Everything went silent.

I blinked, and the world rearranged itself. Hector and Kallen weren't there anymore. The knife I'd seen clatter to the ground was gone. But Drustan still lay on his side, neck broken and an expression of shock on his face.

Faeries surrounded us, staring horrified at what I had done. Ulric was among them. He met my eyes, then touched his fingers to his brow in a salute.

Blood magic was still boiling through my insides, trying to fix me. My stomach contracted, and I vomited, spitting up purple bile. The wine poured out of me in racking waves, puddling at my knees. My head cleared, and as rational thought returned, I realized what had happened. Ulric had poisoned me, and while my grip on both reality and my magic was tenuous, he'd shown me an illusion to make me attack Drustan. But why?

Torin pushed through the crowd of gawkers to stand at Ulric's side. A triumphant look crossed his face. "Guards!" he yelled into the shocked silence. "Seize Princess Kenna. Blood House has broken the Accord."

39

Horror swept over me. I reached a hand towards Drustan. "An illusion," I gasped past my acid-stung throat.

His eyes widened, but he was still paralyzed. I sent magic into his neck to heal him, but before I'd finished weaving the severed nerves back together, a force hit me from behind, knocking me to the ground. My head struck the stone, and my vision briefly blackened.

Caedo howled, racing around and around my wrist. *Destroy them, hurt them, punish them...*

My ears rang from the impact. Through blurred eyes, I saw a Light soldier crouch over me. One of the event guards, wearing flexible leather armor over a white tunic. He grabbed my left wrist and secured a cuff around it.

The metal burned my skin, and pain stabbed through my skull as the magic was sucked out of me. Caedo went silent and still.

Iron.

Panicked, I lashed out with my free hand, but the guard blocked it with a leather-gauntleted forearm. He punched the side of my head, and while I was blinking away the sparks, he locked the second cuff around my right wrist, just below where Caedo curled as a bracelet. I yanked, but the short chain between the manacles held strong. The iron stung my skin like nettles.

Caedo, I thought desperately, but the dagger didn't reply.

The soldier was still crouched over me, gripping the chain between my cuffs in one gloved hand. I lurched up, cracking his nose with my skull, and he shouted and toppled backwards.

"An illusion," I yelled, struggling to my feet. "Ulric showed me an illusion—"

No one heard me, because Torin's announcement had sent the crowd into a frenzy. A roar of sound battered my ears as faeries screamed and shouted, expressions burning with rage and fear. Their mouths formed accusations, and their fingers pointed at me.

No, no, no, I thought, sick with terror. Imogen had told me Torin was eager to end the Accord early so he could start on the butchery, and Ulric had clearly agreed. And I was the weapon they had used.

The guard was on his feet again, running for me. "Please listen!" I shouted, trying to shove through the crowd. "He poisoned me, it was an illusion to make me attack Drustan—"

A faerie in a lavender mask bared his teeth and gripped my forearm, hauling his other fist back like he intended to punch me. Then he went pale and collapsed.

Caedo. Unable to move or speak without our connection, but still able to drink, like it had been in the bog.

The soldier grabbed me by the hair. I spun, swinging my bound fists into his neck. The bracelet hit his throat, and he died, too.

"The chain!" someone shouted. A soldier tackled me, and another bent to hook a longer chain to the one between my manacles. A leash, so they wouldn't have to touch me. He yanked me upright, then tugged again, forcing me to stumble forward. Two more soldiers fell in behind, and I cried out as one jabbed the tip of her spear into my back. "Move," she ordered.

Torin was marching ahead of us, clearing the path to the dais, calling out damning words as he went. "Blood House has broken the Accord! Princess Kenna has broken the Accord!"

The gauntlet of faeries shouted and hissed. A gob of spit struck my cheek, and someone threw a glass at my head. It shattered, spraying me with sticky wine that was quickly joined by blood running from a cut on my skull.

I shouted explanations, but it was no use. Faeries from different houses were already turning on one another, shoving and yelling. It was a silvered event, so only the guards carried swords, but as we passed a Fire faerie fumbling with the ceremonial peace knot securing his dagger, it was clear this was about to get much worse.

The soldiers threw me to the ground before the dais. Imogen stood at the edge, looking shocked. She'd been so certain Torin answered to her.

Torin mounted the stairs, and Rowena emerged from the crowd to join him. "Princess Kenna attacked Prince Drustan," Torin called out. "She turned on him after making a deal with Prince Hector."

"No!" I cried, pushing to my knees. "It was a trick, Ulric cast—" One of the guards backhanded me before I could finish the sentence. Pain exploded over my cheek as blood flooded my mouth.

"This is what comes of trusting a human with power!" Torin shouted. "She violates our sacred traditions. She violates the sanctity of our houses. And now she betrays her own allies. Princess Kenna has declared war!"

The drunken crowd roared and roiled. Someone lunged in my direction, only to be knocked back by a member of Imogen's personal guard. Other guards positioned themselves in a ring around the dais, spears angled outward, but there were too few of them compared to the growing riot. A gap appeared between bodies, and I finally saw Kallen in the distance shoving his way towards me with a determined look. I reached for him with my bound hands. "I'm sorry," I gasped.

The crowd pressed together again, blocking him from my sight.

"Order, order!" Imogen shouted from the dais, hands raised. "Let Princess Kenna face her crimes at trial, as is just. There is no need to abandon the Accord—"

No one was listening. She'd drowned the crowd in alcohol, and everything was spiraling out of control.

Behind Imogen, Torin and Rowena exchanged a look. Torin nodded, then pulled a dagger out of an inside pocket of his tunic and plunged it into Imogen's side.

Imogen screamed. Torin stabbed her again and again, and she collapsed in a heap of puffed pink skirts. The crown fell off her head, landing on the dais with a loud clang. Torin pulled a pair of cuffs out of a pouch at his belt, then snapped them around her wrists.

The nearest onlookers stopped their shoving to gape. My mouth hung open with matching shock.

Torin straightened, holding the bloody knife high. "Princess Kenna started this war," he called out. "I will finish it."

A banging sound at the edge of the room was accompanied by a flash of light and a swirl of thick gray smoke. Through the haze, I saw the door in one of the unicorn heads had been thrown open, and Sun Soldiers in golden armor and white cloaks were pouring through. One of them gutted a Fire faerie with a brutal thrust of his sword.

The room erupted into violence.

The clash of metal was echoed by screams, and flashes of light mingled with waves of darkness and bursts of flame as the most powerful Fae unleashed their abilities. The guard in front of me fell beneath someone's dagger, and a tide of raging faeries swept over him. A boot hit my ribs, cracking them. Someone else kicked from the other side, sending me sprawling. I tried to push myself upright and was instantly knocked back down.

The war had begun, and it was all my fault.

"I'm sorry," I gasped as blows rained down on me. "I'm so sorry."

Now that the disorienting poison was gone, I saw my failures in excruciating detail. I should have run somewhere to vomit up the toxin rather than looking for Kallen to save me. I should have tried to sense heartbeats rather than believing that vision. I should have known Drustan would never make himself a villain in front of everyone, no matter how much he hated Kallen.

But I hadn't done any of that, and now *I* was the villain.

My skull cracked against the floor, and blood spilled over my temple. A faerie stomped on my fractured ribs, but I managed to press Caedo against his ankle, and he collapsed beside me. His corpse took the impact of the next kick, and I was able to get my feet under me. I shot upright, swinging my bound wrists into the side of an attacker. As Caedo turned him into a husk, his fingers loosened, and the knife in his fist clattered to the floor. I scooped it up, needing every weapon I could get.

My broken body screamed in agony, but terror kept me on my feet. Kallen—where was Kallen?

I saw a flash of black in my peripheral vision. He was twenty feet away, mask gone and teeth bared as he battled towards me. He'd untied his daggers and was stabbing his way through anyone blocking him, but there were too many of them, and they turned on him eagerly. He summoned two spots of darkness and ripped a faerie in half, then staggered back when a blinding light burst before him. Someone threw a dagger, and Kallen wisped into shadow an instant before it spun through the air where he'd been standing.

That shadow swirled through the crowd as Kallen raced towards me. A Sun Soldier flung a shining metal net into his path, and Kallen solidified beneath it. He grimaced as he ripped the iron net away, and I saw pink lines marking his face.

He'd just lost his magic.

The Sun Soldier who had thrown the net lunged for Kallen, sword raised. The crowd surged between us again, obscuring him.

I screamed in rage and staggered forward, feeling the hot, spiking agony of fractured bones. My magic couldn't fix the wounds, but my Fae body would heal soon enough, and I had to get to Kallen. I stabbed a faerie in the gut, ripping the blade out so roughly that a glistening slide of intestines followed. The long chain attached to my manacles tangled around my feet, and I kicked it aside.

Drunken, poorly armed faeries were no match for the Sun Soldiers, and the battle was turning into a mass retreat as faeries ran for the exits. Fleeing bodies buffeted me. Some Illusion faeries had joined those from Fire, Void, Earth, and Blood in their retreat, but others had fallen in beside the Sun Soldiers. Ulric was in the midst of them shouting orders.

This was what Torin had been training the Illusion troops for, I realized with the nauseating clarity of hindsight. Torin and Rowena had never planned to let Imogen have the full month to win Mistei over. They'd never planned to support her at all. And in the days I'd spent dithering over my own decision, they'd managed to recruit a portion of Illusion House to their side.

I couldn't see Kallen anymore, but I spotted Hector in the brief slices of space between fleeing faeries. He'd gotten a sword from somewhere and was fighting three Sun Soldiers at once. A fourth tackled him, and his arms were wrenched behind his back before he was bound in iron manacles.

"Kallen!" I screamed. "Where are you?"

A Light faerie tried to stab me, so I slit his throat and jammed Caedo against the wound. A weeping Earth asrai sprinted past, and as I moved out of her way, I nearly tripped over a corpse wearing red. Grief tore through me as I recognized one of my new house members.

They'd trusted me to save them, and I'd killed them instead.

Someone called my name, and I turned to see Aidan shoving his way towards me. Horror swamped me. He looked so small and vulnerable compared to the taller, stronger Noble Fae, and the only weapon he carried was a ceramic wine pitcher. "Get out of here!" I shouted.

"I'll save you!" he cried out, shattering the pitcher over the head of an Illusion faerie.

"You need to run!"

The surge of retreating faeries pushed him back, and he struggled against the flow. "I can't leave you," he said, tears streaking down his face. "And Edric is here, and I can't find him—" His voice broke. "I have to find him."

If Aidan stayed, he would die. "You have to escape," I said, my own tears carving tracks through the blood splattered across my cheeks. "Tell everyone they poisoned me and made me lose control of my senses. Tell them Ulric cast an illusion to trick me."

"They're going to kill you—"

"No, they're not." It was an awful, ice-cold realization, the kind that could only be found in utter defeat. They were chaining the house heads—which meant they had something worse planned for us.

Aidan looked tormented, still shaking his head in refusal. A new group of refugees poured between us, driving us farther apart.

"Please," I shouted, voice raw. "We're going to need someone to save us."

An enormous Sun Soldier appeared behind Aidan, cleaving his way through the crowd. His eyes were fixed on me, but his sword was slicing through everyone who got in his way—and Aidan was directly in his path. I screamed as the blade descended towards my first friend in Mistei.

Edric was suddenly there, bursting through the crowd to grab Aidan around the waist. The Fire lord spun him away, and the sword breezed past them to strike sparks from the stone floor.

Edric didn't let go of Aidan. He started running, carrying him towards the exit. "We'll find you, Kenna!" Aidan cried out over Edric's shoulder.

The Sun Soldier was in front of me now. I aimed my knife towards his neck, but he knocked my chained wrists aside with one gauntleted forearm before slamming into me. I flew through the air, and my back hit the ground hard enough to snatch the breath from my lungs. I wheezed but kept fighting, my blade scraping over the metal greave covering the soldier's shin. He stomped on my bound hands, shattering my fingers in an explosion of white-hot agony. The knife clattered to the floor. Then the Sun Soldier grabbed the long chain hooked to my manacles and started dragging me on my back towards the dais.

My arms felt like they might rip out of their sockets. I sobbed from pain and something far worse. The cavern was emptying of the living, leaving only heaped bodies and a lake of blood behind, just as Caedo had imagined. All this suffering, all this death—all of it my doing.

Where was Kallen? Had he escaped?

I knew better, though. Kallen wouldn't leave Hector or me behind. Terror threatened to choke me as I was pulled through the carnage. I looked frantically to either side, trying to find him, praying to anything that might be listening that he was still alive.

The faerie hauled me past a pile of dead Sun Soldiers, and their pooling blood smeared over my skin and the fine fabric of my dress. They lay sprawled over one another, half of them looking like they'd been cut down trying to escape something terrifying.

At the top of the pile was a single figure in black.

I screamed, grief ripping through me. "No, no, no, no!"

Kallen's face was so swollen it was nearly unrecognizable, and his dark hair was matted with blood. His empty sword hand hung limp at his side, crossed by a delicate silver chain.

I strained against the cuffs, the iron gouging deep into my blistered skin. I could heal him, I could bring him back. I *had* to bring him back. Blood spilled, hot and wet, but the manacles didn't budge, and then the metal was cutting to bone, and I still couldn't get them off.

Kallen didn't move as I was dragged past him. Blood dripped in a steady cadence from his fingers, splatting into the pool on the floor.

A swirl of shadow condensed and took form next to him. It was Una, with a healing cut on her temple and her feathered dress covered in gore. She grabbed Kallen under the arms, yanking him off the heap of corpses. His body hit the ground with a wet thud, and Una threw herself on top of him. Shadows twined around them, forming a cocoon of night. The soldier dragging me leapt towards her, but Una's magic was already wisping the two of them away, and his sword cleaved through empty air.

Tears poured from my eyes, and another scream ripped its way out of my throat, so raw it hurt. He'd looked dead. Was there enough left of him for Void House's healers to salvage, or was Una bringing his body home to mourn?

I couldn't bear it if he was gone.

The Sun Soldier stopped before the dais, still holding the chain taut so my arms were stretched over my head. A shadow fell across me. Through the blur of tears, I saw Rowena silhouetted against the drifting faerie lights. She crouched, eyes bright behind her golden mask as she studied me. Her hem was soaked red with the death she'd orchestrated. "You really must be more careful about what you drink," she said.

Hate filled me, pushing aside all other emotions. I blinked the tears away, then spat at her. She flinched as my pink-flecked saliva spattered across her dress.

"Charming," she said with disgust as she wiped the spit away.

I turned my head, looking to see what was happening now that the battle had been lost. The civilians were gone, and only groups of fighters from Light and Illusion House remained, sorting through the carnage. A soldier had slung Imogen over his shoulder and was carrying her away while she struggled weakly. Drustan staggered behind them, hands chained behind his back as soldiers jabbed him with spears. Relief mixed with agonizing guilt. He'd healed from my attack, but his copper tunic was peppered with bloody stab marks. Hector had needed to be knocked out, it looked like, and was being dragged.

Oriana wasn't there. She wouldn't have sanctioned this, so Torin and Rowena had probably let her escape, knowing she would keep Earth House complacent while they established their new order.

Rowena's cool fingers gripped my chin, and she turned my face towards her. Her attire was pristine except for the reddened hem, and her hair was pinned up perfectly, with diamonds sparkling amidst the gold. "You didn't even pick up a sword, did you?" I asked bitterly. "What a coward."

Her eyes narrowed. "I fight in other ways. Would you like to know what I put in your wine? It's one of my favorites."

I wanted her to suffer as no one had ever suffered before. "Fuck you," I snarled.

She pouted. "Maybe later, then. You'll be getting a good look at my collection soon enough." Her assessing gaze moved over me, from my blood-spattered face to my bound hands. "We need to take care of that," she said, frowning.

Take care of what?

She addressed a nearby soldier. "Cut her right arm off."

His sword swung in a vicious arc, severing my arm near the shoulder.

Lightning cracked through my body at the site of the cut, an agony so immense and overwhelming my brain couldn't process it. Then shock hit, and the pain became a deep, aching throb. *That's my arm*, I thought hysterically, craning my head to see. My lax fingers, my bone and muscle visible at the line of the cut, my blood spilling red.

Rowena held a hand out, and the soldier passed her a key. She unlocked the manacle around my right wrist, then picked up the severed limb and set it down several feet away. I watched, nauseated, as she took the guard's sword and chopped my hand off.

Rowena picked up my arm and shook it, and Caedo slid off the stump of my wrist and clattered to the ground. Just a silver bracelet with a red jewel. "Get that thing in a box," she ordered another Light faerie. "Don't touch it."

As the faerie used his spear to drag Caedo across the floor, Rowena crouched beside me once more, pressing my severed arm back into position. The soldier passed her my hand, and she held it against my cut wrist.

The Fae could heal even an injury this grievous, so long as the missing body parts were reunited quickly enough. Why was she doing it, though? Why fix me?

I'd gone numb from the trauma, but prickling discomfort spread at the top of my arm, like insects crawling over the tear. Then the pain flooded back in, so intense my back bowed and my teeth punctured my lower lip. My immortality was already fighting so many other injuries, but bit by bit, the wounds sealed, and then I had a right hand and a right arm again, bloody but whole. I flexed my fingers, feeling like an essential part of me was still missing without Caedo curving over my skin.

I tried to grab Rowena's throat, but she jerked back, and with my left arm still held tight over my head, there wasn't enough slack in the chain to reach her. The soldier who had assisted her grabbed my free wrist and muscled it back into the manacles.

Rowena sat back on her heels. "That's better," she said. "It's more fun when they start in one piece."

I was lightheaded from blood loss and so terrified I wanted to weep, but I gritted my teeth, determined not to cry. She'd stolen enough from me tonight.

Kallen, I thought desperately. *Please be alive. Please. Give me something to aim for.*

If he was alive, I would find a way to survive whatever was coming. I'd fight my way back to him, even if it took years. So long as I lived and he lived, nothing could break me entirely.

If he was dead . . .

No. I refused to believe it.

I closed my eyes, conjuring a memory of Kallen's dark blue eyes, his secret smile. I imagined a moonless night and a sky full of stars and fixed the memory of him, the hope of him, in that firmament, one star shining brighter than the rest.

Then I imagined locking that dream of a night sky away behind metal gates, where no one would ever get to it. If I let myself hold that hope too close to the surface, it could be used against me. I might use it against myself, too, torturing myself with impossibilities when I needed to focus on survival. But if I buried the dream deep enough, there might be enough of me left at the end to resurrect it.

I opened my eyes to see more Sun Soldiers gathering around us. There would be no escaping. I was Light House's prisoner now.

Beyond them, the hall was filled with dozens of corpses. From the colors of their tunics, they came from every house, but the majority wore the black of Void and the brilliant hues of Fire. Dotted among them were a few spots of dark red. All dead because of me.

If Torin and Rowena didn't kill me eventually, the guilt might.

"Ready, my love?" Torin asked from the dais. His tunic was spattered with blood, and he was wearing Imogen's crown. Mistei would have a king, after all.

It would have a queen, too. Rowena echoed his triumphant smile, then leaned over me. She unhooked a pouch from her belt and loosened the drawstring. "Time to go," she told me in her sweet, girlish voice, as if we were two friends about to embark on a journey. She upended the pouch, pouring powder into my face. It smelled like poppies, and as I breathed in, the world faded.

Soft blackness swallowed me up, clouding my thoughts. My heart slowed. It was almost a relief, this feeling. Sleep reached for me, easy and lulling, promising everything would be all right in the morning.

It wouldn't, though.

I heard Rowena whisper one last thing before my consciousness drowned.

"I'm so glad you like to dance."

ACKNOWLEDGMENTS

Thank you to everyone involved in bringing the next installment of Kenna's story into the world! To my editor, Cindy Hwang—thank you so much for your excellent notes, your patience, your enthusiasm for heaping piles of sexual tension, and your willingness to tackle the longest book I've ever written and get it down to . . . well, still the longest book I've ever written, but a much more reasonable size!

Thank you to Ace and everyone at Penguin Random House who helped with editing, marketing, publicity, sales, foreign rights, production, events, and everything else that goes into creating and promoting a book: Elizabeth Vinson, Jessica Mangicaro (aka president of the Kallen Fan Club), Danielle Keir, Kaila Mundell-Hill, Tawanna Sullivan, Nithya Rajendran, Stacy Edwards, Daniel Brount, Will Tyler, Michael Brown, Stephanie Felty, Andrew Taets, Anika Bates, and the rest of the Penguin Random House staff who helped bring this series to life. Thank you as well to Mia Hutchinson-Shaw for the fantastic audiobook narration!

A massive thank-you to artist Erion Makuo and art director Katie

Anderson for another stunning cover. Kenna looks so fierce, and the details are exquisite. I'm the luckiest author in the world!

To Jessica Watterson, agent extraordinaire—thank you so much for everything. You're my biggest cheerleader and staunchest advocate, and I'm so grateful you're on my side.

Thank you to Jo Segura, Ali Hazelwood, Falon Ballard, and Kate Golden for being my conversation partners for the *Servant of Earth* book tour, and thank you to Village Books, Lark & Owl Booksellers, Meet Cute Romance Bookshop, and The Ripped Bodice for hosting those events. All my gratitude to Village Books for running the preorder campaigns as well—I really appreciate all your hard work making the magic happen. Thank you to all the librarians and booksellers who have supported this series, as well as to all the wonderful authors who blurbed *Servant of Earth* and *Princess of Blood*. It means the world to me.

I'm also grateful to Millie Prestidge, Javerya Iqbal, Jenna Petts, and the rest of the Gollancz team, and to the other foreign publishers releasing copies of both this series and Glimmer Falls. Thank you to Áine Feeney for launching my career in the UK—you're so brilliant and kind, and I was lucky to get to work with you!

I'm very fortunate to have so many friends in this industry, but I want to give extra thanks to Jenna Levine, Jennifer Delaney, Katie Shepard, Julie Soto, the Berkletes, and the Words Are Hard writers. I value your insights, your support, and your memes more than I can say.

To my family and friends—I am endlessly grateful for your support and love. I couldn't do this without you.

And to all the readers who have followed Kenna into the dangerous world of Mistei—thank you so much! Kenna's journey is far from over, and I can't wait to share what's next.

Photo by Mahina Hawley Photography

SARAH HAWLEY is the *USA Today* bestselling author of *Servant of Earth* and the Glimmer Falls series. She has an MA in archaeology and has excavated at an Inca site in Chile, a Bronze Age palace in Turkey, and a medieval abbey in England. When not dreaming up whimsical love stories, she can be found reading, dancing, or cuddling her two cats.